NEW MADRID

BOBBY AKART

THANK YOU

For a copy of his critically acclaimed monthly newsletter, *The Epigraph*, and to get on the list to find out about coming titles, deals, contests, and appearances, visit
BobbyAkart.com
or visit his dedicated feature page on Amazon at
Amazon.com/BobbyAkart

PRAISE FOR AUTHOR BOBBY AKART AND NEW MADRID

"New Madrid is a perfect melding of a fictional story taking on a real-world persona. Akart's works make you stop and think, not if this could happen but when will this happen."
~ Brian Alderman

"Every time I thought the book was going to let me take a breath and relax, it took me right into another life or death punch to the throat. Bobby Akart is the King of Disaster Thrillers!"
~ Colt Payne

"Action, adventure, excitement and heart. This book has it all."
~ Carol Dyer

"As with any of the best novels, this book really captures your attention and makes it hard to put down at the end of the day."
~ Cody McDonell

"New Madrid is not your run-of-the-mill disaster thriller!"
~ Karl Hughey

NEW MADRID

BOBBY AKART

OTHER WORKS BY AMAZON CHARTS TOP 25 AUTHOR BOBBY AKART

New Madrid (a disaster thriller)

Odessa (a Gunner Fox trilogy)

Odessa Reborn

Odessa Rising

Odessa Strikes

The Virus Hunters

Virus Hunters I

Virus Hunters II

Virus Hunters III

The Geostorm Series

The Shift

The Pulse

The Collapse

The Flood

The Tempest

The Pioneers

The Asteroid Series (A Gunner Fox trilogy)

Discovery

Diversion

Destruction

The Doomsday Series

Apocalypse

Haven

Copyright Information

DEDICATIONS

There is nothing more important on this planet than my darling wife, Dani, and our two princesses, Bullie and Boom. With the love and support of Dani and the never-ending supply of smiles our two girls give us, I'm able to tell you these stories. Also, on a special note, *New Madrid* is the novel Dani would've written had she not stepped up to wear every hat a traditional publisher might wear. Thank you for letting me bring your vision to print.

Also, a special dedication to America's first responders—the men and women of law enforcement, firefighters, emergency medical technicians, and hospital personnel. These are the underappreciated brave Americans who run toward danger rather than from it.

Freedom and security are precious gifts that we, as Americans, should never take for granted. Thank you, first responders, for willingly making sacrifices each day to provide us that freedom and security.

EPIGRAPH

Civilization exists by geologic consent, subject to change without notice.
~ Will Durant, American historian and philosopher

A man who comes home to a stout safe cabin and all the ones he loves …
he's the luckiest man in all creation!
~ Davy Crockett, King of the Wild Frontier, 1812, near present-day Obion County, Tennessee

---

Our earth is very old, an old warrior that has lived through many battles. Nevertheless, the face of it is still changing, and science sees no certain limit of time for its stately evolution.
~ Reginald Daly, Canadian Geologist

The Mississippi River will always have its own way.
No engineering skill can persuade it to do otherwise.
~ Mark Twain, *Eruptions*

Extinction is the rule. Survival is the exception.
~ Carl Sagan

A bad earthquake at once destroyed the oldest associations—the world, the very emblem of all that is solid, had moved beneath our feet like a crust over a fluid. One second of time had created in the mind a strong idea of insecurity, which hours of reflection would not have produced.
~ Charles Darwin on the massive 1835 earthquake at Concepcion, Chile

---

Man plans and God laughs.
~ Old Yiddish Proverb

Merciful God! What a horrid situation.
~ Letter to the editor, *Augusta Herald* (Georgia) February 19, 1812

I'll be home for Christmas.
~ Harry Lillis "Bing" Crosby, American Singer

The following is based on a true story.
It just hasn't happened in the modern age yet.

PROLOGUE

Dr. Charlotte Lansing stretched her legs under the speakers' table and shifted her weight on the chair. A seismic hazard and insurance risk specialist droned on about the potential losses to the insurance industry in the event of a catastrophic earthquake along the San Andreas fault. She tried not to allow her inner thoughts to manifest themselves in her facial expressions. Too often, the impact of catastrophic events was measured in terms of damage to structures or economic costs. Dr. Lansing understood there was much more at stake. Namely, loss of life.

When she'd been invited to speak at this year's National Earthquake Conference held at her alma mater, the University of Missouri, she readily accepted. The final day of the conference happened to fall on the anniversary of the first New Madrid earthquake of 1811.

Her research into the timing of large earthquakes based upon mathematical patterns had finally received some recognition by her peers. While it was still a work in progress, especially as it related to the New Madrid Seismic Zone, or NMSZ, her speech at the conference not only gave her an opportunity to discuss the threat this underestimated fault presented, but she was also able to introduce her mathematical pattern theory to the audience.

She looked around the Jesse Auditorium, where she'd spent many days as a graduate student at Mizzou. The doctoral program within the Department of Geological Sciences had enjoyed a reputation as one of the top ten in the nation. While many in her class focused on the environmental issues of the day, she'd sunk her teeth into rocks. She was a science nerd and proud of it.

Unlike most of her classmates, Dr. Lansing was a traditionalist who looked at geology as the study of the Earth—its origin and developmental history together with its structure and composition. The planet was a living, breathing thing in a constant state of flux and evolution. The data derived from firsthand field observations and laboratory analyses of minerals, sediments, rocks and landforms fascinated her.

Growing up in Cape Girardeau, Missouri, Dr. Lansing naturally learned about geology close to home. The small city located on the Mississippi River was an hour north of New Madrid and located within the New Madrid Seismic Zone, or NMSZ. Her high school science and history classes had delved into the subject regularly. Whenever there were extracurricular activities involving exploring caves or studying sediment, Dr. Lansing was the first to volunteer.

She'd spent countless hours in the library, studying old accounts of the 1811 to 1812 earthquake swarm that rocked the region and much of the Eastern United States. As she got older, her fascination with the NMSZ and geology in general led her to a career path as a geophysicist with the United States Geological Survey, or USGS. Now she was the director of the National Earthquake Information Center in Golden, Colorado, commonly referred to as the NEIC.

It was almost her turn to speak, so she sat up in her chair and glanced at her notes, not that she needed them. Dr. Lansing was passionate about her work. She was not shy about public speaking and fashioned herself a bit of a storyteller. Unlike loss-mitigation specialists or structural engineers extolling the virtues of constructing buildings to achieve vertical stiffness while allowing for counter-directional forces, she got to tell them about the drama unfolding beneath our planet's surface.

She helped the attendees understand why the pressure builds and what causes it to release. She left them with the warning that earthquakes can happen anytime, without warning, with deadly consequences. It was never her intention to scare the wits out of people but, rather, to scare the wits into them. To raise their awareness to the sleeping threat that could change the topography of America in an instant.

After introducing herself, she drew in her audience by helping them visualize what was going on underneath their seats. As she spoke, she couldn't help but notice the attendees look down from time to time, wondering if the heinous beast lurking beneath the ground was stirring. She oftentimes wondered that herself.

"Every year, fifty thousand earthquakes are noticed by people without the need for seismic instruments. The ground shudders, swells, and stretches, leading to a massive tweet-storm that reads something like *did you feel it?*

"Social media junkies flock to Facebook and mark themselves safe from the earthquake in X or Y location. Friends commiserate back and forth about how the wine in their glass rippled or Aunt Bessie's vase fell off the mantel. What they really should've been thinking about is what is going on around our planet's mantle.

"Over two hundred years ago on this date, at around two o'clock in the morning, the first of three major earthquakes rocked the New Madrid Seismic Zone. An immeasurable pressure had been building along an ancient plate boundary. Born out of frustration, and feeling underappreciated, the New Madrid fault announced itself with a vengeance.

"You see, five hundred million years ago, the North American

Plate tried to form a plate boundary along the center of the continent, running from north to south. The struggle during these formative years was intense, but the splitting stopped before the new plates could be formed. What we have beneath us are the remnants of this struggle in which the North American Plate is still settling down. In other words, a seismic event that began five hundred million years ago is still in the process of resolving itself. There remains a jagged scar buried below the surface, evidencing this epic struggle. And it's never healed."

She adjusted the wireless microphone attached to her headset and abandoned the podium, much to the dismay of the event coordinator. Dr. Lansing was in the zone, and she wandered along the front of the elevated stage so she could make eye contact with the attendees as she told the story.

"So imagine, if you will, that it's the early morning hours of December 16, 1811. Very few people lived up and down the Mississippi River. The United States had just purchased the Louisiana Territory from France. Our war with Britain in 1812 was brewing but not yet underway. The only means of navigation were canoes, flatboats, and rafts that were one-way in nature, as in downstream only toward the Port of New Orleans.

"Underground, the North American Plate, at this ancient boundary, began to disintegrate in part. The vertical shelves that butted up against one another moved. Not much. Maybe half an inch. However, it was enough for the rock along the boundary to disintegrate.

"The centuries-long stalemate beneath the planet's surface had a change in dynamic. One side of the plate saw an opportunity, an opening, so to speak, to exert pressure on this primeval crack. It forced its will upon its opponent, and the vertical shelves became snagged on one another. As one snag became weaker than the other, one side shifted upward just below the surface of the earth.

"The scrum continued until it held for a minute or so. Then the incredible strength of the always-moving earth pushed again. This time, the snag became an ever-widening crack below the surface, and the first earthquake rocked the region."

Dr. Lansing stopped her casual stroll back and forth across the stage. With a pensive look on her face, she touched her fingers to her forehead and focused on several educators sitting along the front row.

"Remember, it's 1811. Google didn't exist back then. We have to look at the historical record of this event as told by residents in their correspondence and journalists in their newspapers. Obviously, we can only estimate how powerful this series of earthquakes was. Earth-shaking fissures opened up along the fault that were felt far and wide. Boston; Charleston, South Carolina; and Richmond, Virginia. It was felt at the White House, as we know from a letter sent to Thomas Jefferson by our fourth president, James Madison. Even Dolly Madison, his wife, shared accounts of the quake.

"During the third massive quake in February of 1812, vast swaths of land sank while other areas were lifted. Landslides occurred. New lakes, like Reelfoot in West Tennessee, were created. For a brief time, those who relied upon the Mississippi River to deliver goods to the Port of New Orleans found themselves facing the unthinkable. A fluvial tsunami forced the river to run backwards the day of the third earthquake.

"Here's the thing. As geophysicists and those who make a living based on our field of study, we recognize a major event like the 1811–1812 New Madrid earthquakes as a mere geologic blink of the eye. Yet the quakes reshaped Earth's surface. And it had happened before, based upon our sediment study, including major upheavals in 2350 BC, AD 30, AD 900, and AD 1450."

Dr. Lansing paused to catch her breath. It was time to introduce her theory.

"It's natural for those in government whom I have to answer to, or even representatives of the insurance industry, to ask—when will the next big one strike the NMSZ? I believe I've identified a mathematical pattern called the Devil's Staircase."

A murmur went through the crowd as she introduced her designation for her findings. Dr. Lansing wasn't sure if the audience thought she was serious or leading them into a joke of some kind. She got right to the point.

"In conjunction with quake activity, I have been able to identify a mathematical pattern where clusters of large shallow earthquake events were separated by long, somewhat irregular period of seismic inactivity. Heretofore, geophysicists focused their study on the classical seismic modeling that suggested quake activity would occur quasi-periodically based on cycles of buildup followed by the release of tectonic stress.

"In regions like the Ring of Fire, for example, large earthquake sequences, those with a magnitude six or greater, are characterized by a clustering of quake activity in bursts. This is a near-certain predictor of a much greater earthquake event to follow.

"In my study of the NMSZ, the irregular gap between event bursts shows how difficult it is to predict the next major quake event. The Devil's Staircase pattern, as I call it, can be applied to recent large earthquake events in Australia, the plate boundary off the coast of western Algeria, and more recently, at the Dead Sea Transform fault west of the Golan Heights that many labeled as biblical in nature.

"The fact is that these quake events show a pattern of stress transfer between fault segments near identical to the New Madrid fault. What I am suggesting is this. In the United States, most of the public awareness of the devastating impacts of earthquakes is focused on the faults running along our West Coast. Those faults, frankly, are far more predictable than the NMSZ. As a result, warnings can be issued with relative accuracy and in a somewhat timely manner.

"In the case of a fault line like New Madrid, we have what's commonly referred to as a high-impact, low-probability event. An analysis of the Devil's Staircase pattern, which I continue to expand upon, indicates a massive New Madrid earthquake is not as low probability as most contend. In fact, it is a relative certainty based upon the patterns, and most likely will occur in our lifetimes."

PART I

LIVING AT THE EDGE

We live our lives. Work. Love. Play. You never know the day before a catastrophe strikes that it was, in fact, the day before. If you did, you'd prepare your mind, alter your way of life, and even get right with your maker. However, we don't do that. We live on the edge of an unforeseen, unpredictable catastrophe that could be the end of the world as we know it, blissfully unaware of the consequences of our inaction.

And then, one day, the universe says let's shake things up a bit.

CHAPTER ONE

Monday, December 17
St. Louis, Missouri

Jack Atwood had led a charmed life. He was a small-town boy, growing up near Dyersburg, Tennessee, just eighty miles north of Memphis and a dozen miles east of the Mighty Mississippi River. He'd had his share of good luck growing up. He'd been labeled reckless by his parents and a miscreant by his schoolteachers. Then, suddenly, all that changed.

They say cheating death can have a profound effect on a man's soul. Well, it certainly changed Jack. He was a senior in high school when his parents gave him the green light to embark on his first spring break trip with his friends. Like so many his age, they loaded up their cars, stopped by the Short Stop on the way out of town to lie their way towards the purchase of several cases of Pabst Blue Ribbon, and drove nonstop to *Fort Liquordale*—Fort Lauderdale, for those who've never experienced spring break in the Florida coastal city.

His best friend's car was far too powerful for him, or anyone else for that matter. The fire-engine red Chevy Camaro boasted five hundred forty horsepower, way too much power for a teenager.

"This thing will run right out from under ya," his best friend proudly claimed when he first took Jack for a spin. And spin, they did.

Their spring break trip to Fort Liquordale was filled with wine, women, and song. The party never ended until the kids passed out or got arrested. The next day, they sought out the hair of the dog and started all over again.

On the third day of their weeklong drunkfest, Jack's life changed. After about a fifth of Jim Beam being consumed between the two of them, they decided to roar down A1A along the beach, letting the horses run, as Jack's buddy said. The hundred-mile-an-hour joyride didn't go unnoticed by two motorcycle officers, who'd been writing a ticket to another spring breaker for public nudity.

They immediately gave chase, and the Camaro responded. Weaving in and out of traffic, they tried to evade their pursuers and were easily pulling away. That was when the boys realized you can't outrun a radio, as they say.

A roadblock appeared ahead, thwarting their escape and access to the causeway. "I've got this, bro!" his friend exclaimed as he gripped the wheel and slammed on the brakes. The rear end of the Camaro slid sideways as he cut the wheel, an expert maneuver he couldn't reproduce if he tried to replicate it a thousand times while sober. He punched the gas and roared down a side street toward the intracoastal waterway.

Until he ran out of road.

Jack gripped the dashboard and closed his eyes as he braced for impact with the guardrail. His mind raced as he hoped for the best result— the muscle car floating on top of the water long enough for them to swim to safety or be rescued. His mind drifted away, recalling the common myth among teenagers to allow your body to go limp during a wreck to ensure your survival.

The next few seconds could only be described as surreal. It would be many years before Jack repeated his vision to anyone. Just above the hood, floating peacefully throughout the ordeal, Jack saw what he'd inwardly refer to as *butterfly people*. They weren't butterflies per se, nor would he recall them as angels as might be depicted on television or in books. They were an indescribable presence that provided him a sense of comfort. Defying any scientific explanation, he focused on the two who stayed with the car as it whipped to the left and to the left again. Mentally, he felt protected. His body, however, suffered somewhat.

The tires screeched, and he was thrown against the passenger door, cracking open his head against the glass. The centrifugal force exerted so much pressure on him that his body was forced against the side of the Camaro in an effort to throw the locked door open.

Then he was tossed back toward the center console with such a kick that his eyes were forced open just as his head crashed into the windshield. Seconds later, the car was surrounded by Fort Lauderdale's finest with their weapons drawn. And the butterfly people were gone.

Jack's buddy had accomplished the impossible. He'd managed to control the Camaro through a hairpin turn under the bridge. Perhaps with a little help, Jack later surmised.

Initially, he didn't look at the incident as if his life had been saved. In his mind, he'd almost been killed and vowed to never put himself in that position again. As he grew older and replayed the event in his mind, he became convinced the butterfly people played a role in his safety.

The near-death experience, coupled with the presence of the butterfly people, turned his life around. The hospitalization. The arrest. The lecture from his family. All contributed to a real game-changer in Jack Atwood's life, one he'd never take for granted.

He stopped and gazed upward, taking in the six-hundred-thirty-foot-high Gateway Arch. The structure's stainless-steel surface reflected the last vestiges of daylight as the sun set over the St. Louis skyline.

"I can't believe we've never done this." Tony Chandler, his brother-in-law and junior partner in his financial planning practice, interrupted Jack's thoughts. "Naturally, I'd rather be throwing down some oysters and chasin' them with the coldest beer Anheuser-Busch has to offer."

Jack shook his head. He always had his hands full when he and Tony traveled alone to conduct financial planning seminars. Despite the fact he was married to Jack's wife's much younger sister, who happened to be seven months pregnant together with being saddled with the challenges of raising a three-year-old son, Tony couldn't seem to grasp the concept of adulthood and responsibility.

After their second group of seminars in Chicago a year ago, when Jack busted his brother-in-law slipping his wedding band into his pocket while out drinking one night, he curtailed their social activities the best he could. He'd taken to visiting points of interest while they were away from home, like the Gateway Arch.

"Yeah, let's do this," said Jack, although he'd rather be settled in their corporate apartment in downtown St. Louis. After Beth and Tony had their first child, he'd promised his wife to take his brother-in-law under his wing to help him mature. On a business level, Tony was perfect for the firm. On a personal level, he was a handful.

The two men exited their car and were immediately hit with a blast of cold, damp wind. The temperatures had suddenly fallen, and a cold mist had overtaken the city as the afternoon wore on. Jack had watched the weather system that crossed the middle part of the U.S. He hoped the snow would hold off so he wouldn't have to cancel the seminar. This was the last of five he'd been conducting in the cities where his offices were located up and down the Mississippi River.

St. Louis was one of his best producing offices, as it drew prospects from Illinois, Iowa, Kentucky, and Missouri. The cost and logistics of planning this seminar, especially prior to Christmas, were daunting. It was also necessary, as his prospective clients had just a couple of weeks to undertake last minute tax planning before year end.

The guys entered the attraction through the west entrance, and

Jack ponied up the $26 fee to take a tour, including a ride to the top of the Gateway Arch. They boarded the tram that would take them upward along the famous monument along with three other passengers. At six feet four, Jack was slightly claustrophobic during the small tram ride. The ride was only four minutes to the apex, where the observation deck, a gift shop, and a museum were located.

For his part, Tony was enthusiastic. Or, perhaps, Jack thought, it was the attractive young woman who acted as their tour guide. Within seconds of their ascent to the top and the observation deck, Tony had abandoned Jack's side and snuggled up to the tour guide to become her number one sightseer.

Once they exited, the group eagerly followed the young woman, who pointed out the sights as she explained the history of the Arch. Jack took extra effort to locate One Metropolitan Square, where his offices were located and the location of their four seminars that week. From there, he got his bearings to view the St. Louis area and took in the gorgeous sunset.

The tour guide began to take questions, when Jack's cell phone vibrated in his pocket. A smile broke out across his face, and his heart leapt. After ten years of marriage, the mere sight of his wife's picture and name on his phone screen still gave him butterflies in his stomach.

CHAPTER TWO

Monday, December 17
Gateway Arch
St. Louis, Missouri

"I miss my handsome husband," Jill Atwood said sexily into the phone before Jack could say hello. "And, lest I forget, suave and debonair, too."

Jack laughed as he stopped following the tour group. He turned away to whisper to his wife, "Well, maybe I should've stayed home. 'Tis the season to get lucky, you know."

Jill chuckled. "You got lucky last week, mister."

"That was my birthday," he shot back. "I mean, that's a given, right?"

"Yeah, and Christmas is coming. That'll take care of your forty-year-old man-child needs for a while."

"Until New Year's, anyway," he replied with a laugh.

"Good grief. You've been hanging around Tony too much." Jill paused as she held the phone away from her mouth to speak with their daughter. When she returned to the call, she asked, "I don't hear any music in the background. Are the bars and strip clubs closed for the holidays?"

"Very funny," replied Jack, who stepped a couple of paces back toward the tour group. While the other two attendees wandered into the gift shop, Tony had the young guide cornered as he poured on the charm. "No, I convinced our boy to see the Arch with me. He seems to be getting into it." Jack cringed and rolled his eyes as the words came out of his mouth.

"Good. I'm glad you guys aren't headed out for the night. You know he changes when he has a few drinks."

Jack, who helped out on his parents' farm as a boy, responded with the perfect analogy. "Like the difference between a horse grazing and a wild mustang. You know, I can't keep tabs on Tony twenty-four seven. As it is, I've done things like the corporate apartment as a deterrent to him slipping out of a hotel room at night."

"Or slipping something into the room, right?"

Jack sighed. "Yeah, that too."

Jack had his doubts about Tony's fidelity. His keen sense of observation picked up on his brother-in-law's attempts to pick up women. He'd seen him chat up attractive females on numerous occasions, but he'd never actually seen him cross the line. After a while, he found it counterproductive to report Tony's actions back to Jill. It would simply add fuel to a fire that was smoldering within her.

She had a difficult challenge of her own to avoid relaying reports of Tony's disrespectful indiscretions to her sister. Beth was juggling a three-year-old boy with autism along with a near-seven-month pregnancy.

"You've been a great influence on him, honey," said Jill. "Beth knows and appreciates the sacrifices you've made, both financially and timewise."

"I'd do anything for you," Jack interjected.

"It's more than for me. It's for Beth, too. Let's face it. She wants what I have. I'm not saying she's jealous in a pea-green-with-envy sort of way. She'd settle for a husband who simply paid a little attention to her and treated her with respect. Guys like you who worship and adore their wives are few and far between."

"Flattery will get you everywhere, ma'am."

Jill continued. "Listen, she's young, too. They should've never gotten married straight out of college. She visualized this utopian dream of a knight in shining armor doting over her while she had babies. Instead, she got a guy who looks like a prince, but whose eyes, and maybe hands, continue to wander. Sometimes our conversations are consumed about the relationship you and I have rather than anything positive about her own. For Pete's sake, she even wishes she had cutesy names like ours."

"Jack and Jill?" he asked.

"Duh. Cute, right?"

Jack couldn't disagree and then said, "Don't get me wrong. Tony certainly has a problem remembering he has a wife and kid at home. I can't babysit him night and day. From a business perspective, he may have been one of the best hires I've ever made. It enabled me to take my practice in a whole different direction that's paid off for all of us."

Like Jack, Jill was anxious to move their conversation away from the Chandlers' marriage, a topic discussed far more often than they wished to. "So are you excited for this week?"

"Yeah," he quickly replied. "Actually, other than being away from home this close to Christmas, I think it's gonna be a good week for us. Today, we coordinated with the catering staff at the Top of the Met to get ready."

"I'm so glad you were able to get it reopened," Jill added.

"Kemoll's left a big hole when they pulled their restaurant off the fortieth floor and shut down the banquet facilities on forty-two. It didn't seem right to fill the space with only a fitness center. My client, the retired Applebee's franchisee, couldn't wait to fill the void."

"Does he give you a discount?" asked Jill with all sincerity.

Jack laughed. "Hell, he charges me double. Just kidding. No

discount, but he personally supervises most of our soirees. You can't ask for much more than that."

Jill added to the conversation, but Jack couldn't hear her. The Gateway Arch began to noticeably sway back and forth. A child shrieked, and a man yelled, "What's happening?"

"Honey, what's wrong?" Jill asked.

"Um, nothing," Jack mumbled as he turned in a full circle to get a grasp of what was happening. "Listen, let me call you back tonight once we get settled in, okay?"

"But, sure. Why do you have to—?"

"I love you!" he said emphatically into the phone as if it were the final words spoken between them.

Jack rushed down the observation deck toward the group as the swaying subsided. Ever the gentleman, Tony held the attractive tour guide to help her stay on her feet. The disheveled young woman fixed her hair and shyly smiled to show her appreciation. Jack had seen that kind of look between people before. It was often the precursor to something else.

"It's okay, everyone," she said loudly in an effort to calm down the dozen or so people who rushed onto the observation deck from the other areas atop the Arch. "This is not out of the ordinary."

"Was it the wind?" asked an older man who'd been in Jack's tram.

"No. Probably a slight tremor," she replied. "There's nothing to be afraid of. We get them here in St. Louis from time to time. That's one of the magnificent aspects of the Gateway Arch. Its structural design is truly a wonder of engineering."

She spun around and immediately adopted her tour-guide persona. "The first three hundred feet of the Arch consists of carbon-steel walls with reinforced concrete in the middle. All of these are covered with stainless-steel skin, kinda like two slices of bread creating a sandwich. This combination of stressed-skin design connects at the top to make it resistant to earthquakes much stronger than the little tremor we just experienced. In fact, it can sway up to eighteen inches in either direction during a quake while also withstanding hurricane-force winds up to one hundred fifty miles per hour."

"What's the strongest earthquake in St. Louis since the Arch was built?" the older man asked.

The young woman, who'd regained her composure, clasped her hands together as she adopted a schoolteacher posture. "That happened in 1968, only five years after the Arch was completed. The magnitude 5.5 shock was centered just south of here and was felt in twenty-three surrounding states."

"Wow, that was a big earthquake!" exclaimed a young boy, who still held his mother's hand with a death grip.

Jack wandered away to study the now-illuminated St. Louis skyline. He muttered to himself, "Not as big as it could be."

CHAPTER THREE

Monday, December 17
Atwood Residence
Cordova, Tennessee

"I love you back," Jill Atwood replied as Jack disconnected the call. He'd seemed to rush her off the phone, which wasn't like him. She shrugged it off, chalking it up to something Tony related. She set the phone down on the kitchen island amongst the cookbooks, recipe cards, and her iPad opened to CountryLiving.com, her go-to website for holiday meal planning.

Jill was organized in a frantic week-before-the-family's-arrival sort of way. Notepads and multicolored pens were used for meal plans, shopping lists, and an agenda of daily activities. Sure, there were apps for all of that. However, Jill had learned about running a household from her grandmother, who wanted nothing to do with those *newfangled thingamajigs*.

"Mom! Can we change the channel? We've been watching these movies since Halloween. I've seen this one at least three times."

Her twelve-year-old daughter, Emily, had been by her side for most of the Christmas decorating. One of their family traditions during the holiday season was watching the Hallmark Channel. Each year, the network would begin presenting their Christmas-themed programming earlier and earlier. It used to be considered bad form to start the Thanksgiving and Christmas celebrations prior to Halloween.

As retailers began inching their holiday merchandise releases into October, Hallmark followed suit and began to show their Christmas movies earlier, too. Now, in October, you could watch Freddy Krueger slash open some poor soul on Elm Street on one channel, or switch over to see Candace Cameron Bure serve up chewy ginger cookies on Hallmark's version of Elm Street, USA.

Jill returned to the family room, where their Christmas tree stood partially decorated near the fireplace. The flames flickered through the split-oak firewood, providing plenty of heat and an abundance of ambience. Her mantel was decorated with garland, stockings, and their holders. Above it, the TV showed a young couple falling in love below the mistletoe, staring dreamily into one another's eyes as faux snow fell around them. It was the quintessential happy ending to a Hallmark Christmas movie. She'd seen it so many times before, and it always warmed her heart.

"Okay, Em. Whadya wanna watch?"

"The Grizzlies are on," mumbled her son, Tate. The fifteen-year-old never took his attention away from his iPhone as he scrolled through the timeline of one social media app or another.

"No!" Emily voiced her objection. "We watched football all day yesterday. Basketball sucks anyway."

"Language, young lady!"

Emily looked at her mother and tilted her head as if she had no idea what she'd said wrong. Somehow, the word *sucks* had eased its way into the American vernacular as a way to describe something undesirable or disappointing. Few people regularly using the term realized it derived from the term meaning to perform oral sex.

Tate, who was generally indifferent to television unless it involved a sporting event, made a suggestion. "We've got *The Walking Dead* season finale in the can from last night." *In the can* was

Tate's way of referring to the movies and shows stored on the cable box DVR hard drive. Jack used *in the can* to announce where'd he'd be when it was time to go to the bathroom. They were boys.

"Eww, gross," Emily objected again.

Jill rolled her eyes. Tired of acting as a referee between the kids, she switched the channel to digital radio so she could listen to Christmas music. *Nowadays, television programming sucked,* she thought to herself, generating a slight giggle.

She turned to the kids and put her hands on her hips. "Okay, let's get back to the job at hand. We've got a tree to decorate and lots of boxes to put away. Who's ready?"

Emily's arms shot up. Tate didn't move.

"Okay, Em. I'll have you help me with the Shiny Brites. Tate? What about you?"

He raised his eyes from his phone for the first time. He glanced around the room before responding, "I'll take cleanup."

"Okay. Okay. That's good. You can repack the empty boxes and put them in the garage. But don't you wanna help decorate the tree? I could use some help with the star tree-topper."

"How about I get the ladder?" he offered.

Jill studied him for a moment. In the six months since he'd turned fifteen, his attitude toward family events had changed dramatically. He was a sophomore at Memphis University School, a private school for boys in grades seven through twelve. It was a very disciplined college-preparatory school that he'd attended for two years. His grades hadn't fallen off, and to the contrary, he was excelling in most of his subjects.

His extracurricular activities centered around sports. The entire enrollment of MUS was around seven hundred boys. Their sports program was limited, so many of the young men showing an interest in athletics played multiple sports. Tate, as a sophomore, had been invited to play football, baseball, and basketball on the varsity teams. He was tall for his age, making him an ideal addition to the basketball team, but football was his first love.

Every parent was warned to watch for sudden mood changes in

their teenagers. It could be an indication he was running with the proverbial wrong crowd. Maybe drinking or drugs were involved. She and Jack discussed it from time to time as they watched for the telltale signs, including secretive behavior, failing grades, or a general lack of interest in anything other than new friends or social media.

Social media had always been a concern for them. Other than his after-school practices, Tate spent any extra time away from his studies interacting with others on Instagram and Facebook. Tate despised Twitter, constantly referring to the app's users as vile human beings. Jill checked out the Twitter feed from time to time and found herself both agreeing with her son and admiring him for the good sense to avoid it.

"Okay, big guy," she replied. "You grab the ladder while Emily and I adorn this magnificent tree with the brightest Shiny Brite ornaments known to man. Right, Em?"

"Right! I'll start with this one." She pulled out a pink mercury glass bauble with a snowy scene depicted all around it.

The Shiny Brites, along with their home, were something Jill and her sister, Beth, inherited from their grandmother. Like their family roots stretching back to Germany, Shiny Brite ornaments were of German descent. They had been created by German-born Max Eckardt following World War I. He and his brother were toymakers. Soon, the popularity of the glass ornaments stretched across the Atlantic to America. In 1937, he formally founded the Shiny Brite company, so named because the insides of the ornaments were coated with silver nitrate in order to remain shiny Christmas after Christmas. By 1940, he'd partnered with the Corning glass company to produce three hundred thousand ornaments a day. After the war, he assisted in the rebuilding of Germany by adding ornament factories there.

Jill's grandmother used to talk about German work ethic and the pride their toymakers took in creating Christmas decorations. Jill and Beth would spend hours listening to their grandmother explain what Christmas meant to her, both as a family gathering but also as a way to celebrate the birth of Christ. One of her favorite sayings was *remember the reason for the season*. It was her grandmother's strong influence that gave Jill the strength to persevere during a period of great emotional loss. That same strength would serve her well in the near future.

CHAPTER FOUR

Tuesday, December 18
USGS
Golden, Colorado

Dr. Lansing liked to jog to the USGS offices located on the campus of the Colorado School of Mines in Golden, Colorado. The weather conditions had little impact on her decision unless the sidewalks were covered with ice. It was her way of allowing her two worlds to meet. A transition, of sorts, between life at home with her husband and live-in mother-in-law and the job she loved.

Despite being the middle of December, temperatures were in the low fifties courtesy of the jet stream trapping cold air in the polar regions. She'd left the house thirty minutes earlier to burn a few calories picked up during her three-day stay in Missouri. Between the carb-filled foods at the earthquake conference and the delicious meals served up by her mother in Columbia, Dr. Lansing had gained ten pounds. She was sure of it.

She picked up the pace as she passed the marijuana dispensaries on Ford Street. The increase in homelessness in suburban Denver continued despite arguments from the pro-legalization lobby.

Denver had become the unofficial legal marijuana capital of America. The homelessness rate leapt eight percent the first year following the implementation of the marijuana legalization initiative.

To counter the negative publicity surrounding the influx of Californians seeking a Rocky Mountain high, old unprofitable hotels were converted to government-run affordable housing. The newly arrived homeless were given a free place to live. They now had an address. Therefore, they were no longer homeless, technically speaking. Problem solved.

Except there were still homeless people huddled near the intersection of Ford and Tenth, where Dr. Lansing jogged back and forth to work most days. Usually they ignored her. Sometimes they didn't, which made for a few uncomfortable confrontations.

As she ran, she glanced over at Coors Brewery, one of the few vices she allowed herself. Empty calories, to be sure. Another favorite vice in which she indulged only occasionally was Bob's Atomic Burgers to her right. The retro-style burger joint was a local favorite, especially in the summer, when patrons sat outside to enjoy an incredible view of the South Table Mountain, a mesa just beyond the brewery.

She slowed her pace to a walk as she approached the National Earthquake Information Center. The NEIC, part of the USGS, was tasked with identifying, as rapidly and accurately as possible, the location and size of significant earthquakes around the world. They would then disseminate the data to associated national and international agencies, catastrophic response entities like FEMA, and lastly, after approval from the White House, to the public.

The NEIC was also a data-gathering entity. It was a central hub to collect extensive seismic reporting and research compiled from digital helicorders around the world. Prior to advanced technology, these devices recorded signals from seismometers onto a piece of paper wrapped around a drum. A pen drew the signal on the paper, jumping at small intervals when seismic activity occurred. The bigger the shake, the bigger the quake.

Now, the raw data was processed digitally and strained, as they say, through a band-pass filter to separate global events from localized ones. The public didn't realize some earthquakes were of such a large magnitude they could be felt in other parts of the world.

For Dr. Lansing, landing the position of director at the NEIC was like allowing a kid alone in a candy store. There was never enough data for her to analyze. Everything that happened, even on the dull and mundane days, caused her excitement and was worthy of study. She considered herself more than a trained geophysicist. She was Mother Earth's personal physician.

She made her way into the lobby of the NEIC and was immediately greeted by the receptionist.

"Good morning, Doc!" The young intern from the Colorado School of Mines worked for minimum wage when she wasn't attending to her studies. She was one of several students who had been selected out of hundreds of applicants for the opportunity to simply work inside the hallowed halls of the NEIC. It was a résumé builder for them.

"Hi, Jasmine," said Dr. Lansing, returning the young woman's beaming smile.

Jasmine stood and handed the director a stack of phone messages. "Also, here's your copy of the FEMA Daily Operations Briefing."

"Thank you," said Dr. Lansing as she began to make her way to the operations center, her normal first stop upon arrival. Jasmine stopped her.

"Oh, I almost forgot. This is for you." She handed Dr. Lansing the morning copy of the *Golden Transcript*, the second oldest newspaper in Colorado.

Dr. Lansing playfully scowled as she turned the newspaper over and examined it. "What's this?"

"A newspaper."

"You mean they still make these silly things?" she asked with a grin on her face.

"Sure, people still read them. Besides, everybody likes to read about themselves in the paper."

Dr. Lansing opened it to view the headline on the front page. The Colorado governor had just resigned after allegations of campaign finance fraud. *Not everybody*, she thought to herself. She flipped it over to check the headlines below the fold.

"Are you saying I'm in here?"

"Yes, ma'am. About your speech at the conference."

"Why would the local paper care?"

Jasmine laughed and then replied, "Are you kidding? When you talk about sexy things like Devil's Staircases, what media outlet could resist?"

Dr. Lansing wasn't sure if the Devil's Staircase reference was quite as sexy as a soon-to-be-indicted governor, but she'd take it. Then a look of concern came over her face.

"Were they kind to me?"

"They said you were knowledgeable and informative. You know, generally great."

"Generally?" asked the woman who was arguably one of the nation's leading geophysicists.

"Well, yes. Except for the part about you being the prophetess of doom."

Dr. Lansing scowled and muttered to herself, "Nice."

She made her way into the operations center, debating whether to drop the paper in the trash or read about herself somewhere on page six.

"Hi, Dr. Lansing," said one of the geologists who assisted her in the field on most research projects. "I watched the closed-circuit broadcast of your presentation. I thought you were fantastic. Newspapers are really stupid for many reasons. You know what they say about—"

Dr. Lansing waved her hand to cut him off before he finished. She caught his drift. "Would you mind getting me a bottle of water and a banana?"

29

He turned to retrieve both items off his cubicle desk. He was one step ahead of her.

"I figured you'd take a longer run today."

"Because of the article?" The whole *prophetess of doom* reference was eating at her. She'd never incorrectly pulled the trigger on any earthquake warning. In fact, her forecasting capabilities were second to none. However, New Madrid was unique, and she'd take every opportunity to remind the scientific community of that.

"No," he replied. "Because every time you travel, you complain of weight gain. It's never really the case, but you say it every time."

These people know me too well. "Okay. Follow me."

She walked into the center of the operations center, where cubicles, computer monitors, and maps encircled her. Geophysicists of all levels of expertise were manning their stations.

She raised her voice to announce her presence. "So how's our patient today?"

Most of the personnel swung around in their chairs. They acknowledged the arrival of the woman they all highly respected and enjoyed working for.

Oliver, one of her longest serving geophysicists, who hailed from England, replied, "Good morning, mum. She's a little gassy this morning."

The group laughed. Dr. Lansing decided to play along.

"Well, that would make any woman fussy. What exactly did she eat to produce this gassiness?"

"Mum, we've recorded a series of quakes along the AFZ in Northern Chile," he explained. The AFZ was an acronym for the Atacama Fault Zone. Chile was one of the most active seismic regions in the world.

"Can you classify it as a swarm?" she asked.

"Yes, mum. We can. It's actually triggered some volcanic activity in the region. There are reports of gas and nonexplosive lava emissions around the Puyehue-Cordon Caulle volcanic edifices. The ash from the emissions has floated in a southwesterly direction toward Bariloche in Argentina."

Dr. Lansing grimaced. *Not again.* The quaint hamlet in Southern Argentina had been covered in a thin ashy powder mixed with sand and pumice stone just three years prior when the Chilean volcano had a moderate eruption. It was a reminder of how the study of seismic activity can be directly related to volcanic eruptions.

"Okay, keep me posted on developments," she said with a nod of thanks. "Anything closer to home?"

Another geologist assigned to the Mississippi River Valley region and the Upper Midwest responded, "We have reports of tremors in Chicago as well as Cairo, Illinois. They might be false positives."

Dr. Lansing smiled. Residents of Illinois and people who studied geography knew to pronounce the city's name as *care-ro*, not *ki-ro*, as in Egypt.

"Ice quakes?" asked Dr. Lansing. An ice quake, sometimes referred to as a frost quake, occurred when rock saturated with water or ice began to crack or expand. The sudden changes exerted on rock formations often generated a seismic warning. It was common for ice quakes to occur in the Upper Mississippi River Valley during the winter months.

"We're monitoring them now, ma'am," he replied before continuing. "We're exploring a possible connection to tremors felt in St. Louis yesterday afternoon. The surface temperature readings don't suggest a correlation, but we're exploring it nonetheless."

Dr. Lansing slowly nodded her head. "Send me everything you've got on both seismic events, please." She wasn't a believer in coincidences.

CHAPTER FIVE

Thursday, December 20
Advanced Retirement Strategies
One Metropolitan Square
St. Louis, Missouri

One Metropolitan Square, commonly known as the Met, was a striking granite skyscraper that had long been an architectural landmark in St. Louis. The forty-two-story, amenity-rich tower housed a wide variety of American and international tenants. Ideal for business meetings, guests were treated to beautiful art-filled lounges, modern workspaces, and twenty-two thousand square feet of retail shops as well as restaurants. Within a ten-minute walk, visitors could see a game at Ballpark Village or enjoy the nightlife at a number of restaurants and bars.

Jack had chosen the Met for his first Advanced Retirement Strategies office location outside Memphis because it provided his firm instant credibility for prospective clients. After he'd graduated from law school at Memphis University, he joined a firm specializing in tax and estate planning.

The U.S. tax laws had gone through a tumultuous decade as the politics in Washington swung from one side of the political spectrum to another. For retirees, or those approaching retirement, it had become increasingly difficult to plan their estates. Jack found a niche in the estate-planning area of his firm and soon became one of the most highly respected lawyers in Memphis for this field of practice.

In college, Jack had been friends with a man and a woman who were studying to become accountants. Eventually, the two earned their CPA designation and opened up their own office. Jack saw an opportunity for the professional fields to help one another. He was astute enough to realize that estate planning and federal income taxation were inseparable. The decisions made by both a CPA and an estate lawyer had a profound effect on a mutual client's finances.

However, there was still a missing link to the entire process of helping a retiree with their estate planning—investments. By a fortuitous stroke of luck, or the result of an evil curse placed upon him by a cunning witch, Tony Chandler came into Jack's life by virtue of marriage to Jill's sister, Beth.

For all his shortcomings, Tony was an expert salesman. And, make no mistake, any investment advisor was primarily a salesman of financial products. Whether it was life insurance, annuities, stocks, or bonds, the investment advisor makes money from commissions or fees while managing his client's life savings.

Jack saw an opportunity to wrap all three critical aspects of someone's retirement under one roof, and Advanced Retirement Strategies was formed. It was an unusual type of practice in which attorneys, accountants, and financial brokers worked under one roof to provide their clients a comprehensive retirement plan.

His vision became a huge success. After St. Louis, he rapidly expanded his practice to include Baton Rouge, where Tony and Beth lived following their graduation from Louisiana State University. Later, offices in Des Moines, Minneapolis, and New Orleans were opened.

The firm advertised in local newspapers and online resources for those interested in taking advantage of the unique method of estate planning. Following an elegant lunch, they held afternoon seminars discussing the three aspects of the firm's practice. Tony handled the investments discussion while a local accountant discussed the tax benefits of the firm's recommendations. Finally, Jack finished off with the most emotional aspect of the seminar —death.

He'd just finished up their third seminar of the week. In the conference room, Tony was reviewing all of the information provided by their guests, who'd indicated their primary concerns surrounding their individual estates. He was instructing his assistants to call these individuals that evening to schedule free consultations for the next morning if they were interested in the firm's assistance. Otherwise, he could set up a couple of days between Christmas and New Year's.

As he excitedly went over the information and organized the prospects from most promising to least, Jack wandered to his office window and stared out toward the Gateway Arch. Officially, the Arch was a memorial honoring Thomas Jefferson's role in opening the West to the pioneers who helped shape its history.

Jack looked at it from another perspective. The Arch could also be looked at as a monument to a person's life. We all start from the ground up. As infants, we learn to crawl before we walk. We grow as young adults, find our way in the world, and eventually reach a high point in life that may be defined by our successes financially or through the love of family. As we age, Jack thought to himself, we start to wind down. People, like his clients, retire from their jobs or businesses. Eventually, we all grow old and pass away, returning to the earth from which we started.

His mind wandered to Jill, as it often did throughout the day. He recalled the circumstances under which they'd met. She had been a young mother of two. Her son, Tate, had just turned four, and her daughter, Emily, was still an infant crawling across the floor. She was married to a loving man who was taken from her when a drunk driver crossed the median on Interstate 40 one evening and struck his car head-on. He was killed instantly, and her dreams of a long life with him were crushed.

Jill was at a loss. She tried to lean on Beth, who was nine years younger and still in high school. She was estranged from her parents, who chose a life of political activism rather than raising their children. Jill and Beth had been raised by their grandparents. Primarily their grandmother, who lived in Cordova, a small community just east of Memphis, cared for the girls as they grew up.

Then, within weeks of her husband's death, her world came crashing down on her again. Her grandmother passed away. Jill was left virtually alone, with a mountain of debt accumulated by her and her husband and no job or life insurance to pay it. Her grandmother left her entire estate to Jill and Beth. Beth was a party animal at LSU and was not mature enough to receive their grandmother's home, belongings, or savings.

Jill had nowhere to turn, so she hired Jack Atwood. The two estates were a mess. The debts she amassed with her husband would have to be bankrupted. She'd lose her home and have to find a job to take care of her young children. Her grandmother left a will that required probate and the possible challenge of Jill's parents, who could suddenly return from Portland to contest the distribution.

Jack saved the day. He shielded the sisters from their parents and managed to shepherd the estate through probate without a lot of legal fees and with minimal tax implications. In the end, Beth received a handsome spendthrift trust that paid her over several years. Jill was deeded her grandmother's home in Riverwood Farms located east of Memphis in the bedroom community of Cordova.

The happy ending didn't end there. After the estate was settled in probate, Jack and Jill, who'd struck up a close friendship during the proceedings, began to date. They'd become best friends, and then they became lovers. A year after meeting, they were married, and Jack immediately adopted Tate and Emily.

Now, ten years later, he smiled to himself as he looked at the apex of the Gateway Arch. Just a few days before, he'd provided himself a subliminal pat on the back as he stared at One Met, a testament to his success in business. Tonight, he provided another pat on the back for being a loving husband to Jill and a caring father to the kids.

CHAPTER SIX

Thursday, December 20
Atwood Residence
Cordova, Tennessee

Jill was in a jovial mood after she hung up with Jack that morning. He was ready to start day three of his seminars in St. Louis. The kids were off to school for their last two days of semester exams. She would be jetting off to Trader Joe's for groceries and then back home again to get ready for everyone to pile in on them the next night. She was half humming and half singing as she looked over her shopping list and checked the cupboards one last time. She allowed Bing Crosby, however, to do the heavy lifting with the singing part.

"I'll be home for Christmas.
"You can plan on me.
"Please have some snow and mistletoe."

Jill hummed the rest of the refrain as she retrieved her list and wrote the word *mistletoe* followed by a question mark.

She looked through her kitchen window at the sunny skies

reflecting off the lake behind their home. Kids were playing in the park on the other side. In the sky, the Goodyear blimp floated by. It was going to be a big sports weekend in Memphis, and the nice folks at Goodyear had decided to advertise their products overhead.

Just as she was reaching for her jacket to pull it on, her cell phone rang. She studied the display. It was her sister, Beth.

"Hey, Bethie!" Jill greeted cheerily. "Are you on your way yet?"

"Almost," her younger sister replied. "Anthony was being a pill, so we're getting a late start. But we'll easily be at Mrs. Chandler's house before dark."

"Honey, when are you gonna stop calling her Mrs. Chandler?" asked Jill as she cradled the phone between her jaw and shoulder so she could pull on her jacket. The wonders of technology allowed her to take this conversation with her, because Lord knows she didn't have time to chitchat.

"As soon as she lets me," replied Beth. "I tried to call her Mom once, and she shot me a look that gave me the heebie-jeebies. I could see myself being chopped into little pieces and turned into hamburger."

"Whoa! That's an awful visual for a pregnant mother to conjure up."

"It's true," said Beth.

Jill asked, "What's the deal, anyway? Y'all have been married for years. You've got a three-year-old and a second baby in the hopper."

"Beats me. Honestly, my insecurities cause speculation to run rampant through my head. I mean, does she not want to get attached to me or something?"

Jill snatched her keys off the wall hook by the back door. She glanced around the kitchen one last time to make sure she didn't leave any candles burning, and then slipped through the Dutch door leading to the back deck. She wanted to fill the squirrel feeder before she left.

"What do you mean by attached?" Jill asked.

"You know. Like, maybe she thinks I'm not gonna be Tony's wife for long, and therefore I can't call her Mom as if that might somehow make our marriage permanent."

"It is permanent, Beth. You gotta believe that."

Jill let out a noticeable sigh. She'd spent most of her phone conversations with Beth the last two years talking her off the cliff of divorce.

"I don't think she believes it. To Mrs. Chandler, her Tony shoots the moon and can do no wrong. Somehow, it never dawns on her that I'm the one who comes to visit. I'm the one who drags little Anthony out of his comfort zone. You know how he can be around unfamiliar people. Heck, her house smells like mothballs. That freaks me out. Imagine the effect it has on my autistic little boy?"

Jill slid in behind the steering wheel of her full-sized SUV and pressed the ignition button. She turned down the radio and turned on the seat warmer. Despite the temperatures being seasonally normal in the fifties, their car was parked on the north side of the house and seemed to always be in the shade. She transferred the call to the hands-free feature on the SUV's sound system. Her life experiences compelled her to be a responsible driver.

"Can you hear me?" she asked Beth to confirm.

"Yes, why?"

"I have to take you to Trader Joe's with me, so I transferred you to the truck speakers."

Beth hesitated, and her tone became dejected. "Oh, okay. I know you're busy. I'll let you go."

"No, Beth. Don't hang up. We've got plenty of time to talk. Now, listen. You're a good wife and a great mom. You've got another beautiful baby on the way. Tony just needs to step up. He shouldn't force you to see his mother alone, especially at Christmas."

"Work keeps him busy. You know how it is."

The guys had an extraordinarily busy December, but that would likely result in greater financial security for both families.

"Yes, I do. Jack puts in long hours. Usually six days a week. However, he always makes family a priority when he can."

She could hear Beth sigh through the phone. Then Anthony could be heard yelling.

"Bird! Bird! Bird!"

Beth politely corrected him. "No, honey. That's a helicopter."

"He's adorable," said Jill. She always praised her sister's son. It had been a difficult time for Beth and Tony when they confirmed Anthony was autistic. Complicating matters was the fact Beth learned she was pregnant after Anthony's diagnosis. A debate raged in the Chandler household about Beth having an abortion over fears that all of their children might have autism spectrum disorder, or ASD. Beth refused to even consider an abortion, and now she was twenty-eight weeks pregnant.

"He is and I do love him so. I won't lie, it's a challenge."

Jill was anxious to change the subject. "Well, I hope you're ready for a whirlwind of a Christmas week. Tomorrow night, we'll have a potluck kinda supper. Charcuterie boards. Lots of dips. Desserts."

"I've been eating like a horse lately. Count me in."

"Good. Then on Saturday, Jack is gonna take Tony on a turkey shoot out in the country past Fisherville. We'll go shopping and then head into the city to watch Tate's championship game against Webb School out of Knoxville."

Beth enjoyed talking about her sister's family. It was what she dreamed of for herself. "I bet Tate's fired up."

"He is. He loves this new guy from Savannah. His name is Coach Joe Carey, and he led their team to back-to-back championships at the single A level."

"I've got my MUS sweatshirt he bought me for my birthday. Smart kid. You know, getting me an extra-large."

Jill laughed. "Don't start with me. After Anthony, you lost that baby weight so fast it made my head spin. I was chubby for a year after Tate and Emily."

"Is Emily nervous about the Christmas pageant on Sunday?" asked Beth.

"She's trying not to show it, but I can tell she is. I hear her rehearsing every night. I've tried to encourage her to relax. She shoots me down. She talks about this being her big debut and all of that."

Beth and Jill laughed. Then Jill continued. "Anyway, Sunday we'll head over to the Halloran Centre early to let her get comfortable. After, if we want, we'll hit downtown Memphis to tour the Pyramid or see the ducks at the Peabody, and then wolf down some ribs at the Rendezvous."

"Wow! You're checking off all the boxes on my Christmas wish list. There's one you forgot, though."

"*Au contraire*, sis," said Jill in her best French accent. "You will see Graceland in all its holiday splendor Christmas Eve if you want. Maybe Elvis will make an appearance?"

Beth laughed. Jill always made her feel better. "Love me some Elvis."

"He's all yours, honey."

"Come on, Jill. A little bit of shimmy. A little bit of shake. A lot of rock and a lot of roll. What's not to love?"

"Okay. Okay," Jill relented before continuing to lay out the week's agenda. "The rest of Christmas Eve, I thought we'd play it by ear. If there's something we missed or that you want to do, like last minute Christmas shopping, we'll do it. That night, we'll have a big dinner and open presents. On Christmas Day, it's all about chillaxing. We've got college football to watch. The Grizzlies play on TV. We'll eat leftovers and desserts and lie on the couches, moaning in pain."

Beth was laughing hilariously in the background at her sister's description of the daily activities. "What about Wednesday?"

"The day after Christmas? Yes, the best day of all. That's the day y'all get out of my house and go home so I can pass out."

Beth was in tears as she giggled. "You're so rude!"

"Aren't I though? I love you, Bethie. Please drive safe and give Mrs. Chandler a kiss on the cheek for me."

"No way! She's got the cooties!"

"Bye, you silly sister."

The two disconnected the call, and Jill allowed her smile to continue across her face. She loved her sister and she loved Christmas. It was a lot of fuss between the decorating and entertaining but worth every bit of effort.

This was gonna be the best family Christmas ever.

CHAPTER SEVEN

Thursday, December 20
Home of Tony and Beth Chandler
Baton Rouge, Louisiana

After Beth disconnected the call, she set about getting the car loaded. She'd purchased presents for everyone, including Tony. As she loaded them into oversized red velour Santa sacks, she couldn't help but notice none of the packages were for her from Tony. This wasn't out of the ordinary for him. He was one of those men who rushed out a day or two before Christmas and picked out whatever happened to grab his attention at the mall. She imagined as they grew older together, he'd just provide her the credit card and tell her to go buy whatever she wanted.

Beth had done her level best to reduce her expectations of what marriage should be like. Certainly, like many young girls growing up, she'd envisioned her prince charming. She'd hoped for a man who'd sweep her off her feet, then provide, protect, and dote over her until their dying days.

Tony did sweep Beth off her feet. They were popular in college and enjoyed the nightlife of downtown Baton Rouge with innumerable friends. So much so, they purchased a condominium overlooking the Mississippi River within walking distance of Tony's office as well as their favorite evening haunts.

Beth rubbed her protruding belly, which held their unborn baby. She set one of the Santa sacks near the door and wandered over to the window overlooking the river. Flood warnings had been issued due to the days of heavy rain they'd experienced. The region had recorded fifteen inches so far, resulting in the U.S. Army Corps of Engineers working long hours to reinforce levees and place sandbags in front of vulnerable businesses.

News coverage of the flood event had dominated the airwaves. Many were comparing the current rain event to the August 2016 floods, which resulted in over thirty thousand people requiring rescue and over a hundred thousand seeking FEMA financial assistance.

"I'm gonna miss this view, Anthony," she said to her son, who was sitting on the sofa, studying a toy. He didn't always respond to Beth when she said his name. Oftentimes he avoided contact with her and preferred to sit alone in his own little world. She'd gotten over the feeling of rejection. Between advice from Anthony's doctors and her own autism research, she'd come to accept his aloofness was just a part of who he was and not something she should take as rejection.

She glanced around their condo. After Anthony was born, she'd begun to press Tony about moving out of the downtown area to the suburbs east of Baton Rouge. They weren't part of the nightlife scene anymore. Tony's commute into town wouldn't be that onerous, as Baton Rouge was a fairly small city despite being the Louisiana state capital and the home of LSU.

He'd argued they'd have plenty of time to find another place. As soon as Anthony turned five, they'd start looking. Then Beth became pregnant with their second child.

What a surprise?

No, not really. Not to Beth, anyway.

Her marriage to Tony had been rocky and cold of late. She

remembered the attention he'd given her when she was pregnant with Anthony and thought she could rekindle that flame with him by having another baby.

She'd miscalculated.

After he got over the shock, he became concerned that a second child might have autism as well. It was a stressful first eight weeks as the couple debated whether an abortion, which they both vehemently opposed, would make sense for medical reasons. In the end, they agreed she should have their baby.

Tony did change in his attitude toward their marriage. He became even more distant. He found excuses to travel to other offices. He worked longer hours. Her insecurities caused her imagination to run wild. When he hesitated to advance their plans for finding a new home, she immediately wondered if he had a girlfriend in the city somewhere.

Finally, Tony relented and agreed they could purchase a home after Christmas. While Beth was thrilled with the decision, she would've preferred to move before she got so big in the belly that she threatened to topple over a lamp every time she turned around. Nonetheless, she was excited about the coming weeks, and Tony seemed to be more accepting of the direction their life was taking. Between the upcoming visit to Memphis, the house hunting, and the birth of their new daughter, the life of Mr. and Mrs. Chandler was looking up.

But first, she had to do her duty as a wife and daughter-in-law to visit Tony's mother—Mrs. Inez Chandler.

Ugh.

"Well, she isn't really that bad, I guess," said Beth aloud, lying in case her son could hear her thoughts.

Mrs. Chandler was widowed and lived in the Chandler family home in Winterville, Mississippi, a small town near the river about three miles north of Greenville and four miles south of Lamont, not that any of that registered with anybody outside Washington County.

Over time, Tony gradually was saddled with far more important things to do, related to the business, that prevented him from visiting his elderly mother. Beth, on the other hand, he'd determined, had plenty of time to make the three-and-a-half-hour trip up the back roads to let his mom visit with Anthony.

When Beth objected to being alone with her for the better part of two days, Tony always had the perfect comeback. "Would you rather she come here to stay with us for a week? Or two?" Case closed. Tony should've been an attorney.

Beth had everything sitting by the door, ready to go. She double-checked to confirm she had all of Anthony's things and that he was mentally calm to hit the road. She stuffed several of his favorite toys into his Minions backpack and set it on the pile to be loaded into her crossover. Then she called the concierge desk of the condominium and requested assistance to load up.

Nobody used the building's bellhop service except for the old ladies looking for attention and Beth because Anthony would sometimes lose it if he was left alone. It broke her heart the day she discovered that about him and vowed to never leave him alone again.

After she called, she wandered back to the ceiling-to-floor windows that overlooked the Mississippi. Her mind wandered as she observed the bustle of activity and the water lapping over the top of the levees.

She wondered aloud, "Just where does all that water go when it's over?"

CHAPTER EIGHT

Friday, December 21
USGS
Golden, Colorado

Dr. Lansing had arrived at the NEIC just after dawn that morning. She'd been troubled by seismic readings in the Central U.S. as well as reports of unstable groundwater in the Southern Mississippi River Valley. She'd told Oliver, her number one guy as it related to the region, as well as the other geophysicists who routinely compiled the NMSZ data, to plan on arriving early that Friday.

There was a reason Dr. Lansing referred to the seemingly unrelated seismic activity prior to a major earthquake in a region like the NMSZ as the Devil's Staircase. Like the devil, these types of faults issue warning signals, tantalizing hints, in the days and weeks before a larger earthquake.

The signals began as tiny shocks along the fault. After the tremors increased in strength ever so slightly, there would be a period in which they remained constant. Then they'd begin to increase in intensity again. Level off. And start increasing to tremors large enough to rattle houses. On a graph, the results would appear as a staircase rising upward until that final rip into the earth occurred—the appearance of the devil.

Making a link between these precursors and the so-called *Big One* was often controversial in the arena of quake forecasting. Laboratory studies and real-world seismic activity didn't always mesh. As Dr. Lansing tried to point out in her seismic modeling, not all earthquakes have foreshocks, as the preliminary shakers were known.

Besides, attempts to apply laboratory models that suggested an earthquake warning was appropriate didn't necessarily translate to accurate real-world alerts. Faults in the Earth were filled with fluids, heated to extreme temperatures, that undergo complex stresses. Modelling couldn't accurately take into account all the variables and their interaction with one another.

In recent decades, man had introduced hydraulic fracturing into this complicated relationship. Commonly known as fracking, the process of injecting liquid at high pressures into boreholes and subterranean rock had become popular to open existing fissures to extract fossil fuels.

Generally, the fracking process produces small earthquakes of magnitudes smaller than one. Dr. Lansing had created quite a stir years ago when she pointed to fracking as being directly related to a magnitude 4 earthquake in Texas. Subsequently, some geophysicists alleged an M5.8 earthquake may have been triggered by wastewater disposal in Oklahoma.

Late Thursday afternoon, Dr. Lansing began to notice a pattern in the seismic activity stretching from Corona, Tennessee, approximately thirty-five miles north of Memphis, to Keokuk, Iowa, on the Illinois border.

In addition, Keokuk was experiencing spring-like flooding from groundwater aquifers despite relatively modest levels of rainfall. The lower Mississippi River Valley was another matter. The earth from Greenville in Northern Mississippi down to New Orleans had been battered by heavy rains for nearly a week. The flooding had a profound impact on the groundwater levels.

The Mississippi River Valley aquifer was one of the largest in North America. It was located within a huge underground layer of water-bearing permeable rock. Some of these underground reservoirs lay just below the surface and provided water to vegetation and streams. Others were deeper underground, separated from Earth's surface by a thin layer of rock that kept it contained.

Dr. Lansing had pored over hydrograph reports the night before. She found there was extraordinary water accumulation in Mississippi and abrupt draining of lakes on both sides of the river from Memphis to Northern Illinois. One of the geophysicists had just handed her the most recent data.

"I'm starting to suspect a correlation here," she began. "These tremors could be part of a larger preseismic wave train that's building. If, in fact, we're witnessing step changes in groundwater levels, the question is, where is the most likely location of deformation? Arguably, the preseismic stresses could be anywhere along a thousand-plus-mile stretch of the Mississippi River Valley. This deformation is altering the fluid pressures within the aquifer system, both up and down, depending on location."

"Mum, we're expecting updated data within the next few hours from the NWIS," said Oliver. The NWIS, also a department within the USGS, stood for National Water Information System. Real-time hydrographs were available to Dr. Lansing's team, but the expert analysis from the Hydrogeophysics Branch lagged behind by several hours.

She stood from her round conference table and wandered through her office. Her job was frustrating in that most often she was forced to react to an earthquake after it was detected. The NEIC would compile the data in an attempt to locate the epicenter. Then they'd determine its size and intensity.

In recent months, back-to-back earthquakes south of Mexico City occurred where two subducting plates bent and then pulled apart. The first earthquake measured M8.1, and the one that followed nine days later in the same locale measured M7.1.

The purpose of pinpointing this information was to warn the public of possible aftershocks or the potential of soft sediment near the epicenter of the quake causing destruction in the days that followed.

That part of the job was expected of the NEIC. Dr. Lansing wanted to take it a step further. If she couldn't predict the initial quake, then she wanted to be able to predict the second one. Lives could be saved if she was accurate.

"Do we need to issue an earthquake forecast for the NMSZ?" asked Oliver.

She pointed at his white legal pad, indicating he should be ready to take notes. She began to wander through her office, periodically staring at a large relief map affixed to the wall to the side of her desk.

"Okay, any of you can answer as I go through the checklist. If someone disagrees with a response, speak up. We can't mess around with this. Ready?"

They all nodded that they were.

"First of all, let's deal with a magnitude 3 or greater. When was the first one?"

"Arnold, Missouri, Monday the seventeenth at 2:00 local time. There were several more in rapid succession in the St. Louis metropolitan area."

She shook her head in disbelief. Her Frontier Air flight had left for Denver just an hour before that.

"Since Monday afternoon, how many M2s or greater have been recorded?"

"Forty-seven," replied Oliver. "That's if you include the NMSZ and its periphery."

"When?" she asked.

One of the other geophysicists responded, "Thirty-three in the second burst of activity Wednesday afternoon the nineteenth. The remainder have taken place throughout the day yesterday and especially overnight into this morning."

Dr. Lansing stopped pacing the floor. "Officially, let's note the swarm began Monday afternoon. Now, when and where was the largest quake?"

"Last night, 11:17 local time, at Wright, Tennessee, which is on the north side of Reelfoot Lake."

"What is the current water level of the lake?"

Nobody responded. Dr. Lansing looked them all in the eyes. She pointed at one of the geophysicists. "Please look it up."

The young man furiously banged away on his keyboard. "Let's see. Spillway elevation is two-eighty-three. Greatest depth is eighteen, approx. Um, current depth is … Hang on. Eight-point-four. Wow! That's a full inch below its record low in 1953."

"Drought conditions?" asked Dr. Lansing.

He made several keystroke entries to check rainfall totals over the last fourteen days. His response was simple, but it raised concerns for Dr. Lansing.

"No."

She wandered back to the relief map and pointed to Reelfoot Lake in upper West Tennessee. "Here we have a lake that was literally created by the second and third New Madrid quakes in 1812. Now, during this current swarm, it's lost its volume and depth to levels below its record almost eight decades ago. I don't believe in coincidences."

The group watched Oliver make his notes. He then looked up to Dr. Lansing. "Do you want us to calculate a probability forecast?"

"Absolutely. Who's our statistician?"

A young woman waved her hand in the air for a brief second before she returned to her laptop. She was one step ahead of them. She grimaced and then looked up to Dr. Lansing.

"I'm showing a one-in-three-thousand chance of a magnitude 7-plus in the vicinity of the swarm. I would put the chances of a 5-plus outside the NMSZ as one in forty-five hundred."

She turned her laptop around for Dr. Lansing to study the data. After nearly a minute, Dr. Lansing began to wander again as she spoke.

"Okay. Okay. I see three scenarios possible of what could happen in the next seven days. Scenario one, the least likely, would be a larger earthquake along the magnitude of 5 to 6.5 on the fringes of the NMSZ.

"Scenario two, the next less likely of the three, or our middle-ground position, is that a larger quake of M6.5 or higher could occur within the next seven days within the defined boundaries of the NMSZ.

"Scenario three, the most likely, is that these tremors will continue as part of a long-lasting swarm. If recent history is considered, this swarm will continue through Christmas, and then New Madrid will settle down."

Oliver leaned back in his chair and raised his hand slightly. "Mum, what if we're looking at the Devil's Staircase playing out as the kind of pattern you've envisioned?"

Dr. Lansing never answered his question because she didn't want to put it out into the universe. She still resented being referred to as the prophetess of doom by the local paper, but just in case, she didn't want to say it aloud.

She dismissed the group to gather more data. She turned to the relief map and ran the tips of her fingers along the raised terrain that made up the Mississippi River Valley. She muttered to herself, "What's going on with you?"

CHAPTER NINE

Friday, December 21
Winterville, Mississippi

That Friday morning, Beth woke up praying for a sunny day to travel. She even had designs on skipping out on Mrs. Chandler immediately after breakfast so she could catch her niece's rehearsal for the Christmas presentation. When her eyes opened and were ready to focus, she saw the gray light seeping through the curtains and heard the steady patter of rainfall on the old home's metal roof. Her early release from the custody of Tony's mother was thwarted.

Then the aroma of sausage found its way under her door and into her nostrils. Beth swung her legs around, supported her baby with her left hand, and slid off the tall four-poster bed in the guest room. She fought her urge to pee and made her way to the door first. She cracked it open and heard Mrs. Chandler chatting away with Anthony, explaining the art of Southern cooking. For all of her social faults, Mrs. Chandler was one of the best at serving the delicacies of the Old South.

Beth quickly got ready and joined them in the kitchen. As was usually the case, she was forbidden from lifting a finger even when it came time to clear the table and wash the dishes. Her pregnancy was not the issue. This was Inez Chandler's house, and her rules were expected to be followed.

Fortunately, Mrs. Chandler never really wanted to engage Beth in conversation. It wasn't that the two clashed with one another, as long as Beth bit her tongue. It was that they had nothing in common except her son.

Beth always apologized for Tony's nonappearance at get-togethers like these. Before she could begin to spout out the lame excuses, Mrs. Chandler took care of that for her.

My son is a very important man. People trust him with their life savings.

His hard work pays for all the nice things your family enjoys.

We retirees need smart men like my Tony to shepherd us through these difficult times.

Blah. Blah. Blah.

Beth always agreed with her mother-in-law because it was easier that way. She could never have an honest conversation with her about the state of their marriage and how her son wasn't necessarily the golden boy Mrs. Chandler made him out to be when it came to his family.

The only saving grace that kept the two women from coming to verbal blows was that Tony's mother never advised Beth on how to raise Anthony or how to manage her pregnancy.

Never. Not once.

Beth clearly saw that as the exception to the commonly accepted rule. Heck, there were whole books on her Kindle device advising expectant mothers how to deflect the unwelcome advice of others. For some reason that Beth could only explain as pure apathy and indifference, she was one of the few daughters-in-law on the planet to dodge the unsolicited advice and instructions of her mother-in-law.

The day passed, and after countless glances at her watch as well as the digital clock on the oven, Beth announced it was time for her to get on the road. She had a stop to make as she drove up the highway, and she planned on arriving at her sister's home about the time the rest of the family returned there as well.

Mrs. Chandler had baked an apple pie and wrapped it in foil for the trip. She helped load up Beth's crossover and provided Anthony a couple of cookies in the back seat for the road. Beth double-checked the five-point restraint to ensure it was locked, provided her son a kiss on the forehead, and shared an obligatory hug with Tony's mother. With a steady rain continuing to pelt the southern half of Mississippi, Beth was happily on the road.

"Okay, Anthony. Next, we'll have a quick pit stop in Rosedale. I've been craving Miss Barbara's hot tamales. You probably don't remember this, but when I was pregnant with you, I used to be a great wife and came to visit your grandma. Really, I wanted an excuse to pick up a Tupperware container full of Miss Barbara's tamales."

Beth glanced in the rearview mirror. Anthony didn't seem to care that she was talking to him. He'd become fascinated with the shape and texture of the sugar cookies. It was if he was analyzing them to determine which one was bigger or contained more icing. Maybe he was counting the number of sprinkles embedded in the icing? Beth never really knew what was on her son's mind. His unresponsiveness didn't bother her as long as he was happy.

Seeing that Anthony wasn't in a very talkative mood, Beth turned on the radio and listened to SiriusXM Channel 10, pop hits of the 2000s. She tapped her fingers on the steering wheel as one song after another played commercial-free.

She was in a good headspace that afternoon as she rocked along Highway 1, which ran parallel to the river. There was only an occasional car headed southbound, and the rain had lessened compared to when she woke up. She enjoyed spending time with Emily and Tate, both of whom were model kids that she'd love for her children to grow up like. She tried not to admit it—too often, anyway—but she truly envied her sister's life. Everything about it. Jack was a hero and an incredible man. The kids were perfect. Their home was perfect. Jill's life could've been the model for any young girl growing up.

As Beth continued toward Rosedale, mindlessly daydreaming of what could've been, she failed to notice the water rising on the west side of the two-lane highway. The fields were flooded, and as she passed through the small community of Scott near Arkansas City, it was apparent that the river had expanded well beyond its normal boundaries. What Beth didn't know was that water was rising rapidly throughout the lower Mississippi River Basin.

The thirty-minute drive had flown by, and she was full of excitement when she eased into the parking lot at the White Front Café. The nondescript white clapboard front would've caused most unknowing tourists to keep driving by in search of golden arches or some guy holding a red-and-white bucket of chicken.

The sign next to the single door read White Front Café, Joe's HOT TAMALE Place. That's what brought 'em in the door. Tamales. It was the Mississippi Blues Trail Marker sitting to the side of the parking area in the grass that provided the historic nature of the business. Joe Pope, the oldest of ten children, had founded the restaurant in the seventies, and it had been a family business and part of Mississippi history ever since.

It was Friday afternoon, so Beth wasn't surprised that several cars were in the small parking lot to pick up dinner. When she and Anthony entered, the patrons were abuzz with chatter as they watched the four o'clock news on a Jackson news station. The rainfall and flooding dominated the programming.

Beth shrugged it off. She knew it had been raining and the water was threatening Baton Rouge. There wasn't anything she could do about it except wish it would stop. She was only a couple of hours away from Memphis.

She handed Miss Barbara the large Tupperware container over the counter. With a big grin, she said with a laugh, "Fill it up, please. I'm eating for thirty." Beth stepped back away from the glass counter so Miss Barbara could see her belly.

"You sure are, young lady. You know Joe's hot tamales gonna bring that baby right out of there kickin' and screamin'."

"I don't know, Miss Barbara. They might, but it's still a little early. I'll be driving back through town a week from now. I'll bring two Tupperware containers. I'll freeze them and eat one every morning with my prenatal vitamins. Then we'll see how she kicks and screams."

"A baby girl." Miss Barbara beamed. She looked down at Anthony. "Does this young man like hot tamales, too?"

"He did when I was carrying him," replied Beth with a laugh.

She reached down and pulled her son close to her hip. He was a good boy. Beth was certain he took in everything he observed. He studied his surroundings. Watched people interact. With an intense curiosity, he analyzed anything mechanical. And then he catalogued it in his brain somewhere for future reference. When he was ready, he'd share the incredible power of his brain with the world. For now, he was in the learning stage.

While Miss Barbara prepared the tamales, Beth wandered back toward the television. Suddenly, the door was forced open, swinging hard against the wall. The Bolivar County sheriff and one of his deputies lumbered in, bringing the rain with them.

"Hey, Walter," said one of the men focused on the television. "This rain's playin' hell on all our fields. The news says—"

"Jimbo," the burly sheriff interrupted, "here's all the news you need to know. We're evacuating the county."

Jimbo and the other patrons who'd glued their eyes to the television turned around to give Sheriff Walter Baldwin their undivided attention.

"Whadya mean, Sheriff?" asked one of the women.

He tipped his cap to Beth and slid past her to the counter. "Miss Barbara, I need you to listen up, too."

She finished stuffing the hot tamales into Beth's Tupperware and handed them past the sheriff.

He began to explain, "Folks, we're under mandatory evacuation from the governor. It started with the levee breach in Natchez. Here in Bolivar County, we've got levee breaches from Eutaw all the way up to Beulah. What's worse, and ain't nobody explained it to me, but there seems to be some kind of springs or something that's addin' to the groundwater between here and Highway 278."

"Groundwater?" asked Jimbo. "You mean floodin'?"

"Both," replied the sheriff. "Here's what I'm sayin'. The river has blown past all the Corps of Engineers levees to the south. To our east, the waters in the fields are risin', and not just 'cause of the doggone downpours. I mean lakes are showing up out of nowhere."

"Come on, Sheriff," said Jimbo. "I've never heard of such."

"Believe it. We just came across Highway 8 from Cleveland. It's pert near underwater."

The group started to talk excitedly among themselves, so Beth used it as an opportunity to get some advice.

"Sheriff, I'm going to Memphis. I planned on driving up to Tunica and then cutting over to I-55. Is that way okay?"

"It is for now, ma'am," he replied politely. "I'd suggest you be on your way."

Beth nodded her appreciation and then waved goodbye to Miss Barbara, whose face revealed her concern. Her small building was no match for the encroaching Mississippi River.

CHAPTER TEN

Friday, December 21
Cordova, Tennessee

Jill waited impatiently on Sanga Road in front of Cordova Middle School, where Emily was finishing up her final day of the semester. Ordinarily, she'd ride her bike around the lake to get to school. It had been raining on and off all day, so that wasn't an option. Besides, today they had to scoot across Cordova to pick up Tate from MUS and then head downtown. There, Emily would join the other kids from Cordova Presbyterian for their one and only rehearsal in the Halloran Centre before Sunday's event. Apparently, several other mothers had the same idea, or they were picking up their kids to leave town for Christmas.

She checked her watch. 3:25. Plenty of time, she reminded herself, so she took a deep breath and exhaled. A few cars moved forward, so Jill inched along behind them. This morning, Emily had been awake at the crack of dawn. Jill had gotten up to make coffee and found her daughter dancing through the living room. Periodically, she'd stop to practice her lines before continuing to dance. Jill had watched from around the corner of the dining room wall. There was little doubt her daughter was ready, assuming nothing happened to panic her.

It took several more minutes for her to wheel her truck in front of two sets of double doors leading inside the school. Emily was waiting somewhat impatiently near the flagpole. Both of her arms were full of books and her first semester science project.

She'd created a model of the sun emitting a solar flare toward a much smaller Earth. The papier-mâché project had taken a week to build with the help of Jack. Jill had never seen the beautiful aurora created by a solar flare hitting Earth. She wondered if a really strong solar flare might bring the hues of blue and green as far south as Tennessee someday. *That would be cool*, she thought to herself.

She jumped out of the truck and opened the rear hatch. Emily carefully set down her solar-flare project and meticulously spread her books around so they wouldn't topple over and damage the project. The two hugged and kissed one another before Emily slid into the back seat. Once Jill was settled in, she looked at her daughter in the rearview mirror.

"I won't bite, you know. You can ride up here with me before we pick up Tate."

Emily had already unzipped her pink and white duffle bag she'd bought for herself at Victoria's Secret last spring. "That's okay, Mom. I want to go ahead and change so I'll be ready when we get there. Are we on time?"

Jill glanced at the LED clock on the dashboard. "Close enough. You change and get comfortable. No worries, okay?"

Emily gave her a thumbs-up and began to arrange her outfit. She wrestled out of her jeans and shirt, periodically glancing through the side windows to confirm there were no Peeping Toms around.

Jill motored down Germantown Parkway and then zigzagged her way through Poplar Estates to avoid the retail shopping congestion in Germantown. She imagined Kroger, Hobby Lobby, and the stores on Farmington Boulevard were nutso that day.

She pulled into the circular drive at MUS with ease. Unlike

Emily's middle school, most of the students had cars or carpooled with older kids. Now that Tate was fifteen, he had his Learner Permit, but that didn't allow him to drive alone. He had plenty of friends on the varsity football team to hitch a ride with every day. He'd be able to drive soon enough, a guaranteed added stress for his mother.

Jill drove past all the other cars in the parking lot and made her way to the back of the school between the soccer field and the football stadium that rivaled the size of most small colleges. Emily finished changing clothes and set her duffle bag in the rear storage compartment near her other things. She turned to lean through the seats so she could see through the rain-soaked windshield.

"Where is he?"

"I don't know, Em. He said the offense skill players would be running padless drills on Rogers Field." She searched the soccer fields for any signs of activity.

"There's nobody here. What if he went home with someone else?"

Jill and Emily both had their heads turned toward the empty soccer field and the concession stand next to the parking lot. They never saw Tate sneak up on them from behind. He flung the door open.

"Boo!"

Emily shrieked. "You asshole!"

"Young lady! Watch your language!"

Tate was laughing as he looked inside at the startled Atwood women.

"Well, he is!"

Jill regained her composure and scowled at her son. "I can't argue with that. Get in, mister."

"Hey, how about letting me drive?"

"Hey, how about no chance in you know where?"

"Come on, Mom. I need the practice," he whined.

Jill wasn't having any of it. "Not today, Tate. We're a little behind, and it's Friday afternoon before a holiday. It'll be a nightmare."

Tate rolled his eyes and jumped into the front seat. After he buckled his seat, he turned to Emily. "Hey, squirt. Are you ready?"

"Don't call me squirt," Emily complained, and then she added, "Mr. Tardy Farty."

"Oooh, you got me there, Em. Okay, I'm late, but I didn't need to go with y'all. I could've hitched a ride home with Britney, you know."

Emily immediately mocked her brother. "Oooh, riding with an older woman. Shame on you, mister varsity football player."

"Shut up, Emily. You don't even know what that means."

Jill shot him a glance. "Young man, you'd better not know what an older woman means either."

"Mom, it's just Britney. She sixteen. Big whoop."

"Sweet sixteen," Emily crowed. "Going on seventeen. She's way advanced for her age, Mom."

Emily was kicking his ass, and Tate was getting mad.

"Mom, just let me out. I'll walk or catch an Uber or something."

"Maybe Britney will come back for you unless she found a man her own age."

"That's it!" Tate unbuckled his seatbelt and swirled around to grab at his sister. She leaned against the door and began kicking at his hands.

Jill had to intervene. The drive into the city was going to be stressful enough without the kids at each other. Plus, she wanted Emily to be in the best frame of mind possible to rehearse.

"Enough, you two! Apologize to each other."

Tate spun around and buckled his seatbelt. Emily sat in the middle of the back seat with her arms folded. Neither said a word.

"Out loud, please," Jill ordered.

"Sorry, squirt."

"I'm sorry, too, ah—"

"Emily Atwood! Don't you dare let that word out of your mouth."

Tate started laughing. He stretched his arm over the seat to offer his fist to his sister. She bumped it in return as they smiled at one another. Tate would lay down his life for Emily, and she'd do the same for him. Despite their sibling scraps, at the end of the day, they were very close-knit.

Jill drove east along I-240 across South Memphis. She took I-55 into the city along the riverfront before finding South Main Street, which led directly into downtown. It was 4:10. Emily wasn't supposed to be there until 4:30, so there was time if traffic would cooperate.

"Um, Mom, I don't wanna be late."

"I know, honey. There's a big parking garage next to the Halloran. We'll be okay."

Jill wasn't sure. She looked around the downtown area. The last time she saw traffic this busy, both vehicular and pedestrian, was New Year's Eve several years ago.

"Okay, let's see what we can do," she said as she turned into the Memphis Light, Gas and Water parking garage across the street from the utility's main office and immediately adjacent to the Halloran Centre for Performing Arts & Education.

It was 4:20. Plenty of time.

CHAPTER ELEVEN

Friday, December 21
Downtown Memphis, Tennessee

"Mom, I'm gonna be late," Emily whined. Jill glanced at the clock. It was approaching 4:30. She'd driven to the top of the four-story parking garage, and every space was full. She'd already begun to make her way to the ground level.

"Okay. Okay," she began as she gave the kids their instructions. "Tate, I'm gonna have to find a space somewhere else. Can you take Emily inside so she can meet up with the director?"

"Yeah, sure."

Jill whipped the truck out of the garage and in front of an oncoming delivery van. The man laid on the horn and further expressed his displeasure with the one-finger salute.

"Yeah, Yeah. Sorry." Jill ran through the yellow light as she turned back onto Main Street, leaving the delivery van stuck at the red. That earned her another blast of his horn. She pulled to a stop across the entrance from the Halloran Centre. "Okay, kids. Be careful crossing the street."

"We're gonna be jaywalking, Mom," said Emily.

Jill rocked her head back and forth. Her daughter was such a rule follower and a snitch at this age. She'd grow out of it eventually.

Jill smiled at her and unlocked the doors. "I love you guys. I'll be along in a minute."

The kids bailed out of the truck on the sidewalk without saying a word. Jill drove off, heading north toward Beale Street. She glanced in the rearview mirror long enough to see Tate drag his sister by the arm until they were safely across the street and running toward the all-glass performing-arts venue.

At Beale Street, she got stuck in line at the red light. "This is ridiculous." Downtown was packed because of so many activities at once. The AutoZone Liberty Bowl had been moved up to the twenty-first to accommodate the recently revised and expanded NCAA college football playoff schedule. At the FedEx Forum, the Mid-South Holiday Classic was underway, featuring eight college basketball teams, including Memphis, Villanova, UCLA, and Marquette.

Plus, there were the revelers at Beale Street. Known as America's Most Iconic Street and the Home of the Blues, Beale street featured dozens of bars and restaurants as well as shops. On any given night, thousands of locals and tourists alike packed into the area for barbecue, blues music, and dancing. On that night, the Friday before Christmas, it appeared thousands of partiers were descending on downtown to attend the sporting events and to let loose on Beale Street.

Jill turned right on Beale Street, past the bronze statue of a young Elvis Presley playing the guitar, until she could turn on Second Street. The Bank of America Financial Center was a block up on Peabody Place, and she knew it to have a much larger parking garage than the one adjacent to the Halloran.

After waiting at the light for what seemed an eternity although it was only a minute, she made her way into the garage. It was also packed but had a feature the other garage didn't have—a spaces available board. The LED board at the single entrance to the garage informed new arrivals of how many spaces were available on each floor of the seven-story structure. Each of the first six floors were lit up in red and indicated no spaces were available. The seventh, or top floor, fortunately had eleven spaces.

It was getting dark, and Jill took her chances by driving quickly through the lower floors. She hoped she'd see oncoming headlights or a car's reverse lights before she crashed into them. She calculated correctly, and within minutes, she was at the top of the garage. She parked in the northeast corner of the garage, where she had a straight-on view of the historic Peabody Hotel.

She exited the truck. The cool air and the roar of partiers struck her immediately. It was a jolt of energy coming from a city full of life and vigor. She loved Memphis, and one of her favorite things to do was to visit the Peabody Hotel to witness the March of the Peabody Ducks.

The Peabody was also where she and Jack had professed their love to one another. It was just lunch, but it had led to an honest conversation in which the two revealed their feelings. The Peabody was where they honeymooned. It was where they celebrated their anniversaries. It was their place.

She gazed down the street and visualized what would be happening soon. In just under thirty minutes, at five o'clock sharp, the Peabody Duckmaster would lead the hotel's famed ambassadors, five mallard ducks consisting of one drake with his white collar and four less colorful hens, down the red carpet to the lobby's fountain. The March of the Peabody Ducks had been a tradition since 1940.

Sadly, it was about to end.

CHAPTER TWELVE

Friday, December 21
Top of the Met
One Metropolitan Square
St. Louis, Missouri

The small group of twenty arrived for their noon luncheon. It would be the smallest group of the week but important to Jack and Tony nonetheless. The majority of those in attendance for this final session were from the St. Louis area, and several had brought along family members who'd traveled to visit them for the holidays from around the country. It would give the guys an opportunity to reach prospects they wouldn't ordinarily see.

The Top of the Met was a breathtaking space with floor-to-ceiling windows on three sides overlooking St. Louis, the Gateway Arch, and the Mississippi River. The well-appointed space featured crystal chandeliers, two propane-fueled fireplaces, and a twenty-foot-long bar with nearly two hundred different brands of liquor. Tables were decorated with flowers in crystal vases and stemware for every beverage.

The banquet facility was used for everything from high-dollar political fundraisers to wedding receptions, as well as the occasional financial seminar for Jack's company. The opulent space was rich in contrasting shapes, colors, and textures. The walls and floors were finished in eight different granites and marbles. Select walls were adorned with commissioned art and ornate mirrors. The room catered to the affluent, and Jack wanted his guests to feel special when they joined him for a seminar.

After they enjoyed their choice of a chicken or fish entrée along with wine and dessert, the banquet staff cleared their tables, and the seminar kicked off. Jack took the first half hour to introduce the history of his firm and the locations of their offices. He explained the importance of wrapping under one roof all three aspects of their retirement planning, including living trusts, annuity-type investments, and tax-reduction strategies.

After his introductory remarks, he yielded the floor to his associates, with the CPA being first up. The seminar was partially scripted with certain lines delivered to the attendees for maximum impact. The first words out of the CPA's mouth were always the same.

"Who would like to pay MORE income tax next year?"

The response never varied. Nobody raised their hand, and everyone got a good laugh coupled with a chorus of boos.

"Now, how many of you would like to reduce what you send to Washington?" The crowd was unanimous in their desire to save money on their taxes, and Jack's team had effectively influenced them to agree with what his team would suggest right from the start.

After that, the CPAs laid out their strategy, which included preparing the tax returns for their clients at a nominal charge, an interesting technique designed to create a new client of the firm while also gaining access to the details of their financial investments during the preparation of the return. Every time, without fail, they were able to find a way to save the client money on their income taxes, and the financial planner would step in to show them the investments to achieve that goal.

As always, Tony wowed the group with a combination of his charm while extolling the virtues of fixed and variable annuities. Many of the retired men in attendance were looking for an edge to maximizing the return on their investments. The no-risk benefits of annuities caught their attention immediately. At their age, as Tony put it, they were too old to gamble in the stock market and needed to focus on safety, with enough growth to keep up with inflation.

By the time Jack returned to take the floor, the attendees were often tired and less interested in talking about their ultimate demise as opposed to the excitement of saving on taxes and earning more on their investments. To keep their interest, Jack had to tug on their heartstrings.

When he explained to his team why the living trust aspect of the presentation was so important, he once said, "Guilt is a great motivator." He would oftentimes recall the details of probate cases in which families fought with one another because the deceased loved one either failed to create a simple will or the probate became contested. He explained how a living trust avoided the complications of settling an estate. It also saved an inordinate amount of time and legal expense. Like his representation of Jill, rather than taking nearly a year to settle an estate through probate court, a living trust's provisions made the process take only a few days or weeks.

That afternoon, despite the fact he'd said virtually the identical words and delivered them in almost the same manner as prior seminars, Jack was energized as he thought about driving home that night to join the family. Jill had been finishing the Christmas decorating. She'd promised lots of baked yummies as well as homemade candies. It was a time for family to come together to enjoy one another and celebrate.

Jack opened up the floor for questioning. He never looked at his watch during his presentation. Eagle-eye seminar attendees saw that as a sign of boredom or insincerity. Instead, he'd watch Tony, who stood at the back of the room. He was supposed to give Jack a signal when it was four o'clock. This would allow him to take questions, encourage everyone to fill out their informational forms to hand in, and thank them for coming. Jack knew sunset began around a quarter to five, and he wanted his attendees heading down the elevators by then. Instead of giving Jack the signal, Tony was distracted, flirting with one of the staff.

He took pride in helping the attendees even if they never became clients. He looked them in the eye and spoke to them using their first name as if they'd been friends for years. Discussing one's death and the plans for their family was extremely personal. Jack treated the subject matter with the respect it deserved. However, he sensed time had slipped by on him. He broke his rule and glanced at his watch. It was 4:20.

"Okay, everyone. One last question."

"Jack, one of the things I hoped you would've covered today were the second-to-die life insurance policies. Can you tell me a little more about them?"

Jack caught the eye of Tony, who nodded and winked. A second-to-die life insurance policy was designed for wealthy couples who were trying to avoid the onerous estate taxes due the federal government when the first spouse passes away. In essence, the policy insured both husband and wife, but doesn't pay the beneficiaries until the second spouse passes away. It was designed for more wealthy retirees, so this particular prospective client might provide the firm enough business to justify the expenses of the entire week's seminars.

"Thank you for bringing up that very important estate-planning tool. We don't usually get into a detailed discussion of second-to-die policies during our conversation, as it is only appropriate for certain families. However, let me—"

Jack stopped midsentence. He was struck by a ringing sound that reached his ears. From overhead, or outside the windows, there was a faint chime that hung in the air for a moment. It was joined by more bells rising into a cacophony of clanging. Deep. Metallic. Frantic. Rising high into the air. High enough to reach the ears of the attendees on the forty-second floor of the Met.

The room remained deathly quiet until the glassware shuddered. Ripples flowed across the partially filled water glasses, reminiscent of the scene in *Jurassic Park* when *Tyrannosaurus rex* rumbled past a rain puddle.

Tony stepped forward. Ever the jokester, he attempted humor to lighten the moment. "It appears Santa Claus has landed on the roof a little bit early."

A few people laughed nervously, but most remained still as the building began to vibrate. Nobody uttered a word as the bells continued to sound, ringing loudly in dread, not celebration.

CHAPTER THIRTEEN

Friday, December 21
Halloran Centre
Memphis, Tennessee

The Halloran Centre for Performing Arts and Education was opened in 2005 adjacent to the famous Orpheum Theatre. The CEO of the Orpheum, Pat Halloran, envisioned a theater arts education program designed to not only teach young people about performing arts but also as an alternative for teaching kids other core curriculum using theater as a tool.

The thirty-nine-thousand-square-foot building was sandwiched between the Orpheum to the right of its entrance and a much taller parking garage to the left. Inside, in addition to multiple classrooms, the building contained a state-of-the-art audio-video lab, a forty-person conference table, and the two-hundred-sixty-seat theater with a full production stage.

Tate and Emily hustled across the rain-soaked sidewalk to the double set of glass doors covered by a roof overhang. The door was immediately opened for them by a woman with salt-and-pepper hair framing a beaming smile.

"Welcome to the Halloran theater, kids! I gather you're here for the rehearsal."

"Yes, ma'am," said Emily. "I'm one of the actors."

The woman chuckled. "So you are. Well, most of your fellow actors are already here. Young man, are you in the presentation as well?"

Tate shook his head. "Nah, I'm her bodyguard."

The woman cocked her head and furrowed her brow, not sure how to take his comment. Then she laughed. "Well, I suppose all the famous actors have one. Um, you're not packin' heat, are you?"

Tate smiled and said no. Their gracious greeter led them inside and pointed out a few things as they walked down the corridors.

"I doubt that you'll have a need to wander around other than in the theater itself, but to our left is a boardroom overlooking Main Street, which is used by local businesses for large meetings. Through that door is our lounge with comfortable seating and big-screen televisions."

"Really?" asked Tate, suddenly interested in the nickel tour.

"Yes, but it's closed for this evening. I'm sorry. On the far side of the building is the reception hall. There are some vending machines in there if you need a drink or a light snack. And, of course, through these doors is the theater."

She gestured for Emily and Tate to walk through the open doors. She stood back with pride to allow them to take in the scene. Tate was the first to comment.

"It looks like a movie theater except with a stage."

"That's right, young man. The theater-style seating enables every guest to have an excellent view of the presentation. They rise up so that even tall young men like yourself won't block another's view."

"Look at all of that equipment," marveled Tate as he pointed toward the front of the theater. He was genuinely impressed that his little sister would be performing on a professional stage like this one instead of an elementary school lunchroom full of temporary risers.

"Oh, yes. Mr. Halloran spared no expense years ago when he

created this marvelous theater. The large structure you see at the front is a custom rigging system holding the lighting and audio accessories. From a control panel on the platform above our heads, the production team can increase or dim the lights, change their colors, and adjust the sound depending on the scene. Behind the black curtain you see just in front of the rigging are thousands of feet of electrical wire, enormous subwoofers too large to attach to the rigging, and video cameras to record the presentation for later classroom use."

"That's a lot of red," added Emily, referencing the rows upon rows of padded red seats.

"Emily!" shouted the rehearsal director. "Hurry up, Miss Atwood. We need to get started."

Emily smiled at Tate and hustled off.

Tate shouted after her, "Break a leg, Em!" It was the traditional method of wishing a performer well.

"I will!" she shouted back.

The greeter heard voices in the corridor and turned to leave. "Young man, you're welcome to sit anywhere. Obviously, most of the families are as close to the stage as possible."

"I like it back here, thanks," said Tate as he walked along the back row against the wall.

Tate pulled his cell phone out of his pocket and settled into a comfortable seat. He stretched his long legs through the seats in front of him. Emily was instructed to join the dancer's group, and all the kids were given instructions on how the rehearsal would go. Tate expected his mom to arrive and force him to sit closer to the stage, so he wanted to text his girlfriend, Britney, before Jill arrived in the theater.

T: You around?

B: Hey, you! I'm getting ready to go out. I wish you could go, too.

T: No kidding. Coach Carey has us all on lockdown anyway. I'm in the city for my sister's rehearsal.

B: Bummer. We're all headed out to Scooter's farm toward Macon. You know. Bonfire. Jager shots. The good life.

T: Sucks for me.

Tate scowled. Sometimes, he hated being responsible. MUS was full of kids who had lots of money, nice cars, and parents who were oblivious as to what they did at night. His family lived comfortably, but he realized he would never have been able to attend MUS if he hadn't received a full sports scholarship. He was expected to keep his grades up and fulfill his obligations to the private school's athletic department. If he didn't, the scholarship went away, and he'd have to transfer to Cordova High.

He leaned forward and checked the two entrances to his right and left for his mother. Jill still hadn't arrived. Then he checked his text messages. Britney kind of disappeared, he thought.

T: Hey, where'd you go?

A few seconds later, she replied.

B: Did you feel that?

T: Feel what?

Then Tate felt it. Everybody did.

PART II

SHAKEN FURY

Imagine a city crying out in despair. Not just in the building where you stand. The pleas for mercy were everywhere. Block by block. Street by street. Downtown. Along the riverfront. In the suburbs. Traffic stopped. Many people stood, frozen in shock, covering their mouths to suppress their angst. Others ran out of buildings while some ran into them. Cars forced their way through panicked pedestrians in an effort to escape. Everywhere, people were wailing. Guttural. Primal. Utter fear exuded from their minds through their lungs and vocalized for the world to hear. Many did nothing at all, because they were dead. In cities up and down the Mississippi River, the scene was the same. Pure, unadulterated terror.

CHAPTER FOURTEEN

Friday, December 21
USGS
Golden, Colorado

Several of the geophysicists at the NEIC were winding down their short workday and chatting amongst themselves. Because it was the Friday before Christmas, the director of the USGS in Reston, Virginia, had approved all nonessential personnel to leave early that day by 2:30 local time. In the Golden facility, some of the staff had planned vacations for the following week. Others relished the overtime they'd be making by monitoring their patient, as Dr. Lansing called the planet.

For her part, she had no particular plans and had already told her husband she'd be working late. Since her mother-in-law moved into their house, Dr. Lansing had found a myriad of reasons to stay away.

Her team of computer analysts had completed their preliminary modeling of deformation from the weeklong earthquake swarm. The earth's shift had been negligible thus far and not enough to warrant an official earthquake warning to be issued through FEMA, according to her boss in Washington.

Regardless, she had been instructed to carefully monitor data from several seismometers located up and down the Mississippi. She'd been at it nonstop throughout the day. Several of the weary seismologists had volunteered to work late with her to study the data.

"Let's look at InSAR first," she said to the skeleton crew that remained.

The Interferometric Synthetic Aperture Radar was the most technologically advanced and effective way to measure changes in land surface altitude. It replaced the agency's former reliance upon global positioning satellites. InSAR made high-density measurements over large areas by bouncing radar signals from the ground to low-Earth orbiting satellites. The imagery was measured by calculating the time the signals pinged a target point on Earth back to the satellite.

"Yes, mum," began the ever-present, loyal Oliver. He made a few keystrokes on his computer and showed the results on a large monitor mounted at the center of the curved wall, where maps, televisions, and a whiteboard flanked it. "We're looking at a split screen of two monitoring points along the New Madrid fault. One is at the southernmost end of the NMSZ near Millington, Tennessee, just north of Memphis. The other is located near your hometown of Cape Girardeau."

"Is this real time?" she asked.

"No, mum. The imagery is fixed. I compiled it at four o'clock local time."

"Oliver, can you provide me a side-by-side comparison with the noon readings?"

"Yes, mum," he replied politely. He expanded his computer's reach to three monitors across the wall. "You didn't ask, but I've included the eight a.m., noon, and four p.m. for your reference."

She walked slowly toward the wall of monitors. Her eyes read the data and compared the images from left to right. She didn't seem to blink as she digested what she saw.

"Does anyone else see the pattern? The faulting is indisputable." She paused to point at three particular parts on the images and explained, "The relative displacement, here and here, reflects a dramatic change over the last, um, eight hours."

"Yes, mum. The satellite measurements indicate a continuous movement consistent with the New Madrid right-lateral strike-slip fault. Clearly, the fault has moved laterally to the right. The measurements also lead us to the conclusion that shearing forces beneath the surface are forcing the competing plates to move nearly vertical. It's a classic strike-slip scenario."

Dr. Lansing reached behind her head and gathered up her long hair in her right hand. She pulled it into a ponytail and then released it. She repeated the action three times, a habit she'd developed when she was a teen. She was fidgeting, something she often did when deep in thought.

"Oliver, can you bring up the InSAR data in real time?"

"Yes, I believe I can," he replied. It took a moment for him to enter the information, and then, one by one, the screens changed, and the current time, measured in Coordinated Universal Time, or UTC, was displayed.

Friday, December 21 22:40 UTC; 4:40 CST (UTC-6)

Dr. Lansing focused on the time first out of habit. Then her eyes grew wide as the InSAR measurements were fed from the satellites to their computers.

"My god!" exclaimed one of the geophysicists who'd been observing from the back of the room.

Suddenly, those in the operations center who were only marginally paying attention to the interaction between Dr. Lansing and Oliver jumped out of their seats and craned their necks over their cubicles to view the monitors.

Oliver spoke first. "The surface deformation is extraordinary. This can't be possible."

There were murmurs of disbelief and gasps in amazement.

"This amount of uplift exceeds Sumatra in '05," said one of the geophysicists.

"Easily. With an uplift like this, how much energy might be traveling up and down the fault?" said another.

Then every phone in the NEIC in Golden, Colorado, began to ring.

Dr. Lansing ran her fingers through her hair and turned in a complete circle as the operations center burst into chaos. Tension and energy filled the room. The roar of excited voices and phones ringing was deafening as the New Madrid fault awakened in real time.

She took a deep breath and exhaled before she spoke in a faint whisper.

"And so it begins."

CHAPTER FIFTEEN

Friday, December 21
Friars Point, Mississippi

Beth drove up the highway way faster than she wanted to. She'd covered seventy miles in about an hour with her hands gripping the wheel and her ears glued to the local radio stations. It was just past 4:30, and the dark, rainy skies brought sunset early. The wipers beat furiously across the windshield as Beth fought to adjust her vision to the night.

Her trip northbound on Highway 1 was desolate. No cars were headed south as the word spread up and down the Mississippi of the extraordinary flooding and the unexplainable rising waters inland. The reports began to repeat themselves, so Beth switched back to SiriusXM for a while.

However, as darkness set in, and Anthony fell asleep in his car seat, she elected to direct all of her senses to the task at hand, which was to make her way to Friars Point, where her GPS directed her to turn west toward U.S. Highway 61, better known as the Blues Highway. It rivaled Route 66 as the most famous road in American music folklore.

Water sprayed up from the pavement and caused a steady roar in her wheel wells. From time to time, she'd have to let off the gas as she hit an unexpected stretch of road where an inch or more of water had crossed from one field to another.

The robotic female GPS guide interrupted her thoughts. "In a quarter mile, turn right on Friars Point Road. Continue on for six-point-five miles."

"Right. Left. Right. Left," mumbled Beth as she rolled her head back and forth on her shoulders like a metronome. She loved the back roads, and this was a route she'd taken before when coming to visit Jill. Ordinarily, there was something peaceful about driving through flyover country, as rural America was often referred to. It was a reminder that the world didn't revolve around places like New York, Chicago, LA and DC.

She checked her mirrors and slowed to make the turn, easing into it so Anthony wasn't jostled. After she completed the turn, the steering wheel shuddered in her hands. She glanced down at her speedometer. She recalled that sometimes tires get out of balance at a certain speed, causing the steering wheel to shake.

Beth sped up to forty-five, but the shaking continued.

Now she was genuinely concerned she might have a tire going down. When she'd driven another mile and there was no change in the vibration at any speed, she thought it best to get out and look before she got stuck on the main highway in traffic. The last thing she needed was a tire blowing out.

Beth quickly stopped and exhaled. She slowly released her firm grasp of the steering wheel before she reached into the back seat to retrieve her zip-up half-length raincoat. She wrestled it on and pulled the hood over her head. Zipping it up wasn't an option thanks to the bun in the oven.

Anthony was awake, and Beth explained she needed to step outside the car to look at their tires. He became slightly agitated, so she promised to hurry.

Through all the rustling around with her raincoat and the attention focused on Anthony, Beth discovered as she opened the car door that the problem wasn't out-of-balance or damaged tires. The ground was quivering and shaking ever so slightly, enough for her to recoil and quickly pull the door closed.

The earth began to move with a little more force, causing her car to jump slightly on the asphalt road. Anthony was amused by this, raising his arms up and down as each seismic wave passed under them.

"An earthquake? Seriously?" She shook her head in disbelief and subconsciously wrapped her arms around the unborn baby to comfort her.

Beth started the engine and scanned the AM radio in search of a station. There was a lot of static, but none were broadcasting. Puzzled, she reached for the dashboard to switch from radio back to SiriusXM.

Without warning, her car spun sideways. She frantically looked in all directions to see if she'd been struck by something. She shifted uncomfortably behind the steering wheel as her vehicle turned at a ninety-degree angle to the road. Through the windows, she could see streaks of light shooting up out of the ground like the orangish-blue flames of a gas lantern. Above the flames, bright orbs floated skyward until they disappeared into the rain and darkness.

Then pockets of water shot upward near her, joining the light show as if it were a Las Vegas casino attempting to lure gamblers inside. Beth was witnessing sand boils created by underwater pressure wells aggravated by the earthquake. As liquefaction occurred at the shallow depths from the quake, the ground settled and small pits opened up, forcing water from the underground aquifer upward.

Beth started the car and forcefully put it into drive. She turned the steering wheel to the right and pressed her foot down hard on the pedal. The front-wheel drive caught the pavement, and the crossover lurched toward the right onto the road again.

Relieved, she wasted no time in continuing east on Friars Bend Road toward the highway. Her eyes darted all around, checking her mirrors and Anthony. Her palms were sweaty, causing her to take one hand off the wheel at a time to wipe them on her jeans. With the nervous distractions, she lost her focus. She'd barely traveled a mile when her car hydroplaned, spun out, and came to an abrupt stop bumper deep in a soggy cotton field.

Beth closed her eyes to fight back the tears. She wanted so badly to break down and cry. She wiped away the few tears that escaped her eyes and used her jacket sleeve to stifle her sniffles. She checked to make sure Anthony was okay, and then she rolled down her driver's side window to see how bad the car had plunged into the mud.

The car was half-a-wheel deep in the soggy ground and standing water. Hopelessly stuck. As in, it would take a farm tractor to tow her out.

Now her emotions turned to anger. She slapped the steering wheel several times and bounced the back of her head off the headrest. She silently cursed her husband for not being there when she needed him. She chastised herself for losing her focus moments ago.

Then she turned to her cell phone to call for help.

She dialed nine-one-one and waited. She nervously looked through all her windows. The ground had stopped shaking, and the mysterious lights had disappeared from her view.

Beth furrowed her brow and looked at the display on her cell phone when her call hadn't been connected.

No service.

"Jeez, really?"

The rain was coming down, and her headlights no longer illuminated her surroundings like they had a few moments ago. She rolled down her window again and stuck her head out to get a better look at the ground. The car had sunk to the point where the mud was close to the doorframe.

"Shit! Shit! Shit!" She pounded the steering wheel again as her mind raced to make a decision.

"Okay, Elizabeth Harrison Chandler. You're not gonna sink. This is not quicksand."

She tried to convince herself that the wise course of action was to stay put until morning. By then, hopefully, the rain would've stopped, and surely cell service would be restored at some point.

Then the car lurched to the right, sending the passenger side deeper into the mud. She recalled the words of the sheriff. Unexplained. Springs. Groundwater. Lakes showing up out of nowhere.

Beth had to do something. She couldn't allow them to be swallowed by a sinkhole or drowned by the rising river. She flung open the driver's door and slid out of her seat until her feet sank into the muddy ground. At first, she had trouble picking up one foot after another to move. She thought if she could just get them back to the road, walking would be much easier, and they could flag down a passing car.

She opened the rear door and slid into the back seat next to her son.

"Honey, we're gonna have to walk in the rain. You like that, right?"

"Rain! Rain! Falling on my head!"

One of his favorite songs was an old classic Beth had played for him as an infant—"Raindrops Keep Fallin' On My Head" written in the sixties. She hadn't played it in over a year, a testament to her son's ability to learn and retain information, only to be brought out when it suited him.

She squeezed her body sideways and reached behind the seat to grab Anthony's jacket. She removed him from the car seat and worked with him to get dressed. He struggled with her at first, as he insisted on doing it himself.

"Young man, now is not the time to assert your independence," she grumbled as she helped him with his coat.

She retrieved her crossbody bag from the front seat and pulled the strap over her head. As she did, she began to feel moisture around her feet. The water was oozing into the car.

She turned to Anthony. "Okay, buddy. It's time for a walk in the rain."

His response brought a smile to her face. "Falling on my head!"

She slid out of the car and immediately was submerged in the mud halfway up her calf. Anthony was sitting on the edge of his seat, reaching his arms out to her for an assist onto the ground. He weighed nearly thirty pounds and was off-limits for Beth to carry due to her pregnancy.

She did it anyway. She positioned his arms around her neck and shoulder. He wrapped his legs around her back so his feet dangled just below her belly. She set her jaw and trudged through the muck. By the time she found the roadbed and stepped up into the twelve-inch-deep floodwaters, she'd lost both shoes and her mental toughness.

Beth Chandler looked into the rain-soaked sky and began to cry floods of tears.

CHAPTER SIXTEEN

Friday, December 21
Downtown Memphis, Tennessee

It all happened in a matter of seconds. Jill was violently knocked off her feet. The thrust of the earth heaving upward sent her airborne for a moment before dropping her flat on her back. Then, throughout downtown Memphis, car alarms roared their disapproval. Screams filled the air. The sounds of music emanating from the bars along Beale Street were silenced, displaced by a loud rumbling growl resembling a locomotive roaring through the throngs of partiers.

The impact stunned her and momentarily knocked the breath out of her. Jill's mind was in an incoherent daze. Her first assumption was that a terrorist bomb had been detonated nearby. When the shaking of the parking structure continued, she knew it was an earthquake.

She rolled over and over again to avoid the cars bouncing up and down on their tires. She tried to gain her footing, but the wet surface was slippery, and the ground shaking the parking garage made it difficult.

She crawled back to the half wall where she'd stood a moment ago reminiscing about the Peabody Hotel. Just as she pulled herself on to her feet, glass began to break out of the windows of the adjacent skyscraper. 100 Peabody Place, which housed Bank of America, swayed ever so slightly, just enough for the window frames to buckle, causing the glass to shatter. A minute after the quake had hit, pieces of glass, large and small, joined the rain as they sailed to the ground.

Jill pulled her half jacket over her head to avoid the deluge. She rushed to the far side of the garage, as far away from the building as she could. She dropped to her knees to use a four-door sedan as a shield from the glass while being mindful that the continuous hopping of the vehicles could result in her getting crushed against the wall.

She began to panic as she thought of the kids alone in the Halloran. She reached into her pocket to retrieve her phone. The moisture from the rain, coupled with the constant jarring of her body by the earthquake, caused her to drop her phone repeatedly. Frustrated, she held it down on the wet concrete and tried to dial Tate's number.

It never rang. The phone didn't register any signal at all. In the first thirty seconds of the quake, the cell towers and most emergency communications towers had been destroyed.

The falling glass had taken a brief respite, so Jill decided to run for the down ramp of the garage, located near the center of the parking structure. She pulled herself up by the sedan's door handle and steadied her footing. She bravely rounded the rear bumper and began to race toward the ramp when a series of loud explosions rocked downtown, coupled with a groaning, creaking sound.

Then, from half a mile away, she could hear the enormous series of splashes into the Mississippi. The Hernando de Soto Bridge, which connected I-40 from Tennessee into Arkansas, was falling apart despite a $260 million retrofit. It was a momentary, epic struggle titled *Quake v. Concrete and Steel*—two behemoths wrestling for supremacy over Old Man River. Quake emerged victorious.

However, that was just the beginning.

Jill held onto a pickup truck bed to stay upright. The Doubletree Hotel, located two blocks northeast of her across from the ServiceMaster headquarters, started to teeter and eventually fell over onto B.B. King Boulevard. The Holiday Inn across Union Avenue tipped over as well, crashing into the building where world-famous Charlie Vergos' Rendezvous restaurant was located.

Jill became emotional as she watched the disaster unfold. It was the total destruction of the Peabody that started her tears flowing. The downtown had been shaking violently for nearly eight minutes. The older buildings were beginning to lose their structural integrity. The hundred-year-old Peabody Hotel was no match for the New Madrid earthquake.

Jill watched in horror as the upper floors and roof began to drop down, one by one, until the entire structure was pancaked to the ground in a pile of rubble. Clouds of dust and debris began to float high into the air as the three hotels were destroyed in a matter of minutes. Hotels full of visiting guests who simply wanted to enjoy the special events Memphis had to offer or to visit family for the holidays, crushed by the weight of concrete and steel.

She clamped her hand over her mouth and stifled a scream. Her face was soaked with salty tears and dust-covered raindrops. Jill stood frozen in time, years of memories flashing through her mind. Then a massive lightning strike thundered through downtown. She let out a scream of absolute fright and shock.

Jill was mesmerized as she looked across the horizon to the north and east. Bands of brilliant lights were flickering in the distance. The blues, oranges, whites and reds were beautifully shimmering as they streaked across the sky. The earthquake was putting on a beautiful light show of its own as the hues and vividness of the colors changed as they rippled through the dark sky. Below it all, closer to the ground, a greenish light hugged the landscape, changing intensity as debris floated into the sky before coming back to Earth. It was a riveting spectacle she couldn't pull her eyes away from as the earth continued to shake.

Then Jill got it together. She needed to save her children.

CHAPTER SEVENTEEN

Friday, December 21
Top of the Met
One Metropolitan Square
St. Louis, Missouri

As a child, Jack had learned about the Yellowstone supervolcano, deadly tsunamis, and the New Madrid fault in his earth sciences classes. He'd dreamed about living through a catastrophic event that had the potential of wiping man off the face of the planet. He imagined what he would do. How he'd react. What life would be like if there wasn't another human being around him for miles.

When the ground under One Metropolitan Square began to shake violently, it wasn't as he'd imagined at all. Everything he knew about earthquakes came from the frequent tremors he'd experienced his entire life while living in West Tennessee. He'd never been through anything like the quakes on the West Coast or the ones portrayed in the big-screen movies.

There were no ominous signs like large flocks of birds flying past the tall glass windows at the Top of the Met. He hadn't observed dogs suddenly chasing their tails or fish jumping out of the river. Other than the swaying of the Gateway Arch on Monday, he hadn't felt any rumbles under his feet to be shrugged off as nothing more than a large truck driving nearby.

What he saw astonished him. The ground didn't shake up and down as if some enormous fist were punching the underside of a tabletop to watch the plates and glasses hop. What approached them was more like a giant rollicking wave pounding the beach during a violent thunderstorm. Only, it wasn't raining or even cloudy that day. At least, not until now.

The clouds approaching them weren't big, white, and fluffy. These were gray and dirty, with a hint of orange in them. They were fast approaching from the south, hugging the ground, lending the appearance of ten thousand horses kicking up the dust in the desert. Just in front of the cloud, the ground lifted and dropped. Lifted and dropped. A wave of energy forcing everything in its path to rise and fall without regard to the destruction it caused.

And it was speeding toward them.

When the primary compressional waves hit, they threw everyone and everything not bolted to the floor several feet into the air. The bodies were weightless for a moment until gravity pulled them down hard onto the marble floor, which was now covered with broken glass.

Jack pulled himself up onto all fours, but he didn't want to move. He wanted to take in the spectacle of it all. His fear was suppressed for the moment, although his eyes did dart about, searching for the elusive butterfly people, who'd not shown themselves in over twenty years.

His conscious mind took over as the earthquake continued to jostle the building. "Run! Move away from the windows and get into the lobby!"

He scrambled to his feet and observed the people in the room with him. They were frozen in time, aware of the deadly threat approaching them yet unable to react. Some began to crawl toward the elevators. Others lay flat or crawled to the safety of the few dark wood tables that remained upright.

Then, in unison, many of their cell phones began to emit a variety of notification signals. Some were dings, and others were metallic warning sounds. Many of the locals had catastrophic event warning apps tied into the City of St. Louis emergency management systems. The notifications brought them out of their stupor. Struggling to keep their balance, they turned to run toward the elevators. Tony was there to prevent them.

"No! Not the elevators. The stairwell. Through there!" He pointed toward the illuminated emergency exit sign.

Jack rushed to a table where, oddly, an elderly couple in their eighties continued to sit. The man required the use of a walker to get around, and his wife used a cane. They were feeble and needed help to exit the building.

"Tony! Help me with Mr. and Mrs.—!"

Nobody heard Jack say their name. The deafening roar of another primary compressional wave that hit the Met would've dwarfed a hundred freight trains passing simultaneously. For half a minute, the building shook, causing the crystal chandeliers to sway back and forth and the bottles of liquor to come flying off their glass shelves. When the full energy of the earthquake hit the skyscraper, the enormous power coupled with a deafening groan shocked everyone to their core.

Jack and Tony arrived at the elderly couple's table simultaneously. They brusquely dragged them to the floor and under the round table that was large enough to seat eight. Using their bodies, the two men shielded the man and woman from what happened next.

The windows imploded on all sides. Not a single pane of the hurricane-impact glass escaped the thrust of wind and debris that hit it at speeds in excess of two hundred miles per hour. Screams filled the air as shards of glass, coupled with bits and pieces, peppered their bodies.

Then something pumped up the volume on the outside world. The ringing clarion bells prior to the quake were replaced with a shrill chorus of car alarms, horns, and the loud pops of explosions as if mortar volleys were being hurled across a battlefield. The screaming inside the building only served to add a human element to the macabre orchestra playing throughout the catastrophe.

The shaking of the earthquake had continued for several minutes or more. Chalky dust, a mixture of pulverized plaster, mortar, and brick from the surrounding buildings, entered through the broken windows. It permeated the space, filling their eyes, nose, and then their lungs. For those screaming, they inhaled so much of the debris that they were overcome with violent coughing as they gasped for air.

Then, as quickly as the dust and debris surrounded them, it was sucked out as the quake's energy wave rolled past. The guys, along with the couple they were protecting, were now exposed as the vacuum effect of the outside air pulled the table away from them and sucked it out the window. Glass-filled tablecloths that had fallen to the marble floor now became ghostly apparitions filled with sharp fragments of glass that tore through their clothing and skin as they sailed past.

The elderly man underneath Tony let out a guttural scream of pain. A wineglass had broken, and the stem had embedded in his eye. It was a gruesome scene, and Tony froze, uncertain as to whether he should pull it out or not.

The deluge continued as another minute passed. And another. And another. They were locked in the midst of a horror movie that played over and over. Their surroundings were disintegrating and wreaking havoc on their fragile bodies.

The interior of the magnificent skyscraper was not spared from the onslaught administered by the quake. The walls, rather than crumbling like drywall would, fell down in large slabs of granite and marble. Jack and Tony looked in all directions as the carnage unfolded. Anyone near them were crushed in whole or in part. Cries of agony filled the dusty air, which now reduced their visibility to near zero with the loss of power and the sun obscured by the carnage billowing skyward.

Another minute.

"We have to move them!" Jack shouted.

"What do I do about—?" Tony yelled back, although they were mere feet apart.

"Move first. Stay low to the floor."

Tony and Jack dragged the elderly couple through the glass and debris toward the double doors leading to the elevators. Most of the other attendees, at least the ones not crushed under the weight of the fallen marble walls, had made their way to the fire escape in search of safety.

Suddenly, large chunks of the ceiling began to fall around them, crashing into the backs of the guys, who shielded their charges. The crystal chandeliers, which had been swinging violently for minutes, finally worked their way free of the ceiling brackets holding them in place. The heavy bronze and crystal fixtures came crashing downward, landing on bodies and exposed marble.

The quake was relentless. It continued to send shock waves across the Mississippi River Valley. The rupture, spreading out from the New Madrid fault, generated a frequency of seismic waves that was unfathomable. Yet it had happened before.

Now the Met was convulsing, fighting with all of its steel and marble against the unearthly pressure placed upon it from below ground. The building swayed. It hopped. It began throwing off the granite panels admired by all who cast eyes upon them. It begged for mercy, but none was coming. Its suffering was only going to get worse.

CHAPTER EIGHTEEN

Friday, December 21
Halloran Centre
Memphis, Tennessee

Tate never had a chance to pull his legs back across the seat in front of him before the balcony above him came crashing down. The only thing protecting his legs from breaking was the tops of the cushioned chairs they were draped between. Nonetheless, he was covered in sheetrock and steel, the rectangular supports used to create the cantilevered truss system allowing the balcony to be suspended in the air without posts.

The excruciating pain he suffered from being battered by the balcony structure kept him from passing out from the head trauma. He became incredibly coherent in the moment, his senses heightened to all that was happening around him.

The soundproof theater blocked out the intense roar generated by the earthquake outside the Halloran. Passersby were treated to a single blast of broken glass as the entire façade of the building disintegrated all at once. Inside the theater, other than the ringing in his ears from the blow to his head, all Tate could hear was screaming and pleas for help.

"Emily!" he shouted, joining the chorus of parents frantically screaming for their children.

Tate pushed upward on the balcony's flooring system, but it barely budged. He tried again. The young man who could routinely bench press two hundred twenty-five pounds for a dozen or more continuous repetitions was unable to make any headway with the balcony rubble that had collapsed upon him.

He wiggled his legs and then turned sideways in his seat. He scooted forward so that his backside was on the very edge. He steadied his nerves. This was about to hurt.

Tate pulled himself forward to his legs into a crouching position until he fell off the end of the seat. The seat bottom sprang back in place, and Tate landed hard on the carpeted floor, smacking his tailbone, resulting in a brief numbness in his hips.

He kicked his legs and maneuvered his body so he could pull them back from between the seats. His pants leg had been ripped open, resulting in a gash in his right calf. Blood oozed out of his pants and also down his leg into his sneakers.

He shook off the pain, flattened himself on the floor, and began to crawl on his elbows and belly toward the exit. When he got to the down ramp leading to the stage, he saw that it was blocked. He'd have to find another way to the bottom.

He arrived at the double doors leading to the mezzanine encircling the theater. He was able to get his hand on the door push bar to open the outswing door, but it would only open a few inches.

"Now what?" he grumbled to himself. He shoved his shoulder into the door in an attempt to open it farther. It gave way a few inches and then forced its way back closed.

Tate searched in the pile of debris. There was a short piece of twisted steel the size and shape of a two-by-four. He decided to try prying the door open.

Like before, he pressed the push bar and rammed into the door with his shoulder. At the same time, he shoved the piece of steel in the gap so it remained open. He was able to press his face to the three-inch gap to get a look inside the corridor.

He didn't expect to see the mangled body of the woman who'd greeted them upon arrival, together with an older couple who'd been crushed by the upper floor of the Halloran. Their lifeless eyes stared at him, while the other woman's face was missing.

Tate recoiled from the horrific sight and immediately vomited under the back row of seats. He hurled and retched until the contents of his stomach were emptied. He wiped his mouth on his right sleeve and rubbed the tears out of his eyes before falling back against the wall.

He was trapped. He assessed his predicament as he tried to gather his thoughts. The rumbling of the earthquake continued, and the screams of the survivors had reached a fevered pitch. His anxiety reached a high as he was overcome with a tremendous sense of urgency and responsibility for his sister. If he'd just sat closer to the stage, he might've been able to do more.

He looked up and around him. The back wall stood strong, but the exit door was blocked by bodies and building. His only way to the stage would be through the theater seating. The upper balcony had held at its main supports where it came out of the back wall, but the bulk of the cantilevered structure had bent down, creating a lean-to effect.

Tate started crawling downward, hoping the structure had crashed in such a way that an opening was left for him to shimmy through. He eventually had to drop to his belly again to where the front edge of the balcony had landed atop a row of seats. He worked his way down that row, looking for any kind of opening or a point of weakness he could push through.

He found it.

In the center of the balcony, where the production desk was located that controlled the lighting and audio effects, a gap had been created on impact. The half wall of the balcony had been broken apart by the desk and equipment used by the producers.

Tate positioned himself on the floor with his back to the seat bottom and his legs drawn tight against his chest. Then he kicked as hard as he could. There was some give in the half wall on his first effort, which emboldened him. He kicked hard again, and a portion of the half wall was pushed forward. He reared back and kicked a third time, landing a perfect strike against the aluminum supports holding the wall together. They tore away from the half wall and into the row in front of him, leaving a hole just big enough for him to pull his way through.

"I'm comin', Emily!" he shouted, thinking she was standing on the stage, waiting for him.

Tate forced his way through the small hole, ripping open his shirt on a sharp piece of metal. Blood soaked his Harvard-crimson long-sleeve tee shirt, the blood blending in with the MUS school colors.

The protective older brother was undeterred. He thrashed through the debris until he was able to stand in a place six rows in front of his original seat. His eyes grew wide as what he saw shocked him.

CHAPTER NINETEEN

Friday, December 21
Top of the Met
One Metropolitan Square
St. Louis, Missouri

Tony helped the elderly man to his feet, grasping him brusquely under the arms and disregarding the blood gushing down his face. "Come on, sir. We have to move."

"I can't," he groaned, speaking in between gasps for air. "My legs. Won't support me. And the pain. Too much."

Jack crouched down and lifted the man's wife in a cradling motion. He rushed past Tony toward the exit located at the center of the forty-second floor.

"Pick him up," he said calmly as he passed. Just as Tony scooped up the husband, the ceiling came crashing down on them.

Plumbing pipes had ruptured above them and soaked the drywall. Gallons upon gallons of water rushed through gaping holes in the ceiling, soaking the already slippery marble floor. Both Jack and Tony lost their footing. They landed hard on their backs, and the sound of their heads hitting the marble would make anyone cringe.

Unfortunately, the two people they were trying to carry to safety took the brunt of the ceiling's collapse. With the guys flat on their back, the drywall broke loose, bringing the ceiling, the water, and the floor from the storage room above them downward. Their old, feeble bodies never stood a chance. Both suffered severe crushing injuries to their heads and chests, killing them instantly.

"Tony! Are you okay?"

"Yeah. Cut up."

"Me too. Let's try to help these people under the marble."

Jack gently pushed the dead woman's body off him. Her carotid artery had been severed, and she was bleeding out onto the floor. The continuous flow of water out of the building's roof-mounted reservoir was washing it in a steady stream toward the east side of the building.

It had been over six minutes, but the ground continued to oscillate, rocking back and forth as secondary shear waves passed under it. The building strained under the immense pressure being placed upon its foundation. It was built to certain standards but certainly not the level of earthquake protection afforded West Coast structures. The massive weight of the three rooftop heat and air-conditioning units began to take a toll on the roofing system. The shaking and jostling, the rapid up and down motion, caused the roof to sag. It was just a matter of time before gravity hastened its collapse.

The quake managed to reverse-engineer the entire forty-second floor. Ceiling and wall finishes were falling apart. Electrical fixtures were torn away from their mounts, leaving dangling wires hanging from the ceiling like snakes in the trees of the Amazon rainforest. Water flowed from all directions as the high-pressure fixtures cracked, sending streams of fluids across the room. Any building material not welded to the physical structure of the skyscraper was no match against the violent grip the quake had on it.

Jack crawled through the broken glass without regard to the

wounds his hands were suffering. He was desperate to reach the upper body of a man covered by a collapsed section of wall. When he arrived, he dropped his chin to his chest, dejected at the death of another human being at the hands of the quake.

"I've got one over here!" shouted Tony from across the room.

Jack managed to get to his feet, only to lose his balance and fall hard onto his knees. He tried again but slipped on the wet marble floor. It was a fruitless exercise until the earthquake stopped. He crawled toward Tony's voice. It was almost pitch black in the room except for the ambient light put off by two emergency exit signs dangling from the walls leading to the elevators.

"No! No! No!" Tony began to shout as Jack crawled through the debris.

"What is it?" Jack asked.

"Help me lift this marble."

Jack crawled alongside his brother-in-law and saw the problem. The woman was flat on her back, barely breathing, but a wholly intact slab of granite had toppled off the wall and crushed her from her rib cage down.

The three-quarter-inch slab was roughly four feet by eight feet. It easily weighed four to five hundred pounds. The two guys tried to lift it, but the slab wouldn't budge. Tony frantically cleared some insulation and drywall off the surface of the granite, not that the weight of the debris made a measurable difference. They tried again, to no avail.

Jack lay on his belly and ran his arm under the slab. There was lots of moisture. He pulled his hand out and rubbed his thumb across his fingertips. It was warm and sticky, clearly not water. Blood, and lots of it.

"Tony, it's not gonna matter."

"We gotta try to save her," he insisted.

Jack leaned down to whisper to the woman, "Ma'am, can you hear me?'

Her breathing was shallow, and she stared upward, but she didn't respond. Jack felt for a pulse. It was weak.

"Jack? What if we find a way to pry this off?"

"It's too late for her," he said in a dour manner.

Before Tony could argue his point, a massive explosion could be heard echoing through downtown St. Louis. The sky lit up momentarily as if the backstage lights of a Broadway production had suddenly been turned on. Sparks flickered into the air.

More explosions and more sparks. Jack and Tony crawled toward the windows to look toward the river. A substation and its transformers were self-destructing in East St. Louis on the Illinois side of the Mississippi. It looked like a New Year's fireworks show was underway, but that was not what caught their eye in the brief illumination provided by the fires.

The Gateway Arch was bending and bouncing like a Slinky on a pogo stick. The structure, designed to withstand an earthquake, according to the attractive young tour guide, was now being put to the test. The giant wedding band built to fit the ring finger of Gargantua's bride was being forced down only to spring back into shape. Shaken like Jell-O dumped out of its mold, it quivered under the enormous forces rolling just below the planet's surface.

Loud cracking noises split the air like metallic cannon fire. There was an earsplitting tearing sound, and then suddenly, the apex of the arch started to crumble away. Section by section, the stainless-steel exterior flew to the ground, and the carbon-steel structure, the engineering marvel that it was, allowed gravity to pull it apart. Within thirty seconds, all that was left standing were two bony fingers where each side of the arch rose out of the ground, one flipping the bird to the north and the other toward the south.

"Hey," began Tony. "I think it stopped. It's over."

Well, sort of.

CHAPTER TWENTY

Friday, December 21
Top of the Met
One Metropolitan Square
St. Louis, Missouri

A chandelier hung perilously from a single strand of wire over their heads. The thin copper ground began to fray under the strain of holding the all crystal and polished stainless-steel fixture in place. Much like the building they were standing in that was fighting to hold itself upright, the chandelier swayed ever so slightly in the aftermath of the earthquake that had ravaged the earth along the New Madrid fault.

Jack and Tony stood in unison and wiped the dust and debris off their suits with their bloodied hands. Jack winced as a shard of glass embedded farther into the palm of his hand during the process. Despite the cold temperatures that had invaded the building when the windows imploded, he was sweating profusely. He pulled off his jacket, turned it inside out, and wiped off his face and hands.

"Are you hurt?" he asked Tony, who was picking bits of glass out of the palms of his hands.

Tony shook himself and ran his fingers through his hair. "Freakin' glass stuck me everywhere. My face feels like it was peppered with pea gravel."

Jack buried his mouth and nose in the pit of his elbow and approached the outside edge of the building. There was a slight breeze adding to the chill in the air. A curtain from one of the lower floors lifted slowly into the dark sky before being whisked away to the south. His eyes followed the billowing panel until it disappeared.

"No power anywhere," he observed.

Tony arrived at his side and studied the landscape the best he could in the dark. "Man, there are fires everywhere."

Just as he completed his statement, an explosion could be heard in the distance. Their heads snapped in that direction, only to see thousands of sparks float into the air at the source.

"Transformers," commented Jack. "I saw the substation across the river from the Arch blow apart. These fires may have also been caused by gas line or propane tank leaks."

Tony swung around and faced the remains of the opulent banquet room. He squinted his eyes to assess their situation. Then he remembered his iPhone. He pulled it out of his pants pocket, swiped his thumb down the screen to bring up the device's control panel, and tapped on the flashlight icon. The fifty lumens provided by the phone was equal to a small flashlight, but in the darkness it illuminated the entire room.

"Holy shit!" he exclaimed as the devastation revealed itself.

Jack walked ahead of Tony slightly and assessed the damage. He furrowed his brow as his eyes caught a glimpse of the dead bodies who'd succumbed to the crushing weight of the falling granite or who'd been struck by the flying debris. He retrieved his jacket off the floor and fumbled through its pockets until he found his phone.

The guys, with their flashlights leading the way, searched for any other survivors first. They walked gingerly on the water-soaked marble, being careful not to lose their footing. They checked under the bar and in the banquet servers' workspace behind two swinging doors that were remarkably still in place, swaying in the breeze emanating from outside. Other than the victims they knew about already, it appeared everyone else had managed to get into the central hallway leading to the fitness center on the other side of the forty-second floor or toward the fire escape.

Tony inched closer to the pile of rubble created when the ceiling and contents of the upper floor had fallen into the banquet room. "Of course these walls held strong." He slapped the granite dividing wall separating them from the exit.

"We'll dig through this," Jack said encouragingly. "I don't see any steel girders or anything else immovable."

Tony wasted no time. He set a chair upright and propped his cell phone against the back so the light could shine on the rubble. Jack did the same, and the two men began to pull away large pieces of insulation and ceiling drywall.

Over the next several minutes, a space had opened up at the top of the pile, providing access to the center hallway of the building.

"Want me to shimmy through it?" asked Tony, the smaller of the two men.

"I think it's too unstable," replied Jack. "Trust me, I wanna get out of here, too. I think we've got time."

Tony nodded. "Help me with this hunk of flooring."

He and Jack each grabbed an end of the concrete aggregate slab reinforced with rebar. After a count of three, they lifted it. The men both groaned, as did something outside the building.

"Did you hear that?" asked Tony as they set the chunk of concrete to the side.

Jack had already grabbed his phone and used the light to walk toward the jagged remains of the windows. "Yeah, I did."

He inched close to the outside edge of the building, using the aluminum window frames as a guardrail of sorts.

"Can you see anything?"

Jack leaned forward and allowed his head to breach the plane of the building. A gust of dust-filled wind smacked him in the face. He hurriedly looked straight down and quickly snatched his head and shoulders back into the room. He shook his head side to side, admonishing himself for such a foolish move.

He stepped a few paces back into the room. "Not really. There are car lights on, and I can hear alarms blaring."

CREEEAK!

"There it is again!" shouted Tony, who rushed to Jack's side.

The two men stood side by side, waving their hands in front of their faces as debris continued to swirl in the air around them.

Suddenly, an explosive roar was heard. The sound was gradual at first and then gained in intensity. It resembled a passenger airline buzzing over the top of your head. Then loud pops mixed in with the roar.

That was when the first of the dominos fell. Throughout downtown St. Louis, the structural integrity of the tall buildings failed. Residential high-rises and office skyscrapers began to collapse into themselves.

The men were enthralled by the falling structures they could only hear and not see. The screams of their fellow man and cries for help rose high into the air, sending chills up their spines.

CREEEAK!

"That's close!" yelled Jack as the carnage continued to unfold below. Seconds later, it was One Metropolitan Square's turn to be part of the macabre game of skyscraper dominos.

Below them, the twenty-three-story Broadway Tower fell over into the building across the street. The steel and granite listed toward the north ever so slightly until gravity began to pull it across Pine Street into the adjacent building known as St. Louis Place.

Located at 200 Broadway, and directly across from the entrance to the Met, St. Louis Place was a uniquely designed structure. It shared the corner of Pine and Broadway with the other two skyscrapers. To differentiate itself from the others, the architects had designed it with a large opening on the street corner such that the upper floors were supported with a single steel and concrete beam stretching sixteen stories until it reached the upper floors.

While this structural support was designed to hold up the

building under normal circumstances, it was no match for the massive weight of 100 Broadway when it crashed into it. Imagine a four-legged stool holding up a hundred tons of building and then one of the legs gets kicked out from under it.

It happened in just seconds. Just like that.

Broadway Tower toppled across Pine Street and crashed into the south side of St. Louis Place, effectively kicking out the fourth leg of the stool. When this happened, St. Louis Place fell across Broadway and crashed into the lower half of the Met. The impact was felt throughout the building, especially at the top.

Jack and Tony were knocked to the floor. The building swayed back and forth as if it too would topple over. As it did, they began to slide along the wet marble.

"My god, Jack. Is the damn thing gonna fall over?" asked Tony as he scrambled onto his hands and knees and made his way toward the center of the building.

Jack, who was closer to the window opening, was having a difficult time. It was if he were being pulled out by the gnarly fingers of a demon crawling up the side of the building. Just as he'd manage to get onto all fours, he'd slip backwards.

"Go! Hurry!" Jack yelled as he began to panic. He was being pulled toward the edge because the Met was in fact teetering. Furniture, broken dinnerware, and bottles of liquor were all sliding toward the front edge of the building as if being drawn by a massive magnet.

Tony continued to crawl up the slight incline and arrived at the rubble blockade first. He turned his flashlight toward Jack to light up the path. "This way!"

"I see you. Just dig us out!"

Tony drew upon what was referred to by scientists as *hysterical strength*. There were urban legends of a mother going toe-to-toe with a polar bear in Northern Quebec to protect her son. A twenty-two-year-old woman raised a BMW off her father when it had toppled off a car jack. Teenage sisters hoisted up a toppled tractor to save their dad.

Tony's adrenaline increased exponentially. Norepinephrine released directly into his muscles, giving him brief but superhuman strength. Without Jack's help, he began to toss large hunks of concrete flooring off the pile like they were throw pillows.

Jack clawed his way to the pile of rubble just as the building began to tilt farther. The two men worked independently of one another to frantically create an opening they both could fit through. Within minutes, as the steel structure of One Met began to strain, Tony led the way through the hole and cleared the way for the huskier Jack to shimmy through as well.

Once in the center hallway in front of the bank of elevators, they scanned back and forth until they found the entry doors to the emergency stairwell.

"There!" shouted Jack. He wasted no time in moving over fallen debris toward the west side of the building adjacent to the fitness center.

They burst through the steel doors into the concrete fire escape just as a loud rumble echoed through the stairwell, preceded by a cracking sound. Along the wall, stress fractures appeared. Tiny hairline splits ran up and down the walls until fragments of concrete began to fall off. The sound grew louder, and the walls began to break apart.

One Metropolitan Square was splitting in half.

CHAPTER TWENTY-ONE

Friday, December 21
One Metropolitan Square
St. Louis, Missouri

The men burst into the stairwell. The emergency lighting had failed. Parts of the upper floor had collapsed through the door leading to the stairs and crumbled downward, making their footing treacherous. Armed with their iPhone flashlights lit up, they began to race against time in an attempt to descend forty floors before the Met was ripped apart.

The air in the completely concrete stairwell was permeated with gray, powdery dust, making it nearly impossible to take a deep breath. Jack covered his mouth and nose by burying his face into the pit of his elbow. However, this slowed his descent.

Tony, who was younger and more agile, was grasping the handrail with his right hand and used his left to hold the flashlight. He was able to take two steps at a time and race around the U-turn landings at each floor exit. After the first five floors, Jack was losing sight of Tony, who was descending at a much faster rate.

"Jack! Come on!"

Jack tried to respond, but it resulted in a coughing fit. "Having. Trouble." Cough, cough. "Breathing."

"Okay," Tony shouted up to him. "We've got this. I'll come back up to help."

"No!" Jack shouted in protest. "I'll be behind you. Keep going." He began another coughing fit.

As instructed, Tony continued downward until he reached the thirtieth floor, where their firm's offices were located. He shouted up to Jack, who was still moving slowly but efficiently down the stairs.

"I'm at thirty! I'm gonna make sure everyone got out!"

Tony didn't wait for a response, so he didn't hear Jack tell him to wait. Instead, impulsively, he pulled the emergency exit door open and entered the hallway near the bank of elevators. He began to race down the south corridor toward their offices, when the east side of the Met began to crumble away.

After the adjacent building crashed into its base, the east side of the Met began to fall apart from the ground up. First, the spacious thirty-thousand-square-foot lobby and retail space, which had been filled with the debris from St. Louis Place, was further cut off as the fascia of the building fell away before landing on top of the sidewalk. When this happened, more of the east façade, made up of granite, began to peel the face off The Met in chunks.

Gradually, the façade disappeared floor by floor, and as it fell, the interior floors began to fall apart. Inch by inch and then foot by foot, the reinforced concrete separating each floor crumbled before breaking lose and crashing to the ground below.

Tony was running full speed toward their offices when he saw the side of the building disappear in front of him. He slid to a stop and lost his balance, landing on his backside. The floor continued to be devoured like Pac-Man chomping pellets.

He scrambled to his feet and began running back toward the bank of elevators. He glanced over his shoulder as the building disintegrated. He made his way to the stairwell, slamming the door open and almost knocking over Jack, who was about to open the door on the other side.

"Jesus!" shouted Jack.

Tony didn't explain. He grabbed Jack by the arm and tugged him roughly toward the stairs. "We gotta go! It's comin'!"

"What's coming?"

"Nothing but air, man! Run!"

Jack sensed Tony's urgency and forgot about his difficulty breathing. The sound of the building breaking down and falling allowed him to conjure up a visual to accompany Tony's words. He had no interest in surfing on a concrete slab thirty floors to his death.

The guys ran past several groups who were moving slowly down the stairs. Some needed medical assistance and begged them to stop. Jack paused to help a woman to her feet who'd stumbled and ripped open her kneecaps. She leaned on his arm as he tried to lead her downward.

Tony stopped, ran back up a few stairs, and rudely pulled Jack aside, leaving the woman standing with her mouth agape.

"Jack, we don't have time for this. We're gonna die if we don't get out of here."

"These people need—"

The shrieks of people in the stairwell accompanied by an enormous cracking sound cut him off. The side of the stairwell had separated on its east side, an open wound that ran up and down for several flights of stairs.

With only a glance at the people in shock behind them, Jack led the way with Tony close behind. They pushed their way past another group of people walking slowly down the stairs. Leaving them behind went against everything Jack believed in. He'd spent his adult life helping his fellow man. However, he had the love of his life and his kids to get home to.

That was when it struck him. If this was the so-called *Big One* that everyone feared might come out of the New Madrid Seismic

Zone, then Memphis might have been impacted. In the chaos at the Top of the Met, he hadn't tried to call Jill.

He tried to keep up with Tony, who was flying down the stairwell now, taking the steps two at a time while using the guardrail as support. Jack tried to navigate the touchscreen of his phone to place a call to Jill. In his effort to do so, he lost his focus and stumbled at the bottom of a flight of stairs. He tumbled forward and crashed into the wall, dropping his phone in the process.

"You okay?" Tony stopped at a landing below and shouted his question up to Jack.

Jack got to his feet, located his phone, and studied the display. There was no signal.

"Yeah. I'm coming."

The men continued their downward race to the bottom, stepping over debris and dodging others who frantically wanted to escape the building. They'd passed the fifth floor, and suddenly, they found themselves rushing into a crowd of fifteen people blocking the stairwell.

Tony shouted at them, "What are you doing? Keep going!"

Several of the women who were huddled together at the rear of the group turned to Tony and made a path for him to walk through. He studied their distraught faces before slowly walking down the stairs to the next landing. He turned the corner through the rest of the group and immediately realized the problem.

The emergency stairwell had come to an end. Four stories above the ground.

CHAPTER TWENTY-TWO

Friday, December 21
Halloran Centre
Memphis, Tennessee

The front five rows of seats located on the flattest part of the theater immediately in front of the stage had been crushed by the ceiling above them. The entire rigging system holding up the speakers and lighting had come crashing down onto the front of the stage. The families attending the rehearsal in those first five rows were killed or severely injured. Tate could have been one of them.

He rushed to the collapsed ceiling and tried to look for survivors. There were people crying and muffled voices asking for help. There was so much debris from the ceiling and the lighting was so dim that Tate was unsure how to proceed in rescuing them.

The sound of a crying child brought the focus of his efforts back to Emily.

"Emily! Can you hear me?"

No response.

Tate ran up and down the rubble, looking for a path through it leading to the stage. He grimaced and cursed in anger as he realized the access was completely blocked by the collapsed ceiling and the stage rigging.

He tried climbing across the debris, but it gave way, and he got his leg caught. He tried to free himself, and then a hand grabbed his ankle. Somebody was alive under all the collapsed ceiling.

"I can't. I'm sorry," he said to the faceless victim who was trying to get his attention. Tate yanked his leg out of their grip and toppled backwards onto the carpet. As he regained his footing, the roof of the building shook just as the earthquake stopped shaking.

Tate thought it was the final hurrah of the devastating quake. But the thump was too loud. He equated the noise with someone dropping a heavy medicine ball on a hollow wood floor. Only this medicine ball caused more debris to come crashing down.

Whomp!

This blow caused a portion of the roof to open up, and water came pouring in on top of the collapsed ceiling. Tate's mind raced as he presumed the entire building was about to be crushed. He ran to his right toward a green, illuminated Emergency Exit sign. It now provided the only light in the theater other than a few dangling lights toward the center rows just beneath the collapsed balcony.

Then the light fixtures suddenly grew much brighter before the power surge that caused it took out all the electricity to the building. Tate adjusted his eyes and searched the side wall for the exit sign. The batteries kept it illuminated.

Whomp!

"What the hell?" Tate shouted his question at the top of his lungs.

More of the ceiling collapsed, including the exposed steel trusses that crossed the building from side to side. One of the black powder-coated trusses snapped in the center, allowing the roofing material to drop several feet into this end of the building.

Tate wasted no time racing to the exit. He gripped the handle and turned it. He overpowered the door and flung it open so hard the handle embedded in the drywall on the other side.

He immediately turned to his left in search of an entry door leading to the backstage area. A short corridor led to the restrooms, and Tate noticed it was filling with water. He took the short corridor to the left and found a double set of utility doors. The drop ceiling had collapsed in front of them, but the debris was no match for his adrenaline-filled muscles.

Whomp!

Tate jumped just as he cleared the path to the door. More debris fell from above on top of his head and blocked the door. He frantically dug it out of the way. He noticed the wall to the left of the doorway was starting to buckle and crack.

He flung the door open and pushed his way inside just as the front end of a Cadillac STS came crashing through the roof and smashed into the hallway where he'd stood seconds ago. Tate now knew that perception wasn't always reality. He could deal with medicine balls. But cars falling out of the sky?

Behind the stage was a tall wall that ordinarily contained a theater screen and, above it, several rolled-up backdrops to be used during the stage production. Props of all types were built on skids with casters to be rolled into place during scene changes. All of this had either been toppled over or crushed by the falling ceiling.

"Emily!" he shouted. "Where are you?"

Tate had to focus. He thought he heard her call his name, but the voice was muffled. He moved past the fallen props toward the back wall of the theater. He hollered for her again.

"Emily! If you can hear me, knock on something."

What happened next caused the hair to stand up on the back of Tate's neck and caused his skin to crawl. Dozens of tiny hands began to knock on the bottom side of the wooden stage. They were gentle at first, like a young trick-or-treater shyly knocking on a neighbor's door at Halloween. Then they grew to a crescendo as everyone trapped underneath the stage began to pound their fists upward against the raised wooden structure. Their chorus of screams were a combination of *help*, *down here*, and *please*.

"Okay. Okay. I hear you! How did you get under there?"

Tate yelled his question, but the trapped kids couldn't hear him, as they never stopped pounding the floor or yelling for his help.

Whomp!

"Jeez, enough already!" Tate shouted. Between the barely-holding-on survivors, the kids pounding the floor, the chaos that had found its way into the Halloran through the hole in the ceiling, and the doggone cars pounding the roof like some kind of possessed pile driver, Tate strained to focus as he frantically searched for the access panel to underneath the stage.

He began to throw lightweight props to the side, and the heavy ones he slid out of the way. There had to be a hatch. Then he found himself at the back of the stage's center, where the piano sat. He thought it was in an odd place. He struggled to remove a heavy part of the rigging that had toppled over a large prop.

He found the production's director crushed underneath, with blood streaming out of her ears. He pulled her body to the side, and then he saw the outline of the hatch door leading underneath. The woman was a hero. She'd acted quickly to shuffle the children to safety and then moved the piano over the hatch so it wouldn't get covered by the damage caused by the earthquake. She'd given her life for those kids.

Rain was pouring into the ceiling, and the people buried under the rubble were screaming louder now. The access to the seating area was completely blocked by the ceiling. Tate knew the entire building could collapse within itself if it kept getting pummeled by the cars that were somehow coming out of the adjacent parking garage.

"I've got you!" he shouted as he flung open the hatch. Although it was dark, he could make out the outline of half a dozen tiny faces looking upward at him through the hatch. He positioned himself on his hands and knees. "Grab my hand."

The first child, a girl about Emily's age, gripped his hand and wrist. Tate flexed his powerful biceps and back muscles as he pulled the child through the opening and onto the floor beneath the piano.

"Thank you!" she yelled through her tears.

"Is Emily down there?"

The girl didn't respond, but Emily did.

"I'm here! I'm here!"

Tate bent down and dropped his arm through the hatch. Emily put a death grip on his wrist and forearm. He jerked her upward and onto the stage floor. She immediately hugged him and began to cry.

"Where's Mom?"

Tate hesitated before he responded, "Um, I don't know."

"Oh, my god! We have to find her!" Panicked, Emily tried to stand and busted her head on the bottom of the piano.

Tate tried to calm her. "Emily, hold on. We have to help the others. Mom's probably outside waiting for us."

"I'll go look!"

"No, it's too dangerous!" Tate was exasperated by Emily's failure to listen.

"Why can't I go—?" she began to argue when she received her answer.

Whomp!

Another car crashed through the roof and the remaining ceiling structure at the front of the stage, until it fell over backwards, further crushing those in the first five rows.

"That's why," Tate said calmly as he reached into the hatch to retrieve another child.

CHAPTER TWENTY-THREE

Friday, December 21
Downtown Memphis, Tennessee

Jill raced down the ramps of the parking garage, brushing off pieces of glass that had embedded in her jacket and hair. She burst out onto the street, where hundreds of people were scampering in all directions, seeking safety, unsure which way, exactly, was less dangerous. She didn't care what was safe. She cared for her children and knew where she needed to go. Like a bull in a china shop, Jill pushed and shoved her way through the crowd toward the Halloran Centre.

She dodged cars attempting to force their way east out of the city. It was a fruitless exercise. Some drivers grew angry at the pedestrians running in between their front bumper and the car in front of them. Several panicked revelers were struck or run over in the chaos.

Jill ran between two stalled cars and crossed Beale Street onto the sidewalk packed with people fleeing the riverfront. She pushed through them onto the wet grass surrounding the Memphis Light, Gas and Water building. She was in an open space and began to sprint until she tripped over the bronze statue of Elvis strumming his guitar.

She face-planted onto the wet turf and skidded eight feet until she crashed into the legs of people hustling by. Covered in wet grass and some mud, Jill was unfazed by the collision. She was singularly focused on getting to the Halloran.

By the time she arrived at the entrance, the glass had blown out of all the windows, littering the pavement. The front roof overhang that cantilevered outward had dropped down and crumbled into large chunks of concrete. Interior rooms lining the exterior of the building were filled with debris from the ceiling and the upper storage rooms.

She ran to her right toward the Orpheum, looking for a way in. All the access points through the broken windows were blocked by the rubble.

She ran back past the main entrance toward the south side of the building, which was adjacent to the parking garage where they'd tried to locate a space at first. She thought she found an opening, and just as she lifted her leg over the windowsill, she heard the cracking of concrete and the groaning of steel. The building was struggling to remain upright.

Jill instinctively looked toward the roof, presuming the front of the building was about to collapse. She hesitated briefly, and then a man on the sidewalk yelled at her, "Get out! It's gonna fall!"

She spun her head around, and the man was waving his arms frantically for her to come into the street. She didn't know why she trusted him, but in the moment, she was glad she did.

She rushed toward him and then slid to a stop on the broken glass. She turned her body just in time to see the wall separating the Halloran from the parking garage give way. The top two floors of the parking structure began to tilt toward the theater building. That was when the high-pitched squeal of rubber fighting against concrete filled the air.

As the wall collapsed, the top floor of the garage tilted dramatically toward the theater. The cars on the upper level slid across the wet concrete until they crashed into the half wall and broke through. The first vehicle came crashing through and landed hard on the roof of the Halloran.

Jill joined other onlookers in screaming as the disaster unfolded.

The car tires continued to squeal, indicating their approach to the edge of the structure. One teetered for a moment as the weight of the engine in front acted as a counterbalance to the lightweight rear end. Soon, gravity won the day, and the sedan fell over and landed on top of the other car.

The determined mother had seen enough. She wasn't gonna stand there while her children got buried alive by falling cars. She threw caution to the wind and went back to where she'd approached the building moments ago.

Suddenly, the transformers around downtown Memphis began to blow. The explosions, coupled with the intense bursts of sparks, knocked out power to the city. People shrieked and began yelling, none of their voices discernible over another's as the scuffle to escape reached a very ugly level of panic.

Jill took a deep breath and forced herself to remain calm. She pulled out her cell phone and powered on its flashlight. She stepped across the rubble and into the building. Jill paused, beads of moisture pouring down her face as she tried to figure out where to go. She'd never been inside the Halloran before.

Following her instinct, she pushed her way toward the center of the building, climbing over fallen ceiling debris and stud walls. As she made her way deeper into the darkness, Jill would occasionally catch a glimpse of a body part protruding through ruins. She fought back the bile building in her stomach. There was no time for throwing up.

Whomp!

A third car had come crashing on top of the Halloran. Jill shrieked and instinctively covered her head with her arms. Then she chastised herself for being weak. Besides, she thought to herself, if a car was gonna come crashing down on top of her, her measly arms weren't gonna stop it.

With less fear than when she entered and several hard kicks with the bottom of her foot, she tore her way through a hole in an interior wall that led to a forty-seat conference room. It was remarkably well preserved except for wall fixtures being knocked down and a part of the drop ceiling collapsing on top of the exquisite walnut table.

Jill studied her surroundings for a moment and then considered how she'd entered the building. She had a hunch the theater was in the center and likely behind the longest wall of the conference room.

She pounded the wall with the back side of her fist, listening to its hollow sound until it became more solid. She'd done this a hundred times years ago when looking for a stud to hang her pictures. There were millions who relied on apps like Stud Finder for smartphones. The app used a phone's compass to pinpoint metal studs, nails, and screws embedded in walls.

Jill didn't have a fancy app. Her knocking technique worked just fine, and she was able to find the weakest point of the drywall between the studs. Then she turned to find a makeshift tool of some sort to break through to the next room.

A solid brass candleholder that had toppled off the conference table did the trick. She turned it over, and using the base like a hammer's head, she began to flail at the drywall. Within seconds, she'd broken through, allowing her to shove her arm through. She clawed the sheetrock away from the studs and dug out the soundproofing insulation. Soon, a sixteen-inch-wide gap appeared, enabling her to swing her candlestick-turned-hammer against the inside of the next wall.

She hit it hard, but it barely budged. She smacked it again even harder. It gave way.

Whomp!

Startled, Jill jumped and screamed again. "Stop that!" she begged the car-dropping-gods for some relief. The ceiling of the conference room collapsed further as the aluminum grid system gave way and crashed mostly into the center of the room.

Undeterred, Jill began beating the drywall with a renewed sense of urgency. Finally, it broke through, and that was when she realized the difference in its resiliency. She had, in fact, found the theater. The inside walls of the theater space were covered with foam soundproofing panels ranging in depth from six to eight inches. The panels were glued onto the drywall and gave the sheetrock material additional support.

Jill didn't care. Like a crazed lunatic, she began to pound the inside of the wall until it began to fall inward in large chunks. She abandoned the candlestick and began to kick at the wall. Then she turned around backwards, held the conference room wall with her elbows, and forcefully mule-kicked the lower part of the drywall opening until it was open to the other side.

She stuck her head through the wall and screamed out her children's names. "Emily! Tate! Are you in here?"

She could hear the moans of people in the theater and a few muffled cries for help. She called out their names and focused on listening. The chaos outside the building was louder than the voices trying to respond in the rubble. She looked back and forth, using her flashlight for illumination. She hoped to see the kids or a better way to enter the theater than the present option.

Because the rows of theater seats gradually dropped to a pitlike area in front of the stage, her elevation in the conference room was about eight feet above the sloped floor below her. To complicate matters, there was ceiling debris, as well as the foam-covered drywall she'd just demolished, in the aisleway. It didn't leave her much of a landing area once she jumped.

Her first hurdle to overcome was the sixteen-inch-wide space to squeeze through. Her *birthing hips*, as her ob-gyn called them, made her far too wide to pass through head-on. Her *voluptuous chest*, as her husband liked to call her breasts, would have to be mashed down for her to slide through sideways.

So Jill turned sideways, held in her breath, pulled her right breast as flat against her chest as she could, and forced it through the opening. Once the stud wall was wedged into her cleavage, she repeated the process, this time holding her left breast tight against her chest as she pushed her way into the theater.

Now that she was in, she had to find a way to safely jump down.

Whomp!

Another car fell on top of the ceiling, and the explosive sound was deafening inside the confines of the theater. She heard screams emanating from the stage area.

"Emily! Tate! Can you—arrrgggh!" Jill lost her focus, and her feet slipped off the ledge created by the hole in the wall. She fell sideways toward the theater floor, crashing first on top of the drywall pile, and then she rolled over, slamming a row of seats with her back.

She lay there for a moment, allowing her breath to come back into her lungs and her mind to assess whether any of her parts were broken or badly bruised. After a quick self-examination, she used the seat armrests to push herself up. She walked down a couple of rows over the debris until she found her cell phone lighting up the bottom of a seat cushion.

Jill carefully stepped over the debris, moving gingerly down one row after another until she reached the pile of collapsed ceiling and stage parts that covered most of the lower seating area.

"Emily? Tate?"

She no longer yelled their names. No. She asked, almost begged, for them to respond. She couldn't imagine they were underneath all of this destruction. She directed her light toward the stage. It, too, was littered with parts of the building.

Tears began to stream down her face. This was where her son would've been seated during the rehearsal. She looked back to the stage. That was where her daughter would've been showing how her practice and hard work was paying off as she danced and sang and recited her lines for the Christmas presentation.

She was unsure of what to do, hesitating for just a moment. Then, without warning, she almost died.

Whomp!

CHAPTER TWENTY-FOUR

Friday, December 21
One Metropolitan Square
St. Louis, Missouri

"Seriously?" asked Jack as he caught up to Tony. His tone of voice was matter-of-fact, drawing a chuckle from his brother-in-law.

"We need a plan B," replied Tony.

"No shit. There has to be another way."

"Follow me." Tony led the way up the stairwell past the dumbfounded people who stood staring into the abyss. He presumed they were waiting to be rescued. He didn't want to take the time, nor was he inclined to explain to them the building was about to collapse. He made his way to the sixth-floor emergency door and opened it for Jack.

Once they were both in the center hallway, Tony wandered for a few seconds, glancing down at his cell phone twice. The side of the building was completely gone, leaving partial sections of offices dangling over the edge of the structure.

"The light is draining my battery."

Jack walked away toward the elevator doors. "Hey, find something to pry these doors open."

"Whadya thinkin'? Slide down the elevator cables like Spiderman?"

Jack tried to force his fingers between the middle of three sets of elevator doors. "No. Think about it. People have to be able to escape from an elevator through the roof. Emergency service personnel have to be able to climb up or down to help them. I'm thinkin' there are ladders attached to the walls of the elevator shaft."

"Hell yeah!" exclaimed Tony. "You're right. Hang on."

He powered on his flashlight again and walked down the center hallway. He located the fire extinguisher and the box affixed to the wall with a glass door marked IN CASE OF EMERGENCY BREAK GLASS. Instead, he broke the wire holding the flat piece of eight-inch-long steel designed to gain access to the fire alarm. He hustled back to Jack's side with the tool and a fire extinguisher under his arm.

"Try this." He handed Jack the tool.

With his fingers, Jack separated the elevator doors just enough to wedge the tool in between them. Then he pushed hard to force a four-inch gap to appear. When it was open enough for the fire-extinguisher to fit, Tony shoved it between the doors at the base.

"Good work," said Jack. "Now, each of us take a side and pull the damn things open. I understand why they make it difficult, but gimme a break."

Each of the guys grasped the side of the elevator doors and pulled in unison. They got to a point where the doors finally gave way and opened fully, exposing the elevator shaft interior. Jack used his phone to light up the inside.

"Here we go," he said, pointing to a ladder just to his right. He leaned in slightly and looked to his left. There was a second ladder attached to the wall.

Jack moved his phone so the flashlight pointed downward. The fifty lumens didn't provide sufficient light to see the bottom, but there didn't appear to be anything obstructing them.

"Works for me," said Tony. "Listen, I'm gonna let the others know. We're first, though. Okay?"

Jack nodded in the dark. "I get it. We got one shot at this. We led them to an escape. Now it's on them."

Tony darted for the emergency stairwell. He hollered for the evacuees and explained they'd opened the elevator shaft to access the ladders. He was back within twenty seconds.

"Let's go," he said when he arrived.

"Where are they?" asked Jack.

"Thinkin' about it, I guess," Tony replied. He stepped into the shaft, clutching the sides with a death grip. "This doesn't require groupthink, people. Run for your damn lives. Right?"

Jack shrugged. "Agreed. Down we go."

The two men moved slowly and carefully at first, ensuring they had a proper footing on the ladder rungs as they climbed down. One floor after another, they got closer to the bottom. As they passed the second floor, they heard voices and shouts from above. At least some of the other evacuees were following their lead.

"I feel cool air," announced Tony as they approached the bottom. Just as before, he was well ahead of Jack.

"Don't overshoot the ground floor!" Jack shouted down to him.

"Whadya mean? The ground is the ground." Tony kept going.

"No! This leads to the underground parking." Jack stopped at the elevator doors where two of the cabs were parked. He pulled his phone out again and illuminated the back of the third door. A large letter *L* reflected back to him. He stepped off the ladder onto the roof of one of the cabs. "Come back."

Jack dropped to his knees and fumbled around for the latch to the emergency access installed in the ceiling of the cab. He flipped a latch and turned the handle, causing the door to slam toward the inside, swinging violently on its hinges.

"Shit," he muttered as he discovered the cab's doors were closed. He'd left their tool five floors up, and he didn't want to fight through two sets of doors to get out. He sat back on his knees and shined the light toward Tony. "Try the door on the top. See if we can get out that way."

Tony hopped onto the top of the cab, causing it to bounce up and down somewhat. "Whoa!"

"Careful!" Jack shouted at him. Then Jack's elevator cab shuddered under his feet. This was followed by concrete dust and debris raining on top of his head. "Hurry!"

Tony fumbled with the latches but eventually got the ceiling hatch open. "Bingo!"

Jack didn't hesitate. He stepped off the roof of the cab and grasped the ladder. He walked along the eight-inch wide I-beam to cross over to where Tony waited on the roof of his cab. He reached out his hand and helped Jack on top.

Jack exhaled and looked into the cab. "I'm over this shit. How 'bout you?"

The building shook again, causing the cab to lurch upward slightly and then drop again until the brake caught it.

"Ya don't have to tell me twice," quipped Tony as he dropped feetfirst into the interior. He stood to the side and waited for Jack to join him. They exited the elevator together and entered the lobby of the Met, which now resembled a landfill.

CHAPTER TWENTY-FIVE

Friday, December 21
USGS
Golden, Colorado

"St. Louis has been hit the hardest, mum," shouted Oliver as he cupped his hand over the telephone to prevent bursting out the eardrums of the person on the other line. "There are eyewitness accounts of liquefaction along both sides of the Mississippi. It's widening."

As the ground shook, the resiliency of the river's banks, its strength and the stiffness of the soil were lost. As water rushed in to fill the voids left by the unstable conditions, the ordinary solid material began to liquify into a muddy, almost quicksand-like dirt.

Imagine standing next to the water as it laps on the shore of a beach. As it washes over your feet, they gradually sink below the sand and eventually disappear from view. Like quicksand, liquefaction changes the composition of the soil such that heavier objects sink into it.

That was what was happening to St. Louis. Brick by brick.

Building by building. As the earthquake forced underground water and liquified sand to the surface, the massive structures built along the river began to lose their structural integrity and collapse into the earth.

Dr. Lansing had a full house now, including off-duty observers standing at the rear of the room, ready to jump in if somebody needed a break. Within fifteen minutes of the earthquake, the world's media was abuzz with the news. Her team had raced back to work to assist.

She rushed across the operations center and tapped one of the geophysicists on the shoulder. "Do we have the NSA satellite access?"

The young man nodded and pointed at his monitor. Minutes after contacting the USGS director in Reston, he'd made arrangements for her to tap into the national security satellites over the Central United States. Despite the dark conditions, the extraordinary technology could zoom in and read the license plate of an automobile headed home from work in St. Louis, if there was one.

"See if you can identify any lateral spreading," she instructed the man.

She was concerned about the river expanding into the voids. Rivers were alive. Water was always looking for the lowest point in whatever surface surrounded it. Bends in the rivers resulted in the banks eroding and pushing outward over time as a part of their natural evolution. A slight curve becomes a noticeable bend. A bend becomes a horseshoe. A horseshoe longs to connect one side to the other to create a lake. If you were able to view a time-lapse video of the Mississippi River over the last three thousand years, its shape would twist and turn like an angry snake.

The extent of lateral spreading, the cracking and movement of the ground toward natural deformations like rivers and streams, would provide Dr. Lansing some insight into the magnitude of the earthquake as well as the location of its epicenter. She knew the

New Madrid fault like few other geophysicists in the world and had studied thousands of scenarios. Her boss, and ultimately the White House, would be looking to her for answers.

She took a deep breath and exhaled. She paused for a minute to process what was happening. She recalled the day she had been accepted into the earth sciences program at Missouri-Columbia. An obscure news article had caught her eye. FEMA had identified four hazards in the U.S. that would be categorized a catastrophic natural disaster.

They were a category five hurricane hitting Miami, bigger than Andrew in '93, she presumed. A major hurricane hitting New Orleans, which happened in '05 after she'd finished graduate school. A significant earthquake hitting LA, and a giant earthquake hitting the Central U.S. in the New Madrid Seismic Zone.

The often-used phrase "it's happened before and it will happen again" certainly applied to earthquake activity. During the winter of 1811 through 1812, when the three M7+ quakes struck the sparsely inhabited frontier along the Mississippi River, the landscape changed dramatically.

The surface of the planet had slipped deep under the settlement at New Madrid, opening up chasms and cracks across the region. The Mississippi River was diverted in several places, filling the disappearing ground with its waters. Liquefaction threw trees to the ground and landslides into the river. The widening rift along the fault created magnificent waterfalls.

Meanwhile, new lakes, such as Reelfoot in upper West Tennessee covering twenty square miles, were created. Existing lakes were turned inside out as the liquefaction process created holes in the earth's surface, spewing volcanoes of sand and water into the air. Unsuspecting travelers heading toward the Gulf of Mexico were swamped by the tsunami-like waves traveling along the Mississippi.

The earthquakes' tentacles were far-reaching. New Yorkers were jolted out of their beds. Church bells rang in Charleston, South Carolina. People in Toronto, Ontario, Canada, were knocked off balance. President James Madison felt the tremors in the White House and recounted his experience in a letter to Thomas Jefferson.

Dr. Lansing had studied the history. She devoured every family letter, obscure news article, and geologic study she could find regarding the NMSZ. This fault was considered the least understood seismic zone in North America, and her warnings generally fell on deaf ears.

Her frustration with politicians almost cost her her job a few years ago when a contingent of congressmen toured the NEIC facility in Golden. She'd implored them to insist upon infrastructure improvements to the NMSZ not unlike those along the West Coast. She'd referred to an M8 earthquake or greater as a very real possibility during their lifetimes.

When one congressman referred to an earthquake of that magnitude as being fictional and an overhyped demon that would cost the American taxpayers hundreds of millions of dollars in needless infrastructure improvements, her boss gave her the look, and the conversation was over. It was Dr. Lansing's one and only foray into the political arena.

She did find allies, however. One of the congressmen took her pleas to heart and contacted the Central U.S. Earthquake Consortium, or CUSEC. Their board of directors included top-level personnel in the divisions of emergency management for all states adjacent to the NMSZ. Their mission closely aligned with Dr. Lansing's goals: the reduction of deaths and economic loss resulting from earthquakes in the Central U.S.

The movers and shakers at CUSEC, pardon the pun, were tapped into the political apparatus within the halls of Congress. Their lobbying efforts resulted in programs like the Great ShakeOut Earthquake Drill held annually. Dr. Lansing no longer had to fight the bureaucracy within the USGS. She now had an outlet to make a difference.

Now, unfolding before her eyes, the worst-case scenario had arrived. She'd sensed it was coming. She'd alerted her boss, who didn't want to create an unnecessary panic so close to the holidays, especially on a busy Friday. Besides, he said, statistics showed there was only a one-in-ten chance of an M7 or greater.

Well, one was more than none.

CHAPTER TWENTY-SIX

Friday, December 21
Halloran Centre
Memphis, Tennessee

Jill sensed the motion from above although she never saw the minivan coming before it landed nose first into the front-row seats of the Halloran. She leapt backwards and fell into a handicap-accessible seat in the sixth row. Somehow, she had the presence of mind to bring her knees into her chest. As the minivan fell sideways on top of the pile, it gradually crushed everything beneath it and tilted over so that the frame fell hard to the carpeted surface just where she had been standing seconds earlier.

Jill let out a primal, throaty scream that pierced the air inside the theater. She began to sob uncontrollably as she assumed Tate was among those buried beneath the pile of debris and then smashed further by the falling two-and-a-half-ton vehicle.

She screamed his name in despair. "Taaate! No! Please, no." She began to sob, and then she heard something.

"Mom?"

It was Tate's voice.

Emily joined in. "Mom! Mom! We're back here!"

Tears that came from desperation and hopelessness soon turned to joy.

"Kids? Are you okay? Where are you?"

"We're at the back of the stage," replied Tate. "We're trapped. Stupid cars have been falling on us."

Jill spontaneously slapped the bottom of the minivan with the palm of her hand as if she were giving it a spanking.

"Hold on! Let me find a way to get to you!"

"Mom!" Tate shouted back to her. "Try stage right!"

Jill scooted out of the handicapped seat and pushed herself into the row behind it. She held her arms wide as if to decide which way was stage left and which way was stage right.

"Your left, Mom!" Emily lended an assist.

The tears flowed once again, and Jill began to laugh. "Okay! I'll find a way. I'll get you guys out."

"Hurry, Mom!" Tate shouted. "The back wall is starting to crack."

Jill had heard enough. Nothing was gonna take her kids from her. She rushed around the side of the rubble and began to toss pieces out of the pile. She could hear Tate shuffling large objects on the other side of the pile of curtains, such as the fallen ceiling and the stage audio-visual equipment.

Then she heard voices. Several. Working together. Not panicked.

They were the children. Girls, young and younger. Boys, longing to be men, at the age of nine or ten.

"We can carry this one!"

"I'll hold on to you while you pull!"

"Keep the little ones away from the wall!" said one child to another.

Jill set her jaw and used the strength of several moms. She ripped away the parts of the ceiling blocking their path. The aluminum supports for the drop ceiling were next. She rolled a speaker out of the way, dropping it on her toe in the process, not that she cared.

A dead woman lay underneath a long black curtain panel that Jill removed. She was young. Maybe in her late twenties. The mother of one of the youngest children fighting their way to safety. Her body had to be moved and then hidden from view. There were likely several orphans on the other side of the remains of the Halloran's ceiling. They'd have to process it another time, as Jill could hear the squeaking tires above her. She suspected another car was sliding along the wet concrete toward the edge.

"Hurry, kids! You can do this!"

She could, too. She continued to clear a path, and now she was able to step onto the stage. There was a sliding panel that disappeared into a wall to her left. She used all her strength and then her weight to lean against the edge to force it out of the way. This cleared another eighteen inches.

That was all it took.

Emily greeted her mother first. She forced her body through the space created and immediately crashed into her mom for an emotional reunion. Tate reached through the space and touched his sister's head and then his mother's face. All three Atwoods were crying as relief poured out of them.

Then reality set in for Tate. "Mom, we don't have much time. We're losing the wall."

Jill pulled Emily through and pointed to the wall behind her. Emily's eyes grew wide as she noticed the minivan on top of the front-row seats.

"Mom," she began hesitantly.

"Not now, honey. We have to get everyone out. Help keep the kids calm. Can you do that for me?"

Emily nodded, stood a little taller, and wiped the tears off her face.

A loud creaking sound could be heard, followed by more tires fighting to grip the pavement before they fell off the top of the garage.

"Mom!" Tate raised his voice to get her attention.

Jill handed the phone to Emily. "Keep the light shining over here." She spun around to assist the first child through the narrow space.

In less than a minute, Tate and Jill worked together to usher all the children off the stage and against the wall. Then Jill led them up the walkway, lying to several of them about the whereabouts of their parents. Truthfully, she didn't know for certain what had happened to them. It didn't matter at the moment anyway. They could ill afford a distraught child breaking away and running through the Halloran.

Jill waited for Tate, who was bringing up the rear. She pointed up to the opening.

"That's the way out?" he asked.

"Everything that way has collapsed," she said, pointing toward the entry doors of the theater. "Hopefully, this is still open. I had to dig my way in and then bust my way through the wall."

Tate looked around the floor and said, "Okay. It'll be better for me to push their weight up to you. You can pull and I'll push as far as I can. Whadya think?"

"Fine, but …" She hesitated. "How will you get out?"

"I'll figure that out in a minute. Let's get started."

Tate led his mom to just beneath the opening. "I'm gonna clasp my hands together. I want you to face the wall, and I'll push you upward. Use the jagged edges of the foam walls to hold on or get a foothold. You should be able to reach the opening. When you're ready, I'll shove you through."

"I have to go through sideways," she said.

"Okay, just try to get a knee on the edge. You should be able to stand and turn."

"Let's give it a try," said Jill. She instructed Emily to light up the opening as they worked together to get out.

As planned, Tate used his powerful forearms to hoist his mom high up the wall. She was easily able to grasp the edge of the opening. Then Tate, like the cheerleaders do on the sidelines of his football games, took the soles of her feet and pushed her even higher until she could easily reach the opening. Jill disappeared into the wall and then reappeared on her hands and knees, with an arm dangling out to accept her first child.

"Good work," she said to her son.

"Dad always said to move the heaviest weight first."

"Hey!" protested Jill.

"You know what I mean," he defended himself with a chuckle.

Jill smiled. "Send me up the smallest one first so I can get a system down. Em, keep the light on us."

"Okay," Emily replied.

Tate selected a young girl who was nine, but smaller than the eight-year-old who stood next to her. He hoisted the child up, and she grabbed Jill's hand. With Tate pushing the child up and his mom pulling on the other end, the little girl was soon in the conference room.

"We've got this!" shouted Jill. "Keep 'em comin'!"

Tate sent up another. And then another. He worked quickly as several of the kids began to ask more pointed questions about the whereabouts of their parents.

"Why isn't my mom helping, too?"

"Are they all right?"

"Is my dad waiting outside?"

It broke Tate's heart to hear their innocent, yet logical questions. He knew where they were, and he suspected they were either dead or would eventually die there.

Whomp!

Another car crashed onto the roof, or what was left of it.

Emily jumped and lost her grip on the phone. It fell down into the debris pile they were standing on.

"Holy crap! That scared me!" she exclaimed.

"Where's the light?" asked Jill.

"No time, Mom," replied Tate. He turned to Emily. The two of them were the last to climb out. "Get in position."

"Not without you," she responded to his instructions with her arms crossed, defiant.

"I have a plan, Emily," he lied. "More cars are coming. We don't have time."

She reluctantly got into position. Tate hoisted her up, and Jill used the last of her strength to pull her daughter into the space in the wall.

Tate did not have a plan. All that he knew when he'd made the statement to his mother earlier was that every second wasted on figuring out an exit strategy might endanger the young kids.

He turned around and rummaged through the debris to find his mother's phone. He scraped his forearm on a nail that protruded through the drywall, adding another wound to the ones that were all over his body.

"Tate? What are you gonna do?"

He flashed the light up to his mother. "I can't climb this wall, and you're not gonna be strong enough to pull me up. I have to find another way."

"I'm not leaving you here."

"Mom, you gotta get the kids out. I'll figure something out, I promise."

"No," she insisted.

The back wall of the Halloran began to crash into the stage area. The ceiling and the remainder of the rigging fell hard to the floor, causing dust and debris from the parking garage to fly inside the theater.

Tate shined the light around the theater space from front to back. He took a few steps up the aisleway toward the fallen balcony.

"Mom! I've got it. Get the kids out. I'll see you outside."

"But—" she began, but Tate cut her off.

"Go! Hurry!"

Tate hustled up toward the balcony. He moved carefully down the row toward the point where he'd crawled under the newly formed lean-to.

"Sometimes to go down, you gotta go up first," he said aloud. His father and uncle would reach the same conclusion in St. Louis.

CHAPTER TWENTY-SEVEN

Friday, December 21
Halloran Centre
Memphis, Tennessee

Tate climbed up the steep slope of the collapsed balcony, using the rows of seats like a ladder. He reached the top and then assessed how he would get to the door opening. Fortunately, the solid wooden door was open. However, the slope was too steep for him to walk up without something to grab onto. He used the flashlight app to survey his options. He did see that the hallway outside the door appeared to be intact.

He was hesitant to try leaping off the back of the chairs to grab the doorjamb. If he was unsuccessful, he'd likely slide down the slope and crash onto the theater floor more than twenty feet below.

If he could only get a running start, he thought to himself. He stood on the back of the seat supports that were bolted to the floor. They were sturdy. He looked up toward the open door and noticed it had a latch-type handle. He'd have to watch his footing. One slip and he'd tumble down.

He heard the telltale squeal and creaking sound emanating from the stage area. Another car was about to pile onto the Halloran. It was now or never.

Tate kept his balance and walked backwards three seats. There was sufficient ambient light from car headlights outside the building for him to focus on the handle. He set his jaw, tensed his muscles, and quickly walked on the back of the seats until he reached the last one. Then he pushed off with his right leg, leaping upward until he could reach the door handle. He hung on, his muscles straining to stop the effect of gravity pulling him backwards.

First with his right hand, and then with his left, he firmly grasped the door, hoping the hinges wouldn't come ripping out of the doorjamb. Then he walked himself up the carpeted balcony floor, thankful that it provided him some grip until he was able to swing his right leg onto the still-level hallway outside. With one more effort, he called upon his weary muscles to pull his body up and out of the balcony.

Whomp! Whomp!

Two at once. The proverbial straws that broke the camel's back. The roof of the Halloran was struck with a car and a truck near simultaneously. This caused a chain reaction in which the roofing system, the interior walls, and the floor joists succumbed to the crushing weight of half a dozen vehicles.

Tate didn't pause to watch the total collapse into the theater. He immediately turned to find a way out. What he discovered was that he was standing on the equivalent of a catwalk with no way down. Other than a stretch of corridor reaching to the west side of the building, everything else on the second floor except a narrow hallway had already collapsed.

He tried the street side first, hoping for a soft landing spot. He was sixteen to eighteen feet above the ground. The debris pile below him made the drop a shorter distance. However, it was anything but soft. Jagged concrete, metal supports, and broken furniture were everywhere.

He wasted no time in abandoning this side of the building. He rushed in the other direction, and his prospects improved. Although the west wall had collapsed into the building, the steel fire escape still stood. It was not attached at the top, but it was still bolted to the lower portion of the building.

"Better than nothing," muttered Tate as he turned his body to climb down. Rung after rung, he descended the ladder. Once on the ground, he had to crawl over the rubble to get to the street, but at least that was manageable.

Now that he was outside, he was able to experience the chaos on the streets of Memphis. Sirens screamed. Car alarms relentlessly blared. He could hear the shouts of people and the sobs of the injured.

He crawled over the piles of debris, careful not to cut himself further. He slipped at the very end and landed on all fours. Bits of glass embedded into his hands and knees. But he didn't care.

Tate's smile almost broke his face when his sister and mom helped him to his feet. The ordeal was over. Or, he briefly asked himself, was it only the beginning?

CHAPTER TWENTY-EIGHT

Friday, December 21
Western Mississippi

"Cold, Mama. Cold. Cold." Anthony was tugging on Beth's arm as they waded through the water. It had continued to rise and was now up to her knees. It had soaked Anthony's pants and was now just above his waist. There was so much water, Beth periodically wandered off the pavement because she couldn't differentiate between the asphalt and the submerged cotton fields. She certainly knew when it happened, however. The jagged limestone that made up the shoulder worked like those rumble strips designed to keep wandering drivers on the straight and narrow. Each time she found the shoulder, streaks of pain jolted her body from the soles of her shoeless feet upward.

She'd tried to carry her son to give him a respite from his little body sloshing through the cold, rising water. She found she could only go thirty or forty feet at a time before she had to set him back down. Her back was screaming in agony, and her arms were exhausted. Mentally, she was barely hanging on.

Beth had no idea how long it had been since the car spun out and then the floodwaters carried her off into the muddy field. She'd always relied upon her cell phone to tell her what time it was, and she'd stupidly left it in the car. Well, actually, she'd angrily thrown it into the passenger seat, and it had bounced onto the floorboard. She'd forgotten to bring it with her.

Every once in a while, she experienced a tremor. The orangish-blue flames were no longer spitting out of the ground. She suspected that was because the ground was covered in water. But the tremors persisted, although not quite as frequent.

The rain began to dissipate, and soon only a mist was surrounding her. The water levels also began to recede, or she was reaching higher ground. She really wasn't sure which. She just needed relief before she lost it again.

Beth's hopes began to rise when she saw powerlines cut across what used to be a cotton field to her left, and they began to run parallel to the road. The water level had dropped from her knees to mid-calf.

To her left, she caught a glimpse of the top of a natural gas valve and the white PVC piping marking its boundary. She walked farther, and the water levels receded more. She caught a glimpse of the highway markers in the distance. She unconsciously picked up the pace, dragging little Anthony by the arm.

Closer now, Beth chuckled as the arrow pointing to the left for the Highway 61 sign was accompanied by a sign above it that read NORTH. Only, the sign had lost a bolt and turned upside down. That kinda summed up how her world felt right now.

Beth had never been so happy to see a four-lane divided highway. It was a simple thing. But most importantly, it wasn't totally flooded. That meant there would be cars, and that meant someone would give her a ride to the next town so she could get help.

She and Anthony stood in front of the stop sign on the elevated island and looked up and down the highway for several minutes.

There were no cars in either direction. Anthony was shivering, so she removed her jacket and wrapped it around him. Her body took on the burden of his shivers.

Beth couldn't recall if there was a town to the south, but based upon the sheriff's report about rising water, she took her chances on the northbound side of the highway. They ran across the four lanes and slowed upon reaching a parking lot in front of an abandoned metal building. The light blue structure had once been a chapel, but now it was mostly destroyed courtesy of the remnants of Hurricane Delta, which had roared across Louisiana and Mississippi several years prior.

Beth waited and waited for a vehicle to come upon them to give them a lift northbound. She couldn't remember exactly, but she thought Tunica was only a few miles from them.

She heard the roar of an eighteen-wheeler headed in their direction. She got a firm grip on Anthony's hand and inched toward the highway but not too close. She began waving her hands long before the driver would've been able to see her.

Suddenly, Anthony, upset at the roar of the oncoming diesel rig, squirmed in her hands and pulled himself free. He raced back toward the partially demolished building, screaming.

"Noise! No noise!"

Beth looked toward the approaching truck and then back to Anthony, who was distraught. She chose her son. She ran to him and scooped him into her arms just as the driver of the semi roared past them. He probably never saw them huddled by the roofless building.

It took several minutes to calm Anthony down. When his emotional outburst subsided, she knelt by his side.

"Hey, you wanna go for a walk?"

"No rain."

"That's right. No rain. A beautiful night for a walk." She shivered from the cold as she spoke. She'd endure anything to keep her son protected from the cold and safe from whatever came their way.

Beth stood and shifted her feet. She wasn't sure if her feet could take a long walk, but she was certain she could make it a couple of hours, the length of time it would take to get to Tunica.

Or so she thought. It was actually twenty-three miles to Tunica, Mississippi, and Beth was only able to make it a few miles before both she and Anthony gave out after an hour and a half.

After crossing what amounted to a raging river beneath a short span of highway bridge, she came upon a guardrail beneath a sign advertising the casinos at Tunica Resorts. That was when she began to cry again. It read twenty miles. They could never walk that far.

They huddled at the base of the three-foot-diameter steel pole and fell asleep, with Anthony curled up in his mom's jacket. During their fitful sleep, two cars had passed, awakening Beth. However, she was unable to scramble to her feet in time to flag them down.

She had to find a way to stay awake. She coaxed Anthony to his feet, and they moved closer to the highway. The two of them sat on the shoulder and leaned against the cold steel guardrail. That way, Beth surmised, if a car came along, they'd stop because they saw them.

Once again, out of pure exhaustion, she drifted off to sleep. She and Anthony used their body heat to survive the falling temperatures coupled with the moist air.

Then bright lights shining in her eyes woke her up with a start. She instinctively held Anthony in her arms as she tried to block the lights coming from a vehicle parked thirty or forty yards away.

A shadow passed in front of the lights, then out again, temporarily blinding her view. The silhouette was unmistakable.

A man.

A large man was approaching. His body wandered back into the lights, so she could make out the outline of his body as he approached. She could see his right arm reach toward his waist and then swing away from his body slowly. Her eyes grew wide, and fear swept over her.

Gun! she screamed in her mind. The man had pulled a gun from his waist. She gripped Anthony and tried to pull him behind her as she turned her body to place it between the oncoming man and her lovely, innocent child.

As he got closer, she swallowed hard and begged, "Please, mister. Please don't hurt us."

CHAPTER TWENTY-NINE

Friday, December 21
USGS
Golden, Colorado

"If we are at flood stage on the Lower Mississippi, it's the worst of the worst-case scenarios," said Dr. Lansing as she drank another Red Bull. She took pride in her health and rarely indulged in anything deemed *not good for you*. Tonight was an exception. She needed *wings*, as the company's advertising stated.

She paced the floor, her mind racing as to all of the various aspects of the massive earthquake that needed to be assessed. She'd been in continuous contact with her boss in Reston and was told to be prepared to address the president's crisis management team sometime on Saturday. As all of these things filled her already anxious mind, she continued expelling her inner thoughts to her dutiful team.

"Because of these heavy rains the last several days, we have saturated earthen levees that are already breached or are in jeopardy of overtopping. The water has been threatening to flood inland for days, and now the earth is shaking as far south as Natchez, Mississippi."

"Aquifers are adding to the problem, mum," said Oliver. "The waters are emerging from below the normal barriers holding them in place. We suspect the rising waters inland are not just from the heavy rainfall. We believe the aquifers are the primary culprit."

Dr. Lansing stopped and studied the continuous satellite imagery that scrolled across the screens mounted throughout the operations center. "We know the river is gonna take the path of least resistance. It's occurring in the Lower Mississippi Valley and—"

"Dr. Lansing, my apologies," interrupted a voice from the back of the room. "In that regard, we just received this from our Region 4 office in Atlanta."

She spun around and approached the rear of the room, where two analysts on loan from FEMA were working at their assigned stations. The young man rose and stepped a few paces toward her with a multipage report. As she glanced at its contents, he continued.

"Here are the highlights. There are twenty-two miles of levees in Memphis. The Corps of Engineers, with limited resources at the moment, mind you, has been checking for irregularities like boils and obvious slides."

"Boils?" asked Dr. Lansing.

"Yes, ma'am. Boils occur when water finds its way underneath the levees. The earthquake has disturbed the embankment upon which the levees rest. The downward pressure of the water has increased seepage and the resulting piping—cavities forming from the erosion that are either at risk of collapsing or have already done so."

"How prevalent are these boils?" she asked.

"Seven major slide events thus far," he replied and then explained, "Once the structural integrity of the levee has failed, water finds its way through the boils and pops up on the other side. As of yet, this has not occurred. However, the saturated ground is on a slope. There is evidence that the slope is beginning to separate in seven different locations. The intense pressure exerted by the river will eventually cause both sloped sides of the levee to collapse, opening a large breach."

"Seven?" she asked.

"Yes, ma'am. So far, anyway."

She rolled the report into a long cylinder and tapped it on the palm of her hand. Another geophysicist weighed in.

"This is similar to what is happening in Mississippi except for different reasons," he began.

"Are you referring to the aquifers?"

"Yes."

Seismic waves resulting from earthquakes impacted groundwater levels in two ways. One was known as oscillations, and the other was from what scientists deemed permanent offsets.

Oscillations were part of the seismic wave train that roared beneath the surface, causing expansion and contraction of the underground water reservoirs known as aquifers. If the pressure from the seismic wave was great enough, the aquifer would force groundwater throughout its contained area below ground. These changes resulted in water looking for a way out and breaching the surface through wells, sinkholes, and spring-fed creeks, whichever was the path of least resistance.

Offsets were more explosive and resulted from thermal pressurization due to upward movement as the seismic waves passed through the aquifer. Scientific study following the massive earthquake in Alaska in 1964 found the seismic-wave-induced water pressure lasted long after the seismic wave train of the earthquake ceased.

The results of this significant change in the groundwater aquifers stretched beyond the obvious problem of expansive flooding. With the intense shaking of the earthquake, an influx of sediments from the earth invades the aquifer. These particles could include harmful leach nitrates and arsenic compounds, as well as the probability of bacterial contamination in raw water supplies. It was feasible that if the aquifer beneath Mississippi and Louisiana continued to sustain damage, the water supply to that region could be tarnished for decades, if not longer.

"We've got to issue water-quality warnings to the entire region," she instructed.

"Ma'am, um, there's more."

"What?"

"Warnings can't be issued because there is no electricity. Power from Baton Rouge to Des Moines is out. Even emergency communications towers are inoperable in an eight-state region along the Mississippi. Everyone is in the dark, even emergency response personnel."

PART III

SILENT NIGHT

When the world is falling apart around you, it's natural to seek a place of respite. A spot where you can think, process, and cope. It's all about finding tranquility in the chaos. As you age, you learn to stop trying to calm the storm that swirls around you. You focus on calming yourself, knowing the storm will pass. However, in the back of your mind, something always nags at you. Because no matter how hard you try to convince yourself, you know …

A storm is coming.

CHAPTER THIRTY

Saturday, December 22
South of Tunica, Mississippi

Beth was trembling as the man approached. His heavy boots splashed the rainwater accumulated on the pavement. He drew his hand close as he approached and then holstered his weapon. His deep Southern drawl was comforting as he spoke to her.

"Now, ma'am, there's no reason to be alarmed. It's just procedure nowadays. My name is Willie Angel, and I'm a sergeant with the Mississippi Highway Patrol."

The older, heavyset black man knelt down a few feet away from Beth so the headlights of his patrol car could shine on his face and uniform. He removed his hat and produced a toothy smile.

Beth was still somewhat frightened by the trooper's sudden appearance and the fact he'd pulled his weapon to approach her. After what she'd been through, she expected the worst.

"Hi, I'm Beth Chandler, and this is my three-year-old, Anthony. We're traveling to my sister's home in Cordova, um, Memphis."

"Out east, right?" asked Willie.

"Yes. Yes, sir. We heard about flooding, and then I turned toward the highway. We got washed off the road and stuck in a field." Beth's eyes welled up in tears as she relived the circumstances that got her into this predicament.

"That ain't fittin' for the holidays, now is it?"

"No, sir," she replied as she warmed up to the apparently kind, nonthreatening stranger. "I thought we could walk to the highway and find a ride. The water was deep, and when we finally got here, nobody stopped for us."

"Well, Miss Chandler, I think I can help you out."

Willie stood and held his hand out to help her off the ground where the two had remained huddled next to the guardrail. She accepted his hand and held her belly as she rose to her feet.

"Thanks. Um, I'm carrying quite a load, as you can see." She turned and helped Anthony stand.

"Look at you, Miss Chandler. Congratulations. I'm no expert, but you seem like you're quite a ways along."

"Yes, sir. Twenty-eight weeks. Please call me Beth. And this is—"

"Anthony, my name is Willie," the trooper said, finishing her sentence. He bent over and stuck out his hand. "It's nice to meet you, young man."

The three-year-old stood emotionless, staring at the man without moving. Beth tried to encourage him to shake hands, but he wouldn't.

"I'm sorry, sir. He's, um, autistic. He's a little shy around strangers."

Willie stood and placed his hat back on his head. "That's quite all right. As long as he feels safe. Miss Chandler, you can call me Willie. I happen to be off duty right now, headed back to my home in Tunica. The only people who call me sir are the ones I pull over. Lord knows, they're just suckin' up to get out of a ticket."

Beth started laughing. "I believe it. Okay, Willie. Again, you can call me Beth. And I'm Mrs. Chandler. My husband is in St. Louis on business. He and my brother-in-law, Jack, are heading back to Cordova to celebrate Christmas."

"All right, Miss—" He hesitated. "All right, Beth. I can give you a ride up to Tunica. There's some things in the news you apparently don't know."

Willie and Beth got Anthony settled in the back seat before the adults slid into the front. As soon as Willie pulled onto the road, Anthony became agitated because he was alone in the back, separated from his mother by the steel-mesh screen separating the two parts of the patrol car. Beth allowed him a minute to get adjusted to the seating arrangements. After another mile, as Anthony became increasingly distraught, Willie pulled over, and Beth joined her son in the back of the patrol car.

As they drove toward Tunica, Beth leaned up onto the edge of the bench seat as best she could to talk with Willie through the steel mesh.

"I feel like a perp," she said with a laugh.

Willie smiled and glanced back toward her. He gently rapped the steel divider with his right knuckles. "Not all of our cars have these. Normally, when an arrest is made, we hold the suspect until local law enforcement arrives. As drug trafficking on I-55 increased between *New Awlins* and Memphis, more and more of these busts came under the feds' jurisdiction. The state guys were required to deliver the prisoners to Jackson. It was a safety thing."

Beth was impressed that Willie didn't pronounce New Orleans as N'awlins. He might not have been from Louisiana, but he certainly didn't refer to the city like a tourist.

"You mentioned there was some news? I was told about the flooding when I stopped for food in Rosedale."

Willie looked at Beth through the rearview mirror. "Miss Barbara's?"

"Yeah. You know it?"

"There's nuthin' better than those hot tamales."

"I know, right? I had to leave them in the car."

Willie slowed and chuckled. "Maybe we should turn around and fetch 'em?"

Beth began to laugh so hard her belly shook, which caused her a twinge of pain. Anthony, who'd remained perfectly still throughout, seemed to relax as his mother did. He giggled although he had no idea why.

"No, thanks. They're probably flooded anyway. Tell me, what else is in the news?"

Willie had to slow down to drive along the right shoulder of the highway. Beaverdam Lake to their left had swollen well over its banks. The water washed onto Highway 61 for a couple of thousand yards. Once he cleared the floodwaters, he passed by several industrial buildings on the outskirts of Tunica. They, too, were flooded.

The pause in the conversation while he focused on the road gave him time to choose his words carefully. He didn't want to unduly frighten Beth.

"Here's what I know. There was an earthquake, Beth. It seemed to stretch along the Mississippi River from just below Memphis to north of St. Louis. Before the upper half of Mississippi lost power, the news reports were kinda sketchy."

"When?" she asked, forcing herself forward to the edge of the seat again.

"Around 4:45 today. Well, sorry. I mean yesterday. Late afternoon. They say it lasted nearly ten minutes."

"Good god," said Beth as she covered her mouth. "How bad is it?"

He took a deep breath. "You know, with the power out, we really don't have all the details. I think it was localized along the river."

Willie hesitated just enough as he spoke for Beth's intuition to pick up on the white lie.

"Willie, please. Tell me what you know. My sister would've been in downtown Memphis at that time, and my husband would've been in St. Louis."

"Honestly, this is all I know. The power went out almost immediately up there, and then there was a rolling blackout extending into the adjoining states. Our dispatch asked me to stay on for a whole 'nother shift after mine ended at five yesterday."

Beth turned in her seat and reached for Anthony's hand. She slid back on the dark blue vinyl and arched her back to relieve some of the pain she was experiencing. She tried not to cry.

"Here we are," said Willie softly.

Beth looked forward through the windshield and then side to side through the rear passenger windows. "Where? I can't see anything."

"Oh, it's there. With no lights, you just can't see our fair little town."

Willie slowed as he eased through town. A few fast-food restaurants and two gas stations came into view. At that hour, they would've been closed anyway, but the lack of any ambient light was disconcerting.

"You live here?" she asked.

"Sure do. For the better part of forty years, I s'pose. My wife and I moved into my folks' house on Gay Street. Raised three young'uns, shipped them off to Alcorn State, and been here ever since."

Beth felt her maternity jeans for money or a credit card. They were empty because she normally kept everything in her crossbody bag.

"Willie, um, I don't have any money for a hotel room. Do you think they'll—?"

He politely raised his hand and cut her off. "You haven't met my wife yet, but in a few minutes you will. If she knew I found a seven-month pregnant woman and her toddler on the side of the road and stuck her in the no-tell motel over on Main, she'd give me a tongue-lashin' like no other. And that's while she's takin' a switch to my backside. She's reminded me more times than I can count what my Momma used to say. *William Angel, you ain't never too old for a good old-fashioned ass whoopin'.*"

Beth laughed, and then the tears flowed at the same time. "Willie, you are an angel. Thank you."

CHAPTER THIRTY-ONE

Saturday, December 22
Downtown Memphis, Tennessee

Temperatures had dipped into the upper forties, and the last of the rainfall still caused damp conditions along the river. It had been hours since they'd emerged from the collapsed performing-arts center. While Jill and Emily comforted the children, who were now realizing their parents were dead or missing, Tate set out in search of any first responders who could help rescue survivors from the Halloran's remains.

For a couple of hours, Tate wandered the streets of Downtown Memphis in search of police and firefighters. He quickly learned how cataclysmic the earthquake had been. No building had been spared the destructive force of the quake. Entire high-rises had toppled. The bridges across the Mississippi River had collapsed or were considered too dangerous to pass.

Broken gas lines caused leaks throughout the city, especially in residential areas, where homes relied upon the natural gas for heat. As the colorless gas permeated buildings, broken power lines caused sparks that ignited the highly combustible mixture of the gas with oxygen in the air. Throughout the night, the deadly combination resulted in a small-scale equivalent of a thermobaric weapon, commonly known as an aerosol bomb.

The explosive, in this case the natural gas, coupled with oxygen, generated hundreds of high-temperature explosions around the city. The blast wave could be so intense, the overpressure ruptured people's lungs if it didn't burn them completely.

The aerosol bombs caused fires that swept through the mounds of debris. The misty drizzle that continued overnight had little effect on the out-of-control fires. Fire trucks were stymied by the fallen buildings, broken water mains, and damaged cars that blocked the roads. Memphis had become a massive firestorm that couldn't be fought by conventional means. They would have to burn themselves out.

Tate found his way to the closest fire hall, Memphis Fire Station #5, located several blocks away toward the river. The fire trucks were parked in their stalls, covered with debris from their own roof cave-in. The buildings along the river had taken a beating. Most had crumbled and fallen into the city streets. They were certainly impassable for large fire trucks.

Firefighters removed the hoses from their fire engines and dragged them through the streets to fight the closest fires first. They worked frantically to rescue the living and confirm others to be dead. Tate begged two of them to assist in rescuing the parents of the children who'd survived the collapse of the Halloran. They ran with him through the streets, but by the time they arrived, more of the parking structure had collapsed on top of the theater, making rescue efforts too dangerous.

The firefighters were unable to make contact with their 911 operators via handheld two-way radios. The earthquake had snapped millions of fiber-optic cables and telephone lines. Cell towers and emergency relay towers were toppled, cutting off communications between first responders while rendering landlines, cell phones, and internet connections inoperable.

It was well after midnight when the firefighters left Jill, Tate, and

Emily alone with the fifteen children they'd saved. Emily, who knew them all, and Jill, who was friends with many of their parents, tried to comfort the kids. They did their best to offer them a ray of hope. However, when the firefighters left the children alone, they began to cry.

It was Tate who suggested finding a church that was still standing. They would take the children there and seek counseling for them. It turned out to be a wise decision. They led the children east on Beale Street toward the Medical District.

Emily held her mother's hand as they walked. Once, she paused and pointed up to a skyscraper and commented, "Look, Mom. Those buildings lost their skins." Jill grimaced as she looked upward. The historic Beale Street Baptist Church was engulfed in flames, and the orangish glow revealed the broken glass and crumbled façades of the surrounding buildings.

Tate led everyone around the FedEx Forum. The arena, used mainly for basketball and concerts, was a logical place for refugees to gather. They soon learned the ceiling had collapsed during the earthquake, killing many of the fans attending the basketball tournament.

They kept walking. Past people who lay on benches or under the canopies of bus stops. Past the fires and the demolished buildings and the broken-down vehicles. They joined a herd of refugees walking slowly forward, shuffling their feet without a word spoken between them.

After an hour, they merged onto Union Avenue, which crossed by the hospitals. During that time, explosions rocked the downtown area. Most likely, they would've been badly injured if they'd waited any longer.

Another hour passed, and they kept walking, although the large group they'd become a part of began to stop or peel off to join in the looting of fast-food restaurants or drugstores. They reached I-69, which ran north-south through the east side of the city. The overpasses had collapsed, but pedestrian traffic was moving steadily toward the north. When they arrived at the interstate, Tate questioned several of the refugees. He was told FEMA and the National Guard had set up a relief station at the Mississippi Boulevard Christian Church a quarter mile away on Jefferson Avenue.

Tate shared the information with his mom, but he didn't want to get the kids' hopes up. He simply led them along the highway until the large Christian church came into view.

Known as *The BLVD*, the church's campus spanned several city blocks in all directions. Once they came upon the church grounds, Jill immediately recognized it from the interstate. She knew the finance chair of the church, Holly Sanders. They'd worked on a fundraiser to help victims who'd lost their homes as a result of asteroid IM-86 colliding with the planet years ago.

They followed dozens of other people as they climbed up the grassy embankment next to the collapsed Jefferson Avenue overpass. In the parking lot adjacent to the interstate, tall generator-powered lights revealed the National Guard and FEMA staging a recovery effort. Humvees, troop carriers, and school buses were scattered across the church campus.

Several white tents had been set up at the entrance parking lot. Barriers were positioned to lead refugees and victims through a cattle-style corridor so they could be processed. Jill took over from there.

She explained to the FEMA personnel the situation. Within seconds, they'd sent word into the church, and two of The BLVD's elders emerged to help. After FEMA obtained the personal information on each of them, they were led inside the church, where dozens of parishioners immediately stepped up to provide love and comfort to the kids.

FEMA explained that they would keep the children there as long as necessary to find any of their family members. Jill asked for the list of children's names and addresses. She promised to help by going to their homes that were near her own.

That was when the Atwoods got the best news of all. At sunrise, the school buses would begin transporting refugees to the east.

Some would be dropped off at exits off I-40 along the way, while others would be taken to Jackson, almost a hundred miles to their northeast.

They said their goodbyes to the kids and thanked the parishioners who devoted their time to looking after them. Then they got in line to catch a bus.

By eight o'clock that Saturday morning, a caravan of three buses was moving slowly along Sam Cooper Boulevard through the residential neighborhoods of East Memphis. With each street crossing, the houses appeared to be less damaged than the ones before them. The family became convinced the earthquake hadn't impacted their home in Cordova.

The buses slowed to a stop as they reached the giant cloverleaf where I-40 and I-240 merged. Ordinarily, Sam Cooper Boulevard ran underneath the massive overpasses of the two heavily travelled interstate highways. During the quake, the tallest two of those overpasses, with the vehicles on top of them, had collapsed to the ground below.

Massive Army bulldozers had been working for hours to move the concrete, steel, and destroyed vehicles to the side in order to create a lane wide enough for the buses to fit through. It was a reminder to the family that the destruction caused by the quake spread far and wide.

Once they cleared the cloverleaf, the buses were able to gain speed, as now two eastbound lanes had been cleared. The westbound lanes of I-40 only contained the occasional emergency or military vehicle.

Exhausted, Jill leaned against the window on the right side of the bus and closed her eyes. Emily, who was sandwiched between her mom and brother, leaned over onto Jill's shoulder. Tate tilted his head back and dozed off.

Suddenly, a murmur began to build within the bus as the other passengers began to talk in hushed whispers. Several of them left their seats and leaned over the passengers on the left side of the bus to look out the window. Their voices began to rise, stirring Tate awake.

"My god," said more than one.

"I've never seen anything like it."

"Those poor people."

Tate was fully awake now and curious. He stood in the aisle of the school bus, pushing his head into the adjacent seat so he could get a look. His eyes grew wide and he gasped. He slowly backed up and plopped into the bench seat, awakening his mom and sister.

Jill was still half-asleep when she noticed the commotion on the bus. "Huh. Um, what's going on?"

"Mom, you gotta see this."

CHAPTER THIRTY-TWO

Saturday, December 22
St. Louis, Missouri

The waters of the Mississippi River had rolled into St. Louis with the sunrise. Jack and Tony had to climb over dead bodies and mounds of debris to escape the lobby of the Met. What they discovered outside the building shocked them. Everything was destroyed. Buildings. Vehicles. People's lives. Nothing remained untouched. And now flooding threatened to crush what hope the survivors had left.

They moaned in pain and cried in despair. Virtually every survivor was bloodied, battered, or broken. Desperate for help, their outstretched arms and pleading eyes forced Jack and Tony to draw together in an unconscious effort to comfort one another. Humanity didn't deserve what the New Madrid earthquake had inflicted upon it. The two men needed to give each other strength to survive and escape the crumbling city.

There were signs that help was on the way. The roar of two Army National Guard helicopters could be heard in the distance. The constant thumping sound of their rotors echoed through the remains of the downtown skyline. Sirens of emergency vehicles wailed throughout the streets. Several massive bulldozers were already on the scene, pushing debris and destroyed vehicles out of the way.

Volunteers worked together to search for survivors among the rubble. Jack and Tony felt compelled to assist the strangers. They spent half an hour in the rubble about a mile from the Met, assisting emergency workers searching for bodies in the crumbled remains of the nearly two-hundred-year-old Cathedral Basilica of Saint Louis, the first built west of the Mississippi in 1845.

A wedding with three hundred in attendance had been caught completely off guard by the rapidly moving earthquake. In their panic to exit, they'd crushed the oldest and infirm among them, causing a pileup at the entrance. The entire cathedral had collapsed upon them, leaving only the granite entrance with the inscription above it—*deo uni et trino*. God one and triune, referring to the Father, the Son, and the Holy Spirit.

As the waters rose and the rescue efforts were abandoned, Jack stormed away from the cathedral and shook his head in disgust. God certainly had his hands full on this day.

As Jack reflected upon the tragedy, One Metropolitan Square came crashing down. The battering of the adjacent buildings combined with the massive earthquake that had rollicked its foundation was eventually too much for the skyscraper to withstand. With a massive groan followed by a rush of debris-filled displaced air, the Met was reduced to rubble, taking another adjacent building with it.

The guys began to run away, not because they were in imminent danger of the building collapsing on them, as it was just over a mile away. It was an instinctive reaction, a fight-or-flight response, in which their minds were in simultaneous agreement. This fight was bigger than they were, and they simply wanted to put the entire ordeal in their rearview mirror.

He and Tony elected to focus on getting home to their families. They'd had discussions with some of the emergency personnel, who advised them the lines of communications up and down the Mississippi had been severed. Their attempts to access a cell tower were without success. Jack silently prayed to God for the safety of Jill and the kids, after apologizing for asking for help on such a busy day, of course.

The men began walking south, veering away from the river as the water slowly encroached into the downtown. Off to their left, the collapsed remains of Busch Stadium resembled the Colosseum in Rome. Most of the structure had fallen away, leaving the stands of steel beams behind. Surrounding buildings appeared to have been stomped on by a giant steel boot. Every window in their field of vision had been broken, leaving glass covering the floor of the concrete jungle.

Those who were capable began moving west away from the river. A few tried to drive around or over the debris but soon learned walking was much faster. To the east, those who waited too long to escape or who relied upon rescuers would likely drown.

Jack and Tony began to pick up the pace themselves, careful to avoid the large fissures that opened up in the ground. These cracks in the earth would soon be hidden by the slightest amount of water. An unsuspecting refugee could easily step from solid ground in what appeared to be a foot of water into a water-filled crevasse hundreds of feet deep.

The guys found their way to Interstate 44, which was slightly elevated over the rest of its surroundings. The lanes were still passable, but few cars were moving, as the entrance ramps to the highway had been blocked by debris or stalled vehicles. I-44 westbound had become a pedestrian walkway of the displaced. Sullen, exhausted, downtrodden people of all walks of life slowly moved toward the suburbs. Some lived there. Others hoped to find a Good Samaritan to lend a hand.

Jack and Tony exchanged very few words as they made their way out of the city. The collapse of the Met seemed to be a game-changer for them mentally. They each tried their cell phones occasionally but then accepted the fact they weren't going to work.

They decided to conserve their batteries in case their wives called them or if it became necessary to use their flashlight apps again.

It was approaching noon when the men reached the twin spans of highway bridge crossing the Meramec River just north of Fenton. The two four-lane bridges had been destroyed except for a narrow stretch on the eastbound lane just wide enough for pedestrians to cross. Many were afraid to risk their lives along the steel girder coupled with the two load-bearing flanges that remained.

Jack explained to Tony the Meramec was known to flood, and it was likely all of the roads between where they stood and the Mississippi were under water. They decided to go for it.

Separated by about six feet, the two men walked the twenty-inch span alone while others watched on. Tony followed Jack's lead.

"As you go across, watch me. I'll be lowering my body's center of gravity toward the steel span. Think of it this way. It's harder to turn over a short stout vase than a tall slim one."

"Makes sense. I'm right behind you," said Tony confidently.

"Also, a quick reminder. Don't look down."

"Not a problem," said Tony after hesitating. He'd already broken that rule and vowed not to do it again. The swift-moving waters were churning up mud, leaving the appearance of a chocolatey froth. Also, oddly, it seemed to be flowing upstream.

The guys made it across and continued walking along Interstate 44. They stopped to rest as afternoon set in. They were both thirsty and hungry. Exhaustion had forced them to hit a brick wall.

"Do you have any idea where we are?" asked Tony.

Jack chuckled. "Not a clue. High and dry. How's that?"

"Yeah, there's that," he replied. He looked toward the sky and glanced at his watch. It was three o'clock. He pointed toward the sun. "That's west."

Jack laughed out loud and slapped Tony on the back. He mocked him as he spoke. "You were a sharp cookie in school. Or was it Boy Scouts?"

"Screw you, man. I was just gettin' my bearings straight. I think we should start heading south, right?"

Jack smiled and nodded. "I was just bustin' your balls. Yeah, we should be far enough away from the Mississippi at this point to avoid flooding. There aren't many buildings out here, but the ones I've seen are damaged. This quake was massive."

"Whadya think? Six or seven?"

"Bigger. St. Louis was leveled," Jack responded and then sighed. "I mean even out here, maybe a dozen miles from downtown, the buildings are all damaged."

Tony stood and stretched. "I've gotta keep goin'. If I stop now, I'll just roll over there in the weeds and fall asleep."

"I get it," said Jack. "Let's pull off at the next exit. Maybe somebody will let us sleep in a barn or something."

They approached an exit sign marked Beaumont-Antire Road. It was labeled Exit 269.

"Over twenty miles," mumbled Jack.

"What's that?"

"The downtown exit was 290. I remember seeing the sign at Jefferson Avenue when we got started. It read Exit 289."

"Damn," began Tony. "I don't think I've ever walked twenty miles in a day, or anywhere close to that."

Jack picked up the pace and pointed in front of him. "There's a pickup parked up ahead. He didn't pass us, did he?"

Tony shrugged. "I don't think so. A few others did without stopping, but I don't remember this one. Maybe he'll give us a ride?"

The two men jogged toward the truck and slowed as they approached so as not to startle the driver. Jack eased up to the window to tap on it, but it was partially rolled down, allowing him a view inside. The driver wasn't taking them anywhere. He was clearly dead.

"What's the deal?" asked Tony.

"I'm guessing he died of a heart attack. His face is contorted like he had a stroke." Jack pressed two fingers against the man's neck to feel for a pulse. His grimace revealed the result.

"Well, shit," Tony complained.

Jack walked forward a few paces and then returned to the

driver's side. He shook his head and mumbled, "Ya gotta do what ya gotta do."

Tony looked into the front seat of the truck from the passenger's side. He and Jack made eye contact.

"I don't like it, Jack. But it's all we've got."

Jack nodded and opened the driver's door.

CHAPTER THIRTY-THREE

Saturday, December 22
USGS
Golden, Colorado

One of Dr. Lansing's aides gave her a ride home just to pick up several changes of clothes. She wanted to explain to her husband in person what her role would be over the next forty-eight hours or more. She also wanted to let him know she wouldn't likely return until Sunday afternoon sometime. She tried to brush aside his response.

He commented she didn't get paid enough for what she did. For some, his statement might be shrugged off as a joke concerning the value of a person to the business or organization where they worked. Her husband actually meant it. In his mind, the near-six-figure salary was insufficient for the hours she put into a government job, as he called it.

He'd never understood her passion, and she resented his attitude. Dr. Lansing wasn't in it for the money. She wanted to save lives.

She walked back into the operations center and studied the

weary faces. Many of them had worked around the clock like she had. There were a few she had to force to go home and get some rest, especially since there were anxious, able-bodied replacements ready to jump in and be a part of this historic catastrophic event.

"Okay, folks. We've gathered the data, and I know many of you have been focusing on modeling. In about an hour, I have to join a teleconference with my boss and the White House."

"Wow!"

"Very cool."

"Will you get to talk to the president?"

She sighed. "I'm not really sure. Maybe the chief of staff or some staffer? It doesn't really matter. My boss is pressuring me for an official determination on the magnitude and intensity of this quake. Let's work through the calculations, shall we?"

She handed her duffle bag to an aide, who hustled it into her office. Dr. Lansing turned to Oliver, her go-to guy when it came to laying the groundwork for discussions such as this one. His organizational skills and clear head would reward him with her job one day, she was sure of it.

"Oliver, we've been gathering data that measures magnitude, energy release, and shaking intensity. People outside this room, including those in the White House whom I'll be speaking with later, often confuse them with one another."

"Yes, mum," he began. "The dependencies and relationships between the three concepts can be quite confusing to a layman."

"Let's start with intensity," she instructed the man who'd been given the role of the team leader within the operations center.

"Yes, of course. We've been able to access most of the borehole seismometers and strong-motion accelerometers that recorded convulsions in the planet during the earthquake event. Using this data, we've assigned a value to each of these identifiers associated with earthquakes.

"The intensity value ranges from not felt at the surface, intensity level I, to extreme, the highest, which is identified as intensity level

X or X+. For the benefit of our friends from FEMA, this is the Modified Mercalli Intensity scale.

"Under accepted definitions of intensity as being the measure of human observations, which are unavailable at this moment for obvious reasons, coupled with instrumental data at each station location, we've determined locations near Memphis and Keokuk, Iowa have registered as level VIII, severe. Ste. Genevieve, our epicenter that's sixty miles south of St. Louis, has registered as intensity level IX, or violent. None of the readings support a level X or greater."

Dr. Lansing worked through his findings and compared them to the types of earthquakes felt in California. A recent M6 near the Hayward fault running parallel to the Pacific Coast outside San Francisco had generated light to moderate damage and was rated an intensity level VI or in some places a VII.

"What about outside the normal NMSZ region?" she asked.

"Up the Ohio River, intensity level VI was the norm, especially in Southern Indiana near the towns of Mauckport and Brandenburg, Kentucky.

"Along the Mississippi, we have similar results. Level V was the norm into the Davenport-Moline area to the north. Level IV intensity is what we've assigned to Natchez, Mississippi, although liquefaction has increased that value to Level V in areas near Tunica, which is just south of Memphis."

She turned to the two FEMA representatives, who'd remained at their stations throughout, except for numerous bathroom breaks to expel the gallons of coffee they'd consumed.

"I assume communications are still down. Is that right?"

The young man responded, "Yes, although our FEMA response centers have been able to communicate on a limited basis within each community using two-way radios."

"Damage reports are incomplete. Is that fair to say?"

"Yes, sorry."

"Hey, no apologies. I can only imagine what they're going through," said Dr. Lansing. She returned her attention to Oliver.

"Before we talk about energy release, we need to determine this beast's magnitude. This is the number all the media types like to refer to even though it is only a part of the picture."

"I agree, mum," said Oliver. "The seismometer readings have varied throughout the United States. This earthquake was so powerful, like its counterparts in the early nineteenth century, it was felt throughout much of North America.

"For point of reference, since you'll be speaking with the White House representatives and they'll ask out of curiosity, we've determined the magnitude in Washington, DC, as M3.3. This was in line with the swarm we experienced in the last five days within the NMSZ.

"At the epicenter in Ste. Genevieve, Missouri, we've registered the moment magnitude as M8.5. That would put it as the strongest outside Alaska in over a century."

Dr. Lansing's shoulders slumped, and she leaned against a cubicle's partition wall. It gave slightly, causing her to jerk her body upright. A momentary wave of despair came over her. She didn't need to see FEMA's damage report. She could visualize it for herself.

CHAPTER THIRTY-FOUR

Saturday, December 22
Shelby County, Tennessee

Barely a thousand feet north of them, running parallel to the interstate, a fissure had opened up that stretched for miles. The jagged-shaped crevasse changed course abruptly from time to time, creating the impression of a lightning bolt cut into the earth as some kind of otherworldly art project. The enormous tear in the planet was so deep there was no evidence of a bottom.

Starting somewhere northwest of the Bartlett exit closer to Memphis, the earthquake had carved its way through residential neighborhoods and retail shopping centers until it reached the Wolfchase Galleria mall several miles away. The mall had been torn in half, with only JCPenney and Dillard's standing. Stores like Macy's and Gap had been swallowed by the earth.

With everyone's noses pressed against the windows to take in the carnage, the bus driver decelerated to take Exit 16 for anyone living in Cordova and Germantown. The startling maneuver caused several people to lose their balance in the aisleway and shriek. The fear-filled utterance was contagious.

The entire bus assumed the worst without looking and began to panic.

Jill fell back into their seat and pulled Emily down with her as passengers irrationally pushed and shoved to position themselves at the exit doors.

"Calm down, everyone! We're making a stop to let some folks off before we head for the next exit."

A man at the rear of the bus hollered, "I live in Bartlett! We should've stopped back there."

"Sorry, sir. I am not authorized to use that exit. The area is too unstable."

The man slumped into his seat and then stood. Then he sat back down. He didn't seem to know whether he should get off now and walk back, or just keep riding in search of a new place to live far away from the New Madrid Seismic Zone.

The driver pulled the bus to a stop and allowed the locals, including the Atwoods, off the bus. A group of eleven plus their three stood dumbfounded for a moment. Tate saw their concern.

"Hey. Where do you guys live?"

A couple responded Germantown. Another one responded Fisherville, which was ten miles to their east.

A woman was in tears when she responded. She was holding another woman, who appeared to be in shock. She had a cut on her forehead and had a makeshift bandage wrapped around it.

"We live in Stonebridge."

Tate knew the neighborhood well, as several of his classmates lived there. Stonebridge Golf Club was one of the courses the MUS golf team practiced on. He turned to them and smiled.

"Ma'am, you're on this side of the interstate. They wouldn't send the bus through there if, you know, there was a problem."

"Do you think? I mean, did you see what happened over there?" She pointed through the highway overpass. The south side of the mall stood virtually intact. Then it suddenly ended right through the middle of JCPenney.

Tate walked up to them and gently placed his hands on their

shoulders. "I really do think y'all are okay. Either way, you gotta go see."

They patted him on the hand and thanked him before they left. Jill spontaneously hugged her son.

"You're a good man, Tate Atwood."

Tate whispered, "Mom, I hope I'm right."

Emily couldn't help herself. Despite the traumatic ordeal she'd been through, she couldn't resist taking a shot at her brother. "I told you, Mom, he has a way with older women."

Tate broke his hug with his mom and snarled, "That's it. Mom, I can't be held accountable for my actions!"

He feigned trying to grab his sister, and she hid behind her mother. For a few seconds, they used Jill as a blockade as they danced back and forth, trying to take a swipe at one another. Jill threw a wet blanket on the silliness.

"Kids, stop. Look over there."

Several hundred feet down Germantown Parkway, the Dick's Sporting Goods was being looted. Dozens of people were running through the broken windows and carrying out armfuls of sneakers, athletic gear, and clothing. The scene was the same at the adjacent Kohl's department store.

Tate grabbed them both by the hands and tugged them toward the road. "Let's cross here and make our way down Rockcreek Parkway through the subdivisions. We don't want any part of that."

"Good idea, Tate," said Jill as she double-checked the street was clear both ways. The three of them dashed across Germantown Parkway, a street normally packed on a Saturday at lunchtime. Today, the only cars on the move appeared to be those interested in stealing from the local businesses.

They approached Riverwood Farms. The houses were intact for the most part. Brick chimneys on some of the older homes had toppled and crashed across rooftops. Broken windows were the norm rather than the exception. They rounded the lake and began to notice people in their yards. Many of them had propane grills in their driveways. They were cooking their refrigerated or frozen foods.

Other homes appeared abandoned. Garage doors were open and emptied. Others were loading up their vehicles and topping off their gas tanks with cans of fuel used for their lawn equipment.

The water levels of the eleven-hundred-acre lake in the middle of the development had dropped at least fifteen feet. The pole supports of the small boat docks used for paddleboats and Jet Skis were well above the waterline. Jill commented that in her entire lifetime spent in this neighborhood, she'd never seen the water level that low. Not even close.

When they turned onto River Rise Drive, first Emily, followed by Tate, began to run down the middle of the street. They waved to familiar neighbors but didn't bother to stop.

"Hey, wait up!" shouted Jill, who hadn't run this far in years. She vowed to get into shape and then began to consider where they would get their food. She tried to block the future out of her mind. She immediately began to think of Jack and wondered if he'd somehow made it home. She picked up the pace, and soon she was stretching her long legs to catch up with Emily. Tate was long gone.

The three of them turned down the cul-de-sac. "Mom! The gazebo is still here!"

The white gazebo in the grassy center island of the cul-de-sac was one of Emily's favorite play spots. This had been her place to hang out throughout her childhood in the only home she'd ever known.

It had been Jill's favorite spot to hide from an abusive mother and a father who consumed drugs, not recreationally, but as if it were a sports competition. Her memories of the gazebo had not always been fond ones, but Emily's love for the spot had helped her to erase what her childhood was like.

She rounded the cul-de-sac, and their home came into view. Tate and Emily stood in front of the mailbox, staring at their two-story all-brick home that had been in the family for decades. Jack's vintage Jeep sat in the driveway, unharmed. However, there was no sign of Beth's car. Throughout the entire ordeal, Jill assumed the earthquake had been localized, or at worst, stretched up toward New Madrid. She presumed Beth would've heard about it on the news and returned to Baton Rouge. With all forms of communication out of service, she had no way of knowing for sure, so she forced herself not to worry.

She studied the house and the yard. The windows were all intact. No trees had toppled. And other than the lake dropping out of sight over the slope of the backyard, nothing had changed at the Atwood home.

"Do you think Dad's here?" asked Tate.

Emily reached over and squeezed his hand. "If he's not, we'll get everything ready for him. I know he'll be home for Christmas. He promised."

CHAPTER THIRTY-FIVE

Saturday, December 22
Atwood Residence
Cordova, Tennessee

Reality hit the three of them as they realized Jill had left her handbag, with her wallet and credit cards, in the truck. Tate had lost his mom's cell phone in the process of climbing out of the Halloran. His own phone had disappeared somewhere between the balcony falling over the top of him and dodging the Cadillac that had come crashing through the ceiling. Like so many families, they didn't have a telephone landline. Communications were conducted by cell phone, Zoom video calls, or social media messaging services via the internet. They'd have no way to get in touch with Jack and Tony, or Beth.

As expected, the power was shut off. They had no electricity, running water, or heat other than their wood-burning fireplace in the family room. Despite the sunny day, their home was shaded by large oak trees that made it cold inside.

Tate's first job was to get a fire going and to relocate their stack of firewood into the garage to keep it dry. Emily was tasked with picking up all the family heirlooms, photo frames, and other tchotchkes that had fallen or broken during the quake. Jill set about cooking all the perishable foods on their propane grill.

By her estimation, the power had been out sixteen hours. Their side-by-side refrigerator-freezer in the kitchen had kept the food cold enough to prevent spoilage. However, with each passing hour, the temperature would rise, putting the perishables at risk of spoiling. She started with the kitchen refrigerator and saved the deep freeze in the garage for later.

The night before, she'd purchased deli meats and cheeses for everyone to snack on as they arrived at the house. She spread it out on the counter and encouraged the kids to grab what they wanted, as that would be their food for the day. Then, like her neighbors, Jill fired up the propane gas grill on their back deck. She cooked the chicken and burger meat from the refrigerator and saved it in Tupperware containers.

"Mom, we only lost one ornament off the Shiny Brite tree," announced Emily as she carefully brought the remains of the broken glass ornament into the kitchen for her mother to see. "A lot fell off, but they rolled around in the presents and fake snow."

Jill led her daughter to the garbage can. "Just one ornament isn't too bad. Heck, I've broken more than that over the years by accident." She turned her head as Tate emerged from the garage.

"Hey, Mom. It's gonna get cold at night. Should we bring our mattresses into the family room? We can move the sofa back against the wall, and the other chairs can be pushed into the living room. That way we can sleep on the floor by the fire."

"Great idea," said Jill.

"A slumber party," Emily added. "But what about Aunt Beth and Uncle Tony?"

"We'll let them have our bedroom," Jill replied. "Before it's over, the family room may be covered with mattresses for us and Anthony."

Jill sighed and turned away from the kids. She stared through the kitchen window at the lake, which seemed to have lost more water. She presumed the lake had originally been created by a sinkhole or something, but she never imagined it going dry. Her thoughts turned to Jack, Beth and Tony.

She was still firmly convinced that the earthquake hadn't affected Louisiana and Mississippi, at least not the southern part. Surely, she thought, Beth turned around and went home. As for the guys, St. Louis was a long way from here. This earthquake was bad, but could it have reached almost three hundred miles?

Then her mind switched to the visual of the chasm created in the ground only a few miles away. It looked like a canyon had suddenly appeared and swallowed everything around it. She furrowed her brow as she contemplated whether this canyon could grow. What if it started to rain and the ground washed away? Could it reach their home? Where would they go?

Tate interrupted her thoughts. "Mom? Do you know where the keys to the Jeep are? I think I'll bring it in the garage after I gas it up from the mower cans."

"You were reading my mind," said Jill as she turned around and smiled at her son. "They're in the top right desk drawer in Dad's study. But, Tate, park it in front of the house by the sidewalk away from the trees. You know, just in case we have to, um, go."

Tate nodded and smiled. He located the keys and went about his business. Jill and Emily worked together to strip the bedding and push the furniture around to make room for the mattresses. Five or six minutes later, Tate appeared in the front door and got his mother's attention. He had a serious look on his face, so she suspected something was wrong.

"Emily, head upstairs to the closet and bring down all the extra pillows we have. Doesn't matter which ones. I'll be right back."

Emily nodded and took off up the stairs.

Jill approached Tate. "Son, what is it?"

"Mom, um, I found a Nashville radio station that's broadcasting."

"Good! What did they say?"

Tate shook his head from side to side and grimaced. "It's not good. You need to come listen."

CHAPTER THIRTY-SIX

Saturday, December 22
USGS
Golden, Colorado

Dr. Lansing gave instructions to her team not to disturb her unless, heaven forbid, a second earthquake struck the New Madrid Seismic Zone. She was prepared for the teleconference with her boss, who'd traveled from Reston, Virginia, to the White House Situation Room to meet with the president's chief of staff and other members of his emergency response team.

Once the teleconference started, she was introduced as being available for questions or comments, but the course of the meeting focused largely on the damage to the region, with a particular focus on sending in federal government resources to assist the various states.

She was receiving insight into the magnitude of the damages and the number of deaths associated with the M8.5 quake, which was not to be disseminated to the public, their staffs, or even their families. She was reminded, as was everyone in attendance, that the discussions and revelations were not to leave the room, whether they were there in person or virtually. The circumstances were dire, and the president didn't want people flocking to the scene of the disaster to hunt for loved ones, to loot, or seek out photo opportunities to share on social media.

The president's chief of staff conducted the meeting in a very calm, workmanlike manner.

"Let's move on to the situation in Crittenden County, Arkansas. This area is directly across Shelby County and stretches from Tunica, Mississippi, in the south to just past Millington in Tennessee. The principal city is West Memphis.

"The issue at hand relates to the superfund sites located in Crittenden County. The Gurley Pit, located a few miles west of the Mississippi River, has been used to dump waste sludge containing PCBs as well as heavy amounts of barium, lead, and zinc.

"Also, in West Memphis, we have a situation at the South Eighth Street Landfill, also a superfund site, that contains in excess of twenty thousand cubic yards of highly acidic oil sludge containing lead, PCBs, and pesticides. The groundwater there is at risk of lead, arsenic, and manganese contamination."

He paused to remove his glasses and look into the camera. "For those unaware, a superfund site is a landfill and waste disposal facility that has been identified by the EPA as posing a potential risk to human health and the environment.

"We've received reports that both of these superfund sites have undergone a significant amount of quake activity. The ground surrounding the sites has begun to sink, and the toxic sludge levels have dropped significantly. I don't have to paint a complete picture of where this hazardous waste is going.

"There are dozens of superfund sites in Arkansas, and dozens more along the Mississippi River in the affected states. The EPA has advised me that these superfund sites are most likely going to seep their toxic sludge into the groundwater. They want to dispatch inspectors to these locations to conduct a complete assessment before we decide how to clean up the damned mess.

"In addition, there are fifteen nuclear plants located in the New

Madrid Seismic Zone. Homeland Security has assured me that these facilities are constructed to withstand an earthquake of this magnitude, um, 8.5, as I'm told by the USGS. They claim we are not at risk of a Fukushima-type nuclear disaster because the temblor itself didn't cause structural damage to the Japanese plant, it was the tsunami.

"However, I was advised that these plants may not necessarily fare that well if severe aftershocks were to strike the region. I need to ask, um, let me see, Dr. Lansing with the USGS if she's been able to forecast the timing and intensity of the aftershocks, if any. Dr. Lansing?"

She perked up in her chair. "I'm here, sir. Dr. Charlotte Lansing with the NEIC in Golden, Colorado.

"Sir, most large earthquakes are followed up by aftershocks. They're basically smaller earthquakes than the mainshock, as we call it, that make up an aftershock sequence. Just because they are smaller doesn't mean they are less damaging or deadly."

A male voice off camera interrupted her explanation. Suddenly, everyone in the Situation Room pushed away from the conference table and stood at attention. The President of the United States had arrived and made his way to the head of the conference table.

"Welcome, Mr. President," said his chief of staff.

"I have a question for Dr. Lansing," he began without acknowledging the other attendees. "These aftershocks, are they going to be smaller?"

"Not necessarily, Mr. President," she replied nervously. She'd expected him to be there and had been somewhat relieved when he wasn't. It was easier for her to speak to a chief of staff or some off-camera generals than the leader of the free world. "A small fraction of earthquakes are followed by a larger seismic event. In that case, the first earthquake is reclassified as a foreshock."

"A small fraction?" he asked.

"Yes, sir. If I may, by way of example, in 2011, the M9.1 Great Tohuku earthquake and tsunami in Japan were preceded two days before by an M7.3 foreshock. At the USGS, when the first quake occurred, it was called the mainshock and later recharacterized."

"Two days?" he asked.

"Yes, Mr. President, but every seismic event is different."

"Stand by, Dr. Lansing. I'll be back to you in a moment," said the president. He turned to the FEMA administrator. "Give me your most up-to-date damage assessment."

"Yes, Mr. President. Within the eight-state affected region, we have estimates of nine hundred sixty thousand buildings damaged or destroyed. Damage to critical infrastructure—essential facilities like hospitals, utilities, transportation and communications—is substantial in the one hundred seventy counties throughout the rupture zone. We have thirty-eight hundred damaged bridges. Over forty-four hundred breaks or leaks to both local and interstate pipelines. The households without power number in the several million. Hundreds of thousands of Americans are dead, and millions are injured or homeless."

The president allowed the FEMA administrator's words to hang in the air. He sighed, clasped his hands in front of him, and leaned on the conference table toward the camera.

"Dr. Lansing, I have to give the order to send in the largest rescue and recovery effort in the history of modern mankind. I've been on the phone with world leaders, which was the reason I was late, and instructed my chief of staff to get underway. We have commitments from forty nations to send in personnel, supplies, and equipment to help us."

He paused again. His steely eyes bored through the videocam lens as if they were mere inches away from hers.

"I'm about to commit the entire resources of this nation to help those in need. I'm asking foreign governments to commit their people to assist. I want to know if I can safely do so. I want you to tell me whether this thing is over."

Dr. Lansing stared back at him. "Mr. President, I don't believe it is."

The room burst into conversation as the resident expert on the

New Madrid Seismic Zone revealed her opinion that this seismic event might continue.

After the murmur calmed down, the president addressed her. "Dr. Lansing, I'm in a damn tough position here. We've got to help our citizens, but I can't in good conscience send many thousands of people into a precarious situation like this, especially if I'm effectively signing their death warrants. I need you to be sure."

"Mr. President, at the USGS, we make an aftershock forecast that can provide situational awareness for decisionmakers like yourself. We try to predict the number of aftershocks as well as the probability of subsequent larger earthquakes.

"Our goal is to provide as accurate a model as possible to delineate the expected number of smaller aftershocks, M3 or greater. We also predict the aftershocks that could do more damage in the realm of M5 or greater. But we have to also consider the possibility for future moderate M6 to larger M7+ quakes.

"We look at the present data and, this is important in the case of the New Madrid Seismic Zone, past quake sequences. The last time an earthquake of this intensity and magnitude struck the region was in the winter of 1811 through 1812. Those three quakes, occurring over a seven-week timeframe, ranged from M7 through M7.7 based upon our study of the geologic record. But the three additional aftershocks following the initial M7.5 mainshock on December 16, 1811, ranged from M6 to M6.5. They took place the same day and into the next day."

The president raised his hand to interrupt her. "If aftershocks of this magnitude took place now, they'd be just as devastating as the first, right?"

"Under the circumstances, yes, sir. Keep in mind, the M8.5 we recorded last night is one hundred times bigger than an M6.5 aftershock, and its energy release is one thousand times stronger. However, if multiple aftershocks were to occur in rapid succession like in 1811, the impact would be the same as if it was a larger quake."

"Dr. Lansing," the president began, "what if we have a situation like Japan in 2011? Another magnitude eight or even a nine?"

"Mr. President, the size of the earthquake, its magnitude, is largely a function of the length of the fault line. For example, the largest recorded earthquake, an M9.5, occurred in 1960 in Chile along a fault that approached a thousand miles. New Madrid is nowhere near that."

The president appeared confused by her statement. "So it can't get any worse, yet you're telling me it's unsafe to send our people in."

"Mr. President, there is a difference between the size and the energy released. It's the strength of the quake that determines, for the most part, the amount of damage. The size determines how widespread an area is impacted. In the case of the current seismic sequence, I believe additional quakes are possible, also in the M7 or greater range.

"I hope this isn't out of line, but you could liken it to a heavyweight boxing match. A boxer might be able to withstand a single punch to the head. However, punches two, three and four, even if they were a lesser intensity, might knock him out. That's what we're dealing with here."

"Large aftershocks?" he asked.

"Or, sir, additional M7+ earthquakes in their own right at other trigger points along the New Madrid fault or in the immediate vicinity. My hypothetical models have shown multiple quakes can occur during a seismic sequence like this one, with epicenters ranging from Memphis to above St. Louis, or other points within the two-hundred-mile boundaries of the New Madrid Seismic Zone."

The president had heard enough. He thanked Dr. Lansing for her candor, and she was abruptly dismissed from the teleconference. She didn't take it personally. She presumed decisions were about to be made that would upset millions of people more than they were already.

CHAPTER THIRTY-SEVEN

Saturday, December 22
Tunica, Mississippi

It was approaching dawn when Beth, Willie, and Carla Angel stopped talking about the events of the last twelve hours. All of them were spent when they made their way to bed. Naturally, Beth was anxious to get to the Atwoods' home, but she had to get some sleep for the sake of the baby. Besides, as Willie later confirmed, there weren't any car rental places in Tunica, and the hotels in Tunica Resorts up the highway were all without power. Beth only had one way to get to Cordova. Willie, after insisting with the help of Carla, said he'd drive Beth and Anthony up there himself. The only downside was they'd have to wait until Sunday morning.

After sleeping 'til midafternoon, Beth spent the day talking with Carla about a myriad of subjects ranging from babies to husbands to the movies they'd seen about earthquakes. Carla was an incredibly loving grandmotherly type who talked Beth off the cliff several times as she began to worry about Tony and the Atwoods.

Carla gave Willie a sack lunch of baloney and cheese sandwiches to munch on during his shift. He promised to be safe, and he expected to be asked to work another double shift. Willie promised that after he got some sleep, they'd leave around nine in the morning.

With Willie off to work, Carla returned to the conversation about movies. "Honey child, you know those movies are over the top. I mean, think about the one with The Rock. He's a gorgeous hunk of man, but who can leap from one tall building to another? He ain't no Superman."

Beth laughed. She was about to comment, but Carla was on a roll.

"If you want to see a great earthquake movie, you gotta go back to the classics. You're too young to remember Charlton Heston, Lorne Greene, and George Kennedy. They were giants of the big screen."

"I know Lorne Greene. He was on *Bonanza*. And Charlton Heston was Moses, right?"

"That's right. Classics. That's all I watch anymore since Willie finally forked over the dough for a satellite system. I swear we were the last family in Tunica to have satellite and internet. Before, it was like livin' in the stone age."

Like now, Beth thought to herself. She wondered how long people could survive without power being restored. She thought of her kitchen cabinets in the condo. They ate out so much that she and Tony would run out of food within days. Satellite television would be the least of their problems.

They had a good talk. Later Carla took Beth and Anthony for a walk to meet some of the Angels' friends. They exchanged information that had been gathered through gossip. They speculated what was truth and what was fiction. Beth digested everything she'd learned but resigned herself to the fact that tomorrow was going to be a big day, and today she'd simply enjoy relaxing with the lovely family who'd rescued her from the side of the road.

That night, she slept well, but the odd sleeping habits finally caught up with her. She woke up when Willie arrived home from his overnight shift. Without meaning to intrude on her hosts, she sheepishly wandered out into the hallway in a housecoat loaned to her by Carla.

Willie briefly brought the women up to speed on what he'd learned. He was frank with Beth.

"Beth, I will tell you what I've heard, but just know it's rumor. Without electricity, and because the president has issued a disaster declaration, no one is allowed into Memphis or St. Louis unless they are law enforcement or military."

"I understand. How bad is it?"

"Both cities took a lickin'," he replied as he set his hat on the kitchen table.

Carla gave her husband a baby Coke, as they called it. The eight-ounce bottles were two-thirds the size of a typical can of classic Coca-Cola. He reached for a jar of Planters peanuts, grabbed several, and plunked them into the bottle. He took a long sip before the carbonation created by the mixture flowed out of the bottle.

She provided Beth a glass of warm milk, her second of the night. She'd had one before going to bed to help calm her nerves. Carla explained all the so-called experts might say a glass of warm milk doesn't help people rest, but she'd been using it to relieve her anxiety associated with Willie's job for decades and swore by it. Beth was convinced, and both times, she found herself instantly relaxed. She did, however, make a mental note to try one of those baby Coke and peanut concoctions as soon as her baby girl was out of the hopper.

"You know," she began after she took a sip of milk, "I could easily be freakin' out right now. Somehow, something inside tells me they're all okay."

Willie nodded in agreement. "I wish we could jump in the car right now, but I need a little sleep, and also, the roads are dangerous. It's just not a good time to be driving at night."

Beth affectionately reached out and touched Willie on the shoulder. "You have no idea how much I appreciate your help. So many bad things could've happened to me and Anthony. You're a godsend, Willie. And you too, Carla. I'll never forget the two of you."

Carla smiled and clasped her hands in front of her. "Honey, we're glad to help. Listen up. Both of you need to shuffle off to bed. I'll have some breakfast for you in the morning. While Willie gets a pass on going to church tomorrow, I'm gonna be over at the First Baptist Church. Pastor Parker isn't gonna give any of God's children a pass on Sunday services just 'cause the power's out."

CHAPTER THIRTY-EIGHT

Saturday, December 22
Mark Twain National Forest
Eastern Missouri

The man had not been dead for long. After a brief debate in which taking the truck was a foregone conclusion, the guys agreed it would be a bad idea to wrap the man's body in one of the tarps located in the pickup bed. If they got stopped, trying to explain the stolen vehicle would be easier than a dead body wrapped up in the back. The man had some gardening tools, including a hoe and a shovel. Jack drove down to the bottom of the exit ramp. Together, the guys buried the man by the side of the road. After paying their respects, Jack took the first turn behind the wheel and followed the F-150's GPS navigation to work his way south through the Mark Twain National Forest. Tony was asleep within minutes, curled up in the back seat of the four-door pickup.

It was approximately two hundred sixty miles to the I-40 bridge in West Memphis. The drive from Memphis to St. Louis on I-55 running parallel to the Mississippi River was one Jack had made a hundred times. Under normal circumstances, he could easily make it in just over three hours. That evening, forced to use the back roads due to the threat of rising waters and the likelihood that the epicenter of the quake was somewhere south of St. Louis, Jack took a route through East-Central Missouri.

The Mark Twain National Forest had been a place his family frequented when he was a young boy. It was a fairly quick trip from Dyersburg in upper West Tennessee to the campgrounds of the park. They'd pull their pop-up camper behind the family SUV, load up food for several days plus fishing gear to supplement what his mom made at home, and rough it, as his father called it.

He'd spent a lot of time fishing as a boy. Some of their favorite spots were located at Reelfoot Lake, halfway between Dyersburg and the town of New Madrid. The lake had been created as a result of the massive New Madrid quakes of 1811 and 1812. Fishing fueled Jack's curiosity about the water, and he quickly gained an affinity for exploring the Mississippi.

As soon as he got his driver's license, he traveled up and down the river on day trips. Sometimes, he'd take his dates on picnics or road trips to various points of interest. He'd drive as far north as the confluence of the Mississippi and Ohio rivers and then work his way down toward Memphis.

He used to comment the river seemed to take a vacation of its own along that stretch. He imagined kids like Tom Sawyer and Huck Finn floating along on a homemade flatboat, meandering along serpentine curves that swooped and turned past New Madrid towards Tennessee. In fact, at New Madrid, the Mississippi appeared to become confused. It cut to the south along the Missouri-Tennessee border, made a U-turn back to the north, and then took another U-turn toward the south. There was a stretch of farmland along old Highway 22 that was in the midst of three states, all surrounded by the river.

Similar geographic oddities occurred farther south near Dyersburg. When the river flooded, it seemed to move the borders between Tennessee and Missouri with it. When it was dry, like in late summer, farmers in Tennessee suddenly found themselves owning parts of Missouri. Even during the Civil War, the river was modified to suit a particular side's purposes.

In the end, the Mighty Mississippi was called that for a reason. It was the centerpiece of the second largest watershed in the world, covering over a million square miles. It was fed by tributaries from thirty-three different states as well as two provinces in Canada. It began as a tiny creek near Lake Itasca, Minnesota, in the north and emptied nearly twenty-four hundred miles later into the Gulf of Mexico. Quite simply, as much as man tried, the Mighty Mississippi was too big to be tamed.

Jack had no idea what was happening to his east as he drove down the desolate county roads through Missouri. They'd stopped once to ask for directions when the GPS seemed to take them way off course. He began to wonder if the satellites feeding the device information had become confused by the massive earthquake. To confirm he was headed in the right direction, he chatted up a group of people commiserating about the quake in their front yard.

Most of them had little news to report. AM and FM radio stations had ceased broadcasting. Jack was frustrated that even the satellite radio in the truck they'd borrowed provided nothing but static. He found it odd that an earthquake in the Central U.S. would cut off access to the rest of the world.

He tried to stay positive. However, the worst-case scenarios concerning Memphis continued to creep into his head. Their home was well east of the river, about twenty-two miles or so. Flooding might occur, but he doubted it would affect where they lived. He'd even been required to purchase flood insurance even though they lived on the banks of a small neighborhood lake.

The problem with his imagination was he loved Jill and the kids so much that it was easy for worry to overtake his conscious thought. If he could only call them and make sure they were okay. He gripped the steering wheel and picked up his speed as the two-lane road opened up into a highway.

Woot-woot, he said to himself. *Now I've got yellow stripes and a shoulder to rely upon. Maybe I won't drive us into a ditch if I fall asleep.*

"Are you sleepy?" Tony stirred in the back seat.

Jack had to check himself to determine whether he'd said out loud what he thought he was thinking to himself. Maybe he should give Tony a turn behind the wheel. They still had two hours to go, and it was after midnight. He looked into the rearview mirror and responded, "Nah. Well, sort of. It's slow going. I miss the interstate."

"I'm guessin' a lot of people are missin' it, too. Probably under water. Hey, I've gotta pee."

"Lucky you," said Jack, who'd consumed the sixteen-ounce bottle of Diet Coke he'd found underneath the driver's seat. Tony had opted for the two beers in the man's cooler.

Jack looked at his side mirrors to confirm it was safe to pull over on the side of the road. He rolled his eyes at himself and smiled. They hadn't encountered a single vehicle in over two hours. Everyone else was smart enough to stay put.

He stopped the truck, and the guys relieved themselves on the side of the road. Tony was refreshed after the quick nap and took over the driving duties. Within seconds of pulling away from their makeshift rest stop, Jack was blissfully snoring in the back seat.

Jack had no idea how long he'd been sleeping when he heard Tony yell his default phrase when surprised by something unpleasant.

"Holy shit!" The pickup swerved hard toward the northbound lane of the county road until its left wheels were hugging the gravel apron.

"What?" Jack shouted his question. He shot up in the back seat and leaned forward to get a better look. On the right side of the road, the trees were toppling over. Most fell parallel to the road, but the wide canopies of some made their way onto the pavement.

"Hold on!" screamed Tony as he pressed the gas pedal to the floor, quickly accelerating to nearly eighty miles an hour. He kept looking into the rearview mirror, prompting Jack to turn around.

Behind them, the moonlight afforded him enough illumination to see a stitch appear in the asphalt pavement as if a giant sewing machine had gone off the rails. On the passenger side, parts of the earth were disappearing, causing the trees to topple or get sucked into the ground altogether.

"Keep going!" Jack yelled.

"Duh!" was Tony's smart-aleck response.

On both sides of the truck now, trees and branches were splitting with the noise decibel of a high-powered rifle's gunshots. The jagged fissure continued toward them until suddenly it stopped. Tony never let up, racing away from the beast that had threatened to devour them until Jack gently patted him on the shoulder.

"Hey, I think it's over."

Tony was breathing heavily, so much so Jack became concerned he might hyperventilate. He leaned forward and rested his forearms on the backs of the bucket seats. Tony regained his composure.

"I see some kind of business up ahead. Maybe a gas station or something. I think I shit myself."

Jack laughed and then pretended to sniff the interior of the pickup. "Sure enough. You soiled your britches, young man."

A scowl came over Tony's face, and he reached between his legs to feel between his crotch and the seat.

"No, I didn't. But I was close."

He pulled over to the side of the road and slowly entered the parking lot of an abandoned gas station. The windows had been broken out years ago. The building appeared to be falling down, and the kudzu vine was taking it over before winter made it dormant.

Jack looked at his watch and then at the GPS display. "Listen, I'm anxious to get home, too. However, it wouldn't kill us to get a couple of hours' sleep and cross the river in the morning. We won't do our wives any good if we wrap this thing around a tree or accidentally drive into the center of the Earth 'cause we missed a humongous crack."

Tony wiped his sweaty hands on his pants. "No arguments from me. But if the damn earth starts shaking again, we're outta here."

"Agreed."

Jack traded places with Tony, and the two men quickly dozed

off. It's funny how the body has this internal alarm clock. Jack's was no different. If he went to sleep at midnight, he'd wake up at five the next morning. If he was exhausted from a strenuous day and fell asleep at nine the night before, once five a.m. rolled around, he was ready to get up. It didn't matter what time zone he was in or what the circumstances were, five in the morning, Central Time, was his inner rooster's wake-up call.

He didn't bother to wake up Tony, who was zonked out. He slipped out of the truck, took a leak, and got them underway for the final eighty miles into Memphis. He was full of excitement as he followed the GPS directions to West Memphis, taking a slightly circuitous route to avoid potential flooding.

From time to time, the headlights would wash a house or a building in this remote section of East Arkansas. They appeared intact, giving Jack hope that Memphis had been spared. He took a chance and turned on a country road that led him east toward the river on a direct route for the Hernando de Soto Bridge, which held Interstate 40 leading from Arkansas over the Mississippi into Memphis.

The sun began to appear on a new day. He picked up speed as mile after mile was ticked off in their quest to get home. The lowlands along the Mississippi became more predominant on both sides of the road as he got closer. His heart began to race as he wound his way through the farms. He crested a rise just as the sun began to show itself in the east. They were close.

A smile broke across his face as emotion overcame him. He glanced over to see if Tony was awake. Jack tried to contain himself as he wiped the tears of joy off his cheeks.

He daydreamed, visualizing the outline of the massive I-40 bridge. In its shadow, the Memphis Pyramid would be standing alongside the river in its thirty-two-story glory. The Memphis skyline would be behind it. A city that he'd called home for two decades. The place where he'd set himself on a path that led to meeting Jill, adopting Tate and Emily, and making a wonderful home for the four of them.

Instead, he found himself abruptly letting off the gas as he cleared the hill, causing the front end of the pickup to dip down, jarring Tony awake. Jack allowed the truck to decelerate until he finally gently placed his foot on the brake and brought the vehicle to a stop.

He closed his eyes and shook his head in disbelief. The imposing M-shaped supports of the I-40 bridge were still there, but the road itself had disappeared. Many of the familiar buildings comprising the Memphis skyline were either reduced to rubble, on fire, or were skeletal remains of their former selves. And the iconic Memphis Pyramid was there, yet it wasn't. All of the glass panels had been broken, and only the misshapen frames remained.

What he saw was utter devastation of his beloved Memphis, a sight similar to what they'd left behind in St. Louis. As the two men sat there in silence, Jack suddenly pushed himself upright in the driver's seat. He did the calculation for the first time. He silently cursed himself for not realizing this until now.

Emily's rehearsal for the Christmas show. It was Friday afternoon. Or was it early evening? Where were they when the quake struck?

"Damn! Damn! Damn!" He pounded the steering wheel as he shouted the words.

PART IV

———————

FRACTURED

If you look close enough, you'll find that everything has a weak spot where it can break, sooner or later. The Earth is no different. Our world has ended five times. It's been fried and then frozen. Gassed with poison. Smothered with ash. Bombarded from space. Despite all of this, the planet's surface remains a beautiful mosaic of continental plates. Some slowly push together, forming magnificent mountains. Others slowly tear the landscape apart, fracturing what was once whole. Leaving scars of the epic battle below.

CHAPTER THIRTY-NINE

Sunday, December 23
Harahan Bridge
West Bank of the Mississippi River
West Memphis, Arkansas

The roads leading through West Memphis, Arkansas, resembled driving through war-torn cities like Beirut, Lebanon; Aleppo, Syria; or Berlin, Germany, toward the end of World War II. Streets had buckled. Buildings had collapsed within themselves. Death was everywhere. And the eyes of the living were hollow, black, and lifeless.

Jack and Tony had to abandon the pickup truck, as the streets were clogged with debris, vehicles, and pedestrian refugees. They stopped at times to speak to those who'd fled Memphis with nothing more than the clothing they wore and maybe a small duffle bag of their most prized possessions.

The city had suffered. While it might not have been as close to the epicenter as St. Louis, Memphis had certainly been pummeled by Mother Earth's rant. They were told older buildings had crumbled first. Similar to what they'd experienced in St. Louis, a domino effect occurred in which the stability of surrounding structures was compromised by the first buildings to fall. People had no time to escape. Even if they could, there was no place to hide from the bulky steel and concrete that fell to earth.

We had no warning.

No idea.

It came out of nowhere.

Phrases that were repeated by the refugees who'd streamed across the river on the last bridge standing.

The Hernando de Soto Bridge carrying Interstate 40 had fallen first, leaving only the H-shaped concrete and steel supports standing out of the water. The entire double-arch truss-suspended deck had broken loose. After it fell one hundred and ten feet to the surface of the river, carrying motorists with it, the bridge system dropped all the way to the bottom of the Mississippi an additional one hundred eighty feet.

Just to the south, the Memphis-Arkansas Memorial Bridge built in 1949 had fared slightly better during the first earthquake. The Old Bridge, so named because it was built before the Hernando de Soto Bridge, remained standing for the most part except for a stretch of a thousand feet on the Arkansas side. Those traveling on Interstate 55 as the quake struck were lifted into the air slightly before being dropped to the road. During the quake, four of the five Warren trusses had held the structure together as it bounced up and down as the primary compression wave rolled through. However, the stress was too much, and one of the trusses couldn't stand up to the massive pressure added by the strong secondary waves.

The fourth bridge entering Memphis, the Frisco Bridge, never had a chance, according to the refugees. The hundred-twenty-four-year-old railroad bridge had fallen first. The weight of four BNSF Railway locomotive engines crossing at the moment the quake hit saw to that.

There was good news that encouraged Jack and Tony and gave them the mental boost needed to begin walking. They learned the Harahan Bridge, also known as the Big River Crossing, was still standing. The cantilevered bridge, owned by Union Pacific, carried two rail lines along its one-mile length between West Memphis and Memphis. Opened in 1916, the bridge had withstood the test of time and several earthquakes in the region. Its caissons were sunk deep into the riverbed. Coupled with the weight of the enormous concrete and granite piers built upon them, they were driven deeper into the earth.

Over time, as the interstate highway system necessitated the construction of the other bridges, the one-mile-long Harahan Bridge had been retrofitted for pedestrian and bicycle traffic as well. The Big River Crossing served as the connection point between Main Street Memphis and its counterpart in Arkansas.

They walked briskly past the throngs of refugees headed away from the river. Conversations regarding the water rising on the banks on both sides could be heard. Jack and Tony didn't waste any more time for updates on conditions across the river. Now their biggest challenge was pushing their way through the thousands of people fleeing Memphis. They were two of only a handful who seemed determined to head into the twenty-sixth-largest city in the U.S.

Soon, their path to the bridge narrowed as the westbound refugees packed the raised railway bed, and the few pedestrians going against the flow were not accommodated. Frustrations boiled over near the entrance to the pedestrian pathway when an elderly couple was being pushed around by the crowds making their way off the bridge. Jack and Tony caught up to the couple and pulled them off to the side.

"Sir, I'm sorry those guys gave you a hard time," said Tony by way of an apology for the inconsiderate refugees.

"Thank you for saying that, young man," the elderly woman replied. "Our home is in Memphis, and we have no place else to go."

"We know it might be damaged, but at least it's familiar to us," her husband added.

Jack stepped off the embankment slightly to get a better look. He returned to the group and relayed his observations.

"Listen, this walkway is maybe six to eight feet wide. We'll be butting heads with them all the way across. There is another option if you guys are up for it."

"What's that?" asked Tony.

"If we backtrack to the railroad bed, we can travel down the center of the bridge. We'll have to walk over the tracks, but there are far fewer people than what's crammed onto the pathway."

The old couple looked to one another. The husband was concerned about his frail wife. They looked like they hadn't slept since Thursday night. "What do you think, dear?"

"We can do it, with these young men helping us," she replied, looking to the guys with hopeful eyes.

Jack wanted to assist them on a different path across, but he didn't want to be bogged down on a one-mile journey across a railroad bridge with two octogenarians. After seeing the destruction of downtown Memphis from afar, his level of concern for his family skyrocketed. Backtracking would add thirty minutes to their crossing. He and Tony could easily bull their way through the oncoming refugees if they simply continued on the pedestrian pathway.

"Yes, we'll do it," said Tony impulsively without consulting Jack.

Jack wasn't surprised. During the walk out of St. Louis, Tony had expressed regret for not taking the time to help those stranded at the Met. While none of the people in that emergency stairwell were their clients, they'd needed assistance nonetheless. He doubted they would be able to climb through the elevator shaft without assistance.

The four of them turned to join the throngs heading west for half a mile. Then, when the floodwaters were shallow enough to wade through, they helped the elderly couple up the slight embankment and over to the railroad bed. There were some refugees greeting them from the east but not nearly as many as on the pedestrian pathway. After another twenty minutes, they were back to the point of the beginning of the Harahan Bridge where they'd turned around.

"Can we take a rest?" the woman asked sheepishly.

Jack looked to Tony, who shrugged and agreed. The old couple leaned against a rusty railing and encouraged one another. Jack pulled Tony aside to be out of earshot.

"Listen," he began in a hushed tone of voice. "We've got three-quarters of a mile to go. I know that doesn't sound like much, but for these guys, it might as well be a hundred."

Tony sighed. "I know. They're gonna want to take breaks every hundred feet. I mean, how far is it to the house from here?"

"Roughly twenty-three miles from the riverfront. You and I proved we can walk that if we have to."

"My feet will divorce me," quipped Tony in an attempt to add some levity to the situation. Both men were still wearing their suit pants and pressed shirts although they were untucked. Their clothing was smeared with blood, and their pants were torn. However, it was their shoes that provided them the most consternation. Their Johnston & Murphy wingtips weren't designed for twenty-mile walks. Both guys complained of blood blisters and heel pain.

Jack looked toward the couple, who were now standing, a sign they were ready to get going. "Okay. I'll be the bad guy when the time comes. Let's get them started. However, when they ask to stop again, we need to let them go. It's not just the frequent breaks. It's the slow pace."

Tony grimaced and nodded. "I know. I know. Hell, we would've been across already."

With the tough decision made, the guys joined the elderly couple and escorted them onto the railroad tracks. Through the steel mesh, they saw hundreds of people streaming along the pathway. Most didn't look in their direction, opting instead to shuffle along behind the person in front of them and staring at their feet.

As predicted, they'd barely walked ten minutes at a snail's pace when the old couple asked to take another break. The guys stopped with them and complimented them on their perseverance.

But ... There was always a *but*.

But, Jack explained, they had to hurry home to their families, so they wished them well. The couple, while sad, understood and wished them good luck as well. The elderly woman began to shed a few tears, an emotional moment Jack noticed and fortunately Tony didn't. If he'd seen her cry, then he'd have insisted on continuing the escort.

As it turned out, the nearly forty minutes they spent as Good Samaritans might've cost them their lives.

CHAPTER FORTY

Sunday, December 23
Near Lake Cormorant, Mississippi

"You know, sometimes there are things a man don't tell his wife 'cause he don't want her to worry," said Trooper Willie Angel as he drove through a throng of people milling about in Tunica Resorts, Mississippi. The small town of less than two thousand, formerly known as Robinsonville, had become a regional destination for gamblers. Six casinos operated along the Mississippi River, making it the second largest casino destination east of the Mississippi, behind Atlantic City.

"Like what?" asked Beth, who was genuinely interested in what he had to say. She chided Tony often for not confiding in her or revealing his feelings to her. She never knew her father, who'd left with her mother for California soon after she was born. Her grandfather had passed before she was old enough to have such weighty conversations.

"Well, you know. Sometimes money is tight and you love your missus, so you don't want her to feel like she can't buy something or another. Then we might be stressed at work, but we don't wanna burden 'em with our problems. There's medical issues ..." His voice trailed off.

Beth sensed something was troubling Willie. This was her chance to repay him for saving her and Anthony, who had grown comfortable in the back seat of the patrol car.

Carla had allowed him to play with some of her grandchildren's large LEGO blocks known as DUPLO bricks. They were larger than the LEGOs and weren't a choke hazard. With her grandchildren much older, she gave Anthony a mesh sack of pieces to make the Disney Toy Story Train along with the Woody and Buzz Lightyear figurines. Anthony was fascinated by the set and would be occupied for the two-hour drive to Cordova.

"Are you sick, Willie?" she asked.

He sighed before he responded. He wiggled his fingers on the steering wheel as he spoke. "I've got the usual stuff old men get. High blood pressure. Diabetes. Cholesterol. You know. The doc throws pills at me for all of those things, and I keep on livin'."

"Right." Beth stretched the word out slightly. "Is there more? I mean, you don't have to tell me."

Willie grimaced. "Well, to be honest, I wouldn't have brought it up, but I thought I'd ask your advice. I can't talk to my daughters about this 'cause Lord knows they'd be shuffling me off to this hospital or that. Or they'd want us to move in with them. Or, worst yet, one of them would want to move home. That ain't gonna happen."

Beth took a deep breath and blurted it out. The C-word. "Cancer?"

Willie shook his head. "Oh, no. Thank the good Lord. Not that bad, but close. I've got sickle cell disease."

"Oh," said Beth. "I'm sorry to say, although I've heard of it, I don't really know what it means."

"There's no real reason you should. My doc called it the black folk's curse. It's a genetic thing. Some people get it worse than others. My hands and feet started swelling all the time, and I

212

couldn't pinpoint why. My eyes started getting blurry, especially at night. I've had to keep this on the down low from my supervisor, too. I was afraid they'd force me into early retirement."

Beth felt a cramp coming on in her lower abdomen near her uterus. At her last ob-gyn appointment, she was reminded that Braxton-Hicks contractions might start soon. She was just now transitioning from her second to her third trimester. Anthony had come early, and she expected this baby would too.

"Can they treat it?"

Willie quickly replied, "They've tried me on a couple of different meds. The problem is that I've become anemic. I started noticing my eyes turning yellow. You know, jaundice. And then it became more and more difficult to take a really deep breath. Anyway, just this last week, I got my blood results back, and they tell me I'm anemic."

Beth asked the next logical question. It was direct and personal, but she truly wanted to give Willie an outlet to unload his burden. "Um, it's not deadly, is it?"

"They tell me nothing can be said with certainty. The doc was honest with me and said my life expectancy just got reduced by a bunch. I'm sixty-three, Beth. I may only live to seventy. That sounds like a lot of years. Seven. But when you start looking at it like your counting down to the end, it's kind of depressing."

Beth glanced around the highway. The standing water hadn't receded despite a full day, and now morning, of sunshine. Most flooding started to disappear after the rain stopped, and the sun helped the evaporation process. She shifted in the seat and turned to Willie.

"I gather you haven't told Carla any of this."

"That's right."

Beth furrowed her brow. "Have you avoided the subject because you don't want to tell her you have the disease or because you don't want to tell her about the doctor's stupid expiration date he stamped on your forehead?"

Willie chuckled. "Honestly, as you put it, the expiration date bothered me the most."

"Willie, please excuse me for saying this, but that was the wrong thing to lay on you. None of us have an expiration date. Listen, I know nothing about sickle cell, but I do know all of our bodies are different. Minds, too. You can manage this with medication. Maybe proper diet with Carla's help. And you two love each other. A lot. I can tell. You'll help each other find the will to soldier through."

Willie smiled and nodded. "Are you sayin' to tell her about the disease but not about the life-expectancy thing?"

"Yes, absolutely. Willie, you wouldn't be lying because that doctor may be able to read a blood test, but he isn't God. Only God will decide when it's your time."

Willie burst out laughing and then shed a few tears. "Miss Beth, are you sure your last name ain't Angel?"

She smiled and added to the pool of tears in the front seat of the Mississippi Highway Patrol car. "I'm a long way from being an angel, but I'm pretty sure God would agree with me."

They shared a laugh as Willie began to slow the car as he approached an upcoming intersection. Suddenly, the blue flames returned. Any place the ground protruded through the floodwaters, blue flames with tiny orbs circulating around them shot skyward.

The ground began to shake, making it difficult for Willie to hold the steering wheel. A low rumbling sound filled the air, and soon it began to get louder.

A flock of wood ducks was disturbed toward their left. They suddenly raced low along the landscape and across the road directly in front of them. Instinctively, Willie slammed on the brakes and skidded to a halt, sending Beth forward against her seatbelt. The jolting stop then slammed her backwards against the seat. Anthony was tossed about in the back seat and started to cry.

Beth yelled in pain. She reached forward to brace herself on the dashboard.

Willie was angry with himself. "I'm sorry. I'm so sorry!"

He pulled across the divided highway into a Shell station that had been looted since the power went out. He jumped out of the car and ran around to the passenger side to check on Beth. He flung open the door, and she sat there, perfectly still, eyes wide, but staring at the pool of fluid that had accumulated in her seat and on the floor mats.

"I think my water just broke."

CHAPTER FORTY-ONE

Sunday, December 23
USGS
Golden, Colorado

Just after midnight, nearly thirty-six hours after the earthquake struck the New Madrid Seismic Zone, Dr. Lansing felt it was calm enough to go home and sleep. A portion of the staff manned the helm while she recovered from the frenetic pace she'd maintained for a couple of days. Fortunately, there had only been minor aftershocks recorded. However, it appeared the president had delayed sending in the bulk of his recovery resources based upon her warning that multiple earthquakes were possible, especially in light of historic precedent.

By the time she returned late that Sunday morning, the media was criticizing the administration for its tepid response to the disaster. Succumbing to the pressure, the president directed Homeland Security and FEMA to begin the relief effort in earnest. The National Guard was activated in all fifty states and then redeployed to the region. Firefighters drove toward the NMSZ to assist. America's brave first responders did what they were wired to do—run to danger, not from it.

Dr. Lansing wanted to be wrong. She didn't want to go down in history known as the prophetess of doom. She wanted to provide accurate models based upon scientific fact. However, she simply could not disregard the events of 1811 and 1812. History repeats. It might not look exactly the same twice. But it still repeats.

The NEIC had help from around the world. Other geological agencies from developed nations were now sending data into the Golden, Colorado, facility. The global network of seismometers supplemented regional seismic networks like those operated within the NMSZ. All of these monitoring agencies exchanged information, and many brilliant minds were analyzing the data to provide Dr. Lansing various points of view.

The geophysicists who worked under Dr. Lansing were very capable, but none of them were so arrogant to believe that second opinions regarding their patient, Mother Earth, should be disregarded.

Oliver followed Dr. Lansing into her office with a banana and a bottle of water. He gently set them on her desk and studied his boss's demeanor. He frowned as he sensed she appeared defeated.

"Okay, mum. After I finish what I have to say, I will gladly tender my resignation and move back to England if you request. I would be remiss if I didn't speak my mind."

Dr. Lansing managed a smile and gestured for her number one to sit across the desk from her. She took a drink of water and set the banana by her phone.

"You've spoken your mind before, Oliver, and you're still here."

"Yes, mum. I appreciate your patience with me in that regard."

"And I will continue to have patience. Tell me what's on your mind."

He set a stack of emails from all over the world on her desk. They'd been translated and organized from the most influential, highly respected geophysicists to the lesser known but still worthy of considering their opinion.

"It's a who's who, mum. I've read them all. There's no need for you to do so."

She laughed and reached for her banana. "I realize they don't know what I said to the president yesterday or what my official position is on the potential for aftershocks, etcetera. That said, they are smart enough to see our country's actions, or inaction, regarding the recovery effort. They know I'm the one who advised the president. It doesn't take a rocket scientist to know I've rung the clarion bell warning the president away from sending in significant resources at this time."

Oliver raised his chin, and his lower lip protruded outward. He lent the appearance of a much thinner version of Sir Winston Churchill.

"Here is the consensus, mum. The reoccurrence of the huge earthquakes over the last four thousand years culminating with the 1800s sequence leads to a logical conclusion. The 1811–1812 quakes were nothing more than a continuation of a consistent pattern along this ancient plate boundary. Each time, the strain has been relieved and the fault is vitiated. The seismic event of Friday was a one-off, freak occurrence that will calm the region for another few hundred years, if not longer due to its intensity."

"One and done," she mumbled.

"Yes, mum."

She stood and walked around her desk toward the wall-mounted relief map. Oliver spun in his chair to follow her.

"Maybe they're right," she began. She pointed toward Oklahoma. "It wouldn't be the first fault in the Central U.S. to go on an extended hiatus. Consider the Meers fault. It's been dormant for twelve hundred years. Prior to that, it produced M7s with regularity."

"Mum, we know that intraplate faults like New Madrid turn on and off. Eventually, it doesn't have the energy to turn back on. Think of the quake storm of 2016. Your predecessor raised the threat level for the NMSZ, and nothing happened. Years later, many, including yourself, opined that these were simply aftershocks of the 1811 event. Just because an M4 rears its head in the NMSZ doesn't mean the big one is coming soon."

"I know, Oliver. I know this, too. However, it's also true these intraplate quakes may disappear in one fault zone and pop up where no one's expecting. The epicenter for this quake was in Arnold, well to the north of New Madrid. There was significant pre-quake activity in the Memphis area. It fits the pattern we've seen on other continents where the epicenters hop all around a fault."

"Like the unmapped faults in China?" Oliver asked.

"Yes, exactly like that," she replied. "Here's the thing. It's science, but it's not an exact science. We learn from seismic events and then adjust our models accordingly. In the case of New Madrid, we identified a mid-continent fault, and then you get a large quake outside the defined norm. All you can ask is *for Pete's sake, there's a fault running that way, too?*"

Oliver laughed. "It's like playing a giant game of whack-a-mole. If the New Madrid fault has shifted, or even expanded, we truly don't know where to monitor next."

"Exactly. If we put all of our resources into the same location, it's like having an entire police department staking out the last convenience store that was robbed. Who's gonna be watching the other 7-Elevens?"

"I get it," Oliver responded.

She stared at the relief map. "We don't know for certain what's gonna happen next. We analyze the data. We apply history. We prepare or react accordingly."

She pointed to a plaque on the wall given to her by her grandfather when she received her doctorate. It was a quote written by Charles Darwin as he revealed his own primal unease after experiencing the devastating earthquake in Concepcion, Chile, in 1835.

A bad earthquake at once destroys our oldest associations: the earth, the very emblem of solidity, has moved beneath our feet like a thin crust over a fluid—one second of time has created in the mind a strange idea of insecurity, which hours of reflection would not have produced.

A young woman burst into the room without knocking. "Dr. Lansing, come quick! You need to see this!"

CHAPTER FORTY-TWO

Sunday, December 23
Atwood Residence
Cordova, Tennessee

Jill put on her best face as she cooked the last of the scrambled eggs in a cast-iron skillet together with some Tennessee Pride sausage. Emily poured each of them a glass of milk that was on the verge of being spoiled. For the most part, it might appear to be any other Sunday morning before the family went to church. However, the elephant in the room threatened to sit at the table at any moment, demanding attention.

All of them had hoped, or expected, that Jack would've returned from St. Louis by now. It had been forty hours since the earthquake struck Memphis. The radio broadcasts from WLAC-AM in Nashville painted a bleak picture. Highway bridges up and down the Mississippi River had collapsed. From as far south as Natchez, Mississippi, all the way to the Upper Mississippi River area near Hannibal, Missouri, bridges of all types had been destroyed or rendered too dangerous to cross with vehicles.

The reporting wasn't specific as to whether there was National

Guard assistance in crossing the river or if any of the railroad crossings stood intact. It was partly due to the inability to get information that Jill decided to walk through the neighborhood after breakfast to see what other people knew and to enlist help in locating the families of the children who survived the disaster at the Halloran theater.

"Mom, can I go check on Britney and her family?"

Jill had just taken a bite. She swallowed her food and responded, "Um, I don't know, Tate. I might be gone for an hour or so. Maybe you should stay here with Emily? Your dad might return, and you wouldn't wanna miss him."

Tate frowned. "Mom, I won't be long, I promise. I'll cut through the woods along the lake. I'll even see if her family has a portable radio with batteries we can borrow. Her dad is into that ham radio stuff."

Jill thought for a moment. "Don't those things reach all over the country?"

"The world, even," replied Tate. "I can see if he's heard anything. He might even loan us one of his portable ham radios. I saw one sitting on their kitchen counter one day."

Emily weighed in. "Mom, I'll be okay. I'll wait for Daddy to come home. My iPad has half a battery left. I think I'll just hang by the fire and play video games."

Jill shrugged and finished her breakfast. The thought of having access to information from other parts of the country through a ham radio was a plus. The Nashville station was providing some information, but it was only what the government was providing them. She was curious what people like her family were going through.

"Okay," she agreed reluctantly. "But no more than an hour. Okay? Check on Britney and her family. See if they have any information, and get your butt back home. Got it?"

"Yes, ma'am. Thanks!"

Tate pushed away from the table and put his paper plate with the plastic fork he'd used into the garbage. The family only had one case of bottled water, and they were conserving it to be divided between the three of them, not to mention Jack and Tony when they arrived.

Earlier that morning, Jill had taken an inventory of their food and drinks. Almost all of her refrigerator space was devoted to the upcoming holiday visit from Beth and Tony. The freezer had the usual things in it. Ice cream. DiGiorno Pizza. Chicken nuggets and frozen French fries. The ice cream had been consumed the night before, and the other items were on tonight's menu.

She was especially disappointed in herself from the drink standpoint. They had more cans of soda than they had water. Even Tate's Gatorade supply was running low. She just wasn't one to stock up on food and drinks. When you had a Costco, Trader Joe's, and Kroger store within a few minutes' drive, why bother? Now she knew better.

Emily settled in by the fire with her iPad. Tate dressed to impress. It seemed a young man had to put his best foot forward when meeting with his girlfriend during the apocalypse. Jill pulled on a sweater and grabbed her sunglasses. Temperatures seemed to be rising into the upper fifties with the sun shining. Under any other circumstances, it would've been a glorious late-December day.

The Riverwood neighborhood of Cordova where they lived was a typical example of urban sprawl in which urbanized areas, such as low-density residential neighborhoods and supporting retail businesses, gradually spread from the cities into the rural areas surrounding them.

Her grandparents' home was one of the six original houses built on the lake. The rest of the surrounding land had been owned by farmers who gladly accepted the big money offered by developers as Memphis exploded in population. The changes Jill had experienced over her nearly forty years were untold. The streets she was walking on now to chat with her neighbors were once paths taken by cattle when it was feeding time.

Initially, Jill was surprised by how few of her neighbors were home. She couldn't decide if it was because they'd traveled elsewhere for the holidays, or perhaps they'd been caught downtown like she was. In any event, the first three places she sought out in order to visit with women she'd met through church or the kids' school functions were devoid of activity.

She walked farther out of the neighborhood toward Germantown Road. She tried one more house of a family whose daughter was in Sunday school class with Emily. Only the mother was home. Her husband had taken their daughter, a child of her previous marriage, to meet her ex-husband at the airport. The ex-husband lived in Dallas and had flown up to pick up the child for a week's stay. She hadn't heard from them since.

The woman was too distraught to help find the parents of the possibly orphaned children and was too clingy for Jill to stay with her much longer. Jill said goodbye and walked another two blocks to try one more acquaintance. She was already becoming concerned. She'd been gone for over an hour and was uncomfortable leaving Emily alone to begin with.

She started up the street and struck up a casual conversation with a man and his wife talking in their front yard with another couple. She relayed the news from the Nashville radio station to them, but they offered nothing in the way of information in return. They did have a couple of gallons of spring water to offer Jill, who graciously accepted them. She promised to have one of the kids run back a twelve-pack of Coke, but they said that wasn't necessary. They were glad to help.

As she was leaving their home, she felt a tremor. It was so slight she wondered if her mind was playing tricks on her. The two women exchanged glances and looked around the house.

There was another one. Stronger than the first and it left no doubt what was happening.

"Aftershocks?" the woman asked.

Jill set the water on her foyer table and said without turning, "I have to go."

She raced past the three adults who'd suddenly appeared in the front yard, nervously looking in all directions. Before she could reach the asphalt road, the ground lifted and threw her upward several feet before she landed hard on her side.

The impact knocked the wind out of Jill. She gasped for breath, her eyes wide as she looked all around her. If this was an aftershock, it was gonna be a big one. Breathing hard to the point of hyperventilation, Jill found her footing and began running down the street as fast as she could.

The intensity of the tremor increased. Behind her, the asphalt began to crack until a gap of more than a foot appeared. Jill ran, frantically looking over her shoulder as the stitch in the road chased her.

"Leave me alone!" she shrieked as she zigzagged down the street, running toward the curb on the right to avoid the developing fissure, only to have it follow her. Or so it seemed.

Suddenly, the fissure took a hard left and cut through a yard. It swallowed several trees, a riding lawn mower, and a red Kia parked in the driveway.

"No! No! No!" she shouted three times as she turned the corner toward her house. Several of the homes were starting to succumb to the second round of seismic activity. Bricks were falling off their façades. Glass was breaking out from the twisting and turning of the window frames. Trees were being lifted out of the ground and uprooted before being tossed to the ground.

But it was the mini-explosions erupting from the ground that puzzled her and eventually sent her tumbling down the street, ripping and tearing at her arms and legs. She crawled on her bloodied knees to the grass. She fought through the pain to stand. Jill stood in awe and shock as the asphalt street began to break into chunks before disappearing into the ground several feet.

Her eyes grew wide as a huge explosion accompanied by a fireball occurred behind her. Then there was another one. The area around Germantown Road sounded like a war zone.

Jill forgot her pain. She brushed off her bloody knees and elbows. She ran like the wind to find her children.

CHAPTER FORTY-THREE

Sunday, December 23
Atwood Residence
Cordova, Tennessee

Emily was enjoying the quiet solitude of the family room. She'd been one who always enjoyed her private time away from school, activities, and family gatherings. She loved to read, and one of her favorite pastimes was immersing herself in the latest video game apps for her iPad. Regardless of the latest and greatest game, Emily always seemed to gravitate back to *Candy Crush*. The game had been around for years. It had been continuously upgraded with new artwork and unique board designs. Hundreds of new stages challenged players of all capabilities. Plus, it was relatively brainless. When Emily wanted to relax, she sought out brainless activities.

She'd played for a while and then decided to mosey outdoors and enjoy some sunshine. The weather was exactly the way she liked it. She enjoyed bundling up in a sweater or a loose-fitting sweatshirt. There was something about the leafless trees with the occasional evergreen mixed in. A fire coupled with a mug of hot chocolate couldn't be beat. In some respects, Emily was twelve going on thirty as she emulated the simple enjoyments preferred by her mom.

In addition, it was years of the family placing an emphasis on Thanksgiving and Christmas. The Hallmark Channel playing continuously created an atmosphere of love, family, and reflection. Even for a twelve-year-old, growing up in this kind of environment had a profound impact on how she developed. Her mom had avoided the kind of life led by her mother. Instead, raised by her grandmother, Jill epitomized the Norman Rockwell mom in an apron, serving up the fresh-baked cookies. When Emily visualized her future, that was what she saw as well.

The Atwoods' backyard wasn't particularly large, but it was directly on the lake in the center of the neighborhood. They had a fixed wooden dock capable of holding a flat-bottom boat or a canoe, neither of which they owned. Emily enjoyed walking to the end, removing her shoes, and dangling her feet in the water during the summer. Ever the show-off, her more athletic brother liked to do backflips and somersaults into the lake.

Another favorite pastime, especially in the winter months, was when migratory waterfowl stopped by to take a break en route to warmer climates. Memphis was in the heart of the Mississippi Flyway, a watershed twenty-three hundred miles long stretching from the top of the Mississippi River to the Gulf of Mexico.

Old Man Winter didn't discourage the regular feeder birds like chickadees, sparrows, and finches from hanging around. Emily saw them most of the year. She loved what she began to call the Big Show. It was the time when the ducks and geese arrived in large numbers. She'd even purchased from the TWRA, the Tennessee Wildlife Resources Agency, a laminated identification card that Jack had punched a hole through and affixed to the garden bird feed bucket.

Growing up, Emily constantly glanced out the back windows of their home, hoping to catch a glimpse of a ring-necked duck or a red-breasted merganser. Sure, the Canada geese and mallard ducks were regulars, but it was the exotics that thrilled Emily the most.

She'd stood on the deck that late Sunday morning with her binoculars, scanning the ever-withering lake. She was amazed at the exposed bank all the way around the water's edge. Grass that still retained a hint of green turned to brown and then mud as it approached the current water level. After decades of being under water, the soil leading into the lake was moist and muddy.

A flock of ring-necked ducks circled and landed in the lake near the Atwoods' backyard. Emily's heart raced as she saw them washing themselves and milling about. There were dozens of them, prompting her to swiftly, but casually so as not to frighten them, make her way up to the house to fetch her garden seed bucket.

When she returned, the ducks were still doing what ducks do. Emily opened the lid of the bucket and grabbed the galvanized steel scoop. She filled it with a generous helping of sunflower seeds, crushed corn, and oats. She reached back and slung it toward the water. The feed fell woefully short, and the ducks didn't even seem to notice.

She tried again but failed to reach the water's edge with her toss. A slight breeze blowing across the withering lake toward her didn't help matters. Emily was determined to feed the visitors, who bred near Thunder Bay in Ontario, Canada, and wintered throughout the Southeastern United States.

Frustrated, she lifted the three-quarters-full, five-gallon bucket and walked back toward the house to exit the dock. She carefully made her way down the slope, beyond the dormant grass marking the end of their yard, and down into the muddy, somewhat slippery exposed lake bottom.

She pushed the heel of her sneakers into the soft mud to keep her stability. She worked her way closer to the water's edge, keeping her strides to twelve-to-fifteen inches at a time. She cautiously approached the lake until the ground became too muddy and wet to approach further.

"Okay, you guys," she advised the ducks. "Now you'll get some treats."

She set the bucket down in the mud, scooped up the feed, and tossed it underhanded toward the paddling ducks. They immediately responded and scrambled toward the feed before it sank under the water's surface.

Pleased with her first effort, Emily threw out another scoop. The ducks happily ate it up although there was a group to the side who stubbornly refused to partake in the feeding frenzy.

"You can't have any pudding if you don't eat your meat!" Emily repeated a sentence her dad often used when encouraging the kids to finish their meal. She had no idea where it came from. It was a parent thing, she'd surmised.

She scooped up another heaping portion, so much so that some of it fell out of the scoop. She heaved it toward the nonparticipating ducks with an extra effort.

Emily slipped ever so slightly. Her eyes grew wide in panic as she tried to keep her footing. The scoop fell out of her hand, and the bucket tipped over by her side. The lip of the opening stuck in the mud, preventing it from rolling into the water. However, it didn't stop it from spilling all of the feed at the edge. She waved her arms in a windmill motion to maintain her balance. She started to fall backwards, but she was able to plant her right hand and push herself upright.

Emily had avoided slipping into the lake. Then Mother Earth's shaken fury threw Emily in anyway.

When the earthquake hit, she was immediately tossed several feet into the air until she landed in the murky water. By the time her head popped back above the surface, the ducks had taken off in a flurry, further startling the young girl. Emily shrieked and covered her head with her arms, causing her to dip slightly below the surface. She kicked with both legs to push her body upward.

She tried to tread water, but the cable-knit sweater she was wearing weighed her down, causing her arms to fatigue. Emily kicked harder to raise herself higher out of the water in order to shout.

"Help! Help me!"

Gravity pulled her beneath the surface. She flung her arms

about, desperate to get her head above water. The sweater fought against her, causing her to panic. Like Houdini in the midst of a magic act using a straightjacket, Emily tore her arms out of the sweater until it floated away from her. All of her gyrations forced her farther away from the bank.

Her head bobbed above the surface once again. A deafening roar filled her ears. All around her, the ground was shaking. The water had developed waves, some with whitecaps atop them. And the wind had picked up considerably. The combination of the two seemed to be pulling her away from shore.

Emily spun around and looked toward her house. Oddly, the water level had dropped another two feet from where her feed bucket was embedded in the mud. She kicked as hard as she could to raise her head and shoulders out of the water as each wave swept over her. The mud line was growing. She realized what was happening.

The water is draining out of the lake!

Emily began swimming aggressively toward the house. The dock was obscured from view by the rollicking waves on the normally still lake. As she swam over a crest, she could catch a glimpse of the dock, encouraging her to keep swimming.

She was making progress. She was twenty feet away. Ten feet.

Suddenly, a tall, mature oak tree from the neighbor's backyard groaned and cracked before falling sideways along the bank. It crashed into the Atwoods' dock, breaking it into splinters. The leafless tree then started to slide down the muddy embankment until it came to rest halfway between where the dock once stood and the new waterline, four feet below where it was just minutes ago.

Emily's energy was waning, but she fought for her survival. She swam harder. Her resolve to live was there. She made her way to the edge. She tried to get her footing beneath the water to climb out. At first, she slipped backwards and had to start over. She used her small, delicate hands to dig into the mud to get a grip. She pulled her way up and halfway out of the lake.

She set her jaw, and a determined expression came over her face. One hand over the other, she pulled herself up the water-saturated bank as the earth shook in an effort to break her grip. Emily kept digging, pushing off with her feet and clawing with her hands, digging her nails into the steep, muddy slope. She was wholly out of the water now. Up she crawled, a foot or so at a time, but progress nonetheless. The earthquake continued, fighting like a bedeviled bull trying to throw famed rodeo star Cooper Armstrong off his back.

Then the uprooted oak began to slide down the embankment toward her.

CHAPTER FORTY-FOUR

Sunday, December 23
Harahan Bridge
West Bank of the Mississippi River
West Memphis, Arkansas

"Run!" Jack shouted at the top of his lungs. There was no mistaking what was happening. A second earthquake had roared to life. Tony remained frozen for a moment, but Jack racing past him brought his mind back into the present. He glanced back toward the couple they'd abandoned and saw they were gripped in fear. He gritted his teeth and almost turned back when Jack screamed his name again. "Tony!"

The jolt to the earth was massive. Unlike the first earthquake that struck St. Louis with its rolling, ground-swelling appearance, the second quake struck the region with the force of a hundred thousand atom bombs detonating all at once. The impact on North America would be unfathomable. But for Jack and Tony, it placed them in the midst of a textbook unstoppable force paradox.

It was the classic self-contradiction that occurred when an unstoppable force met an immovable object. Both the force and the object were presumed to be indestructible. However, in nature, one or the other must win out.

Jack and Tony would've implicitly rooted for the immovable object, the Harahan Bridge, to prevail over the unstoppable force, the toppling of the close by Memphis-Arkansas Bridge. However, as was most often the case, when two indestructible titans did battle, the only thing that was assured was mutually assured destruction.

And that was what happened. The Old Bridge came crashing down sideways as if only one part of the riverbed sank where the remains of the Frisco Bridge, once equidistant between the two, were laid to rest. It all happened in a manner of fifteen seconds. The northernmost piers of the Old Bridge gave way first, causing the top-heavy steel arches to topple toward the Harahan. The weight of the massive structure struck the piles of the old railway bridge comprising its support.

The guys were only able to run a few hundred feet before the railroad tracks began to buckle. The Harahan lurched upward and then began to wobble on its piers.

They were both knocked to the tracks. The men struggled to find their footing during the final seconds in the life of the Harahan Bridge. They contemplated running back toward Arkansas, but it was too late. The entire piling system gave way, and the bridge fell straight down until it smacked the surface of the Mississippi River.

Jack and Tony were airborne throughout the almost one-hundred-foot fall to the water.

The bridge had the kinetic energy of a brick. As the pilings gave way, there was an enormous amount of potential energy associated with the pull of gravity on the bridge structure. The gravitational pull reached up from the center of the Earth and yanked the bridge into the water. As it did, air was displaced, creating a momentary weightless effect for Jack and Tony.

It took four seconds for the bridge to crash to the surface of the Mississippi River. It took five for the men to reach the water. Incredibly, that additional second diminished the force their bodies faced when they met a nearly immovable force—the Mighty Mississippi.

In those five seconds, Jack's survival instincts kicked in. He didn't know what gave him the presence of mind to shout what he did, but it certainly gave them the opportunity to survive.

"Cannonball! Cannonball!"

He tucked his knees to his chest and wrapped his arms around his shins. His first inclination was to go in feet first, but something inside him screamed otherwise.

Jack plunged in first, and before he'd closed his eyes, he saw that Tony had managed to curl into a tight ball as well. Once he hit the water, the force of the impact threatened to knock him out.

Ten. Twenty. Thirty feet deep. He felt the atmospheric pressure build in his ears, so he swallowed hard. Initially, he couldn't feel the pain from the blow his body had suffered on impact. That would come seconds later when his descent was arrested by crashing into several bodies that had fallen with the bridge.

He suddenly found himself entangled in flailing arms and legs. Panicked, broken human beings fought a brutal drowning death with arms and legs that no longer functioned.

Jack had reached the bottom of his descent. He quickly tested his arms and legs. All his appendages worked. His temple ached from getting kicked by a drowning victim. It didn't matter. He was alive, and therefore he had a chance.

The earthquake continued to jostle the planet. He felt like he'd been crammed inside a washing machine as the torrent of swirling waters battered his body. He tried to swim upwards, desperately craning his neck toward the daylight above. Yet he felt like he wasn't making any progress.

A lifeless body floated upward past him. Oddly, his mind complained that it wasn't fair for a dead guy to get a head start to the top.

Jack persevered. He brought his hands in towards the front of his stomach and then extended them over his head. He'd complete the sweeping motion by pushing them wide and down to his hips again, using his open palms as flippers. It was poor technique for a swimmer's breaststroke, but it was far more effective than simply kicking his legs.

He didn't calculate how long he was underwater, but there weren't a whole lot of seconds left in his built-in air tanks. His lungs began to burn, and his eyes began to bug out. His mind was telling his body it wasn't safe to breathe under water, and therefore, it should stop breathing altogether. Or, on the other hand, his mind implored, go for it. You've got nothing to lose. You're gonna suffocate without air.

That's how a person drowns. They give up. Jack wasn't gonna give up.

With one final downward thrust of his arms, he fought the turbulent waters, and his head popped up above the surface. He sucked in air and turned his face toward the sun. He spontaneously began laughing, an odd reaction. Then he returned to reality.

He was freezing. The air temperature had hovered in the mid-fifties, normal for that time of year. The full sun helped in that regard. However, the water temperature, after being shaded overnight, was in the upper forties at best. He suddenly found himself shivering uncontrollably. Mentally, he tried to talk himself out of the shivers, but the water temperature was somewhere between chilly and just plain oh-my-god cold. He had to warm up his muscles.

He began vigorously treading water and wiggling his appendages in an effort to get the blood flowing to them. His efforts to stay afloat in the river worked. He was no longer approaching a state of numbness, and his mind had reached a heightened sense of clarity. Then he thought it was playing tricks on him.

He spun around, searching for the approaching freight train. He'd never heard a roar so loud. Naturally, there was no train. Only the continuation of the second earthquake. He'd lost track of time in his struggle to survive, but he was certain this quake was longer than the first one two days prior.

"Tony!" he shouted although he couldn't be heard.

Shit! Where's Tony?

He began spinning around again in search of his brother-in-law. There were bodies floating facedown everywhere he could see. Every few seconds, another one popped up out of the water. Jack swam toward them, turning over any man with a white shirt on.

The river had begun to calm after the force of the bridges collapsing was finished displacing the waters. The earthquake caused swells similar to those in the middle of an ocean during a storm, but they were widely spaced and didn't impede Jack's search.

"Tony! Tony!" He shouted his name again. The roar of the earthquake continuing to rumble along the Mississippi drowned out his voice.

"Jack! Over here!"

He was alive! Jack frantically spun around and called out his name again. "Tony! Where?"

"Over here! On the bridge!"

Jack was puzzled by the response and then began to wonder if the blow to his head underwater was causing him to hallucinate. Tony shouted to him again.

"Over here!"

A swell came along and lifted Jack high enough to get a better view. Barely two hundred feet away, Tony had wrapped his arms around the upper chord of the Harahan Bridge's truss system. Like a sketch of the fictional Loch Ness monster, the top trusses remained above water, protruding above the surface every hundred feet or so.

"I see you!" Jack shouted back. He began to swim toward Tony, fighting the current that was pulling him to the side. Occasionally, another body would bob to the surface, startling him and impeding his progress.

"Almost here! Keep swimming!" Tony shouted words of encouragement.

Jack was slowing. His body was giving out as he willed it to swim to safety. Another swell came along, bigger than the others. He was swept upriver along with a few of the dead.

"You're going too far! Turn right! Turn right!"

Tony implored him to change direction. If Jack didn't grab the steel trusses, he'd have to fight the swells to get back, and his energy levels wouldn't be there for him.

Jack took a deep breath, gritted his teeth, and kicked his legs while his arms fought through the water.

"You've got this! Come on, Jack. Almost!"

After Jack completed one more breaststroke, Tony reached down and grabbed him by the back of the shirt and pulled him close. Jack climbed into Tony's arms, and the two men hugged one another in relief and joy.

Tony laughed. "This really sucks, you know?"

Jack laughed and coughed up some of the murky river water from his throat. He tried to talk, but the coughing fit took over. Tony held him against the support until he could recover.

"Yeah, no shit. I'm over it."

Tony took a deep breath and moved to the side so Jack could get a grip on the steel supports. The two men looked around at the floating carnage. The dead bodies rose and fell with each swell flowing across the river.

"Freakin' cold, too," said Tony. He and Jack were both looking from the remnants of the Memphis skyline over toward Arkansas. "Whadya think?"

Jack stretched his neck to orient himself. "Right in the damn middle."

"Yep," Tony added. "Pick your poison."

Jack studied their options for a moment. The swells were getting taller and were now tugging at them as they moved over their bodies. Gripping the bridge structure was becoming more difficult.

He pointed to the west. "Damn! Look!"

A jacked-up pickup truck with large tires was bobbing along in the water toward the south. It was riding the swells and rocking back and forth. The doors were just above the waterline. Inside, a girl was screaming at the top of her lungs for help.

The truck turned in a complete circle when its tailgate struck the bridge a hundred yards away from them. Like a pinball, it hit another support before continuing on its northward course.

Jack, who'd regained his ability to breathe normally, turned to Tony. "Something's wrong."

Tony chuckled. "What was your first clue?"

"No, I mean with the river. It's flowing backwards. Everything is headed upstream."

The guys turned around and followed the pickup truck until it disappeared behind a wave, and observed the dead bodies floating upriver. For over a minute, they rested and watched the Mississippi change course to flow backwards.

It was the sudden eclipse of the sun that caused them both to scream in unison.

CHAPTER FORTY-FIVE

Sunday, December 23
Atwood Residence
Cordova, Tennessee

Tate was excited to see Britney. The two had grown closer as he played a more prominent role on the MUS varsity football team. She was very attractive and came from a good family. Her popularity made her a catch for all the guys at school, and the girl most of the others admired.

Tate was not an aggressive teen. The best way to describe him was *workmanlike*. He was polite and well-mannered. A trait that was lacking in many young men those days. He placed an emphasis on studying while enjoying the athletic program he was recruited into rather than seeing it as a springboard to college. Jack had made it clear that his college would be covered financially, and the most important thing he could do was keep his grades up to ensure acceptance.

Britney was somewhat of the same mindset until she turned sixteen when her parents bought her a car. She now had a freedom Tate hadn't experienced yet. He couldn't drive to the mall whenever he wanted. On nights and weekends, he couldn't head over to a buddy's house or drive the half hour to Meeman-Shelby State Park to hang out by the river. He had to rely on others to offer him a ride.

He understood from his dad he'd have to get a part-time job to pay for his car. Jack and his mom agreed to cover his insurance costs, but the payments, gas, and maintenance would be all on him. He hadn't thought that far ahead. He'd be turning sixteen just as summer started, and there were plenty of jobs available for him to save for a car.

Tate moved quickly through the woods, anxious to see the girl with whom he'd struck up a high school romance. They were both aware of the second-base, third-base, home-run type of boundaries their parents expected of them. Tate was cool with that, and as a result, Britney trusted him.

It took a little over twenty minutes to reach her house. Before he exited the woods, he caught his breath, fixed his hair, and adjusted his clothing so it looked like he was on a casual stroll and just happened to stop by 'cause he was in the neighborhood.

He walked along the front of the house, slyly glancing in the windows to see if he'd been noticed. Nothing so far. He walked up the wide brick steps and pushed the doorbell. He stood there for a minute and then silently cursed himself for forgetting the power was out. He physically shook himself, asking why he was so nervous. *It's just Britney, you idiot.* And that was why he was nervous. She had that effect on him.

He knocked on the door and waited.

Nothing.

Tate knocked again, a little more forcefully this go-around. Still nothing.

Disappointed, he walked around to the side of the house where the garage was located. Britney's car was in the driveway. He looked inside the small windows inset into the three garage doors. Both of her parents' cars were there. Puzzled, Tate walked to the end of the driveway and around the back corner of the house. He thought they might've been sitting outside on the deck.

Other than the patio furniture, the deck was empty. He glanced down toward the water's edge. They didn't have a dock like the Atwoods, but Tate couldn't help but notice how far the water level had dropped.

He stood on the deck for a moment and spun around, running his fingers through his neatly groomed hair.

"I don't get it. Where are you guys?"

Tate knocked on the patio doors. All the curtains were drawn closed, so he couldn't see inside. He stood on his toes to peer through the kitchen window. Everything was neat and tidy. Lastly, he took a chance and tried the patio doors to see if they were unlocked. They wouldn't budge.

Befuddled and dejected, Tate exited the deck and walked up the driveway toward their street. He glanced down the road and saw a man gathering tree limbs that had fallen in his yard. Tate took a moment to inquire about Britney and her family. The man said he'd seen them Friday, but nothing since.

Tate finished the conversation when he felt the ground sway. Slightly at first. Then, as if he were standing on a sheet of ice and hit with a gust of hurricane-force wind, he was thrown sideways until he struck the man's mailbox.

His body, still suffering the battering he took in the Halloran theater, screamed in pain. Tate responded with a long groan but quickly found his footing. He held on to the mailbox post embedded in a concrete footing for stability. He struggled to keep his balance.

The next earthquake was just getting started. Britney's neighbors ran out of the house, looking at the sky as if the evildoer came from above rather than below the planet's surface.

Tate was knocked off his feet again. He held his position on all fours, hoping it would end shortly after starting. Instead, it continued and grew in intensity.

Windows began to shatter in the surrounding homes. Tate stood and moved away from a mature oak tree that began to tilt. His eye caught a glimpse of the lake behind Britney's house. He furrowed his brow and concentrated. Something was different. It was lower.

More windows exploded out of the homes. The shattering glass caused Tate to remember his sister.

"Emily!" Tate shouted as he ran clumsily across the yards toward the woods.

He stumbled twice but picked himself back up. He didn't care if he fell down a thousand times. He had to get to his little sister, who was home alone. He took off across the yards, twice hurdling a short picket fence adjacent to Britney's lawn.

As he crossed the sidewalk leading to her house, the angry earthquake punched the concrete upward as if it had a mind of its own, devilishly intending to prevent him from getting to Emily.

In that moment, Tate saw the quake as something demonic. It was a powerful, supernatural force, choosing its victims and tormenting its survivors. He entered the woods along the lake without regard for his safety. Saplings smacked his face as he ran over them. Low-lying tree branches grabbed at his arms and body like the gnarly fingers of a giant ogre.

And the ogre roared. A throaty, fear-inducing growl that came from the depths of the planet.

Tate dodged falling tree limbs as he ran down the path that was becoming increasingly difficult to identify. He hurdled a fallen southern pine, a tree that was top heavy by nature and easily knocked over. He ducked under a partially fallen oak and entered the backyard of another lakefront home.

His eyes darted between the water level of the lake dropping and the crumbling of the back of the stately home that had been there for as long as their home had been. The retaining wall holding up the driveway had collapsed, and a shiny red Corvette had rolled nose first into the rubble.

As Tate glanced to his left, the ground to his right suddenly gave way. What was once solid turf, albeit on a slope, was now opening up into a hole all the soil and sod was collapsing into. Tate cut left as if he were trying to avoid a defensive back after a catch. He never saw the black water hose that had been left in the yard by the homeowner.

His feet got tangled, and he flew headfirst into the bank and rolled repeatedly until he crashed into a cord of firewood stacked at the edge of the woods.

He moaned in pain, yet again. His body longed for the whirlpool tubs of the MUS locker room, designed to relax battered and bruised football players. But the game wasn't over.

Tate pulled himself up and continued. The trees were uprooting with more frequency as the ground near the lake started to disappear into the water. His race to the house was slowed, but he continued without stopping.

"Help!"

It was Emily. Tate was close enough to hear his sister's voice, and she was in trouble.

"I'm coming! Hold on, Emily!"

Where is she? he thought to himself as he fought through the underbrush of the woods. He'd completely lost sight of the well-worn trails he'd used for years. Or they were buried under the forest now. *Did she go outside like we were taught in school?*

"Emily! Where are you?"

It was Tate's mom. She was at the house. Tate got a burst of energy and ran like the wind as the woods opened up to their property. He appeared in the side yard near the driveway just as his Mom was turning in circles, searching for her youngest child.

"Emily!" screamed Tate.

His mother joined in. "Honey? Where are you?"

There was no answer.

CHAPTER FORTY-SIX

Sunday, December 23
Harahan Bridge
The Mississippi River

The numerous swells had now reached heights of fifteen feet. They easily obscured the smallish, one-hundred-eight-foot-long barge that had broken free from the Vulcan Materials facility located a mile to their south. The deck barge, with a sideboard measuring sixteen feet high, was filled with crushed stone.

Jack didn't see any good options. He tugged at Tony's shirtsleeve to get his attention. "We have to go under. We'll use the steel truss supports to pull ourselves along. We've got to get out of the way of this thing."

"We won't be able to see anything in this crap," said Tony. "Just stay close to my feet. I'll pull my way along with my arms."

The swell lifted the barge higher in the water, giving them a view of its approach. It was floating aimlessly on the river and getting closer.

"After you," Jack said with a nod. He took a deep breath of fresh air, held it, and dropped below the surface simultaneously with Tony.

Arm over arm, the two men began to pull themselves along the collapsed steel truss system of what used to be the Harahan Bridge. The murky waters afforded little visibility, and the sediment stirred up by the fast-moving current caused specks of sand to enter their eyes. They'd only dropped fifteen feet below the surface, giving them ample opportunity to rise for air when necessary.

Most of the dead bodies had become buoyant, floating out of the underwater graveyard to the surface, only to be carried upriver, odd as that sounds, by the current. The only trace of humanity in the murky water was earthquake-created litter carried by the swiftly moving current. There was more debris in the water than when the bridge collapsed. Large trees from a timbering operation floated beneath them like matchsticks, fighting their way to the surface but held back by the bridge trusses. Sheets of corrugated metal floated in all directions like the pieces of paper carried by the wind outside the Met. Occasionally, the men's bodies were bumped by suitcases, Christmas packages, and car parts that managed to float.

The most surreal aspect of their escape from the coming barge was the noise. Underwater, there was a deafening rumbling sound. Jack could hear the faint release of oxygen bubbles as he moved along behind Tony. But the thunderous roar of the earthquake was magnified underwater compared to what they heard topside.

The men pulled themselves along, glancing upward at the sunlight of morning. Occasionally, they held their breath, hoping to see the barge pass. Yet it never did.

It had been a minute.

Tony had stopped and turned to Jack. He put his face in front of Jack's and gave him a thumbs-up sign to surface. Jack nodded and looked upward as he prepared to kick his legs.

Gradually the sunlight disappeared. A total eclipse as the day seemingly turned to night. Then an angry force tried to dislodge their grip from the remnants of the Harahan Bridge.

The barge had crossed directly over them and was now battering the trusses.

The sound of steel rubbing and scratching joined the groaning of the earth. Jack's eyes grew wide although he was almost blinded by the lack of light. The bridge trusses were being slammed repeatedly with every swell that propelled the barge upriver.

Tony's body had turned horizontal at the same time Jack's did. The current had picked up, and the two men were now holding onto the steel support to prevent being swept away. Jack's grip loosened, and he desperately struggled to hold on. His air was disappearing, and he knew he was getting near his two-minute limit.

The truss slipped out of his grasp, and he was whisked away twenty feet until he crashed into the next truss support. The impact almost knocked out what little air he had left, but he managed to hold onto it.

He grabbed the support and looked back toward the darkened water of the barge. A shadow. A mass of some kind was hurtling toward him.

It was Tony.

Jack reached out and grabbed him by the wrist, nearly dislodging his grip from the truss. He held on, even as the barge was battering the other side of the truss system. The momentum of Tony's body continued to tug him away from the support, but Jack held tight. They were in the sunlight now. The barge couldn't get past the exposed trusses. But it wasn't for lack of trying. The swells, which were growing in height and frequency, heaved the barge without stopping, bashing it continuously into the bridge truss.

Jack and Tony were close enough to make eye contact. Tony's eyes were wide and his cheeks were puffed out. He was shaking his head vigorously from side to side. Jack understood what he wanted to say.

He was giving up.

No! Jack was shouting in his mind. *Do not let go. You'll die!*

He gave Tony a stern look and gripped his wrist harder. He

refused to let Tony go. He thrust his head closer to Tony's face as if to say, *Fight!*

The bridge shook with the most force yet as the hulking barge, aided by the Mighty Mississippi, which had reversed course, tag-teamed the old warrior in a concerted effort to put it down once and for all.

Jack pulled and furrowed his brow with determination.

The bridge was slammed again. Harder this time. He instinctively gripped the steel I-beam and Tony's wrist.

A glimmer of light found its way beneath the surface. The shadow had shifted as the massive rectangular barge began to turn ever so slightly. It was not running parallel to the shore, and as another swell lifted it out of the river, it surfed past the fallen bridge.

Then it happened. Tony found his will to live.

He swung his right arm around and gripped Jack's forearm. With a slight smile and a herculean effort, Jack pulled Tony against the current until he could grab the bridge truss for himself. The two men squeezed one another's arms in a show of support. They rapidly pulled themselves up the steel truss, hand over hand, until they broke the surface.

They gasped for air and wrapped their arms around the remains of the Harahan Bridge. It had held firm against the onslaught of the Mississippi River battering it with the weight of the seventy-thousand-ton barge.

Without saying another word, Jack nodded toward Memphis. The guys filled their lungs once again and dropped below the surface, where they pulled their way across the river, which was now flowing backwards.

CHAPTER FORTY-SEVEN

Sunday, December 23
East Bank of the Mississippi River
Memphis, Tennessee

The battle between the barge and the fallen Harahan Bridge raged on, periodically knocking the guys' grips off the steel supports. They were within a hundred yards of the new shoreline when a second barge joined the fray. The swells powered the barge's attack, walloping the bridge until it started to sink farther beneath the surface. The guys were losing their ability to stay above water, and then with a final crashing sound that carried across the river, the bridge lost the fight. Jack and Tony lost their lifeline.

The two men struggled in the swift current as they frantically tried to swim toward what used to be Martyrs Park, a landscaped area honoring those who helped others during the 1878 yellow fever epidemic that ravaged Memphis.

They continued to swim toward their next landmark, the fifteen-story River Tower condominium complex. However, for every twenty feet of progress, they were carried upriver another fifty feet by the swells. Their bodies were near exhaustion, but they stuck together, encouraging one another as they came closer to Tom Lee Park and the crumbling high-rises of Downtown Memphis, some of which were on fire.

The water levels had risen at least twenty feet, and the swells had forced water over the lower half of the park. Waves lapped over Riverside Drive and covered most of the Riverwalk. The paved trail that ran from the south end of downtown, across famed Beale Street, until it moved north toward Mud Island on the other side of Interstate 40, had been sitting on top of a levee overlooking the river. Now it was mostly submerged or destroyed as the levees began to fail.

Many of the eight-foot-tall floodwalls that had been built as part of the levee system at Memphis were now threatened by the rising water. Several breaches in the levees had occurred just north of downtown, allowing water to rush into the city streets, causing massive flooding. The lower levees were still intact, but the floodwaters inside them were clawing away at the earthen dams to join with the rest of the river that had previously eroded the banks.

Tony was the first to reach land by grabbing a handrail bordering the levee. He waited for Jack to swim by and extended his hand to lend an assist. He pulled Jack toward the rail until both men were able to swing their legs over. They collapsed on the levee, panting for air and allowing the warm sun to bake their shivering bodies.

Jack was the first to speak. "Well, let's try not to do that again."

The men laughed. Tony added, "You know, as I was swimmin' my ass off, there were several things I swore to. One was to move someplace where they don't have earthquakes. Two, never go on a bridge, in the water, or up a high-rise ever again."

Jack leaned up and untied his shoes. He removed his shoes and socks to reveal his swollen, bloodied feet. He looked inside his shoe and tossed it to the side.

"You can add never wearing these things again to the list."

"Oh, yeah. We're wearing Reeboks or Adidas to all of our seminars from now on. Folks will just have to understand."

Jack chuckled, then buried his face in his hands. He ran his fingers through his hair and then looked at their surroundings.

"Our business is screwed. The markets are probably as destroyed as the cities up and down the Mississippi. And we're probably broke. God only knows what's gonna happen to the markets tomorrow."

Tony stood and retrieved Jack's shoe. "You'd better put them back on before your feet swell too much. Otherwise, you'll be walking barefoot twenty-some miles to the house. Besides, Jack, don't worry about our finances. I've got our backs."

"What are you gonna do, go into the money-printing business?"

"I already did, sort of. Here's the thing. I got a little spooked on top of the Gateway Arch the other day. The markets have been blah anyway, so I decided to make a couple of moves."

Jack was intrigued. He winced as he forced his shoes back on over his wet socks and battered feet. He was barely able to tie the laces.

"Like what?" he asked as he rose to his feet, his face scrunching as he shifted his weight from one foot to the other.

"Like, um, I moved all of our family and business holdings into gold or foreign currencies in the Zurich and Hong Kong markets."

"Really?"

"Yeah. All I could think of was where should we park our investments if a quake hit the middle of the country. I thought, you know, for a week or so, we'd just play it safe."

Jack laughed and grabbed the shorter man by the shoulder. "You know what this means, don't you?"

"Yeah. Good news is an understatement. I bet the value of our gold certificates doubled ever since the first quake hit."

Jack wrapped his arm around Tony. "You're a genius. Thank you."

Tony's shoulders slumped and his head drooped. Jack noticed the difference in his demeanor, so he stepped away to get a look at his face.

"Hey, what's up?"

Tony looked at the sky and sighed. He began to tear up, so he turned away from his brother-in-law and watched the barges work their way upriver.

"I've been a shit husband, but you know that already."

"Hey, listen. Marriages are tough. They require work."

Tony laughed. "That's psychobabble from Dr. Phil or some crap. Either you wanna be married and a good husband or you don't. If you do, then do it right."

This was a conversation Jack had wanted to have with Tony for years but never could find the right opportunity to bring it out in the open. This was apparently the time.

"Do you wanna be married?" His question was blunt and to the point.

Tony wandered away and stuck his hands in his pockets. He pulled out a handful of sopping wet dollars and chuckled. He symbolically tossed them in the river and watched the current carry them away.

"Yeah, at first. I loved Beth, and we had fun together. She was my best friend. We traveled. Went out to eat. Partied with friends. You know what it's like."

"I thought you guys were happy," added Jack, who'd never had that kind of relationship with Jill. After they fell in love, he was plugged into a built-in family. He wanted to keep his side of the conversation to a minimum. This was Tony's moment. "What changed?"

"I feel like an asshole for saying this," he began in response. "We had Anthony. Don't get me wrong. That was exciting at first. You get a lot of attention. You watch him grow and develop. You dream of playing ball with him and stuff."

"You can do all those things," said Jack.

"Sure. But in the process, I feel like I lost my wife. Beth began to focus her entire existence on Anthony. I know. I know. I'm being a selfish prick. I wish I wasn't. Over time, our family became Beth and Anthony, not Beth and Tony."

Jack took a deep breath. He wasn't sure this question was

necessary or appropriate, but he had to ask so Tony could let it all out. The man was releasing his burdens, and there was no sense in stopping now.

"Have you cheated on her?"

Tony furrowed his brow and looked upward. "No, thank God. I hate to admit it, but all of my messing around with young girls was some kind of way to prove I've still got it, you know what I mean?"

"The mojo," said Jack, trying to lighten the mood. In the moment, under the circumstances of what they'd just been through together, he believed that Tony had been faithful, to an extent.

Tony laughed. "Yeah, the mojo. You know, the ability to make a move on a woman and have her show interest in return. But, eventually, the more I felt sorry for myself, the more I considered actually following through with it. You know, if a girl made the first move or something."

"But that never happened."

"Nope, I swear."

"Then you're still good. That is, if you wanna be. You've got another kid on the way."

Tony leaned against the rail and watched as the two barges got hung up on the remains of the M-shaped supports of the Hernando de Soto Bridge to their north. The swells were subsiding, but the water continued to rise.

"Having another baby was Beth's idea, of course. She thought it would bring us closer together. She totally misread my feelings."

"Have you ever told her how you feel?" asked Jack.

"Nah, man. Are you kidding me? She'd lose it if I said I'm falling out of love with you because of Anthony and the baby on the way."

Jack walked up to him and put his arm over his shoulder again. "Tony, this has been eatin' you up. I can see how you immerse yourself in our business. You always jump at the opportunity to travel. It's just an escape mechanism."

Tony hung his head again. "I know."

"All right, so let me say a couple of things. First, Beth loves you very much. You and I can never understand about a mother's love for her children. It's something innate within them that we can't completely relate to. Second, I know she would do anything within her power to make your marriage better. She's seen the strain between the two of you because she talks to Jill about it."

"She thinks you guys are the greatest. She's commented more than once about how great your marriage is."

Jack nodded. "It is great. I won't lie to you. Earlier, I said it requires work. Maybe work isn't the right word. Sacrifice and compromise might be better ones. You learn to do the things she likes that you might not. If she has a bad habit or tends to get under your skin about certain things, you ignore it or blow it off. But if you aren't going to address it, don't let it fester and eat at you. In that case, you gotta raise it and talk it through. She should be able to do the same with you."

Tony understood. "Beth wanted to see a marriage counselor, so I agreed. We went through two sessions, and I'd had enough. All she did was beat me over the head, and the counselor agreed with her the whole time. I came out of there madder than when I went in."

Jack didn't say anything because he felt Tony wasn't finished. He was right.

He sighed and turned back toward the river. "Something happened to me when I was in that water. My mind weighed the options of living or dying. If you had let go of my wrist, I would've floated off and died. In that moment, I realized I didn't want to die. I saw Beth's face next to mine on a pillow. I saw myself sitting on the family room floor, playing with Anthony. I saw our new baby in a crib, swatting at those mobile things like they were the greatest invention known to man. It was their faces that gave me the will to fight for my life."

"Are they more important than having a wife freed up for Friday night dinner dates or Saturday day-drinking?"

"Damn straight. There's nothing more important."

Jack wrapped his arm around Tony's neck and squeezed it. "Let's go home, shall we? I think we both miss our families."

CHAPTER FORTY-EIGHT

Sunday, December 23
USGS
Golden, Colorado

The NEIC in Golden was frenzied. The first earthquake along the New Madrid fault got the juices flowing. The second, with an estimated magnitude of 8.6, coupled with aftershocks as far north as Illinois and all the way to Natchez, Mississippi, absolutely caused their heads to explode. The seismometers delivered information on the compression and shear waves of the earthquakes faster than the geophysicists could process the data.

"It's tearing us in half!" hollered one of the geophysicists. "We have fissures opening up along the Reelfoot Rift, the Mid-Continent Rift, and even in part of the Southern Oklahoma Rift."

"It's migrating," said Oliver as he delivered a satellite image to Dr. Lansing. "I've never seen anything like it on a plate boundary, mum."

"Neither have I, Oliver," she responded calmly. Now was not the time to panic. What was happening across the Central U.S. into Canada flew in the face of all prior earthquake modeling. "In the past, New Madrid seismic activity was concentrated along the Reelfoot Rift. We know the continent contains many fossil structures that would seem equally likely candidates for this kind of concentrated seismicity."

"Dr. Lansing! We have an estimated M6.3 centered just north of Evansville."

"Wabash?" she asked.

"Yes, ma'am. The epicenter is right in the heart of the Wabash Valley Seismic Zone at the border of Indiana and Illinois, forty miles north of Evansville."

Dr. Lansing shook her head in disbelief.

"Oliver, it turns out we may all be right," she began, referring to the opinions of other geophysicists.

"How so, mum?" he asked.

"Well, those who claimed that New Madrid's heyday was over pointed at other nearby faults as the so-called new kid on the block. Wabash Valley is one of them. Think about it. There hadn't been an M6 in New Madrid for over a hundred years until this weekend. Wabash Valley had experienced three M5s in the last two decades. I've seen evidence that Wabash has produced M7s or greater in the past."

The North American crust was filled with cracks and faults where an earthquake could occur at any time. Many faults remained undetected and weren't placed on the geologic map until they unexpectedly revealed themselves.

When the North American continent tried to separate hundreds of millions of years ago, it left behind crust cracks and ruptures that could sometimes pull apart. The rock comprising this part of the world was one-point-seven billion years old, and the seismic waves could travel very long distances through Earth's crust.

This stood in stark contrast to the western U.S., where the rock was hotter and thus the shock waves were dampened and contained. Then again, the superheated rock was part of Earth's complex volcanic plumbing, which presented a whole different set of problems, such as the Yellowstone supervolcano, an extinction-level event waiting its turn to erupt.

"Dr. Lansing, we're registering minor earthquake activity in the Precambrian rock outcrop of Michigan's Upper Peninsula. These tremors could be nothing more than the Wabash wave spreading."

"We can't assume anything at this point," said Dr. Lansing. She moved to the center of the room. "We are in the midst of an historic seismic event. As scientists and geophysicists, we'd love to grab the popcorn and watch it unfold like a real-life disaster movie. However, our job is to analyze and advise those who are trying to save lives. Let's calm down and focus. We're going to reassign tasks based upon the breadth of this event. Oliver, split the team up according to the current heat map."

The USGS had the technological capability to generate a heat map during an ongoing earthquake sequence. The infrared map revealed heat flow from the earth as earthquakes opened up cracks and fissures.

"Yes, mum," he replied.

She took a look around the operations center and then walked with purpose to her office, where she closed the door behind her. She needed to get away to clear her head. Ordinarily, she'd task Oliver or another member of her team to perform predictive models of subsequent aftershocks. This time, she felt compelled to do it herself.

It was time for the prophetess of doom to prognosticate.

CHAPTER FORTY-NINE

Sunday, December 23
Near Lake Cormorant, Mississippi

Beth shrieked as a surge of energy from beneath the ground threw both the car and Willie into the air. He landed hard on his back against the gas pump island. His hat fell off and rolled toward the highway intersection. Then a fierce wind blew across the standing water, blowing moisture across them and picking up his hat until it landed next to the car.

"Arrrgggh!" screamed Beth, a soprano's groan that accompanied the baritone's growling noise that accompanied the building earthquake. She was going into preterm labor. "Nooo! It's too early!"

Willie recovered from being knocked across the parking lot, and he made his way back to the car. "What can I do? The closest hospital is Baptist Memorial in Southhaven."

"How far?"

Before Willie could respond, the ground around them opened its jaws and began to swallow hunks of the earth. To their north and east, the ground was heaving up in waves until splits in the earth became large cracks. The water near the cracks rushed into them, draining the field but soaking the dirt further. The cracks began to run in several directions. They crossed the highway and then stitched through a field across Star Landing Road, which led toward the interstate.

Willie began to run around the car to the driver's side. He yelled, "We'll go back. It's only a few miles. We'll try to find a way through the flood."

"We can't—arrrgggh!" Beth's contractions were coming fast and furious. Something was wrong. "No time!"

"What?" asked a panicked Willie, who was standing at the front bumper. He held the hood with both hands as the ground continued to generate a roar that sounded like a fleet of dump trucks roaring by at a hundred miles per hour. He was knocked to the ground again and crawled around the car until he reached Beth's open door.

She was breathing heavily, gasping for air every few words. "Can't wait. We have to. Do it. Here."

Willie's eyes grew wide and looked around nervously as he spoke. "I don't really know—"

Beth caught her breath and reached out to touch Willie's hand. "Just listen to what I say."

An earsplitting screeching sound could be heard, followed by a series of loud pops and snaps. Beth turned sideways in her seat and looked toward the highway. Willie stepped away from the car.

The power poles on both sides of the Shell station's entrance had cracked, and the power lines were snapping loose from the transformer. A wheezing sound accompanied the transmission lines as they were released from the poles and snapped across the parking lot until they lashed the white, yellow, and red canopy over the gas pumps. The power lines acted like giant whips, tearing open the thin metal bearing the Shell logo. The whiplike force started to topple the canopy over.

"Close your door!" he shouted to Beth, who groaned as she reached for the handle. A part of the canopy collapsed and landed across the pavement just in front of their car. Another piece scraped across the hood until it landed on the driver's side. The shaking earth caused it to rattle and bounce around until it rested against the sidewalk adjacent to the building.

"Willie!" Beth shouted as another contraction gripped her. They were becoming stronger, longer, and more frequent. She was breathing quickly to deal with the pressure exerted inside her.

He came racing back to her. She was opening the door and exiting the car.

"Where are you going?"

"The back seat. Please put Anthony in the front."

Beth held both hands under her belly and grimaced as she stood outside the car. Willie opened the back of his patrol car and hoisted Anthony up and out of the back seat. Remarkably, her son had remained calm throughout the melee.

Beth only had the strength and breath to muss his hair. "Thank you for trading seats with Mommy."

Anthony hesitated when he saw his mother's amniotic fluid on the floor of the car. Willie helped Beth into the back and then gave Anthony the DUPLO blocks to occupy him. He paused to pat the child on the head and then began to close the door, glancing downward to ensure none of the young toddler's limbs were in the way. He knelt down and retrieved his hat. He manipulated it back in shape and placed it on Anthony's head. For the first time, the young boy smiled at Willie.

He took a deep breath. It was time for him to man up. He found Beth inching her way backwards across the seat until the back of her head rested on the armrest. He pushed up the sleeves on his navy-blue sweatshirt with the Mississippi Highway Patrol insignia across the front. The state didn't mind their troopers using their vehicles on select occasions for personal purposes for so long as they wore some form of apparel identifying them as a trooper. Most of the guys wore the windbreaker-style jackets. In the winter, Willie donned his sweatshirt.

"Okay. What do you need me to do?"

Beth was still having difficulty breathing. After each word, she gasped for air. "Towels. Blanket. Knife. String."

"Okay. Stay here." Willie dashed toward the inside of the Shell convenience store before Beth laughed at her comical instructions. She moaned in pain as punishment for the chuckle.

"Momma. Hurt."

The sound of Anthony's voice comforted her. "No, honey. Not hurt. I'm having a baby."

"Not a baby. Not a baby."

"I know, honey. You're my big boy. You enjoy your blocks, and Momma will be done in a—errrrr."

Beth couldn't finish her sentence as another contraction struck her. She tried to stifle her reaction to the pain, and she immediately wondered if she'd be able to contain the screaming as she gave birth. She was certain it would upset Anthony.

The earthquake continued to rumble across the landscape of Northern Mississippi. She'd grown accustomed to the rhythmic shaking and wondered if the rocking might actually assist her with delivering her newborn.

Beth began to breathe rapidly again. She closed her eyes as she prepared herself to give birth. She'd have to abandon all modesty as she revealed herself to a stranger. She pushed the elastic waistband of her maternity jeans down until they were around her ankles. She gently kicked them out of the back seat onto the asphalt. Then she eased off her panties and kicked them out as well.

Willie appeared at the open door just as her panties hit the ground. He immediately averted his eyes and looked toward the front seat.

Beth took a deep breath before she spoke. "Willie, you're gonna have to look."

"What? Where?"

"My, you know. My maternity ward." Beth giggled at the joke, and then, as before, she was punished with a strong contraction that caused her to yell.

"Arrrgggh!"

"No. Why?" he asked.

"Because." Gasp. "When I push her out ..." Gasp. "You have to catch her." She gasped again and took a deep breath and exhaled rapidly.

Whoosh. Whoosh. Whoosh.

Beth couldn't see the expression on Willie's face, as he was still looking away, but in that tense moment, she could only imagine.

CHAPTER FIFTY

Sunday, December 23
Near Lake Cormorant, Mississippi

He'd done as well as could be expected on his limited shopping expedition into the Shell station. Between the looters and the destruction caused by the earthquake, the small convenience store was in shambles. He was able to find a couple of packages of shop towels, several green beach towels bearing the logo of the Lake Cormorant Gators football team, and some fishing line. He also grabbed a few bottles of Evian water, which was the only beverage remaining in the store's inoperable refrigerated coolers.

Willie got it together and forgot about the immodesty of the birthing process. He had a job to do, which was to be there to help Beth through it and, as she said, catch her child when the time came.

Beth had moved into the transitional phase of her labor. She'd been through it once before and swore she'd never forget the pain she endured. She promised herself and the universe she'd never give birth again without an epidural. She had to break that promise, unfortunately.

Willie had not been in the hospital room when his daughters

were born. For one thing, he was too squeamish, and secondly, Carla forbade it. She was surrounded by her mother and ladies from the church. That's just how things were done in Tunica. Over the years, Willie had experienced all manners of bloody horrors. Mangled bodies from vehicle accidents and gunshot victims were just two of the most common tragedies he came across every year. However, despite his lack of experience in the birthing process, he gave Beth some excellent advice.

"Just do what feels right."

Beth nodded as her face scrunched together. She began to push as her body felt her daughter enter the birth canal. There was an unmistakable urge for her to bear down on her child, urging the young life to come out into the world.

"Arrrgh!" she shouted, abandoning all attempts to muffle her pain for Anthony's sake. She began to breathe heavily.

Willie had played high school sports many decades ago, but he knew when someone was starting to hyperventilate. He knelt into the back seat and reached for Beth's hand. It was a touching gesture that calmed her almost immediately.

"Breathe, Beth. Easy though. If you pass out, who's gonna tell me what to do?"

Beth chuckled and then scowled. She took a deep breath. "You can't make me laugh. I'm having a baby!"

This caused her to laugh again, and seconds later, she felt the urge to push.

"Arrrgh!"

She started breathing fast again but then immediately controlled herself.

Willie was still holding her hand. "That's it. That's it. Steady, now."

She continued to breathe in and out. Barely ten seconds had passed, and it was time to push again.

And push she did. A long, sustained, I-wanna-get-this-over-with push.

"Arrrgh!"

"I see her head, Beth. Sure 'nuf. I see it." Willie's excited voice caused Beth to smile. She closed her eyes, took a deep breath, and then waited for the signal from her body. One second. Two seconds. Three. Now!

"Arrrgh!" She pushed again. She didn't need a nurse, or her husband, or even Dr. Willie Angel to encourage her to do so. She knew what to do.

Willie eased back and supported the baby's head in his massive hands. Beth didn't have to instruct him on what to do. Something primal and instinctual guided Willie that day.

"Her head is really big, but I've got it," said Willie.

Beth grimaced. She contemplated all of the things she would do to Willie when this was over for that comment. However, it was time to push again.

"Arrrgh!" *Whoosh-whoosh-whoosh.* She breathed quicker and easier now.

"I've got shoulders. Two of them!" Willie's exuberance was the most unexpected aspect of the birth of Beth's second child. That, and the earthquake, of course.

"Lift them slightly," said Beth as she prepared to push again.

With one final groan and a mighty shove, her newborn daughter came out easily into Willie Angel's hands.

The bluish baby girl was slippery, so he gently rested her on several shop towels, which he determined to be cleaner than the beach towels hanging on a rack.

He began to shed tears of his own as the cool air struck the naked newborn. She filled her lungs with her first breath of air and let out a mighty squall that caused Anthony to begin rocking back and forth in the front seat. He marveled at how small she was, most likely weighing three pounds but certainly less than four.

Willie worked quickly to dry the baby off, and then he swaddled her in clean shop towels with a blanket for warmth. He took another towel and wrapped it around her head to help her retain heat. Then he readied the fishing line, tied it around the umbilical cord a couple of inches from the baby's belly, and severed it. He quickly stemmed the bleeding and used a ripped piece of cloth off a shop towel as a makeshift clamp.

He was as efficient as an expert maternity nurse. Then he leaned forward and presented the beautiful new life to her mother.

Tears streamed down Beth's face as she held her child for the first time. Willie leaned in and unbuttoned her shirt to reveal her skin. Beth had been wearing front-clasped maternity bras for the last several weeks. He looked down at her breasts, and then the two made eye contact. She smiled and nodded, providing him approval to expose her breasts so she could bond with her baby.

Now both stand-in doctor and mother were crying tears of joy. A new life had been brought into the world in the midst of the destruction of part of the planet. They'd done it together under the most bizarre of circumstances. Beth held her baby close and reached up to touch the teary-eyed man who'd saved her life and gave life to her baby girl.

After they shared a moment, Beth was reminded by her uterus there was still some work to do. It had begun to contract ever so slightly in order to separate the placenta from the inside of her body. She looked up to Willie.

"Do you happen to have a first aid kit in the car?"

He rolled his eyes and shook his head. "We're supposed to, but our stock never got replenished after the hurricane two months ago."

Beth sighed and then took a really deep breath. Her baby had fallen asleep on her chest. She felt the contractions in her uterus intensify.

"Um, Willie, my placenta will be coming out soon. I can urge it along by rubbing my belly, but when the time comes, I'm gonna have to push it out."

"Okay. What do I do?"

"First, if you have an extra blanket, would you mind putting it under my butt?"

Willie reached down and retrieved one of several extras. Beth used her heels to arch her back so he could slide the towel underneath her.

"Okay. What's next?" he asked.

"This could take ten minutes, or it might take thirty minutes. I won't lie. There's gonna be a lot of blood, and my placenta, my insides are gonna come out. After that, I really need some gauze bandages to, you know, keep the maternity ward from getting infected and stuff."

Willie backed out of the car and looked around. He saw a building just past the Shell station that was unaffected by the fissure that crossed the two roads. He leaned into the car with his arm resting on the roof.

"How much time do I have?"

"Ten minutes, but probably more," Beth replied.

"Okay, I have an idea." He started to turn, and Beth stopped him.

"Hey, Willie."

"Yes, ma'am."

"Thank you so much."

Willie smiled and nodded. He glanced in to check on Anthony before gently shutting Beth's door to give her some privacy and shield her from the random wind gusts. He jogged across the Shell parking lot and across the road under the watchful eye of a newly minted big brother, Anthony Chandler Junior.

CHAPTER FIFTY-ONE

Sunday, December 23
Atwood Residence
Cordova, Tennessee

Tate rushed past his mom toward the side door leading from the driveway into the garage. He flung the door open, intending to run through the garage. However, the door only partially opened. He crashed into the steel exterior door head-on, causing his body to spin sideways through the opening, where he stumbled over several plastic shelves containing tools and partially filled cans of paint.

Jill rushed to his aid, using her shoulder to ram the door open a little more, allowing her sufficient light to see what had happened to Tate.

"Are you okay?"

"Yeah. Go! Go!" He waved his arms toward the door leading into the kitchen.

While Tate untangled himself from the mess, Jill stepped through the shelves and up the steps leading to the door. She turned the knob and began shouting for her daughter as she entered the kitchen.

"Emily! Emily! Where are you, baby?" She ran from the kitchen, through the breakfast room and into the family room. The fire was burning out behind the glass enclosure, and everything appeared in the exact same condition as when Jill left earlier.

"Emilyyy!" Tate had emerged from the garage and yelled her name. He ran past his mom toward the foyer. He grabbed the newel post and used it to quickly swing himself around to run up the stairs, taking the steps two at a time.

"Emily!" Jill shouted at the end of the hallway where it adjoined the master bedroom suite. Tate's heavy feet could be heard tromping across the wood floor upstairs that connected the bedrooms.

"Where are you?" he shouted his question. The response he got was unexpected.

The windows of the upstairs rooms began to crack and then break. The roar of the earthquake had stopped, and the last shaking of the ground subsided. Nonetheless, the strain on their home had taken its toll. A sound similar to nails on a chalkboard caused the glass to split. Then, seemingly all at once, the upper windows shattered and fell inside the house. Tate checked the last empty room and pulled the door shut behind him as if to keep the destructive demon locked inside.

He rapidly walked down the oak treads of the stairs until he met his mother in the foyer. She opened the front door and screamed Emily's name again. This time, they got an answer.

"Mom!"

They both rushed onto the front stoop and into the yard. The two of them walked in opposite directions, screaming her name.

"Help! Back here!"

"By the lake!" hollered Tate as he spun around and ran across the driveway to the side yard where he'd arrived through the woods. He slowed as he approached the lake. The grass turned to moist dirt and then mud.

"Emily! Where are you?"

"Behind the tree! Tate! Please hurry. The water is coming back!"

Tate was confused. He'd seen the water levels dropping at Britney's house. How could it be rising here? He glanced at the lake as he moved closer to where their deck once stood. There were some waves but not very high.

Jill came around the other side of the house.

"Mom, over here. She's down by the water."

"What?" Jill couldn't understand why but hustled to join Tate as he climbed through the top of the massive fallen oak. He pushed some branches aside and ducked under others. He eventually caught a glimpse of Emily floating on top of the water. She had a death grip on a partially broken branch that used to be at the top of the forty-foot oak.

"I see you, honey. Hold on!" Jill's adrenaline was flowing through her body as she fought through the tree to join Tate.

"I've tried to pull myself up, but it's breaking."

Tate carefully stepped down the slope, using the fallen tree for support. He saw the branch Emily was holding onto. It was barely an inch in diameter and had snapped midway down. The white inside and the green from just under bark were visible. The remains were starting to shred and separate from the tree.

Tate put a firm grip on the branch holding his sister so it wouldn't go anywhere. "Em, can you hold onto it while I pull you up?"

"I think so," the exhausted child replied sheepishly. "The water is coming back."

Tate furrowed his brow and glanced toward his left. It was hard for him to gauge whether she was correct or not. First things first, he thought to himself.

"Okay, I might break this branch all the way, but I've got you. Hold tight, and let me pull you toward some sturdier limbs. Grab them as you can. Then we'll pull you even closer."

"Let me go in after her," Jill begged in a panic.

"No, Mom. You could slip down the hill. I've got her."

Tate began pulling the branch back toward the trunk of the tree by bending it farther. The shreds of bark holding it to the tree were tearing the closer Emily got to another branch.

"I've got one," she proclaimed as she let go of the original branch.

It snapped back in place, causing Tate to fall on his back. He quickly twisted and grabbed a thick branch, which allowed him to pull his body up the slope.

"Okay, Em. I'll come to you. Just stay there, and I'll work my way 'til I can grab your hand."

"Sure. All right. But the water is coming up. I swear."

Jill had no idea what she was referring to. She looked around the bank, and it appeared to be at the same level as when she got up that morning.

"Just follow your brother's instructions, and everything will be fine."

"Stretch," said Tate as he reached out for Emily's arm. She placed her cold, wrinkled hand in his. He repositioned his grip to include her wrist and forearm as he pulled her slowly through the branches. She was now on the ground and able to walk up the embankment with his help.

"Crap!" yelled Jill. "The tree is sliding down the hill!"

"Get on the other side of the trunk!" ordered Tate.

His mom pulled herself to the trunk and swung her right leg over it, followed by her left. The tree was sliding a few inches at a time, straight toward the water's edge.

"Wrap your arms around my arm and hold on," Tate said to Emily. She followed his instructions, and with a grunt, he lifted her up and over the tree trunk into her mother's waiting arms.

"Oh, god, honey. Thank goodness you're okay."

"I'm sorry, Mom. I just wanted to feed the ducks. Then all hell broke loose."

Instead of chastising her daughter for her potty mouth, Jill began laughing and crying. She held her youngest child tight and waited for Tate to join them.

"Okay, you guys. We still have some work to do. Mom, I want

you to walk parallel to the water using the tree trunk as a guardrail. You know what I mean?"

Jill nodded. She walked sideways along the embankment, holding Emily's wrist with one hand and the tree trunk with the other. Seconds later, they reached the massive root ball of the oak.

Tate was right behind them and took the lead. He used the roots to pull himself above the grade of where the tree tipped over. He pulled Emily and his mom up to him. Seconds later, the three of them had crawled into the crunchy brown grass of their backyard and rolled over onto their backs, allowing the sun to warm their bodies.

CHAPTER FIFTY-TWO

Sunday, December 23
Near Lake Cormorant, Mississippi

Willie hustled across the Shell parking lot toward the Sigma Supply warehouse. As he jogged across the part of Star Landing Road that remained intact, he couldn't help but stare to his right to take in the spectacle of the earth being ripped open. He'd never experienced an earthquake as strong as the one that had lasted nearly as long as it took for Beth to give birth. A tremor that might get folks talkin' on the street corner was nothing compared to the real thing.

Once he stepped off the roadbed and onto the driveway leading to the warehouse, he found himself sloshing through nearly a foot of water. The ground was too saturated to absorb the heavy rainfall or flooded Mississippi River and just simply wasn't allowing the water to recede. For now, that was the least of his concerns.

He needed to find first aid supplies to assist Beth in her recovery and to prevent her from having any type of infection. Sigma Supply was likely to have what he needed. The company was similar to the well-known Uline operation in America, specializing in selling packaging supplies and equipment to businesses of all types.

He arrived at the front entrance and discovered the stress of the earthquake had broken out the plate glass of the double doors. He was glad that he, as an officer of the law, wasn't breaking in. Although, he had no feelings of guilt when it came to procuring the necessary first aid supplies to help Beth. It was an emergency situation, after all.

The front lobby had been jostled, and anything not permanently affixed to the structure had been unceremoniously tossed about. He stepped over fallen bookcases and chairs to make his way down a dark hallway toward the warehouse that made up the vast majority of the building. The deeper into the structure he went, the darker it became as he lost natural light from the front windows.

When he opened the steel door leading to the rear, he was unexpectedly blinded by sunlight. A large portion of the roof had caved in during the quake. He was certain it hadn't happened during the Friday night earthquake, as the interior of the warehouse was still dry.

He stopped, put his hands on his hips, and surveyed the trashed interior. His initial observations would've caused him to turn around and leave. However, he had no choice today. Sigma Supply distributed everything from furniture and equipment to food service and packaging supplies.

He was certain that OSHA, the U.S. Occupational Safety and Health Administration, required the company to keep medical supplies on hand for the protection of their employees. He was sure Sigma also sold first aid kits to their customers, but based on the piles of products littering the warehouse, he was not likely to find them.

He made his way along the common wall separating the warehouse and the front offices. There was an enclosed area near a line of large roll-up doors at the back side of the building. He surmised the trucks were loaded and unloaded through there, and a warehouse manager most likely monitored activities from the office.

It took him a while to crawl over the fallen products and toppled shelves. Parts of the corrugated steel roof had collapsed in this area as well, which hindered his progress. After several minutes, he arrived at a door to the warehouse office, but it was locked.

Willie found a large fire extinguisher on the concrete floor and used it as a hammer to beat his way through the glass. He located several five-gallon buckets of floor cleaner and used them to climb through the broken window onto the desks lining the interior of the office space.

He was breathing heavily as he kicked debris out of the way to clear a place on the floor to stand. In addition to the drop ceiling, anything on the desks and the OSHA safety manuals on the built-in bookshelves had been tossed around the room.

"This has been a lot of action for an old man with a weak ticker," Willie said to himself as he searched through the debris for a first aid kit.

Willie was happy for Beth, but he was also proud of his role. There was a saying that he despised because it was overused. It went something like *taking you out of your comfort zone*. He wasn't sure what that meant until now. He was certainly taken from one twilight zone to another, or some such.

He couldn't wait to tell Carla what he'd accomplished. She probably wouldn't believe him, so he'd have to give her just enough detail so she knew he wasn't making it up. He'd proved all those old biddies from the church wrong. He not only could've been in the room when his daughters were born, he might've been able to do it all by himself, with a little help from Mrs. Angel, of course.

There! He slung a chair away from a desk and found an industrial-sized first aid kit pushed up under the knee space. He opened it up and quickly glanced at its contents. Antibiotic ointment. Gauze pads and rolls of all sizes. First aid tape. Advil. Even an instant ice pack.

He wasn't sure what all he needed, but this was a pretty good start until he could get Beth and the baby to a hospital. He closed the lid and unlocked the office door. He exited the easy way and immediately decided to go out the back rather than climb over the piles of debris between him and the office hallway.

He pushed through piles of fallen boxes filled with toilet paper and paper towels until he reached the first roll-up door. He reached for the chain and pulled downward, expecting it to shoot right up.

Nothing happened. He studied the mechanism and realized it was locked with a padlock. Willie moved over to the next door. It was also locked. He started to walk back toward the office, thinking he might be able to quickly locate the keys to the padlocks, when the building shuddered.

Then, ever so slightly, the ground began to shake. He felt a sense of urgency to get out of there, as he suspected an aftershock was about to hit them. He rushed to the office and then tried to follow the same path he'd taken over the debris pile when he entered.

He fell once, losing his footing on a broken shelf. His right leg fell through the middle of the rubble, causing him to lose his balance and topple backwards. He inadvertently allowed the first aid kit to slip out of his hand, cursing to himself as it dropped through the shelf. As the ground shook again, he was digging through the pile of products to retrieve it.

"Gotcha!" he exclaimed as his meaty hand gripped the handle. He pulled it up through the pile and began his climb toward the office doorway.

The ground shook again, and the building seemed to jump a little. It was a large, hundred-thousand-square-foot corrugated-steel structure. Yet the energy underneath the surface of the planet was able to push it around with ease.

Part of the ceiling collapsed toward the back near the loading docks. Willie just gave it a passing glance as he remained focused on getting out. A crashing sound was heard as if more of the roof was caving in. Daylight suddenly appeared to his rear, but he kept his eyes forward, pushing through the merchandise until he reached the door.

He paused momentarily to catch his breath after entering the hallway. As if it might protect him, Willie shut the steel door behind him and locked its deadbolt. It was an odd, symbolic gesture to block out the threat that lurked in the warehouse, threatening to devour the ground beneath him.

With another deep breath, he proudly strutted out of the building and back into the bright sunshine. He paused for just a moment to allow the warmth to soak into his face. Then the ground lurched upward knocking him off his feet.

Willie scrambled forward, digging and clawing at the gravel parking lot. He tried to scream but his voice was lost. His attempts to find his footing were in vain. He crawled to escape. The trembling earth kept knocking him down.

The planet emitted a wolfish growl as it ate. Hungrily. Ravenous. Voraciously devouring anything on its surface, greedily satisfying its gluttonous appetite. Inch after inch. Foot after foot. Its jaws opening wider and wider until it swallowed Willie Angel.

CHAPTER FIFTY-THREE

Sunday, December 23
Near Lake Cormorant, Mississippi

While Willie was away in search of medical supplies, Beth's uterus continued to contract. She was growing impatient. She gazed at her beautiful daughter one more time and then held her tight against her chest. She decided to speed up the delivery of her placenta. She reached down and gently pulled the cord while exerting downward pressure. With one final push, which caused her to wince in pain, it came out.

Every moment of her first delivery started to come back to her. She recalled the doctor examining her afterbirth to ensure it was intact. If it was torn or missing pieces, it was a sign of trouble. For Beth, there was nothing gross about examining the part of her body that had provided bed and board for her baby the last twenty-eight weeks. Symbolically, it represented the end of one stage of her baby's life and the beginning of a brand-new one.

Satisfied there were no problems, she gently wrapped it in one of the shop towels and rested it on the seat next to her. In a way, Beth was glad Willie wasn't around for this part of the birthing process. It was an intimate and private moment between a woman and her body.

Relief swept over her as she sat upright in the center of the back seat. And so did the chills. It was normal, as Beth recalled. She reached for the last of the high school mascot beach towels and draped it over their bodies. It wasn't much, yet it was comforting.

Beth stared at her child in wonderment as the color of the baby's extremities gradually turned from newborn blue to pretty-in-pink. She spoke in hushed tones, thanking God for keeping them safe, and telling her daughter how much she loved her.

She looked up from her baby in the direction of the Sigma Supply building. "What is taking you so long?" she muttered to herself. Beth turned her attention back to the bundle of joy swaddled beneath the layers of towels. She continued to rock her baby as she blissfully slept against her chest.

Beth glanced up again. What she saw, or didn't see, didn't register with her at first. The parts of her brain that interacted together to analyze what the eyes conveyed refused to believe the signals.

She rocked her baby twice and then froze. She looked back through the windshield. Her eyes grew wide and her mouth fell open.

It was gone.

The warehouse was gone.

It had been sucked into the earth. Swallowed whole.

Like it was never there.

She stared for several seconds in disbelief, oblivious to her surroundings.

Then, inexplicably, Anthony opened the car door and exited. He pushed it closed and walked in front of the hood until he stopped.

Stoic. Trancelike. Mesmerized by the sight of the ground disappearing in front of them.

Beth screamed his name. "Anthony!"

She looked all around her in disbelief. Where the warehouse building once stood, the ground was quickly collapsing. Water began to drain out of the fields, creating a waterfall effect. As the water poured over the edge, more of the rain-soaked soil joined it. It was more than a sinkhole. It was creating a void in the earth.

Beth reached over to the door handle to pull it open. It slid out of her moist hand. She frantically wiped her palm off on the blanket and tried again.

It was locked. She searched the door panel. There was no way to unlock it. She tried the other door, sliding across the blood-soaked seat. It was also locked.

The ground shook slightly.

"Anthony! Come back here!" The front seat windows were barely cracked. Could he hear her? He just stood there without responding. Did he see the earth crumbling?

Her baby started to cry. Beth clutched her tight. Maybe too tight. She tried to release her grip as she rocked her child. The tears began to flow.

Willie was probably dead. Sucked underground while trying to care for her. She'd killed him.

Waves of guilt and fear swept over Beth. Because ... well, just because of everything. She began breathing rapidly, and her rocking motion increased in speed.

She called her son's name out over and over again, but he didn't respond. Beth turned sideways in the cramped back seat. She kicked at the windows, but with each kick, she only propelled herself across the slippery, blood-covered seat to the other side.

She sat upright and centered herself facing forward. She groaned in pain as she pulled her knees as close to her belly as she could. She unleashed a hard double-kick at the back of the steel mesh separating her from the front seat.

"Arrrgh!" she screamed in utter pain as her insides contracted and seemed to shift.

The divider didn't budge.

She began bleeding profusely, but she had to try again.

Beth let out a primeval growl as she kicked the screen again. Her bloodied and bruised feet screamed back as they embedded in the mesh. Yet the screen didn't move.

She was angry now. She pounded at the divider with her free hand. Over and over again, cursing it at the top of her lungs.

It didn't move. It was built to withstand the most fervent of attacks, from drug-fueled rages to the distraught mother of a newborn.

Beth begged for help. She began sobbing and breathing rapidly again.

"Anthony," she plead, barely loud enough to be heard inside the car much less at the front bumper. The ground continued to shudder as the chasm widened. It had begun to eat the asphalt that was once Star Landing Road. The surrounding groundwater aided its advance, moistening the fields that had produced cotton for two hundred years so they could be easily devoured by the monster lurking beneath. Undermining the roadbed to allow the asphalt to crumble.

"Please, Anthony," she sobbed. Her face was covered with tears and mucus. She didn't bother to wipe it off with her free hand. She focused on comforting her crying baby.

The road was gone now.

The back entrance to the Shell station was next. Foot by foot, the gravel and asphalt fell downward in chunks. A telephone pole holding two transformers swayed back and forth like a drunk trying to walk the line after being pulled over.

Then it too succumbed to the hungry beast. The station's dumpster was next. It teetered on the edge of the abyss, and then, just like that, it was gone, too.

"Anthony!" Beth screamed in despair. "Honey, please come open the door for Momma. Puhleeze!"

Oddly, she started laughing as she lost control. This had to be a nightmare. After she gave birth to a miracle child, how could God take their lives away like this?

She closed her eyes and rocked her daughter. Waiting for the inevitable—joining Willie and, next, her son, in the depths below.

Then she heard it. A click followed by a rush of cool air engulfing her body. She immediately shivered, but she was suddenly completely lucid.

"Momma. Cold."

Beth twisted in her seat and there stood Anthony. Her little man. Her three-foot-tall, barely thirty-pound adorable child had opened the door.

The back of the gas station began to collapse as the ground ate the back corner of the building.

Beth clutched her baby and slid across the seat. She stepped out of the car and braced herself on the door until she could get her footing. Then she bent over and kissed Anthony.

"Good boy, Anthony. You are a very good boy."

He looked down at the ground and pointed. "Momma. Boo-boo."

Blood was dripping down Beth's legs.

The Shell station was slipping away, block by block. The chasm was less than a hundred feet away.

"Yes, honey. But I will be fine. Come on. I need you to get in the car."

She grabbed her jeans off the ground, hurriedly tossed them in the back seat, and pushed the rear door closed. She opened the front door for Anthony and kissed him on the cheek. He allowed her a slight smile and dutifully slid into the seat. He adjusted himself in place, reached for the seatbelt, and buckled it. It's something adults do several times a day. Anthony never had, until now.

Beth hustled around the front of the car with a watchful eye on the approaching rift. She stopped for a moment to search for Willie. When she saw the thousand-foot-wide opening in the earth, she knew he was gone.

She clutched her newborn and rushed into the car. She transferred her baby to her left arm, started the ignition, and burned rubber off the tires as she backed out of the parking lot onto the highway.

She backtracked on Highway 61 a quarter mile until she found a road that led to the east away from the river. It was covered in three or four inches of water, but the highway patrol car seemed to sail right over it.

Anthony found his DUPLO blocks, and he was back in his comfort zone. Her new daughter had fallen asleep against Beth's chest. Beth fought to slow her breathing, and then the voice of Willie entered her consciousness.

Breathe, Beth. Easy though. If you pass out, who's gonna tell me what to do?

Tears streamed down her face once again. She managed a smile.

"Thank you, Willie Angel."

CHAPTER FIFTY-FOUR

Sunday, December 23
Memphis, Tennessee

The guys moved toward town along the levee until they reached a raised walkway leading to a parking garage. They climbed up a single flight of stairs to reach the top deck of the garage. Jack led the way to the railing of the three-story structure, where he was the first to notice what was happening.

He had been in law school when devastating floods occurred in the Memphis area during the spring of 2011. A pair of major storm systems had rocked the Midwest, dumping record levels of rainfall along the Mississippi River watershed. Added to the heavy amounts of rain was the usual springtime snowmelt upstream, which caused the Mississippi's rivers and tributaries to rise to record levels.

The river reached its highest level, just over forty-eight feet, that May. Beale Street Landing, the Tom Lee Park, and most of Riverside Drive went underwater. That flood, however, was nothing compared to what was happening now. Jack didn't know what a hundred-year flood meant, or even the term thousand-year flood.

What was happening around them was far worse. The city, or what was left of it, was gradually being immersed in water.

"Well, driving is out of the question," said Tony jokingly.

"Looks like we might be swimming again," Jack added.

"That's marvelous. Which way?"

Jack took in the cityscape. "Damn, Tony. This is almost as bad as St. Louis. The roof of the FedEx Forum has collapsed. Beale Street is on fire. We should be able to see the Peabody Hotel from here."

Jack's mind raced as he recalled the timing of the quake in St. Louis. Had it been the same here? Jill and the kids would've been at the Halloran about that time.

His eyes darted around the Memphis cityscape. Water was eight to ten feet deep as far as he could see. When did the flooding start? Was it after the first quake? Or did it pour in during the second? He desperately wanted to make his way over there, but Tony's comments interrupted his thoughts and reminded him of why it wasn't possible.

Tony stood a little taller and pointed toward downtown. "The whole thing is gone. There's, like, this big void where all those buildings once stood. The rest are on fire."

Jack's chin dropped to his chest. His thoughts turned to Jill. The Peabody held so many memories of their life together. The void he saw where it once stood left a void in his heart.

He fought back his emotions and turned to Tony. "How 'bout the fires?" Jack asked as he pointed to several buildings engulfed in flames.

They walked around to the east side of the parking garage. "It seems the water levels are lower over that way. Higher elevation, I guess." He pointed toward the Medical District, the cluster of medical complexes near I-69, a major highway crossing through the east side of Memphis.

"That's the general direction we need to go. Let's try to make our way over to Union Avenue. That's a couple of miles on the other side of downtown. From there, I can take us to the house."

The guys went to the stairwell leading to the ground floor. That was where they entered the floodwaters. They were slightly warmer than the river itself. However, to their exhausted bodies, the water caused them to shiver once again.

They swam over a long parking lot and then arrived at a one-story industrial building. The old brick structure was still standing and not completely flooded. The guys hoisted themselves up over the roof's parapet wall. They walked across the flat roof until they reached the other side. Once there, they identified another building to swim towards.

They continued this approach of swimming to a building, walking across or through it until they reached the other side, and then swam to the next one.

"I feel like a bullfrog bouncing from one lily pad to another," said Tony as they took a break on their fourth rooftop.

"Did you notice how the water is still rising?" asked Jack. "I know these buildings are all different, but we're able to swim right onto the rooftops now."

Tony shrugged and looked around. "Really, it should be just the opposite. The farther inland we go, the lower the water levels. I figured we'd be sloshing through waist-deep water at this point."

"Me too," said Jack, somewhat dejected. He was tired, and they'd just gotten started. He looked toward the sky. The sun was on its downward trajectory, meaning they had three or four hours of daylight left at best.

Tony pointed at a long, rectangular-shaped building across another parking lot. "If we can make it to that one, it's like knocking out two lily pads at a time. Then it looks like there's another one across the street from it that takes us closer to FedEx Forum."

Jack took a deep breath and dove into the water again, converting to a breaststroke from the freestyle motion he'd used for the first few legs of their swimming relay. It was slower but less taxing on his weary muscles.

The guys made it to the first long, rectangular building, crawled through a broken window and walked through the destroyed interior until they reached the other end. The water levels were finally lower but still approached eight feet. They swam to the second building that was identical to the one they just walked through.

It was a slow process, but they were moving east to higher ground. However, darkness was threatening to make their job more complicated. A series of residential projects were next up for the guys. There were dozens of people seen looking out their windows, expecting a rescue effort to come their way. Many stood on rooftops, looking around for any signs of a boat or helicopter. There were none.

Before the men dove into the water to make another leg on their swim-walk journey, Jack asked Tony to wait a moment. He walked toward the north end of the building and looked back toward the Memphis Light Gas & Water building. He dropped his head and began to cry.

Tony caught up to him and turned Jack around to see his face. "Hey, man. What's up?"

Jack pointed in the direction of the Memphis Light building. Just beyond it, adjacent to a concrete parking garage, two structures were ablaze.

"Do you see the fires? Right of the parking garage?"

"Yeah."

"That's the Halloran Centre and the Orpheum Theatre. That's where Emily's rehearsal was Friday night. You know, when the quake hit."

"Shit," said Tony, pretty much summing it up. He tried to look on the bright side. "Hey. Hey. That was over thirty-six hours ago. These fires wouldn't be burning that long. And you know the water started rising with the second quake. At least, the worst of it. Right?"

Jack sniffled and wiped his nose on his soaked shirtsleeve. The pinpoint cotton dress shirt was in tatters. "Yeah. You're probably right."

"Not probably, man. I know I'm right. You need to believe that, too. Okay?"

Jack forced a smile and nodded. "Yeah. That fire just happened, I bet. Come on."

The two men turned in unison and once again dove into the water. They swam for two blocks until they reached a two-story auto repair service. Like all the other buildings in the area, the glass was broken out, and virtually the entire first floor of the business was flooded. They crawled into a window and walked through the company's workshop.

"Do you see anything that might float?" asked Tony. "A boat would be nice."

The guys carefully moved across the wood floor through rubble resulting from the ceiling collapse. Shelves full of tools and auto parts had been knocked over, littering the floor with everything from brake parts to wrenches. They reached the far end of the building having given up the search for any type of flotation device.

Suddenly, there was a crackling sound below them and a metallic scraping sound. Without warning and just seconds later, an explosion rocked the building.

In the center of the repair shop, the floor disappeared, and superheated flames burst upward behind them. Like so many of the older buildings in Downtown Memphis, this hundred-year-old structure had just been gutted by a natural gas explosion.

Jack and Tony ran for the windows to escape the flames. Then the second blast hit. The guys were thrown twenty feet against the outside wall of the brick structure, striking the masonry block with their upper bodies first. They were both knocked unconscious from the impact while the flames soared through the wood floor toward the ceiling like the fires of hell escaping a hole in the earth.

CHAPTER FIFTY-FIVE

Sunday, December 23
Atwood Residence
Cordova, Tennessee

The three of them changed into dry clothes and ate supper. Tate spent a few minutes in the Jeep, hoping to get an update on the second quake from WLAC in Nashville. They were no longer broadcasting. In fact, even the emergency warning system he found on an Oxford, Mississippi, radio station had been replaced by static. When he returned inside, he found his mom and sister standing on the back deck, watching the sun set over the horizon. It produced an orangish glow on the ever-rising lake.

"Is it gonna flood our house?" Emily had asked a logical question that was on all their minds. She was the only one brave enough to say it out loud.

Jill furrowed her brow and leaned over the rail to assess the distance between their basement and the rising water. "Honey, this doesn't make any sense. I was in college when we had a spring storm in May of 2011. It hit us just like a hurricane. The winds were over a hundred miles an hour. The rain flooded everything and left seventy percent of Shelby County without power for a couple of weeks. Granny said the water rose above the dock, but that was it."

Tate pointed down to where the dock pilings still stood. "You can barely see the posts at the surface. It's been rising steadily all afternoon."

Emily was growing concerned. "Do you think we need to leave?"

"I don't know, honey," her mom responded. Tate, however, had a more definitive plan.

"I don't think we should leave. Just move to higher ground."

"What do you mean?" Jill asked.

"First, think about it. When Dad and Uncle Tony make it home, they'll have no idea where we are. It's not like we can leave them a note. I mean, well, I guess we could, but I have a better idea."

"Tell us," said Emily.

"Mom, you said most of the homes you went to were vacant, right?"

"Well, yes. I suppose they just didn't want to answer the door. Or maybe they went to the grocery stores or something."

"Or," Tate continued, "maybe they're out of town. Or they evacuated. Or got caught, you know, in what happened downtown. Either way, their houses are empty. Like Britney's."

"You didn't speak to her?" said Jill inquisitively.

"No. I looked in all the windows and talked to her neighbor. Nothing, which goes back to my point. A lot of these homes are empty. I think we should consider finding a place nearby that's higher up than ours."

"Are you talking about breaking in?" Jill asked.

"You know, um, politely," he replied with a sly grin. "We'll knock first. If there's no answer, we'll go around back and gently break open a window to get inside."

"What about their alarm?" asked Emily innocently.

"No power. No alarm," replied Tate. "Hey, I don't like it, but it beats going off to a place where Dad and Tony can't find us. Besides, if the people come home, we'll just explain and apologize."

"Like 'Goldilocks and the Three Bears'?" asked Emily with a smile.

"Sure. Why not?" Tate rubbed the top of his sister's head. "Face it. They have food that will spoil and go to waste. We're gonna run out ourselves after tomorrow. We need fresh water, especially. I just think that if the house is in danger, we should look around us for help first. I don't hear any fire trucks or police cars, do you guys?"

"No," replied Jill. Then she suggested in all sincerity, "I suppose we could write them a note apologizing. Also, I could leave them a check for the broken window and the food we eat."

Tate shrugged and spread his hands apart. "See? We would be like refugees in need of food and shelter. That's a big difference from the looters running out of Dick's Sporting Goods with their arms full of Nikes."

The three were contemplative for a moment. The temperatures were dropping with the sun, and a chill swept over Jill's body, causing her to draw her jacket tight around her body.

Emily broke the silence and turned to her mother. "If we have to, right, Mom?"

Jill looked into her daughter's eyes and smiled. She'd stand in front of a speeding bus to protect her children.

"You betcha."

Jill wandered back to the deck rail and watched the last of the sun drop below the horizon. Sunday night was about to pass without her husband. She wondered where he could be.

PART V

I'LL BE HOME FOR CHRISTMAS

Never, never, never give up. Let the power of love guide you to the ones you love.

CHAPTER FIFTY-SIX

Monday, Christmas Eve
Fayette County
East of Memphis, Tennessee

Beth was exhausted from giving birth, lack of sleep, and loss of blood. Everything she passed on the highway had either been destroyed, shuttered, or looted. Her heart sank as the Memphis skyline normally seen at night was dark except for fires burning in the high-rise buildings. She imagined the destruction was worse near the riverfront.

As she approached the Tennessee state line, she got a second wind as she realized Cordova wasn't that much farther. Her excitement was doused minutes later when highway safety barriers had been erected, forcing all traffic to exit the interstate and head east. Emergency vehicles were allowed, but she was in a Mississippi Highway Patrol car that was technically stolen, and its trooper's whereabouts were unknown.

She fiddled with the patrol car's scanner and emergency radio, but all she could hear was static. Fortunately, the GPS worked, and she was able to find her way east of the city after backtracking into Northern Mississippi.

The landscape along the state line lent the appearance that a massive hand holding a spiderweb-shaped stamp had crushed the earth. Long lines of relatively thin cracks in the ground, compared to the canyon created near Lake Cormorant, weaved their way along the roads, sidewalks, and yards for miles. At times, whole sections of road had been forced upward on one side, with the back side of the miniature ridge sinking below the surface.

Her navigation consisted of following a road to the east, turning northward for as far as the ground would allow, then zigzagging across Fayette County immediately to the east of Shelby County.

Beth was relieved that her bleeding had stopped. She'd give anything for a bag of ice to ease her swelling, followed by a warm bath. She'd already prepared herself for the fact that neither of those things would be available to her at the house.

Moreover, she was hungry. All she could think about were those hot tamales from the White Front Café floating around a flooded cotton field. Anthony had slept throughout the drive into Tennessee. Unless the ground shook again, she doubted he'd wake up before she arrived at the house.

As for her gorgeous baby, she'd awakened once as Beth was driving along a country road east of Macon. Beth thought she could make her way to the house within thirty minutes, but her daughter, who'd found her voice, wailed until she pulled over to nurse her. She was concerned for her newborn because she was premature. She'd been told babies born earlier than thirty-two weeks were rarely breastfed. However, she didn't have much of a choice under the circumstances.

It forced Beth to catch her breath and assess her situation. She kept reminding herself women had given birth throughout the millennia without birthing suites in fancy hospitals surrounded by a team of medical professionals. The pioneer women in covered wagons did it routinely.

She laughed to herself as she envisioned Daniel Boone's wife screaming for an epidural while giving birth. Heck, her husband was probably off exploring Kentucky or Indiana with his brother Squire anyway.

Once she reached Macon, it was a straight shot to the house. Growing up, Beth had spent a lot of time on the farms of East Shelby County and into Fayette County. Back then, I-269, the long interstate bypass that bisected the farms east of Memphis, didn't exist. It was very rural and suited Beth. Despite the dark conditions, she recognized the farms along Macon Road that led west toward Cordova.

She was able to see Gray's Creek lapping just below the Macon Road bridge. The water had never been that high in her lifetime. She shook her head in amazement as she thought of the flooding she'd witnessed in the last forty-eight hours. The Mississippi River seemed to be expanding to the size of the Great Lakes.

Beth wheeled her way through the S-curves as she approached the side street marking the front of the neighborhood. As she traveled west, the destruction to the buildings became more prevalent. She turned into the entrance with trepidation, as the first home she drove by had been reduced to a pile of bricks.

There was no sign of life, although she wasn't surprised by that at this hour. It was after midnight. She chuckled to herself, causing her baby to rise and fall on her belly. She hoped her sister or Jack didn't come to the door with a rifle. She wasn't sure if she could handle any more drama.

Beth's concern immediately changed as the headlights of the car washed across the front of the house. Jack's Jeep was parked out front, something she suspected was out of the ordinary. There were no cars in the driveway, but they might've been parked in the garage. There were no sources of light inside, whether from lanterns or candles. Again, she wasn't surprised by that.

She slowly pulled forward and placed the patrol car in park. She turned off the ignition and allowed the motor to wind down. The ticking sound of the hot engine filled the night air. She took several deep breaths and allowed the tears to flow down her face. She'd made it.

Beth exited the car, and cold air immediately hit the lower half of her body. She was still half naked and realized she'd never put her maternity jeans back on. She clutched her baby to her chest and rushed around the back of the car to retrieve her jeans from the rear floorboard. She slid them on and adjusted them on her hips.

Out of habit, she made herself more presentable although her shirt was covered with dried blood, as were her hands and arms.

"Okay, Anthony. Let's go see who's home. Okay?"

The sleepy boy rubbed both eyes with his tiny fists. He was barely awake, so he didn't put up a fight as she led him along the sidewalk leading to the front door.

She paused and studied the door as well as the entire front of the house. It was in remarkably good condition from what she could see. Some of the upper windows had broken out, and several bricks had fallen from the box window in front, but that was it.

Clutching her newborn in one hand and pulling Anthony along with the other, she walked to the front door. She gently knocked on the door so as not to startle anyone.

She stepped back a foot or so and waited.

After half a minute, nobody answered.

She knocked more forcefully this time, reminding herself everyone was probably asleep.

She heard movement inside and muffled voices, yet nobody immediately answered the door.

Beth's anxiety shot through the roof. She studied the door handle and the downstairs windows. Maybe someone broke in? They were trying to decide what to do.

She gripped Anthony's hand tighter and backed away from the door to the edge of the front steps. She steadied her nerves and prepared to bolt for the car.

CHAPTER FIFTY-SEVEN

Monday, Christmas Eve
Atwood Residence
Cordova, Tennessee

"Mom, Mom, wake up!" Tate spoke softly as he shook his mother awake. The fire had burned out, and the house was dark. Tate had heard the sound of a car slowly approach the driveway, and he immediately recognized the appearance of headlights washing across the front of the house. His bedroom was upstairs, and he'd seen the headlight effect many times when his dad came home late from a trip.

"Wut. What is it?" she asked in her half-sleepy state. Emily began to stir and shot up on her mattress.

Tate scrambled to his feet and found the rifle he'd left leaning against the front doorjamb. They hadn't experienced any looters in their neighborhood, but after they'd observed what was happening at the stores near I-40, they thought it would be a good idea to have one of their rifles at the ready.

"What's going on?" asked Emily.

Tate held the gun pointed down and stuck his right eye to the peephole in the door. From that perspective, the driveway was out of view.

He half-turned to respond, "I don't know. A car just pulled into the driveway."

Emily crawled across the mattresses spread across the floor, rushed around the sofa, and climbed onto the cushion of the window box seat. She impetuously peeked through the curtains without consideration of the possible consequences. The moonlight provided just enough light to reflect off the car that had arrived. She sat back on her legs and slowly released the curtain so it closed.

"What is it, honey?" asked Jill.

"Um, Mom. It's the police."

Jill immediately broke out into tears, assuming the worse. There was only one reason for the police to pay them a visit at this time of night, and that was to notify the next of kin of a death. Her tears and sniffles elicited a similar response from Emily.

Jill wiped her nose and face. She stood a little taller in an attempt to will herself to look strong and in control.

"Kids, I need you both to go into the kitchen, please."

"But, Mom," Emily and Tate whined in unison.

"No arguments. And, Tate, put that gun away."

He sighed and set it back against the wall where it would rest behind the door when opened. Neither he nor Emily moved toward the kitchen. Jill had to ask again.

"Emily, Tate, I mean it. Kitchen, please. I'll deal with this."

She began to sniffle again, and she tried to nonchalantly wipe away her tears. Tate took Emily by the hand, and the children sheepishly walked around their bedding past the Christmas tree until they were just inside the kitchen entry. They both turned around. Jill took a deep breath. She wasn't going to force the issue. They could stand there and eavesdrop if they wanted to.

There was a gentle knock at the door. It wasn't the expected *thump-thump-thump*, this-is-the-cops-open-up knocking. It was the kind of knock from someone who had bad news to deliver in the middle of the night.

She sighed and tried to gather herself. She summoned all her inner strength by providing herself words of encouragement.

Be strong. C'mon, Jill. You're in charge. Be strong.

The knocking repeated. More forceful this time. It was impatient. An authoritative, this-is-your-last-chance kinda knock.

She emitted a heavy sigh, wiped her face one last time, and dried her hands on her pants.

"Who is it?" she asked loud enough for the visitors to hear.

"It's me," a familiar female voice replied.

Jill's heart leapt out of her chest. The tears of sorrow magically transformed into tears of joy. She nervously fumbled with the bolt lock and handle to open the door. Finally, through the tears and the nervousness and the joyous excitement, she flung open the door.

Her eyes grew wide as the spittin' image of Sissy Spacek from the Stephen King movie *Carrie* stood in front of her, covered in blood, holding Anthony's hand and a rolled-up towel tightly against her chest.

The two women stared at each other for several seconds that felt like minutes. Finally, Beth broke the silence.

"Um, can we come in?"

Emily shrieked and yelled, "Aunt Beth! You made it!"

She left Tate's side and rushed past her mother. She jerked to a stop before crashing into her aunt.

Beth winced. "Um, I had my baby."

"Holy crap!" hollered Tate from the kitchen.

"Mom, isn't this great?" asked Emily as she tugged at Jill's sweatshirt sleeve.

Jill was frozen. Initially, she was overwhelmed with joy the police weren't there to inform her she was a widow. Then the sight of her sister covered with blood and cradling a newborn made her wonder if this was just one more chapter in a nightmarish dream.

Finally, she got her wits about her and wrapped her arms around her sister. The two sisters let out their emotions, allowing the waterworks to pour out of their eyes in buckets.

Emily took charge and reached for Anthony's hand. The two had always had a good relationship. Anthony enjoyed Emily's company and seemed to trust her as much as he did his mother.

Tate came to gently hug his aunt. Then he spoke in a soft voice so he didn't disturb the sleeping newborn. "I'll start a fire to warm the house up."

Jill regained her role as the general of the Atwood clan. "Candles, too. Everywhere, please. Also, Tate, there's enough water in the water heater to run Beth a bath. Will you start that, please? Also, fire up the grill. I want two pots of water boiling immediately."

Tate spun around and hustled to the kitchen. They'd hooked up a water hose to the drain spigot at the bottom of their eighty-gallon water heater. He'd fill the pots up and start them boiling. Then he'd start filling up the tub even though the water would be room temperature at best, which was around fifty at the moment. He'd keep filling the tub with hot water until it could be tolerated.

"Thank you," Beth said through her sniffles. "I'm a hot mess."

Jill laughed. "You gave birth in the wild. You are my hero."

After a laugh, a wave of sadness washed over Beth. "I had help. I'll tell you about it later. I'd really like to get out of these clothes."

Jill lovingly wrapped her arm around her waist and led her down the dark hallway to the master bedroom. Tate had already rushed back there to light up several Christmas candles, which cast a warm, orangish glow throughout the room.

"You'll get to open your presents early for this miracle," said Jill. "I also have a plush robe for you from Barefoot Dreams. It's divine."

"You tried it on?" asked Beth.

"No, of course not. I bought one for myself. We can be twinsies!"

Beth started laughing and then grimaced. "It hurts to laugh, so try not to be funny."

"Hard to do, but I'll give it my best shot." Jill carefully hugged her sister and kissed her on the cheek.

Beth stopped and turned back toward the family room. "Have you heard from the guys?"

Jill pouted and shook her head. "No. Nothing. Beth, it was bad downtown. Bridges collapsed, and the river's flooding like I've never seen before. They could be on the other side with no way across."

Jill held out her hands, and Beth turned her baby over to someone else for the first time since Willie lovingly presented her. The two sisters sat on the side of the bed next to one another while Jill gently rocked the baby. The candlelight flickered, reflecting their facial features and causing the tears on their cheeks to glisten. She turned her head toward Beth.

"I wanna see her."

"She's pink," said Beth, causing herself to chuckle and wince. The resulting pain was her own fault, which oddly made it even funnier. She nodded toward the bundle of shop towels. "She's in there somewhere. I hope."

Jill carefully unfurled the towels, scowling as she did. She'd look over at Beth and then remove a little more.

"Aren't these the kind of rags they use—" she began before Beth finished her sentence.

"In a gas station? Yes. I gave birth in the back seat of a Mississippi Highway Patrol car while parked at a Shell station in the middle of an earthquake."

Jill's eyes grew wide and she shook her head in disbelief. "Great. My niece is gonna be a grease monkey who'll live her life in and out of jail because she likes to shake, rattle, and roll too much."

Beth burst out laughing and then moaned in pain. "Please, you gotta stop. We should be miserable right now."

"Nope. It's Christmastime. There'll be no sad faces at Christmas."

CHAPTER FIFTY-EIGHT

Monday, Christmas Eve
Atwood Residence
Cordova, Tennessee

Tate stepped up as the man of the house at that moment. In addition to rebuilding the fire in the family room, he built one in the master bedroom as well. He explained to his mom that as soon as the sun came up, he'd go forage for more firewood and kindling. He twisted his back to determine if the bruise he'd received while running through the woods still hurt. It did, but it also reminded him of the cord of firewood he'd crashed into.

He also kept the hot water coming and suggested he use their Igloo and Yeti coolers to keep the water warm so Jill could combine it with the room-temperature water gradually. He was displaying common sense in a survival situation that impressed both his mom and his aunt.

When the fire was putting out warmth and the water was ready, Jill shut the bedroom door to provide Beth some privacy from the kids. She slowly undressed her sister by the fire and led her into the bathroom.

Jill assisted Beth as she eased her way into the bathtub so that the colder-than-usual water wouldn't be too much of a shock to her body. While Beth got acclimated and began to wash herself in the shallow water, Jill retrieved an ironstone washbasin that was used as décor in her bedroom. She wiped it out with a clean towel and then poured warm water into it. She closed the toilet seat and set the basin on top so Beth could watch.

Once again, she unwrapped Beth's baby girl. She slowly set her into basin of shallow, warm water and lovingly wiped her off with a soft, Gerber washcloth that was part of Beth's Christmas presents. The newborn wiggled and kicked, seemingly enjoying the warm, gentle touch. Or perhaps she was glad to get the dried blood off her pristine pink skin.

Jill finished her niece's first baby sponge bath. Afterwards, she wrapped her in a pink, plush hoodie-blanket combination that matched the robe she'd bought for Beth. She carefully placed the content baby on a pile of pillows and blankets near the fire, carefully positioning her so she couldn't roll over and suffocate. She then turned her attention to her sister.

While Beth washed her body, Jill washed her hair. She tilted Beth's head back and slowly poured the warm water over her long hair until it was wet. She lathered it with Pantene and gave her a gentle head massage as she worked the shampoo in. Without making it obvious, Jill lovingly removed bits of dried blood off her head and shoulders. After a rinse, she repeated the shampooing process until both sisters were satisfied that Beth could declare herself to be a *new woman*.

Finally, it was time for her to wrap herself in the plush robe Jill had purchased as her Christmas present. Jill had hung it over a chair by the fire to warm it. Beth had never been so pampered in her life. During those fifteen very intimate, touching minutes, the two barely said a word. They didn't shed tears. They didn't allow themselves to express worry over their husbands. It was all about Beth and her baby girl.

Jill helped her sister to bed. She propped her up slightly against the headboard and rested her baby on her chest. She tucked them in. As she left the bedroom, she promised to look in later to make sure the fire was burning and the candles stayed lit.

It was time for mother and daughter to bond with one another in comfort and safety.

CHAPTER FIFTY-NINE

Monday, Christmas Eve
Memphis, Tennessee

The rising floodwaters that chased them across downtown Memphis, threatening to kill them, were also responsible for saving their lives. As the searing hot fire engulfed the ceiling of the ground floor, it began to heat the wood-plank upper floor. The fire began in the middle and immediately began to spread in all directions. With the guys lying unconscious against the wall, they were as far away from the fire's flashpoint as possible. As the fire continued, the floodwaters rose and doused it from below, leaving charred remains except for ten feet of flooring where the men were.

Jack was the first to recover from his semiconscious state. He'd been dreaming, imagining a big dog smothering him in wet, slobbery kisses. What should have been a happy dream was off somehow.

They were in their backyard overlooking the lake. The kids were playing. Jill was setting the picnic table, and he was supposed to be cooking the burgers and hot dogs. Instead, he was lying on his side with this overly friendly pup hovering over him, licking his face, while his pants smoldered from catching fire.

He began to come out of his stupor, and his dreamlike visions turned to reality. The rising water had breached the huge hole in the floor and was now washing up against them. His eyes opened wide in surprise, and he tried to force himself upright.

That was when he discovered the burns on his right leg. The flames had generated shooting embers from the old, dry wood. Some of them had landed on Jack's leg and caught his pants on fire. His flesh had burned on his shin from the top of his ankle to just below his kneecap, the thinnest and most sensitive skin on his leg.

"Arrrgh!" he screamed as his mind woke up and the burnt skin sent signals to it. He reached for his leg to see how bad it was burned, and then the post-concussion trauma to his head revealed itself. He lifted both of his hands to his temples and then his scalp in search of blood. The crown of his skull had a huge knot on it and was very tender to the touch.

Jack tried to get his bearings in order to remember what had happened. His vision was blurry as he looked around the dark room. The early morning sunshine showed through a hole in the ceiling created by the shooting flames propelled by the pressure of the natural gas line. Even that little bit of light hurt his head.

"Tony," he muttered at first. Then he got serious. "Tony!"

Jack fought the pain and pulled himself up using the windowsill as a crutch. He didn't care that his hands were cut on a sliver of glass. That was the least of his worries at the moment.

He felt his way along the wall, moving slowly to mind his footing. Most of the floor was missing, and the area where he walked seemed spongy.

He inched along until his left foot kicked Tony's body. Groaning in pain, he dropped to one knee and then the other. He blindly felt around Tony's upper body until he found his face. Jack gently touched his neck to feel for a pulse. Then he reached over his body and scooped some water in his hands. He carefully wiped Tony's face and neck with the cool water to revive him.

It worked. Like Jack, he awoke with a start, shooting straight up until he was sitting upright. Then his head introduced him to the battering it took.

"Holy shit, that hurts."

"I've got one, too," said Jack. "How are your arms and legs?"

Tony wiggled them and then rolled his neck around on his shoulders. "All there. You?"

"I've got a helluva burn on my right leg. At some point my pants leg caught on fire."

Tony tried to help despite the pain he was in. "Let me take a look."

"Not now. We don't have time. We only have about eight or ten feet of floor, and the water's coming in. It rose at least four feet while we were knocked out."

"What time is it?" asked Tony.

Jack tapped the glass face of his iWatch. "Don't know. Batteries died at some point on my watch and the cell phone. Right after dawn, maybe."

Tony stood and glanced out the window. He looked upward to see if there was a higher point in the building to evade the water. The limited light didn't offer him much of a view. He turned to Jack.

"Can you swim? How bad is it?"

"It's the shinbone."

"Ouch," said Tony. "You couldn't have picked a worse area. Can you bend your leg? At least enough to swim?"

"I don't have a choice," Jack answered truthfully. "We've gotta get out of here because I don't trust this floor, or the ceiling either. Maybe the cool water will help relieve the pain."

Tony bent over and helped Jack to his feet. He turned to the glass window and carefully broke out the jagged, broken panes that were sticking up from the windowsill.

"We'll head toward the hospitals and get you treated."

"They're in low-lying areas and are probably flooded. If we keep going due east, the ground rises. There are some retail stores and offices farther out on Union Avenue. If we can keep going before the river floods more, I'll be all right."

Tony was skeptical, but Jack was right. They had no choice. "After you. Age before beauty, right?"

Jack laughed. "Did I mention part of your hair singed?"

"Shit! Really?"

Despite the pain, Jack crawled through the window and dove into the dark water. His leg bristled at the first contact with the cold water, and then it seemed to respond. The pain subsided, and his swimming pace picked up. The guys were back to lily-pad hopping.

CHAPTER SIXTY

Monday, Christmas Eve
Memphis, Tennessee

For hours, the guys made their way from building to building along Union Avenue. As predicted, the hospitals and medical centers were either flooded with water or flooded with people whose injuries were far worse than Jack's. The Methodist University Hospital was able to see patients on their second floor, but Jack was told it might be many hours before he could be treated.

The guys persevered, pushing through the pain until, gradually, the water levels dropped to five feet deep. They were able to alternate between swimming and wading through the water until soon it was only waist deep.

It was around one o'clock on Christmas Eve when they came across a Walgreens drugstore. The building was still standing, and remarkably the concrete walls appeared to be stable. The glass-pane double doors were shattered, which allowed them access to enter.

Tony asked Jack's opinion. "Everything is probably floating around in there. We can fumble through the store until we locate some burn gel, Neosporin, and some type of bandages. It's worth a try, right?"

Jack nodded and started to hobble toward the door when three young males darted out of the building with their shirts pulled up to their chests. The long-sleeve shirts resembled a kangaroo's pouch. Only, their pouches were full of prescription drug bottles.

They brushed past Jack, causing him to lose his balance. Pain rushed through his leg, causing him to get angry. He almost yelled at the men but caught himself. *They've got their job to do, and we've got ours.*

"Okay. No problem, gentlemen. There's plenty for everybody, right?"

One of the men glanced back at him and scowled. Then they scurried off in different directions with their loot.

"Let me go in first, Jack. And I'll do the talking if necessary. Okay?"

"Be my guest," said Jack, still perturbed at the men's behavior.

He gestured for Tony to enter the doors. They had to duck under the aluminum push bar that crossed the center windowless frame. Once inside, they recognized the daunting task ahead of them. Thousands of products once perfectly arranged on the store's shelves were now floating on top of the water like the last remaining Cheerios in a half-full bowl of milk.

The guys stopped for a moment and considered abandoning their quest. Jack's leg began to throb, and he thought about the bacteria from the water easing into his wound. He decided to begin the search.

"Let's start near the first aid products. Maybe the stuff didn't float far. Remember, we need gauze, Neosporin, and any kind of burn-relief gel. I know that's a long shot. If we can't find that, we'll grab a couple of beers out of the refrigerators if there are any left."

The guys laughed and began the search. Forty-five minutes and half a dozen more looters later, Jack and Tony emerged from Walgreens with several tubes of Polysporin ointment, two large boxes of gauze pads, and a couple of rolls of Kinesio tape generally used to protect athletes from exacerbating their muscle injuries. Jack thought it would hold the gauze in place while keeping pressure on his wound to reduce bleeding.

Outside, they tore the lower half of Jack's pants leg off. They cleaned and dressed the wound and protected it with the gauze bandages. The tightness of the Kinesio tape made Jack's leg stiff, so he had to hobble as he walked. The pressure bandage did prevent swelling and bleeding, and eased the pain somewhat. The forty-ounce bottle of Olde English 800 malt liquor helped, too.

By the time they'd made their way east on Union Avenue for another mile, they were in better spirits and ready to get home. Then they hit a lucky break.

Outdoors Inc. was a local business founded in 1974 when two avid paddlers and outdoor enthusiasts joined forces to sell outdoor equipment and apparel for a variety of activities. Jack was a regular customer of their location in Cordova but had never visited this store until now.

When they came upon the small nondescript building, the walls were still standing, but like so many other storefronts, the windows were shattered. The floodwaters had only reached the sidewalk entryway adjoining the parking lot, but had not yet entered the store. To the left of the store's building was a rack containing five brightly colored canoes wrapped around and around with chain. A padlock secured it to the frame of the rack.

Tony pointed at the canoes as they approached the largest of the plate-glass windows. "How much would we have paid for one of those things yesterday?"

"All the gold in Zurich?" replied Jack, making reference to Tony's shrewd, if not lucky, investment move on their behalf. He pointed to his right. Adjacent to Outdoors Inc. was their sister store that sold Cannondale bicycles. "So what's a bicycle worth to ya? It'll make the last dozen miles go a lot faster."

Tony turned to the west. The sun would be setting over the

Memphis skyline, which now smoldered with black smoke coupled with the occasional flames of fire dancing upward.

"I'll leave them my credit card," he said with a laugh. "Let's go shopping." He led the way through the window, gingerly stepping over the jagged glass protruding up from the aluminum frame.

Jack joined him and marveled at what he saw. "Stuff's knocked around, but it looks intact."

Tony headed toward the clothing racks, which had spilled their contents onto the floor. "I never understood why looters went straight for the drugs, alcohol, and especially the electronics. Do they honestly think those big screens are gonna do them any good right now?"

Jack hobbled forward and leaned down to pick up a pair of bicyclist leggings. "No, but these will. If we're gonna ride through this forty-degree cold air, let's do it in these Gore-Tex, um, tights?"

Tony laughed. He threw a snug-fitting cycling jersey at Jack. The pullover jersey featured screen art that read "never underestimate an old man with a bicycle."

"Here. This suits you."

Jack caught the jersey and held it up to read the inscription. "Very funny. I was thinking more about this." He showed Tony a fleece hoodie.

Tony gave him a thumbs-up and moved deeper into the store. "Jackpot! Pardon the pun. Hey, we've got shoes. Hiking. Biking. Running. You name it. Socks, too."

Jack let out a hoot and stiff-legged his way to the back of the store. The guys were in great spirits as they picked out their outfits and changed clothes. They resembled a couple of stylish city boys headed to Vail, Colorado, for a weekend.

Next, they moved into the darkened space where the bicycles were displayed. Neither of them had ridden a bicycle in many years. The Cannondale line offered a variety of bicycles, but the guys both chose mountain bikes. The wide tires and additional suspension would be useful if they found roads blocked or flooded. Before they left, they loaded backpacks with camping gear, first aid kits, and a tire pump in case they ran across a problem on the way home.

It was after four by the time they left the store. And in those two hours, the floodwaters had risen another foot and began to wash throughout the interior.

CHAPTER SIXTY-ONE

Monday, Christmas Eve
East Memphis, Tennessee

The guys were riding east on Walnut Grove Road toward Cordova. They'd just passed the Galloway Golf Course on their right when they entered a stretch flanked by stately homes with once-magnificent mature oak trees lining the four-lane street. Many of them had been uprooted and thrown in all directions, and parts of the road had buckled. They soon found themselves walking their bikes through the trees, even carrying them at times to make their way over the massive trunks.

Then, remarkably, the quarter mile of Walnut Grove Road that looked like a war zone suddenly turned into a pristine street that appeared untouched. The only thing out of the ordinary from any other sunny day was the throngs of people milling about in front of the St. Mary's Episcopal Church.

The guys walked their bikes through the crowds of men, women, and children—refugees who had traveled on foot, seeking help. The scene in front of Second Baptist Church and Independent Presbyterian down the street was similar. Hundreds if not thousands of people, faces filled with despair, their bodies bloodied and battered, were desperately begging for assistance.

Each of the churches deployed a small army of volunteers and parishioners. They were sorting people according to their immediate needs and then guiding them onto the church property. Those seeking medical attention were given first priority. Single mothers with young children were given their own area away from the rest. The newly homeless residents were told their options for local shelters that hadn't been destroyed by the earthquake.

The hungry? Well, the hungry were promised that the church would do what it could for them. Everyone was hungry. As they politely pushed their way through the crowd, they listened to people exchange their stories.

Some had watched their homes and businesses crumble before their eyes. Others were in a state of shock over the loss of loved ones. There were tales of flooding in places that had never flooded before. Some had seen strange lights and weird flames shooting out of the ground. The fires frightened many because they were out of control. Most questioned the lack of notice for either of the earthquakes.

How could they not know?

Why weren't we warned?

Where is the government to help us?

As they walked through, Jack scanned the crowd for any familiar faces. Not that he wished something had befallen them. Secretly, without admitting it to Tony, he was looking for his family. After what he'd seen and what they'd been through, he didn't care if their home was still standing. As long as Jill and the kids were safe, that was all that mattered.

They passed Mullins United Methodist, and a quarter mile later, the foot traffic began to dissipate. The combination of riding and walking helped Jack work out the soreness resulting from the explosion at the auto repair building the night before. Also, this was an area he was familiar with, and as a result, his mind was beginning to become reinvigorated. Home was practically in sight. They began riding again with renewed energy until they ran into another obstacle that slowed their progress.

Running from northwest to southeast across the eastern part of Shelby County was the Wolf River. Ordinarily, it was a muddy river that was approximately a hundred feet wide. It was the type of waterway that commuters and locals traveled across every day without giving it a second thought. Today was different.

After the earthquakes, the river had flooded and consumed the low-lying areas all around it. The water encroached up the embankment holding Humphreys Boulevard, but anything lower in elevation was flooded. Walnut Grove Road extended over the river, providing a direct route to the house. However, the bridge abutments had been compromised, and it was at risk of collapsing. The police had closed the thoroughfare to all traffic, including pedestrians.

The guys had to travel south along Wolf River Boulevard and then ride parallel to the river into Germantown. From there, they could make their way into Cordova. However, it was entering Germantown that threw the guys for a loop, literally.

They'd just travelled across an overpass above a swollen creek feeding the Wolf River when floodwaters covered the road. The standing water was six to eighteen inches deep in areas, but because the bicycle tires didn't have the same buoyancy effect as a car's, the guys were able to ride through it.

Jack pointed to the Germantown Welcome Sign and provided Tony a thumbs-up. He explained they were only a few miles from the house and could still be there by dark. Excited, he pedaled faster and sped ahead of Tony. Tony started laughing, and the two grown men suddenly found themselves reverting back to the twelve-year-old versions of themselves, racing through the water, challenging one another to go faster.

Jack was a full bike length ahead of Tony when he ran into a submerged streetlight and its steel pole. The quake had dislodged it from its concrete mount and toppled it across the road. The water had covered it from view.

Jack's front tire struck the pole hard, popping it and bending it inward. The sudden stop of his momentum sent him flying over the handlebars until he rolled over and over again on the flooded asphalt.

Tony suffered a similar fate although he managed to apply the brakes and slide into the pole before it threw him sideways off the bike. He suffered significant scrapes and bruises. Jack might have broken his wrist and reinjured the leg hurt from the gas explosion.

The guys groaned in pain. Jack pushed himself upright in the floodwaters and gripped his wrist. He rocked back and forth. His face contorted in agony. The amount of pain caused Jack to assume his wrist was broken.

Tony stood and brushed off the bits of asphalt embedded in his clothing and wiped the blood off his elbows with the standing water.

"Man, I think it's broken," said Jack as Tony approached him. He tried to hold it up for Tony to see, but the pain forced him to bring it back in front of his stomach. Tony knelt to a crouch and patted Jack on the knee.

"Can I take a look?"

Jack let go of his wrist and raised his right arm in front of Tony.

Tony made eye contact with him. "Jack, this is probably gonna hurt."

"It can't be any worse than that bomb blast last night."

"Except you're gonna be conscious for this," said Tony with a smile.

"Good point. Go ahead, Doc."

Tony, who'd played a year of football at LSU before focusing on school, was familiar with sports injuries of all types. He gently took Jack's wrist in his hands and ran the tips of his fingers all around it.

"Good news, so far," he began. "I don't feel any protruding bones. It could still be a hairline fracture, but it's definitely not a complete break. You've got a little swelling. Let's check your range of motion. Slowly rotate your wrist. If you can't do it, I'll help. Give me a pain level on a scale of 1 to ten, and be honest."

Jack barely rotated his wrist and groaned. "Ten. Ten!"

Tony rolled his eyes and smiled. "You didn't even do it," he said as he took Jack's wrist in his hands again. "Loosen up and let me do it."

Jack exhaled and his arm went limp. Tony slowly rotated the wrist, and Jack winced but endured the motion.

"Okay. Okay," said Jack as he tugged his wrist back to his belly. "That's enough for a diagnosis."

Tony stood and walked behind Jack to help him stand to get out of the water. "Was your pain sharp and stabbing. Or was it—?"

Jack cut him off. "It was more of a throbbing, pulsating pain."

"I think it's just sprained. There are no bones poking out, and it doesn't look crooked or anything. Trust me, I had a broken wrist years ago. If it was broken, you'd know it."

Jack shook his head side to side and began hobbling on his reinjured right leg toward Germantown. "I'm too old for this shit."

"We all are," added Tony.

CHAPTER SIXTY-TWO

Monday, Christmas Eve
USGS
Golden, Colorado

It was Christmas Eve on the calendar, not that most people cared at the moment. It was day four of the worst natural disaster in the history of modern mankind. From the Gulf of Mexico to Hudson Bay in Canada, earthquakes continued to rumble across the center of North America.

Power outages and lost communications extended outward from the Mississippi River for a hundred miles. Rescue and recovery efforts were stymied by the continuous shaking, causing roads to buckle and chasms to open. Flooding was widespread as the aquifers were emptied onto the surface of the planet, and the Gulf of Mexico poured upstream along the Mississippi, bringing brackish waters to low-lying areas.

Dr. Lansing had resigned herself to the fact there was no end in sight. Every time she thought the seismic activity had calmed, a new hot spot opened up in the seventeen states directly impacted by the series of earthquakes.

The nation had come to a standstill. Within the areas directly affected by the series of earthquakes, survivors tried to hold on until assistance arrived, not realizing help was not coming any time soon. The president's decision to send in FEMA resources and the National Guard during the predawn hours of Sunday had been met with the second M8+ quake centered near Memphis. Personnel and supplies were lost during the earthquake and the aftermath as the river sent floodwaters rushing into populated areas.

Survivors had no detailed information about what was happening around them, much less within the disaster zones throughout the Central U.S. They waited, sure their government would be able to bring them food and water or provide the displaced a roof over their heads.

The NEIC team continued to work with little sleep and short breaks. They processed the data and disclosed it to Dr. Lansing, who took over the modeling and analysis. She in turn delivered it to the USGS headquarters in Virginia via satellite uplink. All transcontinental communication lines had been cut. The country had been severed in two for all intents and purposes. The ability to cross the Mississippi by vehicle was limited to a single bridge in Minneapolis and the Huey P. Long Bridge in Baton Rouge. Others had either collapsed, been so damaged as to be rendered unsafe, or were flooded by the rising waters.

The nation was in the throes of a heart-wrenching, devastating catastrophe that was too incredible to comprehend.

A gentle tap at the door brought Dr. Lansing back to the present as she tried desperately to push out of her mind the death toll numbers she'd just seen from her FEMA Daily Operations Briefing, the largest of its kind since she'd joined the USGS.

"Mum, you have a phone call."

"Oliver, now's not a good time."

"I think you need to take this one. It's the president."

"Come on," she said with a scowl. "It's not the time for jokes either."

"It's legit, mum. I confirmed it myself."

Dr. Lansing glanced over at her telephone. A single blinking light flashed on and off rapidly as if it recognized the incredible importance of the caller. She shrugged and lifted the handset while dismissing Oliver with her other hand.

"Hello?" she greeted the president as if she was unsure Oliver was accurate about it being him.

"Dr. Lansing, I'm calling to apologize for doubting you. I made a terrible mistake, and we lost many lives and valuable resources."

She took a deep breath and exhaled in an effort to calm her nerves.

"You made the logical decision, Mr. President. I'll be the first to admit my opinion was very much in the minority."

"Well, it was the one I asked for, and I should have relied upon it instead of letting others, especially those with my political future on the forefront of their mind, influence my decision. Sometimes the best decisions may seem politically unpopular at the time."

Dr. Lansing could tell the man was pouring his heart out to her. He just seemed like he needed somebody to talk to. His mood wasn't that different from her own at the moment. She never imagined the president would just pick up the phone and call someone during a time like this. When she didn't respond to his last statement, he continued.

"I've read your updates and most recent reports. This reads like science fiction to me. Fissures. Aquifer ruptures. Rivers flowing backwards. Liquefaction pulling skyscrapers into quicksand. To be honest, when I took office, a reporter asked me what threat I feared the most. Naturally, nuclear war was at the tip of my tongue as well as any event that might destroy our power grid or other critical infrastructure. Then, jokingly, I said I could probably deal with an alien space invasion better than those other things. I never imagined an earthquake would bring our nation to her knees."

"Sadly, sir, I knew it was a possibility. These types of geologic events have occurred throughout the millennia. Only now, our population levels are huge. Our buildings and necessary infrastructure to provide us modern conveniences cover our landscape. When these seismic events occur, they don't discriminate. They don't target one city over another. They simply happen like they have for millions of years. We're just in the wrong place at the wrong time."

The president noticeably sighed on the other end of the call. "It's Christmas Eve, and it should be a time of joy and celebration for all Americans. Instead, it has many, myself included, wondering if the powerful hand of God played a role in all of this. A not-so-friendly reminder that He's in charge."

"Sir, I can't imagine that any god would punish us this way. However, if He's as benevolent as most believe, this too shall pass."

The president laughed under his breath; then he caught himself. "Excuse me, Dr. Lansing. I don't think any of this is funny. I am, however, going to repeat the question I asked you two days ago. Is this over?"

She sighed and paused for a long moment.

"Dr. Lansing," the president continued, "your silence speaks volumes. Please don't mince words or equivocate."

She knew in her heart what the answer was, but she hesitated to punch the distraught president in the gut one more time. In the end, she had to speak her truth.

"Sir, it's quite likely just the beginning."

CHAPTER SIXTY-THREE

Monday, Christmas Eve
Atwood Residence
Cordova, Tennessee

It was the afternoon of Christmas Eve. The Atwood home should've been full of love for family and the excitement of Christmas. It was bustling with activity but not like any of them ever imagined. Everyone had a job to do, except Beth's new baby, whose role was to remain adorable and serve as a reminder that life can spring from the depths of despair. This bundle of love proved Jack and Tony could make their way home to their family.

Emily was tasked with entertaining Anthony and putting the final touches on the Christmas decorations. She found her blunt-tipped scissors, a box of crayons, and a packet of multicolored construction paper. The two of them settled between the Christmas tree and the fire to create some paper ornaments to adorn the Atwood home. With some twine, the two children created a variety of holiday shapes to hang on doorknobs, drawer pulls, and even each other's ears.

Tate was the busiest of the bunch. He'd awakened early to

restock their firewood supply. His first stops were the yards of vacant homes near theirs. After the conversation they'd had concerning the difference between looting for the sake of stealing and foraging for the sake of survival, he was determined his family, especially his new niece, would survive the winter.

In addition to firewood, he gathered several small propane tanks from outdoor grills in the vicinity. There wasn't anything left in their refrigerator to cook, but the necessity of fresh water led him to thinking how he might be able to purify the lake water behind the house.

He hummed a little ditty as he went about his business. *Strain and boil, baby. Strain and boil.*

This led him to another water-gathering option. He devised a way to reroute rainwater through the downspouts, across a coffee filter, and into buckets. Just like with the lake water, boiling out the impurities was the last step in the process.

Jill tried to meal plan with what she had left. She set all of the Christmas cakes and cookies into a separate wall cabinet. Regardless of when the guys made it home, whether it was Christmas Eve, Christmas Day, or after the first of the year, there would be some type of holiday yummy to enjoy.

She made notes on their canned goods and breakfast foods to determine the best way to provide some semblance of a balanced diet. She was the consummate organizer, and through her planning, she was able to come up with seven days of meals with sufficient calories to keep them all satisfied.

Jill recognized, however, this would not be enough when Jack and Tony arrived home. When they did, it would be time to consider entering their neighbors' homes or moving toward the retail stores to assess their options.

Beth took on the role of the family nurse. After her ordeal, she'd become aware of the types of medical supplies the family would need to deal with basic necessities. She worked with Jill to make a wish list of items they should find for their first aid kit. If or when they determined it was necessary to borrow from their neighbors, they'd have a list of what to look for.

Despite the obvious need to prepare themselves for a prolonged power outage and therefore a lack of resources necessary to live day to day, their activities on Christmas Eve gave them a sense of purpose. It also took their worried minds off Jack and Tony, who were still missing. Sitting around the house wringing their hands wasn't going to help them survive from one day to the next.

The afternoon flew by, and the sun began to set over the lake behind the house. Tate checked the stakes he'd driven into the ground at the edge of the lake to determine whether the water levels had changed. Since that morning, the water had risen three inches. On the surface, that sounded minimal. However, based upon his calculations, a continuous one-inch rise per day meant their basement would be subjected to flooding within a few weeks. If aftershocks hit or a heavy rainfall, then everything would change.

Everyone but Emily and Anthony had gathered on the back deck to watch the sunset. Beth had the baby wrapped up snugly and tucked inside an oversized sweater of Jill's. Tate emerged from below by climbing up an extension ladder. The stairs leading to the ground had broken loose from the deck and fallen down the hill. Jill was sitting sideways on the rail, mindlessly watching the orange ball drop over the horizon where the homes once were on the other side of the lake.

Suddenly, the French doors leading to the kitchen swung open. Warm air escaped the house and found its way to the group twelve feet away. Emily poked her head through and addressed them in a loud whisper so as not to startle Anthony or the baby.

"Mom, I think somebody's coming."

CHAPTER SIXTY-FOUR

Monday, Christmas Eve
Atwood Residence
Cordova, Tennessee

Every family had stories to tell. Clearly, some were more memorable than others. A few were repeated often and told to most anyone, strangers included. Others were buried in closets, behind lock and key, or in some cases, in old trunks hidden away in the attic underneath boxes of Christmas decorations. For Jill, Beth, their husbands and children, the events of the last seventy-two hours created stories that would be passed to their grandchildren and then to their grandchildren. Just as the memories of the New Madrid earthquakes from 1811–12 had been told and retold over the centuries.

Jack and Tony hobbled together up the sidewalk to the front door. They'd picked up the pace through the neighborhood as they discovered most of the homes were standing intact. The sight of Jack's Jeep sitting in front of the house indicated Jill and the kids were probably home.

The Mississippi Highway Patrol car in the driveway caught

Tony's eye next, causing him to practically drag Jack along the street out of concern for his wife. Jack gave him a reason to relax.

"Tony, the state police in Mississippi aren't going to hand-deliver bad news in a catastrophe like this. There's too much of that to go around. They'd only deliver something good—your family."

Tony became emotional, and within seconds, both men were blubbering with excitement. They hobbled in unison like two kids participating in the one-legged race in a schoolyard. Before they reached the steps, the front door swung inward.

Emily burst through first and leapt from porch to sidewalk, skipping the three steps before sticking the landing like an Olympian. She rushed to hug the guys, knocking them back a step. Jack groaned, but the pain meant nothing. He began sobbing as Tate followed his sister outside, and then Jill tentatively walked to the edge of the front stoop, her hand covering her mouth.

There were no dry eyes in the Atwood family. Their hearts raced. Their noses ran. Their smiles threatened to reach their ears. Throughout the joyous reunion, God was thanked often, and the words *I love you* were repeated too many times to count.

Tony slipped away from Jack, Jill and the kids. His face became concerned momentarily as he moved hesitantly toward the front steps.

Suddenly, Anthony appeared in the doorway, holding one of the cardboard cutout Christmas decorations he'd created with Emily. It was a white star with red and green sparkles glued on it. He stepped onto the porch and held it out to show his dad.

"Star. Star light. Star bright."

Tony broke down as he dropped to his knees on the steps. "That's right, son. Just like I taught you. Star light, star bright."

Tony had taken Anthony to the rooftop of their building one night to view Comet Oort when it flew in near proximity to Earth. Anthony had become fascinated by the stars, so his dad had repeated the "Star Light, Star Bright" nursery rhyme. That had been a year ago, and he couldn't recall Anthony ever mentioning it.

He closed his eyes as he hugged his son. He squeezed the young boy harder than he meant to because, he presumed, he knew why the Mississippi Highway Patrol car was here. Something had happened to Beth.

He was wrong. Sort of.

He opened his eyes, and there she stood in the doorway. Angelic. The soft glow of the fire and the setting sun on the other side of the house created a silhouette effect.

He blinked several times and then released his bear hug of Anthony and wiped his tears away. She was holding something. His heart leapt out of his chest.

Was it?

He slowly released Anthony and stood. He was crying so hard he couldn't focus his eyes. Tony was unable to speak. He slowly lifted his hand and pointed at her.

A smile came over her tear-soaked face. She nodded rapidly up and down. Tony gently rubbed his hands over the top of Anthony's head. He walked slowly to greet his wife. He fought the urge to hug her like he did his son. Beth was fragile. Delicate. And she'd given birth to their baby.

With the Atwoods looking on, Tony and Beth held one another, alternating between looking into each other's eyes and down to the pink cherub snuggled between them. They whispered to one another, cried more tears, and then began to laugh. If any love had been lost between them over time, it was found and rekindled in their hearts and minds.

Jill, the undisputed leader of the clan, suggested everyone return inside. Darkness would be setting in, and after two consecutive nights of clear skies, temperatures would be falling, making it all the more difficult to keep the house warm.

Tony lifted Anthony onto his hip and followed Beth inside. Tate helped his dad up the steps, followed by Emily. Jill paused a moment and looked around the yard. She gazed toward the sky and said a prayer, thanking God for protecting all of her family and giving them a roof over their heads.

Then she smiled and said to anyone outside their home that might hear her words. "Godspeed and merry Christmas."

Inside, as was often the case during family gatherings, everyone gravitated toward the kitchen. In normal times, it was because food was being prepared or snacks were laid out to munch on. Once a couple of family members or their friends began to hang out around the kitchen island, chatting and munching, the rest did as well.

This evening was different. The family room was covered with mattresses. All of the other places to sit had been moved into other rooms or shoved against a wall. Nonetheless, the kitchen was the heart of the Atwood home, and everyone had gathered there as they recovered from their highly emotional reunion in the front yard.

Jill and Emily worked together to open up crackers, peanuts and chips to munch on. Cans of Frito Bean Dip, Jack's favorite, and jars of salsa were spread across the counter for everyone to enjoy. She even poured a bag of pretzels, a box of Life cereal, and a bag of bagel chips into a large bowl to create her own recipe of Chex Mix.

Jill completely abandoned her post-apocalyptic meal-rationing plan developed earlier in the day. In the joyous moment, she was reminded of how you only live life once. Last Thursday, the day before the earthquakes started, she'd had no idea it was the day before an apocalyptic event. Had she known it was the day before, her purchases at Costco would've looked much different.

That's the way life can be, she thought to herself. *When you're given lemons, you figure out a way to make lemonade.* For tonight, the family would celebrate their survival and reunion. Tomorrow was Christmas. They'd thank the Lord for their blessings and discuss their future, whatever that might look like.

She and Emily retrieved glasses out of the cupboard. Jill had purchased two bottles of sparkling grape juice for Beth to join in the holiday festivities. They opened them and poured drinks for everyone. She imagined the harder stuff would be poured later when the kids were asleep or otherwise preoccupied. Discussion of their future would require a stiff drink for them all.

Jill raised her glass, and everyone, including young Anthony, followed suit. "We have lots of things to discuss, but for now, I hope that we can focus on our family and how thankful we are to be alive. It's Christmas Eve, the night when we come together as a family. It's always been a happy time for us. I propose we enjoy it like always, making the best of the blessings God has given us."

"I agree!" said Tony.

"Same here," added Jack. "Merry Christmas, everyone!"

"Merry Christmas!" they replied, and the sounds of glasses clinking together filled the room. Emily tried to suppress a burp from the sparkling grape juice, drawing laughs from the parents.

Beth wasn't shy about it as she amplified her burp so loud that it startled Jill. She laughed.

"Whoa! I needed that!"

Her husband kissed her on the cheek and held his hand out to hold their newborn. Jill walked up to them and whispered, "Why don't you guys spend some time talking in the bedroom? Tate stacked some logs on the hearth for you. Just come out when you're ready, or go to sleep if you want."

Tony reached for Jill's hand. "Thank you for all that you've done for us. And ..." he began. Leaning forward, he locked eyes with Jill. "There is no better man on this planet than Jack Atwood. I mean that."

CHAPTER SIXTY-FIVE

Monday, Christmas Eve
Atwood Residence
Cordova, Tennessee

Jill was alone with her husband for the first time. Tate and Emily worked together to create some kind of seating arrangement in the living room, easily sliding furniture around on the hardwood floors. Anthony went to the master suite with his parents so the Chandlers could reconnect. Jack sat still with his arm outstretched across the breakfast table while Jill carefully wrapped his wrist sprain.

Tate had offered to check his injured wrist to determine if was sprained or broken. When Jack resisted, Tate said, matter-of-factly, that he'd seen injuries like this a hundred times on the football field. Jack indulged his son, who was smiling as he tried to convince his dad to give him his wrist to examine.

"Not gonna happen," Jack said defiantly. "Your uncle Tony pulled this same spiel on me earlier. Then he tried to twist my hand off to see if it was, in fact, broken. Heck, if it wasn't before, it sure is now."

Tate started laughing and reached for his father's wrist. He swore not to hurt him, but Jack refused. The family got a laugh from the teasing Jack endured, and it served to turn the conversation with the kids away from what they'd been through toward settling in until their ripped-open world could be sutured back together again somehow.

Jill didn't think she had any more tears in her, but apparently a few were replenished. As she wrapped his tender wrist, she glanced up at his eyes. "I never gave up, Jack. But, by this morning, the negative thoughts began to creep into my mind. I thought I'd lost you."

"We've all been through a lot, love," he said as she tucked the wrist wrap into place. Jack pulled it up and tried to bend it slightly. It was a snug fit. "Every obstacle was just another step to getting home to you. I tried not to make panicked, emotional decisions. Tony helped a lot. I'm really proud of him."

Jill leaned back in her chair and nodded. "They've been through a lot. I think, in an odd way, this may have brought them closer."

"At some point, when you're comfortable, you can tell me the details of what you guys went through. For me, it might be a long time before I can tell you everything. It was just so sad, Jill. So many people died. They never had a chance. We tried to help when we could, but we couldn't risk our lives when we had to get home to our families."

Jack closed his eyes and welled up in tears. In those few seconds of silence between them, his mind raced from the moment they first felt the quake at the Top of the Met, to their trek south to West Memphis, to the multiple times they should've died crossing the river. He wasn't ready to discuss any of that. Not for some time.

Jill felt the same way. However, the kids were a different matter. "I think Tate and Emily need to relay their experiences if they can. Tate's girlfriend is missing. In the Halloran, kinda like you, he saved lives, but he had to abandon rescuing others. Emily's experience was different."

"What happened?"

Jill explained everything Emily had been willing to repeat to her after the incident. She'd clearly withheld information from her mother, in part because her brother was around, and he had a tendency to tease her, but mostly because she felt safer keeping it bottled inside. Jill hoped their daughter would open up to Jack.

Tate and Emily appeared in the breakfast room. "I think we've got a pretty good setup. Wanna come see?"

The family moseyed through the family room and then down the open hallway-foyer combination into the formal living room. The kids had done a great job. They'd even centered the ten-by-thirteen Oriental rug in the space. The living room resembled a small version of a dance studio with all the seating facing in and the rug placed in the center, ready for the contestants to *cut it*, so to speak.

"Great job, guys!" said Jack enthusiastically. He started to raise his right hand out of habit to exchange high fives but quickly drew it behind his back. He imagined he'd bump his wrist a thousand times before the sprain healed. Left-handed high fives would have to suffice.

"We need some side tables or even nightstands," suggested Jill. "Um, Tate, why don't you give me a hand?"

Jack, feeling helpless, spoke up. "I can do it with one hand, I think."

Jill shook her head. "Nah. Tate and I can handle it. Why don't you and Emily take a moment to talk?"

Jack understood. She'd created a diversion to get father and daughter alone for a little while.

"Sounds like a plan. Hey, Em. Wanna join me on the loveseat?"

"Cozy and warm?" she asked as she rushed over and plopped down.

"Absolutely," he replied.

The two made small talk for a moment. Then Jack broached the subject of her near-death experience in the lake. Emily never cried as she spilled all the details of what had happened. She'd developed an inner strength through the ordeal that Jack didn't know she possessed. As she relayed the details, she gradually got to the part she'd been unable to tell her mother.

"Daddy, please don't think I'm crazy when I tell you this."

"Honey, everything that happened to us may have been crazy, but we aren't."

"I didn't want to worry Mom. She might not let me go swimming again."

Jack chuckled and whispered into his daughter's ear, "If I told her what happened to me in the river, she'd make us all move to Mount Everest or some other place as far away from water as we can get."

Emily took a deep breath and began to fidget. Her feet kicked against the bottom of the loveseat, and she mindlessly played with her fingers. She found the courage to speak.

"Daddy, one time, I thought I couldn't swim anymore. I couldn't find my way back to the top of the water. It was so muddy down there. And dark. I wanted to breathe so badly, but I knew I couldn't."

Emily's fidgeting picked up. Her legs swung more, and she clasped her hands together until parts of her fingers turned white. The candlelight reflected off her face, showing her consternation. However, there were no tears.

"Honey, if you don't—" Jack began as he gently placed his left hand over hers.

"It's okay. Daddy." She turned in the loveseat slightly to face him. "Um, I had help."

"From who?"

Emily paused again. She took a deep breath and responded after a long moment. "They were people. Except, um, they weren't. Each of them looked like a different butterfly. They were all around me. Even in the muddy water, they were pretty. Elegant like princesses. Except they had wings."

Jack fully understood. He'd experienced them as well. The passage of time had caused the details in his memory to fade. Nonetheless, they were his guardian angels once in his lifetime, and now they'd apparently reappeared to save his precious child.

When her dad didn't say anything, Emily dropped her chin to

her chest, and a few tears dripped down her cheeks. "You don't believe me. That's okay. I saw them."

Jack put his arm around Emily's shoulders and pulled her close to his chest. He whispered to her, "I do believe you, Em. You know why? I've seen them, too. They saved me once. I'll never forget it."

She looked up to his face. Children had an incredible, built-in bullshit meter. Emily could read her father better than Jill could.

"Really? You're not just saying that, are you?"

"No, honey. I swear. One day, when things settle down, I'll tell you my story the best that I can remember it. Let's just say I believe they helped me just like they helped you."

"Kinda like guardian angels, right, Dad?"

"Exactly," he replied. He thought for a few seconds. There needed to be a parental lesson out of this. He didn't want the takeaway from Emily's experience to be that she could throw caution to the wind and live life as a risk-taker. "That said, there were plenty of times in the last couple of days I wish the butterfly people had shown up to pull me to safety. They never did, so you can't really count on them every time."

"I know," said Emily sheepishly. "Maybe only in the most dangerous times?"

Jack leaned back on the loveseat. He tried to process the analysis of a twelve-year-old girl who'd just come off a near-death experience. Maybe the butterfly people knew he'd emerge from the depths of the Mississippi on his own? Maybe they knew he wouldn't collapse with the building in St. Louis? Maybe he didn't need their help? Well, at least this go-around.

"Here we are," announced Jill before she entered the living room. It was her way of warning Jack to wind up the conversation. He felt it was over, although at some point he expected to get quizzed by Emily about his own near-death experience. It would be something the two of them shared as father and daughter.

Jill and Tate began to add tables to the furnishings. Candles were repositioned from other rooms so they now had a comfortable seating area in close proximity to the fireplace in the adjoining family room. The ransacked house was beginning to feel like a home again.

An hour later, Tate and Emily, exhausted from the day's activities, crawled into bed in front of the fire. Anthony wanted to sleep near his cousin. The baby was snuggled in a makeshift bassinette using a laundry basket and the softest blankets in the house. The adults were ready for their cocktail.

Jack and Tony fixed everyone a drink. The group bundled up and wandered out to the back deck overlooking the lake. The moon provided enough illumination to give them a pretty good view across the water. The clear skies enabled them to see the tops of buildings on fire off in the distance.

Although they'd promised during their toast in the kitchen earlier to save the serious conversations for another time, they broke the pact. At least in part. Most of the details of the catastrophe and how they managed to survive it might end up hidden from conversations for years. The more immediate concern as to what happens next was in the front of everyone's minds.

CHAPTER SIXTY-SIX

Monday, Christmas Eve
Atwood Residence
Cordova, Tennessee

After some small talk and a couple of adult beverages, except for Beth, of course, because she'd be nursing, Jill took the floor. "Okay, before we start talking about what's next, let me say that I've been making lists of everything in the house that we use on a daily basis. It's kept me busy and focused rather than sitting around losing my mind over what happened to you guys."

Beth added, "They're really detailed. I have to admit, as I was driving up here, I began to worry about formula, vitamins, diapers, and even postnatal doctor visits. It was weird, actually. It was almost like I was psyching myself up for the inevitable—a world where none of that stuff was available anymore."

Tony asked, "I don't think it's really that bad, do you? I mean, don't get me wrong. Jack and I saw the devastation just like you did. But it's fixable, right?"

"I suppose anything can be rebuilt," replied Jack. "You've heard the old saying. There's nothing that time and money can't solve."

Jill continued. "The real question for me is time. We don't have access to our money, not that there's anyplace we can spend it. Besides, the market probably got crushed."

"No worries, honey," said Jack. "Tony pulled off the financial move of the century. We're probably really rich right now and don't know it. However, it doesn't do any good in the near term."

"What do we do?" asked Beth.

"I haven't mentioned this to you yet," Jill began in her answer to Beth. "There's a huge tear in the earth on the north side of I-40. For miles, homes, stores, and businesses were sucked into the ground. It's hard to imagine."

"I can imagine it," said Beth sadly.

"Anyway, the stores near the exit and along Germantown Road were being looted on Saturday. My guess is they were cleaned out by today."

Tony turned to look toward the west. "We saw something similar in the city at a Walgreens. I'm sure as desperation sets in, that will only get worse."

"Where's FEMA?" asked Jack.

"They were staging on Mississippi Boulevard at that large church," replied Jill. "We saw thousands of people descending on that place Saturday morning. Again, after two days ..." Her voice trailed off.

Jack sighed. "If FEMA is getting set up, I'm sure they'll expand their operation to temporary housing and meal handouts."

"How long do you think it will take them to fix the power and water supply?" asked Jill before adding, "I don't wanna be overdramatic, but in a few days, we're gonna be in a world of hurt."

"It sure seems like our world suddenly got a whole lot smaller," added Tony.

"No doubt," said Jill.

Jack set his empty glass on the rail and walked as he spoke. "Let's consider the government's response first. Listen, so much of this is speculation. Tony and I kinda talked about it in between jumping off bridges and dodging barges."

Jill laughed. "You wish, Mr. Mission Impossible."

Jack and Tony glanced at one another. Perhaps that conversation would need to be postponed a couple of years.

Jack continued. "Anyway, we have to ask a logical question. What if they can't? What if it's so bad that the city and its infrastructure can't be rebuilt. Or, as Beth can attest, the Mississippi may have changed course. I don't know if these two quakes were worse than what happened two hundred years ago. It doesn't matter because our world is a lot different."

Beth moved closer to Tony for warmth and comfort. He tried to temper the conversation.

"I can see where you're coming from, but I think we need to avoid speculation and consider our immediate needs. We need to get from point A to point B or it won't matter."

"Well, I agree," said Jill. "I actually discussed it with Tate on Saturday. We really need more information, and the radio stations aren't broadcasting. In the meantime, we have some resources available to us."

"Like what?" asked Beth.

"Tate and I don't like it, but we may have to break into our neighbors' homes in search of supplies. We've already lost our window of opportunity to empty their refrigerators. If we get lucky and come across a deep freeze, then we could salvage something there if we cook it right away."

"Their pantries may be full," added Jack.

"Fuller than ours, anyway," said Jill. She turned toward the grill and pointed. "Tate has gathered up several propane tanks to boil water and cook with. They will eventually run out. He's been taking firewood from the neighbors, but if this is going to be prolonged through the winter, and if we have to stay, we'll need to cut down our own."

Beth began to cry as her hormonal imbalance continued to affect her. "This is all too much."

"I'm sorry, Bethie," Jill apologized. "We'll figure all of this out tomorrow."

"I agree," said Jack. "We're all exhausted. Tomorrow is Christmas. Let's get some sleep."

CHAPTER SIXTY-SEVEN

Tuesday, Christmas Day
Atwood Residence
Cordova, Tennessee

There were no alarm clocks. No roosters crowing. No sounds of early morning traffic scurrying off to a loved one's home or sunrise services at church. The tired group of survivors were happily sleeping in until the sun rose high enough to begin shining through the front windows. Then, Beth and Tony's baby, who clearly had excellent lung development, demanded her breakfast, again. Anthony and Emily stirred awake next. And within ten minutes of the sun making its presence known, Christmas morning had arrived.

It certainly wasn't the Christmas celebration Jill had envisioned. She'd been planning for weeks. Making lists. Buying recipe ingredients on sale. Juggling schedules to accommodate everyone. It was all going smoothly until just after four thirty last Friday afternoon. Then the earth began to shake.

They made the most of it, happy to be alive and together. Jack did his best to play one-armed Santa. He distributed wrapped presents to the children, Tate included. After the gifts were opened by them, a few more presents were presented to Beth that were mostly for the baby. She loved them all and thanked Jill for her thoughtfulness.

Before turning in for the night, Jack and Jill, out of respect for the others, exchanged their gifts. Jill knew Beth had lost their presents when she had to abandon her car. Tony, who was now referred to privately as the *old Tony*, had planned on scrambling around over the weekend to gather up gifts for his family. Because they got waylaid by the earthquake, the Atwoods elected to save them any embarrassment by not having a gift exchange among the adults.

Tate and Jack traded shifts through the night to keep the fire going. Memphis was not known for harsh winters, but as misfortune would have it, a cold front had crossed over about the time the second earthquake finished destroying everything around it.

"Everybody," said Jill as she stood in the center of the room. "I had big plans for our meals. I have managed to save some Christmas treats we can eat for breakfast. I hope you don't mind cookies and—"

"Let them eat cake!" exclaimed Emily in her best Euro-accent, interrupting her mother. She had no idea the callous, rude remark made by Marie-Antoinette had a negative connotation. For the young girl, it was a way of saying cookies sounded just fine to her. Apparently, the suggestion was unanimous.

Jill laughed and continued. "I do have a little cake, too. They're Little Debbie Christmas Tree Cakes, but they're really good."

Beth started to hand the baby to Tony. "Let me help."

Their hostess raised her hands and politely declined her offer. "Nah, keep your seat. I've got this."

Jill made her way to the kitchen and returned with a platter of Christmas Tree Cakes. She set it on the coffee table they'd placed in the center of the living room. Then she carried the tray of cookies around toward Anthony and offered him the first choice.

"I'm sorry they're mostly broken. Since Anthony is the youngest, we should give him first dibs."

"Hey, she's the youngest, Mom," Emily objected, pointing at Beth and the baby. "Wait a minute. What's her name?"

Tony and Beth exchanged glances. Throughout all the turmoil, and their focus on being grateful their baby girl had survived it, they hadn't taken the time to name her.

"We talked about several girl names a month or so ago but never settled on one."

Jill leaned down to present the sugar cookies to Anthony. They'd been created using cookie cutters in a variety of Christmas-themed shapes. Then she'd frosted them and covered them with multicolored sprinkles.

Anthony reached onto the plate and pulled a cookie from the bottom of the pile. It was probably the only one intact among the broken cookies. Its icing was a bright white with gold and silver sprinkles. He studied it for a moment, raised it into the air, and turned to his mother.

"Angel," he said softly. Then he repeated himself, "Angel."

Beth looked into Tony's eyes. As she did, visions of the lovable, lifesaving state trooper, Willie Angel, raced through her mind. They smiled and nodded at one another.

"Yes. We'll call her Angel."

It would be a Christmas to remember for Jill, Beth and their families. They'd survived the worst catastrophic event in the history of modern mankind. The ramifications were widespread and far-reaching, impacting every corner of the planet in some way.

Sorrow and hardship surrounded them. The devastating result of the massive back-to-back earthquakes extended all up and down the Mississippi River. The North American continent had been torn in half from the Gulf of Mexico through the Great Lakes to Hudson Bay in Ontario, Canada.

America had become a nation divided. Only time would tell whether it could be reconnected.

THANK YOU FOR READING NEW MADRID!

If you enjoyed it, I'd be grateful if you'd take a moment to write a short review (just a few words are needed) and post it on Amazon. Amazon uses complicated algorithms to determine what books are recommended to readers. Sales are, of course, a factor, but so are the quantities of reviews my books get. By taking a few seconds to leave a review, you help me out and also help new readers learn about my work.

WHAT'S COMING NEXT FROM BOBBY AKART?

Get on the list to find out about coming titles, deals, contests, appearances, and more!

Sign up for The Epigraph, my official newsletter, at BobbyAkart.com

VISIT my feature page at Amazon.com/BobbyAkart for more information on my other action-packed thrillers, which includes over forty Amazon #1 bestsellers in forty-plus fiction and nonfiction genres.

READ ON, beginning with my Author's Note, as I provide insight into why I wrote *New Madrid* and my thoughts on the extensive research surrounding this potentially catastrophic threat.

AUTHOR'S NOTE
DECEMBER 16, 2020

The most alarming aspect of telling the story of New Madrid's fault and its history of earthquakes was how little of it I made up. The history speaks for itself. Applying the scientific findings of the 1811–12 earthquake sequence to present day simply reinforces how vulnerable we are.

That said, sometimes one can only grasp the magnitude of a catastrophic event like an earthquake along the New Madrid fault line through the eyes of fictional characters. I may have conjured them up for purposes of telling this story, but the underlying scientific premise is very real.

WHAT LED ME TO WRITE NEW MADRID

I don't get to conduct all my research in person, but there was one trip in particular that gave fruit to many novels. I had the pleasure of appearing on a television episode of George Noory's *Beyond Belief* in 2016 to discuss my nonfiction treatise on electromagnetic pulse weapons and EMPs generated by solar flares. The moral of this story? I should travel more often.

Bear with me as I take you down memory lane for a moment. You'll see how one thing leads to another and to another. Out of that trip, several novels and book series sprang forth.

Due in part to the hacking and coughing of my fellow passengers on the Frontier Air Flight to Denver, I made a solemn promise to my social media followers—*know this, my next novel will be about a pandemic*! I kept that promise, and since then, my medical thrillers—including the Pandemic series (pneumonic plague), the Virus Hunters novels (multiple infectious diseases), and the Odessa trilogy (bioterrorism)—have opened many sets of eyes as to the pandemic threat. And now, here we are in 2020. Enough said.

While in Boulder where the television studios were located, I took the time to visit the Space Weather Prediction Center. I randomly asked the folks I met what existential threat they feared the most. Their responses were varied and reflected their fields of study. I have written about several of them with more to come. The Blackout series depicts a current-day America in which a catastrophic solar flare strikes us head-on, just as it did in 1859 during the well-known Carrington Event. The Geostorm series was another set of novels that dealt with the shift of the Earth's magnetic poles, a phenomenon occurring as of this writing.

As a side note, the professionals at the SWPC introduced me to some brilliant minds at NASA'S Jet Propulsion Laboratory in Pasadena, California. Through my interviews and correspondence, I discerned the threat concerning them was from near-Earth objects, such as asteroids, that wandered our solar system and remained undetected by even the most advanced technology. These planet killers were the basis for my Asteroid trilogy. The geophysicists at the Jet Propulsion Laboratory told me asteroids may be planet killers, but the Yellowstone supervolcano would bury us in ash. I dove into the research and wrote the Yellowstone series, my bestselling to date. Yellowstone Hellfire reached #25 on Amazon Charts list of bestselling novels.

Also, while at the Boulder studios with George Noory, I became acquainted with Dr. Peter Vincent Pry, Executive Director of the EMP Task Force on National and Homeland Security, who has also served as the Chief of Staff of the Congressional EMP Commission. We discussed my book, EMP, and he revealed his biggest concern as the use of low-Earth orbiting satellites by North Korea as a mechanism to deliver a nuclear-tipped warhead to be detonated over the United States. The resulting EMP would destroy our power grid and deliver us back to the 1800s. As a result, I wrote the Lone Star series and was honored to have Dr. Pry write the foreword.

Which brings me to this novel, *New Madrid*. As a result of my phone conversations with the learned scientists and geophysicists at the Jet Propulsion Laboratory that afternoon, I was encouraged to make a quick trip down Highway 93 to the National Earthquake Information Center in Golden, Colorado.

The scenic twenty-minute drive was enjoyable in itself, and it brought back memories of when I visited Golden while in college. Pop and I, along with two of his coworkers, had driven to Colorado during spring break during my first year of law school. We had some time, so we ventured into Golden to tour the Coors Brewery. As an aside, this was before Coors was distributed nationally, so the four cases of beer we smuggled home were a real score. Golden was also where I was introduced to Rocky Mountain oysters (insert green puking emoji here. Just kidding!).

Golden hadn't changed that much from what I could remember, but I was glad I ventured onto the campus of the Colorado School of Mines, where the USGS National Earthquake Information Center was located. First, a note about the university. What's not to love about a small, quaint campus set at the base of the Rocky Mountains. Couple that with a school whose mascot is an ornery-looking mule and whose moniker is *orediggers*, and I just had a great feeling about the side trip.

I was glad I went there for many reasons, including the insight I gathered about what was going on under Earth's surface. To be sure, many of those I spoke with wanted to talk about climate change. I did, in fact, incorporate some of their thoughts and suggestions into the Geostorm series. However, my primary focus was to hear their thoughts on earthquakes that affected the United States. Being a native Tennessean, I was particularly interested in the New Madrid Seismic Zone.

My takeaway from those conversations was this. There has always been a lot of hype about San Andreas and the other faults running along our nation's West Coast into Alaska. Stories, movies, and television programs have featured all types of seismic activity based in California. Now, don't get me wrong, the type of earthquake that could be generated along San Andreas would be devastating.

However, a seismic event in the center of the country, along the Mississippi River and emanating from the New Madrid Seismic Zone, could not only result in an incredible death toll, but it could sever our nation's communications, transportation routes, and other related aspects of our critical infrastructure. The recovery and repair effort would last many years.

Next up, let me give you a brief history lesson, and then I'll reveal, through the eyes of the scientific community, what would happen if fiction becomes reality.

A BRIEF HISTORY OF THE HISTORIC
QUAKES OF 1811–12

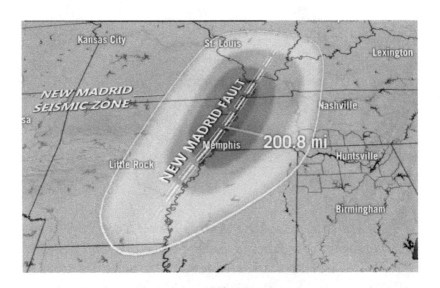

The New Madrid fault line is found throughout Missouri, Illinois, Kentucky, Tennessee, and Arkansas, where the potential for greatest intensity is located. However, depending on the strength of the earthquake and the precise location of the epicenter, Mississippi, Indiana, and Iowa could also be impacted.

New Madrid is made up of two faults. One is a strike-slip

segment oriented toward the northeast, running between the small towns of Marked Tree, Arkansas, and Caruthersville, Missouri. A strike-slip fault is a vertical fracture in which the continental boundary plates have moved side to side. The other is a northwest trending reverse fault lying below New Madrid, Missouri. By trending, scientists mean it's an active area undergoing compression, or squishing. Faults that move the way you expect gravity to move them are normal faults. A fault that moves counter to the law of gravity is a reverse fault.

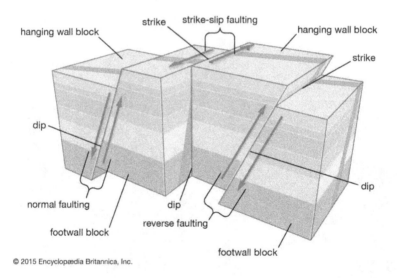

© 2015 Encyclopædia Britannica, Inc.

The main area of the New Madrid Seismic Zone, NMSZ, sits underneath large open farms in the boot heel of Missouri as well as under the rolling hills of Arkansas down to Memphis. The faults in the NMSZ are deep because this area has been the site of some very, very large earthquakes for thousands of years.

Geological studies have revealed that the uplift rates associated with the NMSZ could not have occurred continuously over long periods of time without dramatically altering the topography beyond what it is today. Therefore, scientists agree the seismic activity began approximately sixty-four thousand years ago, making New Madrid one of the youngest seismic zones on the planet.

Based upon the analysis of sand blows (when liquified sand forces its way through fissures to the earth's surface) and soil samples, it's been determined massive earthquakes have occurred there in 2350 BC, AD 30, AD 900, and AD 1450. More recently, in the winter of 1811 through 1812, several earthquakes and aftershocks ranging from a magnitude 6.5 to nearly M8 rolled across the NMSZ.

December 16–17, 1811

The first principal earthquake, or mainshock, occurred at about 2:15 a.m. local time in the vicinity of northeast Arkansas at the Cottonwood Grove fault. Estimated to be an M7.5, it caused only slight damage to man-made structures because the epicentral area was sparsely populated at the time.

Geophysicists believe the future location of Memphis was shaken with an intensity of Level IX on the Modified Mercalli scale. At New Madrid, trees were knocked down and riverbanks collapsed. The first earthquake shook windows and furniture in Washington, DC, and rang church bells in Richmond, Virginia, and Charleston, South Carolina. It knocked the plaster off houses in Columbia, South Carolina. Observers from Missouri to Indiana reported the earthquake as lasting ten to twelve minutes.

Twenty-seven aftershocks were felt from the first earthquake in intervals of every six to ten minutes. Then came what was known as the *Daylight Shock*. Sometimes referred to as the *Dawn Shock*, the M7 aftershock struck at 7:15 that morning with an epicenter in northeast Arkansas. Over the next twenty-four hours, three more large aftershocks jolted the NMSZ, bearing intensities from M6 to M6.5.

January 23, 1812

The second principal shock of the earthquake sequence was determined to be an M7.3 at approximately 9:15 a.m. on January 23. The epicenter was New Madrid, Missouri, on the banks of the

Mississippi River. Although it was the smallest of the three mainshocks, it resulted in widespread ground deformation, landslides, fissuring, and the rerouting of the Mississippi River.

Some geophysicists hypothesized that this mainshock resulted in the rupturing of the New Madrid north fault. This rupturing is credited with extending the fault line and the boundaries of the NMSZ into Illinois. In 2011, an independent expert panel convened by the USGS found that an extended section of the New Madrid fault exists. Further, they hypothesized this north fault in Illinois is still loaded and capable of hosting a great earthquake in the near future.

February 7, 1812

It had only been a little over seven weeks since the first earthquake struck the NMSZ. The estimated M7.6 quake was also the largest in intensity because of its proximity to the Reelfoot fault that extended from the New Madrid fault in Missouri, under the Mississippi River and into West Tennessee.

This final mainshock in the sequence destroyed the town of New Madrid. To the north, homes were severely damaged, and brick structures in St. Louis were toppled. The reverse fault that ran under the river resulted in significant uplift on the Tennessee side. The rise of the ground elevation created temporary waterfalls on the river and a tsunami wave that propagated upstream.

The tremendous upheaval along this fault resulted in the formation of Reelfoot Lake, a twenty-three-square-mile body of water in Obion County, Tennessee. It also caused the Mississippi River to run backward, a scientific phenomenon known as a fluvial tsunami.

1812–1900

The NMSZ has not rested since. Hundreds of aftershocks were felt for several years through 1817. Later in the nineteenth century, an M6 occurred on January 4, 1843, and an M6.6 was felt on Halloween of 1895. The 1895 seismic event, with an epicenter at Charleston, Missouri, damaged all the buildings in the city, created sand volcanoes in the surrounding fields, and cracked a pier as far north as the Cairo Bridge in Illinois.

Recent Seismic Activity

There are geologists who opine that the quake sequence of 1811–12 continues to put off aftershocks. They believe the rift system beneath the Mississippi River Valley that failed to split the continent many millions of years ago has remained a scar, or zone of weakness, deep underground. These ancient faults appear to have made Earth's crust in the NMSZ mechanically weaker than the rest of North America.

As evidence of this and the expansion of the fault into Illinois, they point to an M5.5 earthquake in November of 1968, centered near Dale, Illinois, a small community located sixty miles west of Evansville, Indiana. The quake was felt in twenty-three states, including cities as far away as Boston, Massachusetts and Charleston, South Carolina.

Just a dozen years ago, in the nearby Wabash Valley, a similar M5.4 quake with its epicenter in Illinois occurred. Since 1974 when the first seismic instruments were installed in the Wabash Valley Seismic Zone where the scientists believe the north fault line of the NMSZ extends, there have been over four thousand earthquakes recorded.

WHAT IF FICTION BECOMES
REALITY?

In 1999, FEMA identified four hazards in the U.S. that would be categorized as the worst-of-the-worst likely catastrophic natural disasters. They were a major hurricane hitting Miami, a major hurricane hitting New Orleans, a significant earthquake hitting LA, and a giant earthquake hitting the Central U.S. in the New Madrid Seismic Zone.

In 2008, FEMA issued a report warning that a serious earthquake in the NMSZ could result in the highest economic losses due to a natural disaster in the history of the country. They predicted widespread and catastrophic damages in a dozen states near the NMSZ. Tens of thousands of fatalities should be expected, and that's if only a single earthquake were to occur.

The potential for a reoccurrence of the type of earthquake swarm that struck the NMSZ in 1811–12 resulted in an increased monitoring of ground motion and the study of past quakes to gauge their potential for destruction in modern times.

In October 2009, a research team consisting of scientists from the University of Illinois and Virginia Tech considered a scenario where all three segments of the New Madrid fault ruptured simultaneously with a total magnitude of M7.7, similar in size to the two largest mainshocks of the 1811–12 sequence. Their report revealed dire results.

Eighty-six thousand casualties. Over seven hundred thousand damaged structures. Over seven million people displaced. And the impact zone would stretch far beyond the states comprising the NMSZ. The overall direct economic loss would approach half a trillion dollars.

At the NEIC in Golden, the primary concern of geophysicists is that the small earthquakes of the last two hundred years don't seem to be diminishing in number or intensity. Therefore, they don't believe they are mere aftershocks of the 1811–12 quake sequence.

In 2009, the USGS issued a fact sheet stating a probability estimate of ten percent for a New Madrid earthquake of M7+ by 2059. The probability of an M6+ rose to nearly forty percent during that time frame.

In 2018, just nine years later, the fact sheet was updated, as was the risk assessment. The National Seismic Hazard Model now states an estimate of twenty percent for M7+ and fifty percent for M6+. In addition, a new probability estimate was added—M8+ at two percent.

An M8+ quake has never been recorded outside of Alaska. Yet the USGS scientists now believe there is a probability, albeit slight, that it could happen.

God help us when it does.

A FEW INSIDER TIDBITS ABOUT THE NOVEL

Writing is fun. Seriously, there is nothing about the process of creating, researching, writing, and publishing a novel that I don't like. The best part about becoming an author has been the friendships I've been fortunate enough to create with readers and social media acquaintances. Many of my readers have been with me since I published The Loyal Nine in the Summer of 2015.

I like to reward them with literary Easter eggs—a nod or a message in my novel that references another story already published, or to be published in the future. Like many authors, I insert personal anecdotes into the story. Let me give you a glimpse at a few examples.

This story was set in the days leading up to Christmas. Dani and I love Christmastime. We enjoy watching Hallmark Christmas movies; decorating our home; and adorning our tree with Shiny Brite ornaments. We have a few from my dearly departed mom who was born and raised in Germany. We've collected many others over the years. I was glad to be able to work all of this into the story.

As a kid, I used to ride my bicycle to work at a golf course near my home. In order to get there, I had to ride through the campus of

Webb School of Knoxville. I added Webb to the story to play against Tate's high school for the state football championship.

Another note, or Easter egg, actually. Tate greatly admired his new coach who'd come to his school from Savannah, Tennessee—Joe Carey. Not only is Joe Carey the same Coach Carey depicted in the Blackout series, he is also a real person and a dear friend. You'll note that he's on my team of advance readers.

Now, for some Easter eggs that cross-reference to my fifty currently-published novels. I'm not gonna give you the ones related to future stories. One day, they'll strike a chord and you'll remember.

In Chapter 4, Oliver is updating Dr. Lansing on Mother Earth's condition. He referenced ash from an active volcano in Chile floating toward the quaint town of Bariloche. San Carlos de Bariloche, Argentina, is one of the key locations in the Odessa trilogy featuring Gunner Fox.

In Chapter 31, Jill and the kids arrive at the FEMA staging area at *THE BLVD*, a well-known church in Memphis. She referenced working with a woman following the damage caused by an asteroid colliding with the planet years prior. The asteroid, IM-86, was a reference to the planet killer in Gunner Fox's Asteroid trilogy.

In Chapter 42, while Jill is seeking out her neighbors to learn what she could about the first earthquake, the second quake hits. As she runs home, she is chased by an emerging fissure that swallows trees, a riding lawn mower, and a red Kia parked in a driveway. Readers of 36 Hours, book one in the Blackout series, might recall an *offending Kia* that got in the way of Madison Ryman's Suburban.

Speaking of the Blackout series, if there ever came a time where all of my characters got together for a reunion, of sorts, I'd love to see Alex Ryman and Tate Atwood become close. You see, I'm a hopeless romantic.

In Chapter 43, I described the earthquake as *fighting like a bedeviled bull trying to throw famed rodeo star Cooper Armstrong off his back*. Cooper Armstrong, a fictional rodeo star and the oldest of the

Armstrong's *rodeo kids*, was one of the primary characters in the Lone Star series.

In Chapter 56, as Beth was in labor, her mind wandered to the pioneer days when women gave birth without the aid of a hospital, or even a doctor. She thought of Daniel Boone's wife who gave birth while her husband and brother Squire were off exploring Kentucky and Indiana. This is a cross-reference to the Geostorm series. The characters were direct descendants of Squire Boone and lived in Southeast Indiana near Mauckport.

Mauckport is also an Easter egg. Once again, in Chapter 33, as Dr. Lansing is being briefed on the extent of the earthquake outside of the New Madrid Seismic Zone, reference was made to the intensity of the quake at Mauckport, Indiana.

Now, a not-so-proud anecdote. In the early part of the novel, I wrote about a life-changing experience Jack had while riding in a friend's car in Fort Lauderdale. This came from my own experience as a teen when I sat in the passenger seat of a 1977 Pontiac Trans Am driven by my friend Mike. To this day, I don't know how I lived through those few seconds.

Finally, a note about the Butterfly People. I have not personally experienced the Butterfly People but I am certain I've had either angels or the hand of God himself protecting me throughout my life. If you're interested, search *Butterfly People of Joplin, Missouri*. The stories from the children who survived a vicious tornado in May 2011 (near the same time as the Memphis floods written about in this novel) will warm your heart.

Until next time …

Godspeed Patriots and Choose Freedom!

Bobby

SIGN UP for my mailing list at BobbyAkart.com to receive a copy of my monthly newsletter, *The Epigraph*. You'll also learn about special offers, bonus content, and you'll be the first to receive news about new releases.

VISIT my feature page at Amazon.com/BobbyAkart for more information on my novels or any of my other bestselling action-packed thrillers, which includes over forty Amazon #1 bestsellers in forty-plus fiction and nonfiction genres.

ACKNOWLEDGMENTS

Creating a novel that is both informative and entertaining requires a tremendous team effort. Writing is the easy part.

For their efforts in making *New Madrid* a reality, I would like to thank Hristo Argirov Kovatliev for his incredible artistic talents in creating my cover art. He and Dani collaborate (and conspire) to create the most incredible cover art in the publishing business. A huge hug of appreciation goes out to Pauline Nolet, the *Professor*, for her editorial prowess and patience in correcting this writer's same tics after fifty-plus novels. Thanks again to the newest member of the team, Drew Avera, a United States Navy veteran, who has brought his talented formatting skills from a writer's perspective to create multiple formats for reading my novels. Finally, the incredibly talented, award-winning performer Stacey Glemboski brings my words to life in audio format.

Now, for the serious stuff. Telling New Madrid's story required countless hours of never-ending research and interviews of some of the brightest minds in the world of geophysics.

Once again, as I immersed myself in the science and history, source material and research flooded my inbox from around America. Without the assistance of many individuals and organizations, this story could not be told. Please allow me a moment to acknowledge a few of those individuals whom, without their tireless efforts and patience, *New Madrid* could not have been written.

Many thanks to the seismologists and research geophysicists at the National Earthquake Information Center in Golden, Colorado, who've indulged my questions and theories over the last several years as I prepared to write this novel. You guys put the fear of God into me that afternoon in 2016, prompting me to write this book. In that same vein, a note of appreciation to Brian Shiro, associate director of the Geologic Hazards Science Center, who pointed me in the right direction with my inquiries.

A shout-out to Mike Lynch and Keith Hautula of the Kentucky Geological Survey and the University of Kentucky Department of Earth and Environmental Sciences is in order. They've continued decades of research into the NMSZ at the KGS. Thanks for allowing me access to the real-time recordings of seismic activity within the NMSZ so I can see what's happening beneath Earth's surface through the eyes of seismologists.

At the USGS, Reston campus, a debt of appreciation must go out to the folks in the Publications Warehouse, who helped me compile actual news accounts of the 1811–12 seismic event at New Madrid. Will Seffner, Natalia Korava, and Dave Mason are the best! I hope you'll peruse the news articles and private correspondence compiled in the back of the print editions.

New Madrid, like many of my other novels, could not have been written without the support of my contacts at the USGS and Jet Propulsion Laboratory ... Thanks to you all!

To my friends at GeoScienceWorld in McLean, Virginia, who helped guide me during my initial research into the subjects of earthquakes, volcanoes, and anything else going on under our feet. You folks are way smarter than I am!

Finally, as always, a special thank you to my team of loyal friends who've always supported my work and provided me valuable insight from a reader's perspective—Denise Keef, Joe Carey, Shirley

Nicholson, Bennita Barnett, Karl Hughey, Brian Alderman, Martin McDonell, Cody McDonell, Colt Payne, Leslie Bryant, Melonie Kennedy, Diane Ash, and Carol Dyer.

Thank you all!

Choose Freedom and Godspeed, Patriots!

ABOUT THE AUTHOR, BOBBY AKART

Author Bobby Akart has been ranked by Amazon as #25 on the Amazon Charts list of most popular, bestselling authors. He has achieved recognition as the #1 bestselling Horror Author, #1 bestselling Science Fiction Author, #5 bestselling Action & Adventure Author, #7 bestselling Historical Fiction Author and #10 on Amazon's bestselling Thriller Author list.

Mr. Akart has delivered up-all-night thrillers to readers in 245 countries and territories worldwide. He has sold over one million books in all formats, which includes over forty international bestsellers, in nearly fifty fiction and nonfiction genres.

His novel *Yellowstone: Hellfire* reached the Top 25 on the Amazon bestsellers list and earned him multiple Kindle All-Star awards for most pages read in a month and most pages read as an author. The Yellowstone series vaulted him to the #25 bestselling author on Amazon Charts, and the #1 bestselling science fiction author.

Mr. Akart is a graduate of the University of Tennessee after pursuing a dual major in economics and political science. He went on to obtain his master's degree in business administration and his doctorate degree in law at Tennessee.

Mr. Akart has provided his readers a diverse range of topics that are both informative and entertaining. His attention to detail and impeccable research has allowed him to capture the imagination of his readers through his fictional works and bring them valuable knowledge through his nonfiction books.

SIGN UP for Bobby Akart's mailing list to receive a copy of his monthly newsletter, *The Epigraph*, learn of special offers, view bonus content, and be the first to receive news about new releases featuring Gunner Fox and the Gray Fox team.

Visit www.BobbyAkart.com for details.

REAL WORLD EXCERPTS FROM
1811 – 1812

NOTE: This is a compilation of newspaper reports, personal correspondence and diary entries curated from the Earthquake Information Bulletin, United States Geological Survey and as found in the public domain. The text provided is exactly as written. No attempt was made to correct typographical or grammatical errors in order to preserve the accuracy of the historic record. The entries are not in chronological order.

LOUISIANA GAZETTE (ST. LOUIS)
Saturday, December 21, 1811
Earthquake

On Monday morning last, about a quarter past two, St. Louis and the surrounding country, was visited by one of the most violent shocks of earthquake that has been recorded since the discovery of our country.

As we were all wrapt in sleep, each tells his story in his own way. I will also relate my simple tale.

At the period above mentioned, I was roused from sleep by the clamor of windows, doors and furniture in tremulous motion, with a distant rumbling noise, resembling a number of carriages passing over pavement- in a few seconds the motion and subterraneous thunder increased more and more: believing the noise to proceed from the N. or N.W. and expecting the earth to be relieved by a volcanic eruption, I went out of doors & looked for the dreadful phenomenon. The agitation had now reached its utmost violence. I entered the house to snatch my family from its expected ruins, but before I could put my design in execution the shock had ceased, having lasted about one and three fourth minutes. The sky was obscured by a thick hazy fog, without a breath of air. Fahrenheit thermometer might have stood at this time at about 35 or 40 (degrees).

At forty seven minutes past two, another shock was felt without any rumbling noise and much less violent than the first, it lasted near two minutes.

At thirty four minutes past three, a third shock nearly as tremulous as the first, but without as much noise, it lasted about fifty seconds, and a slight trembling continued at intervals for some time after.

A little after day light, a fourth shock was felt, but with less violence than any of the others, it lasted nearly one minute.

About 8 o'clock, a fifth shock was felt; this was almost as violent as the first, accompanied with the usual noise, it lasted about half a minute: this morning was very hazy and unusually warm for the season, the houses and fences appeared covered with a white frost, but on examination it was found to be vapour, not possessing the chilling cold of frost: indeed the moon was enshrouded in awful gloom.

At half past eleven, a slight shock was felt, and about the same hour on Tuesday last, a smart shock was felt - several gentlemen declare, they felt shocks at other intervals.

No lives have been lost, nor has the houses sustained much injury, a few chimneys have been thrown down, and a few stone houses split.

In noticing extraordinary events, perhaps no attendant

circumstances should be deemed unimportant: This is one of that character, and a faithful record of appearances in such cases as these, may form data for science. Viewing the subject in this way, it may not be amiss to notice the reports of those who have explored the extensive plains and mountains of the West.

On the margin of several of our rivers pumice and other volcanic matter is found. At the base of some of the highest of the black mountains, stone covers the earth, bearing marks of the violent action of fire. Within -0 miles of the great Osage village on the head waters of their river, and 1-0 miles from this town, it is said that a volcano had ceased to burn for the last three years, and it is thought to have now broke out in some quarter of our country. Upon the whole, this has been an uncommon year; the early melting of snow to the north raised the Mississippi to an unusual height. The continued rains in the summer and the subsequent hot weather, and consequent sickness amongst the inhabitants, rendered that period somewhat distressing. - Autumn, to this time, has been unusually mild, and health ____ the ____ in every quarter.

Since writing the above, several slight shocks were sensibly felt, to the number ten or twelve.

LOUISIANA GAZETTE (ST. LOUIS)
   Editor
   Saturday, December 28, 1811

Our correspondent at Cape Girardeau has forwarded us with the following notice of the Earthquake.

Dec. 22, 1811

"The concussions of the Earthquake which commenced at two o'clock on Monday morning still continue. We have experienced five severe shocks which split two brick Houses and damaged five brick chimneys in this place."
   J. McF.

The Earthquake was felt at Nashville, Ten. with like effects, and about the same moment it was felt here.

LOUISIANA GAZETTE (ST. LOUIS)
Saturday, January 4, 1812

The editor of the St. Vincennes paper, notices an earthquake to have been felt there on the same morning as with us -- and at 3 o'clock.

Saturday, January 18, 1812

The earthquake of Dec. 16 &c was felt in the states of Ohio and Kentucky, some houses has been thrown down but no lives lost.

LOUISIANA GAZETTE (ST. LOUIS)
Saturday, February 8, 1812

On Thursday morning last, between 2 & 3 o'clock, we experienced the most severe shock of earthquake that we have yet felt, many houses are injured, and several chimneys thrown down; few hours pass without feeling slight vibrations of the earth. Should we ever obtain another mail, we shall be attentive in recording the progress in every quarter.

Saturday, February 15, 1812

A number of our readers having expressed a wish to become acquainted with the opinions of the learned, on the subject of earthquakes, we have principally devoted this number to the theories which are held in the highest estimation, and which the editors of the (last edition) of the Encyclopedia have selected from the volumes written on geology.

From what we have read on that subject, we cannot find an instant, where the earth's vibration has extended to such a vast portion of country as of the last two months concussion: travellers say that it has been felt in New York, Pennsylvania and Virginia: In Kentucky and the state of Ohio its effects were more distinctive to buildings than in Louisiana. Hunters from the west, three or four hundred miles from this place, aver that the shock felt on the 16th of Dec. was extremely violent in the headwaters of the White river. From these circumstances it would appear, that it is not limited to a particular portion of country; its extent, we believe, will be ascertained to be more wide, than any instance of such phenomena on record.

LOUISIANA GAZETTE (ST. LOUIS)

Editor

Saturday, February 22, 1812

Natchez, Jan. 2

IMPORTANT ARRIVAL

Arrived here on Monday last, the Steam Boat from Pittsburgh which had on account of low water been some time detained at the falls of the Ohio; and is destined to run between this place and New Orleans as a regular trader. She was only 221 hours under way from Pittsburgh to this place, a distance of near two thousand miles.

No very satisfactory account of the shocks of Earthquake, and their effects, which have lately happened could be expected; that received from the gentlemen on board, is rather more to than we anticipated.

The shake or jar, produced by the powerful operation of the engine, rendered the shocks imperceptible, while the boat was under way. While at anchor five or six shocks were felt, two or three more severe than the rest. On enquiry at New Madrid, a small town about 70 miles below the mouth of Ohio, they found that the chimnies of almost all the houses were thrown down, and the inhabitants considerably alarmed. - At the little Prairie, thirty miles lower down, they were bro't to by the cries of some of the people, who thought the earth was gradually sinking but declined to take refuge on board without their friends, whom they wished to collect.

Some distance below the little Prairie the bank of the river had caved in to a considerable extent, and two islands had almost disappeared.

SAVANNAH, GEORGIA EVENING LEDGER

Mr. Evans - The repeated shocks of Earthquakes, which have been felt in this place since the morning of the 16th, having drawn forth some speculations and hypotheses from the scientific. I shall take the liberty of giving as perfect an account of the phenomena as they occurred, as my own observations, assisted by that of others, will enable me to do.

About 3 o'clock of the morning of the 16th, a shock was felt which produced an oscillating movements of the houses, and lasted for nearly a minute. It was not preceded by any noises which usually portend this phenomenon, nor was its approach announced by any other appearance than a great serenity in the atmosphere. An hour afterwards another shock was felt, but of shorter continuance than the other and a person then up, has said, that he observed at the same time a tremulous undulating motion of the earth like the rolling of waves. At 8 o'clock a noise resembling distant thunder was heard, and was soon after followed by a shock which appeared to operate vertically, that is to say, by a heaving of the ground upwards - but was not sufficiently severe to injure either furniture or glasses. This shock was succeeded by a thick haze, and many people were affected by giddiness and nausea. Another shock was experienced about 9 o'clock at night, but so light as not to be generally felt - and at half past 12 the next day (the 17th) another shock was felt, which lasted only a few seconds and was succeeded by a tremor which was occasionally observed throughout the day effecting many with giddiness. At half past 8 o'clock a very thick haze came on, and for a few minutes a sulphurous smell was emitted. At nine o'clock last night, another was felt, which continued four or five seconds, but so slight as to have escaped the observation of many who had not thought of attending particularly to the operations of this phenomenon. At one o'clock this morning

(23d) another shock took place of nearly equal severity with the first of the 16th. Buried in sleep, I was not sensible of this, but I have derived such correct information on the fact that I have no reason to doubt it; but I have observed since 11 o'clock this morning frequent tremors of the earth, such as usually precede severe shocks in other parts of the world.

It is something extraordinary, that these shocks so numerous should not be attended with more formidable effects, or that they should not have increased in their severity. There is nothing extraordinary in their frequency, but as in other countries, not so much subject to the influence of the sun as this is, such frequent shocks usually have ended in mischief and desolation, we ought to have calculated upon similar effects from similar causes.

The mildness of those we have felt can be attributed only to the distance of the cause by which they have been produced. On this subject, of the cause of earthquakes, there are numerous and discordant opinions from the ancient philosopher. An __xagoras, to sir William Hamilton or Mr. Oplomien.

According to the hypothesis of some, earthquakes are occasioned by subterranean fires throwing down the arches or vaults of the earth; according to others the rarefaction of the abyss waters, interior combustion and fermentation, volcanic operations, and lately by the electric fluid.

The latter hypothesis seems to be the most accredited, as it evidently is the most rational. The instantaneous effects of _____ earthquakes prove beyond doubt that electricity __iss be the principal agent in this alarming and terrible phenomenon. Whether according ___ ___, this electricity is superficial, or is buried in and pervades the bowels of the earth, as is supposed by others, is among those _____ of nature, which human wisdom may be never able to ascertain.

The most rational hypothesis to me seems to be, that earthquakes are produced by an _____ of terrestrial and atmospheric electricity, as by the former the heaving of the ground upwards is easily explained as the corruscations and explosions which sometimes precede and accompany earthquakes may be accounted for by the influence of the other.

Volcanic operations may have their influence in the production of earthquakes, by giving an extraordinary impulse to the electric matter which everywhere pervades the interior of the earth, and as no bounds can be fixed to the progress of that subtle fluid, the impulse which may be given by a volcano of the Andes would reach us in the course of an hour, or sooner, in proportion to the quantity of electric fluid affected by the contact.

The celebrated earthquake in 1755 appears from all the facts, as they have been carefully compiled, to have travelled four millions of square miles in about one hour and ten minutes.

From the nature, quality and direction of the shocks felt in this city I am induced from a variety of circumstances to suppose, that they may be traced to some of the volcanic operations of the Cordillera de los Andes, and if the hasty remarks which I now do myself the pleasure of submitting are deemed sufficiently interesting for publication, the subject will be renewed with more method and reflection.

A SUBSCRIBER

Savannah, Dec. 23, 1811

ST. LOUIS

SAVANNAH, GEORGIA EVENING LEDGER

Saturday, February 22

By a gentleman just from Arkansas, by way of White river, we learn that the earthquake was violent in that quarter that in upwards of 500 places he observed coal and sand thrown up from fissures in the earth, that the waters raised in a swamp near the Cherokee village, so as to drown a Mr. Carrin who was travelling with his brother, the latter saved himself on a log. - In other places the water fell, and in one instant it rose in a swamp near the St. Francis 25 or 30 feet; Strawberry a branch of Black river, an eminence about 1-1/2 acres sunk down and formed a pond.

The Earthquake noticed in our list has been felt in various parts of the country. The paper from Richmond, Falenton(?), Wilmington, Charleston and Savannah, mention the phenomenon-- In Charleston, six distinct shocks were felt; the first and most violent about 3 o'clock, and one minute and a half in duration. It was very severe and alarming; indeed, the vibration was so great as to see some of the church bells ringing- the pendulums of the clocks stopped, and the picture glasses in many houses were broken.

Saturday, February 29, 1812
   EARTHQUAKE

SAVANNAH, GEORGIA EVENING LEDGER
   New Orleans, December 26

A letter from Fort Stoddert mentions, that on the morning of the 16th past, two shocks of an earthquake had been felt. This is precisely the time it was felt at Natchez. It is evident that our being on an island and resting on the water, prevented us from feeling part of the shocks.

Cape Girardeau, Feb. 15th, 1812

The concussions of the earthquake still continue, the shock on the 23rd ult. was more severe and larger than that of the 16th Dec. and the shock of the 7th inst. was still more violent than any preceding, and lasted longer than perhaps any on record, (from 10 to 15 minutes, the earth was not at rest for one hour.) the ravages of this dreadful convulsion have nearly depopulated the district of New Madrid, but few remain to tell the sad tale, the inhabitants have fled in every direction. It has done considerable damage in this place by demolishing chimnies, and cracking cellar walls. Some have been driven from their houses, and a number are yet in tents. No doubt volcanoes in the mountains of the west, which have been extinguished for ages, are now opened.

Saturday, March 7, 1812
   Orleans, January 13

THE EARTHQUAKE

By a gentleman who came on the Steam Boat we are informed that this convulsion of nature, (the first, we believe that has ever been felt on the Mississippi since the settlement of the country by the whites,) has destroyed several islands in the Mississippi, and has thereby endangered its navigation very considerably. He also states that it has sunk the land in a number of places on the margin of the river.

Mr. Charless,
   I here give you an extract of a letter, dated Orleans January 16th, from my friend John Bradbury. It will be found to contain some information relative to the effects of the earthquake of 16th Dec. on the Mississippi river and its banks; permit me to add that you have no information from any source which can be more implicitly relied on.
   Yours, H.W.D.
   EXTRACT

"Our voyage was from various causes tedious and disagreeable, we being 28 days from St. Louis to this place, Mr. Comegys has fared worse, being two months. Our progress was considerably impeded by an alarming and awful earthquake, such as has not I believe, occurred, or at least has not been recorded in the history of this country. The first shock which we experienced was about 2 o'clock on the morning of the 16th Dec. at which time our position was in itself perilous, we being but a few hundred yards above a bad place in the river, called the Devils Race Ground:* in our situation particularly, the scene was terrible beyond description, our boat appeared as if alternately lifted out of the water, and again suffered to fall. The banks above, below and around us were falling every moment into the river, all nature seemed running into chaos. The noise unconnected with particular objects, was the noise of the most violent tempest of wind mixed with a sound equal to the loudest thunder, but more hollow and vibrating. The crashing of falling trees and the loud screeching of wild fowl made up the horrid concert. Two men were sent on shore in order to examine the state of the bank to which we were moored, who reported that a few yards from its summit, it was separated from the shore by a chasm of more than 100 yards in length. Jos. Morin, the patron, insisted on our all leaving the boat which he thought could not be saved, and of landing immediately in order to save our lives: - this I successfully combatted until another shock took place, about 3 o'clock, when we all left the boat, went on shore and kindled a fire. Between the first shock and daylight, we counted 27. As day broke we put off from the shore, at which instant we experienced another shock, nearly as violent as the first, by this the fright of the hands was so much increased, that they seemed deprived of strength and reason: I directed Morin to land on a sloping bank at the entrance of the Devil's Race Ground, intending to wait there until the men should be refreshed with a good breakfast. While it was preparing, we had three shocks, so strong as to make it difficult for us to stand on our feet; at length recovered from our panic we proceeded; after this we felt shocks during 6 days, but none to compare with those on the memorable morning of the 16th. I made many and minute observations on this earthquake, which if ever we meet, I will communicate to you, &c."

* 120 miles below N. Madrid

Extract of a letter from Orleans dated Feb. 11, to a gentleman in this place.

"This city has experienced some slight concussion of earthquake, particularly on the 9th, whilst a number of persons were at the theatre and the ball, some of whom were much alarmed, tho' the shock was not severe, nor had done any damage."

Saturday, March 14, 1812

The Earthquake of the 16th of December last was felt as far North as Charlestown, New Hampshire.

Saturday, March 21, 1812

The Indian mode of worship, as happened in consequence of the late Earthquakes.

This alarming phenomenon of nature struck with such consternation and dismay, those tribes of Indians, that live within and contiguous to that tract of country, on the Mississippi, where the severity of the earthquake appears to have been the greatest, that they were induced to convene together in order to consult upon the necessity of having recourse to some method of relief, from so alarming an incident; when it was resolved to fall upon the following expedient to excite the pity of the Great Spirit. [There follows a description of the religious ceremony of the Shawnees.]

We are informed from a respectable source that the old road to the post of Arkansas, by Spring river, is entirely destroyed by the last violent shocks of earthquake. Chasms of great depth and considerable length cross the country in various directions, some swamps have become dry, others deep lakes, and in some places hills have disappeared.

Pittsburgh, Feb. 14

On Friday morning the 7th inst. about 4 o'clock, a shock of an Earthquake was severely felt in this town. The effects of this convulsion were much more sensibly felt, than the one which happened on the 16th of December. Many of the houses were violently shaken.

Saturday, April 18, 1812

Accounts from la Haut Missouri, announces a general peace among the Indians, it is said that the earthquakes has created this pacification.

Saturday, May 2, 1812

Slight shocks of Earthquake continue to be felt here. On Wednesday night last, several who were awake declare, they felt a strong vibration of the Earth.

THE LOUISIANA GAZETTE AND DAILY ADVERTISER (NEW ORLEANS)
Saturday, December 21, 1811

No mail north of Natchez yesterday. Letters from that city state that a small earthquake had been felt there some days ago. From the principles of earthquakes we are surprised it was not felt here. Earthquakes have generally been felt in southern mountainous countries; sometimes located to a small portion of country sometimes more extended. Different nations, near the Adriatic and Mediterranean, have felt the shock of an earthquake at the same moment.

The Comet has been passing to the westward since it passed its perihelion - perhaps it has touched the mountain of California, that has given a small shake to this side of the globe - or the skake which the Natchezians have felt may be a mysterious visitation from the Author of all nature, on them for their sins - wickedness and the want of good faith have long prevailed in that territory.

Sodom and Gomorrha would have been saved had three righteous persons been found in it - we therefore hope that Natchez has been saved on the same principle.

THE LOUISIANA GAZETTE AND DAILY ADVERTISER (NEW ORLEANS)

Thursday, December 26, 1811

A letter from Fort Stoddert mentions, that on the morning of the 16th inst. two shocks of an earthquake had been felt.- This is precisely the time it was felt at Natchez. It is evident that our being our island and resting as it were on the water, prevented us from feeling part of the shock.

Tuesday, December 31, 1811

NATCHEZ WEEKLY CHRONICLE

THE EARTHQUAKE - A hasty Sketch

Natchez, Dec. 18th, 1811

Sir,

Having made a few observations with respect to the Earthquake, which has drawn the attention of the citizens of this place and its vicinity within a few days past, I present them, to you thrown together in a hasty way for publication, if you think fit, under the impression that they may not be uninteresting to your readers.

On the morning of Monday last the 16th inst. several shocks were felt - four have been ascertained by an accurate observer to have been felt in this city. The principal one, as near as can be collected, was about ten minutes past two o'clock, A.M. There was no noise heard in the atmosphere but in a few instances in certain situations-- The shock was attended by a tremulous motion of the earth and buildings - felt by some for about one and a half minutes; by others about five; and my own impression is, that I am conscious of its lasting at least three, having been awakened from my sleep. Several clocks were stopped at two or about ten minutes after. Several articles were thrown off the shelves; crockery was sent rolling about the floor; articles suspended from the ceiling of the stores vibrated rapidly without any air to disturb them, for about nine inches; the plastering in the rooms of some houses was cracked and injured; the river was much convulsed, so much that it induced some of the boatmen at the landing, who supposed the bank was falling in, to cut adrift. The shocks in the morning were at about six or half after, one of them considerable. The vibration of suspended articles was, whenever room would admit them, east to west. Accounts from Louisiana state, that the first shock was felt about ten minutes past 2, A.M. at Black river, thirty miles distant, and at different places on the road to Rapids, where the trees were violently agitated. It was also felt on the river at a considerable distance above and below Vidalia. - The shock was also felt as far up as the Big Black, and at the different intervening towns; in the vicinity of Washington the trees were observed to be much convulsed, nodding their heads together as if coming to the ground.

Another shock was experienced yesterday of fifteen minutes past eleven o'clock, A.M. The houses in several instances shook considerably, and the suspended articles in the stores were violently convulsed. Some clocks were again stopped, and in one of the stores a cowbell was heard to tinkle.

NATCHEZ WEEKLY CHRONICLE
AN OBSERVER
Tuesday, January 14, 1812

The earthquake that was felt at Natchez on the 16th of December, has been severely felt above and below the mouth of the Ohio - we may expect detailed accounts of the damages soon. Travelers who have descended the river since, generally agree that a succession of shocks were felt for six days; that the river Mississippi was much agitated; that it frequently rose 3 and 4 feet, and fell again immediately; and that whole islands and parts of islands in the river sunk.

NATCHEZ WEEKLY CHRONICLE
Monday, January 20, 1812

We have the following description of the Earthquake from gentlemen who were on board a large barge, and lay an anchor in the Mississippi a few leagues below New Madrid, on the night of the 15th of December. About 2 o'clock all hands were awakened by the first shock; the impression was, that the barge had dragged her anchor and was grounding on gravel; such, were the feelings for 60 or 80 seconds, when the shock subsided. The crew were so fully persuaded of the fact of their being aground, that they put out their sounding poles, but found water enough.

At seven next morning a second and very severe shock took place. The barge was under way - the river rose several feet; the trees on the shore shook; the banks in large columns tumbled in; hundreds of old trees that had lain perhaps half a century at the bottom of the river, appeared on the surface of the water; the feathered race took to the wing; the canopy was covered with geese and ducks and various other kinds of wild fowl; very little wind; the air was tainted with a nitrous and sulphureous smell; and every thing was truly alarming for several minutes. The shocks continued to the 21st Dec. during that time perhaps one hundred were distinctly felt. From the river St. Francis to the Chickasaw bluffs visible marks of the earthquake were discovered; from that place down, the banks did not appear to have been disturbed.

There is one part of this description which we cannot reconcile with philosophic principles, (although we believe the narrative to be true,) that is, the trees which were settled at the bottom of the river appearing on the surface. It must be obvious to every person that those trees must have become specifically heavier than the water before they sunk, and of course after being immersed in the mud must have increased in weight. - We therefore submit the question to the Philosophical Society.

NATCHEZ WEEKLY CHRONICLE
Tuesday, January 21, 1812

The earthquake was felt at Pittsburg, Richmond, Norfolk, Raleigh, and various other parts of the United Sates.

NATCHEZ WEEKLY CHRONICLE
Friday, January 24, 1812

A slight shock of an earthquake was felt in this city yesterday morning, about nine o'clock. The wind was from the southward, light and gentle, and the morning fine-- it lasted but few seconds & but few felt it. At that time all is bustle in the city - but many proofs, such as clocks stopping, glass shades, and different kinds of glass ware and crockery shaking, the feelings of many who were either writing or reading, prove the fact. We may expect to hear more on the subject from the northward & eastward

THE PITTSBURGH GAZETTE
Friday, December 20, 1811

On Monday morning last, about three o'clock, the citizens of this town were greatly alarmed by the shock of an Earthquake; a number of persons from the shaking of their houses, were so much alarmed as to jump out of bed. About 7 o'clock, the same morning, there was another shock, though not so evident as the first.

THE PITTSBURGH GAZETTE
Friday, December 27, 1811

By accounts from Meadville, and Waterford, we are informed, that severe shocks of an earthquake were felt at those places on Monday morning the 16th inst. at the same time of those experienced here. At Meadville, the one which happened at 3 o'clock was so sensibly felt, that many persons were awaken by the rocking of their beds, and the trea - - ious motion continued from 10 to 15 minutes - the one at 8 o'clock was nearly as severe, but did not continue so long - the top of the trees in the town were seen to vibrate for about a minute, and the puddles of water in the streets appeared in waves as if a sudden blast of wind had passed over them. On Tuesday about the middle of the day, a third shake was felt, but was slighter than the others.

THE PITTSBURGH GAZETTE
Friday, January 31, 1812
THE EARTHQUAKE

Extract of a letter from a gentleman on his way to New Orleans, to a friend in this place (Lexington, Ky.) - dated 20th December.

"We entered the Mississippi on the morning of the 14th, and on the night of the 15th came to anchor on a sand bar, about ten miles above the Little Prairie - half past 2 o'clock in the morning of the 16th, we were aroused from our slumber by a violent shaking of the boat - there were three barges and two keels in company, all effected the same way. The alarm was considerable and various opinions as to the cause were suggested, all found to be erroneous; but after the second shock, which occurred in 15 minutes after the first, it was unanimously admitted to be an earthquake. With most awful feelings we watched till morning in trembling anxiety, supposing all was over with us. We weighed anchor early in the morning, and in a few minutes after we started there came on in quick successions, two other shocks, more violent than the former. It was then daylight, and we could plainly perceive the effect it had on shore. The bank of the river gave way in all directions, and came tumbling into the water; the trees were more agitated than I ever before saw them in the severest storms, and many of them from the shock they received broke off near the ground, as well as many more torn up by the roots. We considered ourselves more secure on the water, than we should be on land, of course we proceeded down the river. As we progressed the effects of the shock as before described, were observed in every part of the banks of the Mississippi. In some places five, ten and fifteen acres have sunk down in a body, even the Chickasaw Bluffs, which we have passed, did not escape; one or two of them have fallen in considerably.

The inhabitants of the Little Prairie and its neighborhood all deserted their homes, and retired back to the hills or swamps. The only brick chimney in the place was entirely demolished by the shocks. I have not yet heard that any lives were lost, or accident of consequence happened. I have been twice on shore since the first shock, and then but a very short time, as I thought it unsafe, for the ground is cracked and torn to pieces in such a way as made it truly alarming; indeed some of the islands in the river that contained from one to two hundred acres of land have been nearly all sunk, and not one yet that I have seen but is cracked from one end to the other, and has lost some part of it.

There has been in all forty-one shocks, some of them have been very light; the first one took place at half past 2 on the morning of the 16th, the last one at eleven o'clock this morning, (20th) since I commenced writing this letter. The last one I think was not as severe as some of the former, but it lasted longer than any of the preceding; I think it continued nearly a minute and a half. Exclusive of the shocks that were made sensible to us in the water, there have been, I am induced to believe, many others, as we frequently heard a rumbling noise at a distance when no shock to us was perceptible. I am the more inclined to believe these were shocks, from having heard the same kind of rumbling with the shocks that affected us. There is one circumstance that has occurred, which if I had not seen with my own eyes, I could hardly have believed; which is, the rising of the trees that lie in the bed of the river. I believe that every tree that has been deposited in the bed of the river since Noah's flood, now stands erect out of the water; some of these I saw myself during one of the hardest shocks rise up eight or ten feet out of water. The navigation has been rendered extremely difficult in many places in consequence of the snags being so extremely thick. From the long continuance and frequency of these shocks, it is extremely uncertain when they will cease; and if they have been as heavy at New Orleans as we have felt them, the consequences must be dreadful indeed; and I am fearful when I arrive at Natchez to hear that the whole city of Orleans is entirely demolished, and perhaps sunk.

Immediately after the first shock and those which took place after daylight, the whole atmosphere was impregnated with a sulphurous smell."

THE PITTSBURGH GAZETTE

Friday, February 7, 1812
EARTHQUAKE CORRESPONDENCE

New Orleans, December 26, A letter from Fort Stoddert mentions, that on the morning of the 16th inst. two shocks of an earthquake had been felt. This is precisely the time it was felt at Natchez. It is evident that our being on an island and resting on the water, prevented us from feeling part of the shock.

Fort St. Stephens, December 24, ONn Sunday night the 15th inst. the earth shook here so as to shake the fowls off their roosts, and made the houses shake very much, again it shook at sunrise and at 11 o'clock next morning, and at the same time the next day, and about the same time the third day after.

Accounts are brought in from the nation that several hunting Indians who were lately on the Missouri have returned, and state that the earthquake was felt very sensibly there, that it shook down trees and many rocks of the mountains, and that everything bore the appearance of an immediate dissolution of the world! - We give this as we got it - it may be correct - but the probability is that it is not.

NASHVILLE CLARION

Friday, February 14, 1812
EARTHQUAKE

From Mr. James Fletcher, Nashville, (Ten.) January 21, in whose statement we place the utmost reliance we have received the following narrative:

At the Little Prairie, (a beautiful spot on the west side of the Mississippi river about 30 miles from New-Madrid), on the 16th of December last, about 2 o'clock, A.M., we felt a severe concussion of the earth, which we supposed to be occasioned by a distant earthquake, and did not apprehend much damage. Between that time and day we felt several other slighter shocks; about sunrise another very severe one came on, attended with a perpendicular bouncing that caused the earth to open in many places - some eight and ten feet wide, numbers of less width, and of considerable length - some parts have sunk much lower than others, where one of these large openings are, one side remains as high as before the shock and the other is sunk; some more, some less; but the deepest I saw was about twelve feet. The earth was, in the course of fifteen minutes after the shock in the morning, entirely inundated with water. The pressing of the earth, if the expression be allowable, caused the water to spout out of the pores of the earth, to the height of eight or ten feet! We supposed the whole country sinking, and knew not what to do for the best. The agitation of the earth was so great that it was with difficulty any could stand on their feet, some could not - The air was very strongly impregnated with a sulphurous smell. As if by instinct, we flew as soon as we could from the river, dreading most danger there - but after rambling about two or three hours, about two hundred gathered at Capt. Francis Lescuer's, where we encamped, until we heard that the upper country was not damaged, when I left the camp (after staying there twelve days) to look for some other place, and was three days getting about thirty miles, from being obliged to travel around those chasms.

Previous to my leaving the country I heard that many parts of the Mississippi river had caved in; in some places several acres at the same instant. But the most extraordinary effect that I saw was a small lake below the river St. Francis. The bottom of which is blown up higher than any of the adjoining country, and instead of water it is filled with a beautiful white sand. The same effect is produced in many other lakes, or I am informed by those who saw them; and it is supposed they are generally filled up. A little river called Pemisece, that empties into the St. Francis, and runs parallel with the Mississippi, at the distance of about twelve miles from it, is filled also with sand. I only saw it near its bend, and found it to be so, and was informed by respectable gentlemen who had seen it lower down, that it was positively filled with sand. On the sand that was thrown out of the lakes and river lie numerous quantities of fish of all kinds common to the country.

The damage to stock, &c. was unknown. I heard of only two dwelling houses, a granary, and smoke house, being sunk. One of the dwelling houses was sunk twelve feet below the surface of the earth; the other the top was even with the surface. The granary and smoke house were entirely out of sight; we suppose sunk and the earth closed over them. The buildings through the country are much damaged. We heard of no lives being lost, except seven Indians, who were shaken into the Mississippi. - This we learned from one who escaped.

Previous to the shocks coming on, we heard a rumbling noise like that of thunder. They continued until I left the country - some very sincere. - I cannot tell how many there were.

The above account is confirmed by letters from the country. A gentleman attempting to pass from Cape Girardeau to the pass of St. Francis, found the earth so much cracked and broke, that it was impossible to get along. The course must be about 50 miles back of the Little Prairie. Others have experienced the same difficulty in getting along, and at times had to go miles out of their way to shun those chasms.

We have no idea that the principal cause of the shocks originated on the Mississippi - we have not yet heard the worse."

NASHVILLE CLARION
Friday, February 14, 1812

On Friday morning, the 7th inst. about 4 o'clock, a shock of an earthquake was severly felt in this town. The effects of the convulsion were much more sensibly felt, than the one which happened on the 16th of December. Many of the houses were violently shaken.

NASHVILLE CLARION
Friday, February 21, 1812

The following extract, taken from a letter received from Mr. Zadock Cramer, to his friend in this place, dated Natchez, Jan. 23, 1812 serves to corroborate the account hitherto received besides noting other remarkable phenomena in nature, with which we have not before become acquainted.

"This morning at eight o'clock, another pretty severe shock of an earthquake was felt. Those on the 16th ult. and since done much damage on the Mississippi river, from the mouth of the Ohio to Little Prairie particularly. Many boats have been lost, and much property sunk. The banks of the river, in many places, sunk hundreds of acres together, leaving the tops of the trees to be seen above the water. The earth opened in many places from one to three feet wide, through whose fissures stone coal was thrown up in pieces as large as a man's hand. The earth rocked - trees lashed their tops together. The whole seemed in convulsions, throwing up sand bars here, there sinking others, trees jumping from the bed of the river, roots uppermost, forming a most serious impediment to navigation, where before there was no obstruction - boats rocked like cradles - men, women and children confused, running to and fro and hallooing for safety - those on land pleading to get into the boats - those in boats willing almost to be on land. This damning and distressing scene continued for several days, particularly at and above Flour island. The long reach now, though formerly the best part of the river is said to be the worst being filled with innumerable planters and sawyers which have been thrown up from the bed by the extraordinary convulsions of the river. Little Prairie, and the country about it, suffered much - new lakes having been formed, and the bed of old ones raised to the elevation of the surface of the adjacent country. All accounts of those who have descended the river since the shocks give the most alarming and terrific picture of the desolating and horrible scene."

OHIO and MISSISSIPPI NAVIGATOR
February 18, 1812

Messrs. Cramer, Spear & Eichbaum
Printers, Pittsburgh
Gentlemen:
Your being editors of the useful guide, the Ohio and Mississippi Navigator, induces me, for the sake of the western country traders to inform you as early as in my power the wonderful changes for the worse in some parts of the Mississippi river, occasioned by the dreadful earthquake which happened on the morning of the 16th of December last, and which has continued to shake almost every day since. As to its effects on the river I found but little from the mouth of Ohio to New Madrid, from which place to the Chickasaw Bluffs, or Fort Pickering, the face of the river is wholly changed, particularly from Island No. 30, to island No. 40; (see page 185) this part of the river burst and shook up hundreds of great trees from the bottom, and what is more singular they are all turned roots upwards and standing upstream in the best channel and swiftest water, and nothing but the greatest exertions of the boatmen can save them from destruction in passing those places. I should advise all those concerned to be particular in approaching Island No. 32, where you must warp through a great number, and when past them, bear well over from the next right hand point for fear of being drawn into the right schute of Flour Island, Island 33, which I should advise against, as that pass is become very dangerous unless in very high water. Two boats from Little Beaver are lately lost, and several much injured in that pass this season. Boats should hug the

left shore where there is but few sawyers, and good water and fine landing on the lower point of the island, from there the next dangerous place is the Devil's Race Ground, Island No. 36, (page 187). Here I would advise boats never to pass to the left of the island and by all means to keep close to the right hand point, and then close round the sandbar on the lower end of the schute is very dangerous and the gap so narrow that boats can scarcely pass without being dashed on some of the snags, and should you strike one you can scarcely extricate yourself before you receive some injury. From this scene you have barely time to breathe and refresh, before you arrive at the Devil's Elbow, alias the Devil's Hackle, Islands No. 38 and 39 (p. 188) by far the worst of all; in approaching this schute you must hug close around the left hand point until you come in sight of the sand bar whose head has the appearance of an old field full of trees, then pull for the island to keep clear of these, and pass through a small schute, leaving all the island sawyers to the right, and take care not to get too near them, for should you strike the current is so rapid it will be with great difficulty you will be able to save, your boat and cargo.

I shall advise all those descending the river not to take the right hand of Island No. 38, as it appears entirely choked up with drift and rafts of sawyers. When through these bad places the worst is over, only fuller of snags, but mind well the directions in the Navigator and there will be no danger. Run the Grand Cut-off No. 55, (p. 192) in all stages of the water, and hug close the right hand point, this pass is good. Take the left of St. Francis No. 59, left of No. 62, right of large sand bar and Island No. 63, and right of No. 76, in all the different stages of the water. All these channels are much the best and safest. Should this be the means of saving one boat load of provisions to an industrious citizen, how amply shall I feel rewarded for noting this, whilst with gratitude I acknowledge the obligation we as boatmen are under to you for your useful guide, that excellent work the Ohio and Mississippi Navigator, much to be valued for its accuracy and geographical account of this immense country.

I have the honor to be, gentlemen, your sincere friend and humble servant.

James Smith

OHIO and MISSISSIPPI NAVIGATOR
Friday, April 10, 1812
"SIGNS OF THE TIMES"

Has such a succession of Earthquakes as have happened within a few weeks been experienced in this country five years ago, they would have excited universal terror. The extent of territory which has been shaken, nearly at the same time, is astonishing - reaching on the Atlantic coast from Connecticut to Georgia and from the shores of the ocean inland to the State of Ohio. What power short of Omnipotence, could raise and shake such vast portion of this globe? What a tremendous natural agent must have (sed) to produce such mighty effects as stated that in North Carolina a volcano has appeared, and that in an eruption a few days since, a flood of lava poured out which ran to the distance of three quarters of a mile. - The period is portentous and alarming. We have within a few years seen the most wonderful eclipses, the year past has produced a magnificent comet, the earthquakes within the past two months have been almost without number - and in addition to the whole, we constantly "hear of wars and summons of wars." May not the same enquiry be made of us that was made by the hypocrites of old - "Can ye not discern the signs of the times."

PENNSYLVANIA GAZETTE (PHILADELPHIA)
Wednesday, December 25, 1811
Richmond, (Vir.) Dec. 16.

An earthquake was witnessed by many people in the city - about three o'clock in the morning there were three successive shocks; another about 6; and again about 8. Several persons were under a persuasion that thieves had broken into their houses; and in one of the most elevated houses of the city, the bells, both above and below, were set a ringing.

Norfolk, December 16.

This morning two distinct shocks of an earthquake were felt in this place: The first, and (according to most accounts) the most violent, was about 3 o'clock. It was so severe as to awaken a number of persons out of their sleep. The shock, at two very short intervals, might have continued about a minute. The shaking of the beds is described as if a strong man had taken hold on the posts, and shook them with all the violence in his power. Several clocks were stopped. The houses were shaking with great violence. Again about eight o'clock another shock was felt by a great number of persons, as many had risen; this was also very violent. The most sensible effect produced by this, that we have yet learned, was that of throwing a pipe of wine off the skids, in a warehouse, in Commerce street.

PENNSYLVANIA GAZETTE (PHILADELPHIA)
Wednesday, January 1, 1812
Charleston, Dec. 16

An Earthquake - This morning, a few minutes before three o'clock, a severe shock of an earthquake was felt in this city. Its duration is supposed to have been between two and three minutes. For an hour previous, though the air was perfectly calm, and several stars visible, there was, at intervals of about five minutes, a rumbline noise, resembling distant thunder; which increased in violence of sound, just before the shock was felt. The vibrations of St. Phillip's steeple caused the clock bell to ring about 10 seconds. Two other shocks were felt this morning, one a little before 8 o'clock, and the other ten minutes after that hour; both slighter than the first, and of shorter duration: the vibrations of the second lasted probably rather more than a minute, and of the last two or three seconds. Many of the clocks were stopped; and the water of the different wells was much agitated. We have not heard of any damage having been done by these repeated shocks; nor have we heard how far they have extended into the country; except that they were felt at Rantowle's.

Such phenomena, until lately, were very rare. One is remembered to have happen on the 19th May, 1754, about 11 o'clock, A.M.; but it was very slight. Another slight one was felt on the 11th April, 1799, about 1 o'clock in the morning. In the year 1811, on the 13th January, another occurred, and was felt at Columbia and Granby, in this state, and in Augusta in Georgia, but not in Charleston.

PENNSYLVANIA GAZETTE (PHILADELPHIA)
Wednesday, January 29, 1812
Alexandria, Jan. 24.

A shock of an Earthquake was distinctly felt in this town yesterday morning, about 20 minutes after nine o'clock. Its duration was supposed to be about 30 seconds, and its motions from N.W. to S.E. Considerable sensation was excited by this event.

New York, January 24.

Another Earthquake - A correspondent at Jamaici (L.I.) under date of this day, says - "Yesterday morning, at fifteen minutes after nine o'clock, a shock of an earthquake was sensibly felt in this village. Every thing suspended in my store was set in motion for more than a minute. The motion was a steady swinging backward and forward. The shock was felt also by my family, and by several of our neighbors."

We understand that the shock was noticed by many people in this city.

CORRESPONDENCE
Arkport, (N.Y.) Jan. 6

Messrs. Miner & Butler,

A very singular phenomenon took place near Angelica, in the country of Allegany, on Monday morning the 16th of December, which I will state, as related to me by one of the eye witnesses. Early in the morning, about sunrise as sitting at breakfast, he had a strange feeling, and supposed at first that he was fainting, but as his sight did not fail, he then concluded that he was going into a fit, and removed his chair back from the table. - He then had a sensation as though the house was swinging and observed clothes hanging on lines in the room were swinging, as also a large kettle hanging over the fire. He observed that his wife and family appeared to be greatly alarmed, and still supposing that it was in consequence of his apparently falling into a fit, but on enquiry found that all felt the same sensation. This continued as he supposed for at least 15 minutes. There was no noise or trembling, nor any wind, but only an appearance of swinging or rocking, as he supposed, equal to the house rocking two feet one way and the other. - One of his neighbors felt the same, and on the opposite side of the river, at the farmhouse and dwelling house of Phillip Church, the same motions and sensations were felt. Mrs. Church was in bed, and when she first felt the motion, and a strange sensation as if suffocating, she jumped out of bed, supposing the house was on fire. The motion was so considerable as to set all the bells in the several rooms a ringing, and an inside door was observed to swing open and shut.

The same motions were felt up the river, about eight miles above, at a house near a small brook; the people ran out of the house, and observed the water to have the same motion. Accounts state, that the same motions have been felt at sundry other places 30 miles distant.

I could relate many other similar motions felt and perceived at the same time, but leave it for the present. How to account for it I know not. If you think it worthy of notice, you may make it public, and if the same or similar motions have been felt at other places, doubtless it will be communicated. I should like to hear it accounted for on rational principles.

Christopher Hurlbut

CORRESPONDENCE
Baltimore. Jan. 27

Extract of a letter dated West River, January 23.

"This morning, at about 9 o'clock, a friend of mine, Captain Franklin, miss Webster, and myself, had just sat down to breakfast, when Captain F. observed, "What's that? An Earthquake!" at the same instant, we felt as if we were in the cabin of a vessel, during a heavy swell. This sensation continued for one or two minutes, possibly longer. For although I had the presence of mind to take out my watch, I felt too sick to accurately observe its duration. The feeling was by no means tremulous, but a steady vibration. A portrait, about four feet in length, suspended from the ceiling by a hook and staple, and about five eights of an inch from the side wall, vibrated at least from eighteen inches to 2 feet each side, and so very steady, as not to touch the wall. My next neighbour and his daughter felt the same sensation about the same time. The father supposed it was the gout in his head. The daughter got up and walked to a window, supposing the heat of the fire had caused what she considered a faintness. Two others that I have seen mentioned to have felt the same, but none of them had thought of an earthquake. The two last being mechanics, and up late, mentioned that they were much alarmed at about 11 o'clock last night, by a great rumbling, as they thought, in the earth, attended with several flashes of lightning, which so lighted the house, that they could have picked up the smallest pin - one mentioned, that the rumbling and the light was accompanied by a noise like that produced by throwing a hot iron into snow, only very loud and terrific, so much so, that he was fearful to go out to look what it was, for he never once thought of an earthquake. I have thrown together the above particulars, supposing an extract may meet with corroborating accounts, and afford some satisfaction to your readers.

P.S. - The lightning and rumbling noise came from the south - I have just heard of its being felt in several other houses, but not any particulars more than related.

CORRESPONDENCE

Easton, (Md.) . Jan. 25.

The Earthquake - Last Thursday morning, about nine o'clock, the shock of an Earthquake was very sensibly felt in this place. The vibratory motion, which continued nearly a minute, seemed to be north and south, and was so violent that the pendulums of several clocks stopped vibrating, and the weights were thrown into an irregular and confused motion. Considerable giddiness, some nausea, much wonder, and a little terror, were among the consequences.

CORRESPONDENCE

Annapolis, Jan. 23.

An Earthquake - A severe shock of an earthquake was experienced by a number of persons in this city yesterday morning, the 22nd inst. about sixteen minutes before ten o'clock. Its duration is supposed to have been about two or three minutes, from beginning to end, and its direction apparently from E. to S.W. This phenomenon was dissimilar in its nature and effects from any of the kind that we have heretofore heard of, as it was not accompanied or preceded by the usual rumbling noise, nor any sudden concussion of the earth, but a continued roll, similar to that of a vessel in a heavy sea. One circumstance which renders its effect more singular is, that it was very sensibly felt by some, while others altho' in same room, and perhaps within a few feet of them, were not in the least affected by its operation, and those who were in the street, or open air, were insensible as to any extraordinary motion of the earth. The first intimation to those who experienced its effects was from the motion of every thing around them, and a sudden and deadly sickness, accompanied with a giddiness in the head. We judge of the severity of the shock from the motion which was given to substances saspended from the ceilings of houses. The fairest opportunity that was presented (to our knowledge) of judging of its force and direction, was from an ostrich egg which was suspended by a string of about a foot in length from a first floor ceiling, which was caused to oscillate at least four inches from point to point. We are informed that the steeple of the State House, which is supposed to be 250 feet in height, vibrated at least 6 or 8 feet at the top, and the motion was perceptible for 8 or 10 minutes. A number of clocks were stopped, and the ice in the river and bay cracked considerably. Some persons, who were skaiting, were very much terrified, and immediately made for the shore. In the lower part of the city it appears to have been most forcible, some people abandoning their homes, for the purpose of seeking safety in the open air. It is said that a noise like distant thunder was heard about 4 o'clock in the morning, and a slight motion of the earth observed about 8, but neither were very sensibly heard or felt.

There was nothing extraordinary in the atmosphere, except that it was remarkably calm, and rather inclined to be warm, altho' there was a deep snow on the ground, and for several days past it had been extremely cold.

THE NORFOLK HERALD
Wednesday, Feb. 5, 1812

Extract of a letter from a gentleman who in descending the river Mississippi, to his father in Norfolk, dated Chickasaw Agency, Dec. 17, 1811.

"On the 13th we reached the confluence of the Ohio and Mississippi; and on the 14th we entered the father of rivers, on the 15th we passed New Madrid, a small settlement in the upper Louisiana, and at 2 o'clock on the morning of the 16th, we sensibly felt the jar of a distant convulsion, which we conjectured to be an earthquake, caused by eruption of some operations far to the west of the Mississippi. - We hope in God that its seat was far from human habitation. - We have frequently heard a distant noise like thunder since; the 16th was indeed a solemn, awful, and gloomy day; but now all seems quiet and serene; safety has returned our cheerfulness to us, and our hearts are warmed with grateful thanks to the Supreme Ruler of Nature for our preservation. From Natchez or New Orleans I will write you a full and minute account of the convulsions."

THE NORFOLK HERALD
Wednesday, February 5, 1812
THE EARTHQUAKE

Raleigh, (N.C.) Jan. 24

The Earthquake. - A letter has been received in this city, from a gentleman of the first respectability in Tennessee, which states that the Earthquake, so generally felt on the 16th of Dec. was so violent in the vicinity of his residence, that several chimnies were thrown down, and that eighteen or twenty acres of land on Piney river had suddenly sunk so low, that the tops of the trees were on a level with the surrounding earth. Four other shocks were experienced on the 17th, and one or more continued to occur every day to the 30th aft., the date of the letter.

A slight shock of an Earthquake was felt in this city about eight o'clock yesterday morning. It continued only a few seconds.

THE NEW YORK EVENING POST
Wednesday, February 12, 1812

February 8

Yesterday morning, at half past four o'clock, a smart shock of an earthquake was felt in this city. During the last two-months, this city, and every town in the U. States to the Southward of us, have been visited with one or more earthquakes.

From **POULSON'S DAILY AMERICAN ADVERTISER**

EARTHQUAKES

Several distinct shocks for undulations of the earth were felt in this city on Friday morning, a few minutes before 4 o'clock. To several persons it appeared as if their bedsteads were raised under them by a pressure below.

One gentleman described it, as being so violent as to force open the folding doors of a wardrobe in his bed chamber, and others, state, that their chamber doors were thrown open, and articles loosely suspended from the ceilings and walls were kept in a state of oscillation for more than a minute. The undulations were more sensibly felt in the southern, than in the northern part of the city.

Mr. Pouson

THE EARTHQUAKE which happened this morning was, by my watch, at 4 h. 24 m. A.M. - I find by T. Parker's regulator, that my watch was slow 3 M. 30 s. This will give the correct time, 4 h. 27 m. 30 s. A.M. The duration of the trembling was at least 1 m. 30 s. probably 2 m. with short intervals of quickness. The person who awakened me at the commencement stated, that it began with a noise resembling the very quick passage of a dray over hard ground. The motion appeared to be from West to East, or from East to West.

All the furniture in my chamber was much agitated, particularly the bed on which I slept, and the drawer handles of a desk and book case, standing on the west side, which continued rattling for some seconds after the motions of the bedstand had ceased.

I send you these remarks with the assurance that you may depend on the correctness of the time. - Perhaps some other persons may have made similar observations, in different places; by comparing which together an idea may be formed, of the centre from which the numerous late shocks have proceded. Yours, Sc. W.V. Feb. 7, 1812

We are informed (says the Baltimore Federal Gazette of Friday last) by several persons of respectability, that a shock of an Earthquake was very sensibly felt here this morning about half past four o'clock.

THE LEXINGTON REPORTER (Kentucky)

THE EARTHQUAKE

Extract from a letter to a gentleman in Lexington, from his friend at New Madrid, (U.L.) dated 16th December, 1811.

"About 2 o'clock this morning we were awakened by a most tremendous noise, while the house danced about and seemed as if it would fall on our heads. I soon conjectured the cause of our troubles, and cried out it was an Earthquake, and for the family to leave the house; which we found very difficult to do, owing to its rolling and jostling about. The shock was soon over, and no injury was sustained, except the loss of the chimney, and the exposure of my family to the cold of the night. At the time of this shock, the heavens were very clear and serene, not a breath of air stirring; but in five minutes it became very dark, and a vapour which seemed to impregnate the atmosphere, had a disagreeable smell, and produced a difficulty of respiration. I knew not how to account for this at the time, but when I saw, in the morning, the situation of my neighbours' houses, all of them more or less injured, I attributed it to the dust and sot (?), &c which arose from the fall. The darkness continued till day-break; during this time we had EIGHT more shocks, none of them so violent as the first.

"At half past 6 o'clock in the morning it cleared up, and believing the danger over I left home, to see what injury my neighbours had sustained. A few minutes after my departure there was another shock, extremely violent - I hurried home as fast as I could, but the agitation of the earth was so great that it was with much difficulty I kept my balance - the motion of the earth was about twelve inches to and fro. I cannot give you an accurate description of this moment; the earth seemed convulsed - the houses shook very much - chimnies falling in every direction. - The loud hoarse roaring which attended the earthquake, together with the cries, screams, and yells of the people, seems still ringing in my ears.

"Fifteen minutes after seven o'clock, we had another shock. This one was the most severe one we have yet had - the darkness returned, and the noise was remarkably loud. The first motions of the earth were similar to the preceding shocks, but before they ceased we rebounded up and down, and it was with difficulty we kept our seats. At this instant I expected a dreadful catastrophe - the uproar among the people strengthened the colouring of the picture - the screams and yells were heard at a great distance.

"One gentleman, from whose learning I expected a more consistent account says that the convulsions are produced by this world and the moon coming in contact, and the frequent repetition of the shock is owing to their rebounding. The appearance of the moon yesterday evening has knocked his system as low as the quake has leveled my chimnies. Another person with a very serious face, told me, that when he was ousted from his bed, he was verily afraid, and thought the Day of Judgment had arrived, until he reflected that the Day of Judgment would not come in the night.

"Tuesday 17th - I never before thought the passion of fear so strong as I find it here among the people. It is really diverting, or would be so, to a disinterested observer, to see the rueful faces of the different persons that present themselves at my tent - some so agitated that they cannot speak - others cannot hold their tongues - some cannot sit still, but must be in constant motion, while others cannot walk. Several men, I am informed, on the night of the first shock deserted their families, and have not been heard of since. Encampments are formed of those that remain in the open fields, of 50 and 100 persons in each.

"Tuesday, Dec. 24th - The shocks still continue - we have had eight since Saturday - some of them very severe, but not sufficiently so to do much additional injury. I have heard of no lives being lost - several persons are wounded. This day I have heard from the Little Prairie, a settlement on the bank of the river Mississippi, about 30 miles below this place. There the scene has been dreadful indeed - the face of the country has been entirely changed. Large lakes have been raised, and become dry land; and many fields have been converted into pools of water. Capt. George Roddell, a worthy and respectable old gentleman, and who has been the father of that neighborhood, made good his retreat to this place, with about 100 souls. He informs me that no material injury was sustained from the first shocks - when the 10th shock occurred, he was standing in his own yard, situated on the bank of the Bayou of the Big Lake; the bank gave way, and sunk down about 30 yards from the water's edge, as far as he could see up and down the stream. It upset his mill, and one end of his dwelling house sunk down considerably; the surface on the opposite side of the Bayou, which before was swamp, became dry land, the side he was on became lower. His family at this time were running away from the house towards the woods; a large crack in the ground prevented their retreat into the open field. They had just assembled together when the eleventh shock came on, after which there was not perhaps a square acre of ground unbroken in the neighborhood, and in about fifteen minutes after the shock, the water rose round them waist deep. The old gentleman in leading his family, endeavoring to find higher land, would sometimes be precipitated headlong into one of those cracks in the earth, which were concealed from the eye by the muddy water through which they were wading. As they proceeded, the earth continued to burst open, and mud, water, sand and stone coal, were thrown up the distance of 30 yards - frequently trees of a large size were split open, fifteen or twenty feet up. After wading eight miles, he came to dry land.

"I have heard of no white person being lost as yet - Seven Indians were swallowed up; one of them escaped; he says he was taken into the ground the depth of 100 trees in length; that the water came under him and threw him out again - he had to wade and swim four miles before he reached dry land. The Indian says the Shawnee prophet has caused the earthquake to destroy the whites."

THE LEXINGTON REPORTER (Kentucky)
Wednesday, March 11, 1812
Washington, Feb. 29

More of the Earthquakes - The following interesting extract of a letter, on these phenomena, is from a gentleman in Tennessee to his friend in this city, dated January 23d, 1812:

"This morning we were again alarmed by a most tremendous concussion of nature's elements, equal, if not more terrifying than those of the 15th of last month. Its continuation was from 20 to 30 minutes - it shook off the top of one chimney in this town, and unroofed some small buildings in the neighbourhood. It was succeeded by three or four small shocks in the course of an hour. About 4 o'clock, P.M. another was sensibly felt, but in a much lighter degree. The cause of all these phenomena appears to originate a little south of a due west course; which will render the information just received still more probable.

"A gentleman who was near the Arkansas river, at the time of the first shock in Dec. last, states, that certain Indians had arrived near the mouth of the river, who had seen a large lake or sea, where many of their brorhers had resided, and had perished in the general wreck; that to escape a similar fate, they had travelled three days up the river, but finding the dangers increase, as they progressed, frequently having to cut down large trees, to cross the chasms in the earth, they returned to the mouth of the river, and from them this information is derived.

Monday evening - Since Thursday last we have felt 3, 4 and 5 shocks of a day and night, but not very severe."

THE LEXINGTON REPORTER (Kentucky)
Wednesday, March 18, 1812

Russelville, (Ken.) Feb. 26

Arrived in this place on Friday morning last. Mr. John Vettner and crew, from New Madrid, from whom we learn, that they were on shore five miles below the place on Friday morning the 7th instant, at the time of the hard shock, and that the water filled their barge and sunk it, with the whole of its contents, losing every thing but the clothes they had on. They offered, at New Madrid, half their loading for a boat to save it, but no price was sufficient for the hire of a boat. Mrs. Walker offered a likely negro fellow for the use of a boat a few hours, but could not get it. - The town of New Madrid has sunk 12 feet below its former standing, but is not covered with water; the houses are all thrown down, and the inhabitants moved off, except the French, who live in camps close to the river side, and have their boats tied near them, in order to sail off, in case the earth should sink. It is said that a fall equal to that of the Ohio is near above New Madrid, and that several whirls are in the Mississippi river, some so strong as to sink every boat that comes within its suck; one boat was sunk with a family in it. The country from New Madrid to the Grand Prairie is very much torn to pieces, and the Little Prairie almost entirely deluged. It was reported when our informants left it, that some Indians who had been out in search of some other Indians that were lost had returned, and stated that they had discovered a volcano at the head of the Arkansas, by the light of which they travelled three days and nights. A vast number of sawyers (?) have risen in the Mississippi river.

No pencil can paint the distress of the many movers! Men, women and children, barefooted and naked! without money and without food.

THE BAIRDSTOWN REPOSITORY (Ohio)
Earthquake

Sir - The effects produced on the Mississippi, by the Earthquake on the 7th of February, are so great as to render it highly interesting to the community in general, and more particularly so at this crisis, when so many of our fellow citizens are about to adventure their property down that river. Under this impression I have procured the enclosed written statement of Matthias M. Speed, just returned from New Madrid, with a view of giving it publication thru' the medium of your paper. The account I am told is substantially corroborated by another man, who passed through Bairdstown a few days ago. I am, very respectfully, your humble servant,

THE BAIRDSTOWN REPOSITORY (Ohio)
Tho. Speed, (March 3d, 1812)

In descending the Mississippi, on the night of the 6th February, we tied our boat to a willow bar on the west bank of the river, opposite the head of the 9th Island, counting from the mouth of the Ohio we were lashed to another boat. About 3 o'clock, on the morning of the 7th, we were waked by the violent agitation of the boat, attended with a noise more tremendous and terrific than I can describe or any one can conceive, who was not present or near to such a scene. The constant discharge of heavy cannon might give some idea of the noise for loudness, but this was infinitely more terrible, an account of its appearing to be subterraneous.

As soon as we waked we discovered that the bar to which we were tied was sinking, we cut loose and moved our boats for the middle of the river. After getting out so far as to be out of danger from the trees which were falling in from the bank - the swells in the river was so great as to threaten the sinking of the boat every moment. We stopped the outholes with blankets to keep out the water - after remaining in this situation for some time, we perceived a light in the shore which we had left - (we having a lighted candle in a lanthorn on our boat,) were hailed and advised to land, which we attempted to do, but could not effect it, finding the banks and trees still falling in.

At day light we perceived the head of the tenth island. During all this time we had made only about four miles down the river - from which circumstance, and from that of an immense quantity of water rushing into the river from the woods - it is evident that the earth at this place, or below, had been raised so high as to stop the progress of the river, and caused it to overflow its banks - We took the right hand channel of the river of this island, and having reached within about half a mile of the lower end of the town, we were affrightened with the appearance of a dreadful rapid of falls in the river just below us; we were so far in the sock (?) that it was impossible now to land - all hopes of surviving was now lost and certain destruction appeared to await us! We having passed the rapids without injury, keeping our bow foremost, both boats being still lashed together.

As we passed the point on the left hand below the island, the bank and trees were rapidly falling in. From the state of alarm I was in at this time, I cannot pretend to be correct as to the length or height of the falls; but my impression is, that they were about equal to the rapids of the Ohio. As we passed the lower point of the island, looking back, up the left channel, we thought the falls extended higher up the river on that side than on the other.

The water of the river, after it was fairly light, appeared to be almost black, with something like the dust of stone coal - We landed at New Madrid about breakfast time without having experienced any injury- The appearance of the town, and the situation of the inhabitants, were such as to afford but little relief to our minds. The former elevation of the bank on which the town stood was estimated by the inhabitants at about 25 feet above common water; when we reached it the elevation was only about 12 or 13 feet - There was scarcely a house left entire - some wholly prostrated, others unroofed and not a chimey standing - the people all having deserted their habitations, were in camps and tents back of the town, and their little watercafts (mispelled), such as skiffs, boats and canoes, handed out of the water to their camps, that they might be ready in case the country should sink.

I remained at New Madrid from the 7th till the 12th, during which time I think shocks of earthquakes were experienced every 15 or 20 minutes- those shocks were all attended with a rumbling noise, resembling distant thunder from the southwest, varying in report according to the force of the shock. When I left the place, the surface of the earth was very little, if any, above the tops of the boats in the river.

There was one boat coming down on the same morning I landed; when they came in sight of the falls, the crew were so frightened at the prospect, that they abandoned their boat and made for the island in their canoe- two were left on the island, and two made for the west bank in the canoe - about the time of their landing, they saw that the island was violently convulsed - one of the men on the island threw himself into the river to save himself by swimming - one of the men from the shore met him with the canoe and saved him. - This man gave such an account of the convulsion of the island, that neither of the three dared to venture back for the remaining man. The three men reached New Madrid by land.

The man remained on the Island from Friday morning until Sunday evening, when he was taken off by a canoe sent from a boat coming down. I was several days in company with this man - he stated that during his stay in the island, there were frequent eruptions, in which sand and stone, coal and water were thrown up. - The violent agitation of the ground was such at one time as induced him to hold to a tree to support himself; the earth gave way at the place, and he with the tree sunk down, and he got wounded in the fall. - The fissure was so deep as to put it out of his power to get out at that place - he made his way along the fissure until a sloping slide offered him an opportunity of crawling out. He states that frequent lights appeared - that in one instance, after one of the explosions near where he stood, he approached the hole from which the coal and land had been thrown up, which was now filled with water, and on putting his hand into it he found it was warm.

During my stay at new Madrid there were upwards of twenty boats landed, all of whom spoke of the rapids above, and conceived of it as I had done.

Several persons, who came up the river in a small barge, represented that there were other falls in the Mississippi, about 7 miles below New Madrid, principally on the eastern side - more dangerous than those above - and that some boats had certainly been lost in attempting to pass them - but they thought it was practicable to pass by keeping close to the western shore.

From what I had seen and heard I was deterred from proceeding further, and nearly gave away what property I had. On my return by land up the right side of the river, I found the surface of the earth for 10 or 12 miles cracked in numberless places, running in different directions - some of which were bridged and some filled with logs to make them passable - others were so wide that they were obliged to be surrounded. In some of these cracks the earth sank on one side from the level to the distance of five feet, and from one to three feet there was water in most of them. Above this the cracks were not so numerous nor so great - but the inhabitants have generally left their dwellings and gone to the higher grounds.

Nothing appeared to have issued from the cracks but where there was sand and stone coal, they seem to have been thrown up from holes; in most of those, which varied in size, there was water standing. In the town of New Madrid there were four, but neither of them had vented stone or sand - the size of them, in diameter, varied from 12 to 50 feet, and in depth from, 5 to 10 feet from the surface to the water. In travelling out from New Madrid those were very frequent, and were to be seen in different places, as high as fort ,Massac, in the Ohio.

s/ MATHIAS M. SPEED (Jefferson County, March 2, 1812)

THE BAIRDSTOWN REPOSITORY (Ohio)
Wednesday, April 22, 1812

Lexington, (Ken) April 4 - We are informed from a respectable source, that the old road to the port of Arkansas, by Spring river, is entirely destroyed by the last violent shocks of earthquakes - chasms of great depth and considerable length cross the country in various directions; - some swamps have become dry, others deep lakes, and in some places hills have disappeared.

THE BAIRDSTOWN REPOSITORY (Ohio)
Wednesday, May 6, 1812

Richmond, (Vir.) April 24 - A few minutes before 4 o'clock, on Wednesday morning, an earthquake was distinctly felt and heard by several persons in and near this city. The sound was like the rumbling of distant thunder. Pendulous bodies swung, beds were shaken, and several roused from their slumbers. How fortunate are we, that we are so far removed from the scene of convulsion - and saved from the frightful disaster - which has laid the wretched Carracas in ruins.

THE BAIRDSTOWN REPOSITORY (Ohio)
Wednesday, May 20, 1812

Louisville, (Ken.) May 1 - Earthquake - At forty-five minutes after three o'clock A.M. on Friday last, a shock of an earthquake was very sensibly felt, and at forty minutes after ten o'clock P.M. another slight shock was distinctly perceived; the vibration appeared to be from North to South, or rather West of North and East of South; - duration of first shock, about minute, of second shock, about half a minute.

NEW YORK EVENING POST
Monday, December 23, 1811
Richmond, Dec. 17

Our city has been sensibly shocked at intervals, for the last two days, by an earthquake. It was first felt on Monday morning at three o'clock. In the most elevated parts of the city, the citizens were alarmed by the violent concussion, and the house bells in some places set a ringing. On yesterday, at eleven o'clock another violent shock was felt.

It was felt at Norfolk at 3 and 8 o'clock on Monday morning, at which the Hearald says, "The clocks were all stopt, and doors, and things suspended from the ceilings of the shops and stores, oscillated violently, though a dead calm prevailed. Its course was from West to East." It is remarkable that although the higher parts of this city were much agitated, and a gentleman who was then shaving himself was obliged to discontinue the operation, those who live below the hill never felt it at all.

NEW YORK EVENING POST
Thursday, December 26, 1811
Charleston, Dec. 17

Earthquake - Yesterday morning, about three o'clock, a severe shock of an Earthquake was felt in this city. It was preceded by a blowing noise, resembling that made by smith's bellows. The agitation of the earth was such that the bells in the church steeples rung to a degree that some supposed there was fire. The houses shook so sensibly as to induce many persons to rise from their beds. The clocks generally stopped. Another slight shock was felt about fifteen minutes after, and again at eight o'clock, which last shook to such a degree as to make a very considerable rattling among glass, china and other furniture. A looking glass, about three feet in length, hanging against a West wall, was observed to vibrate two or three inches from North to South.

Georgetown, December 18

Earthquake - Several shocks of an Earthquake were experienced in this town between the hours of three and eight o'clock on Monday morning. Great indeed was the consternation of the inhabitants, on the awful occasion. So severe were the shocks that the parade ground of the fort settled from one to two inches below its former level. A tub of water sitting on a table in the barracks was upset by the jarring of the building.

Another severe shock was felt yesterday at 12 o'clock.

Raleigh, (N.C.) Dec. 18

Several slight shocks of an earthquake were felt in this place on Monday morning.

NEW YORK EVENING POST
    Wednesday, January 1, 1812
    Charleston, Dec. 18

Earthquake - A slight shock was felt on Monday evening, and another yesterday at 20 minutes after 12. They continued but a few seconds. We have now had six of these awful visitations in two days.

Savannah, Dec. 17

Four shocks of an Earthquake have been sustained by our town, and its neighborhood, within the last two days. The first commenced yesterday morning between two and three, preceded by a meteoric flash of light and accompanied with a rattling noise, resembling that of a carriage passing over a paved pathway, and lasted almost minute. A second succeeded, almost immediately after, but its continuance was of much shorter duration. A third shock was experienced about eight o'clock in the morning, and another today about one.

Persons from White Bluff, (about eight miles from town, southwardly) felt it very sensibly; and several who were up at the time, state that the movement of the earth made then tether as though they were on ship board in a heavy swell of the sea. Those who were up at the time conceive its direction to have been from southwest to northeast.

On Monday morning, the 16th inst. about three o'clock, the

citizens of the town of Pittsburgh, (Penn.) were greatly alarmed by the shock of an Earthquake; a number of persons from the shaking of their houses, were so much alarmed as to run out of bed. About 7 o'clock, the same morning, there was another shock, though not so violent as the first. - Philad. pap.

ANNAPOLIS MARYLAND REPUBLICAN
Wednesday, January 29, 1812

An Earthquake- A severe shock of an earthquake was experienced by a number of persons in this city yesterday morning, the 22nd inst. about sixteen minutes before ten o'clock. Its duration is supposed to have been about two or three minutes from beginning to end, and its direction apparently from E. to S.W. This phenomenon was dissimilar in its nature and effects from any of the kind that we have heretofore heard of, as it was not accompanied or preceded by the usual rumbling noise, nor any sudden concussion of the earth, but a continued roll similar to that of a vessel in a heavy sea. One circumstance which renders its effects more singular is, that it was very sensibly felt by some, while others, although in the same room, and perhaps within a few feet of them, were not in the least affected by its oscillation, and those who were in the street or ____ air, were insensible as to any extraordinary motion of the earth. The first intimation to those who experienced its effects, was from the motion of everything around them, and a sudden sickness accompanied with a giddines in the head. We judge of the severity of the shock from the motion given to substances suspended from the ceilings of houses. The fairest opportunity that was presented (to our knowledge) of judging of its force and direction, was from an ostrich egg which was suspended by a string of about a foot in length from a first floor ceiling, which was caused to oscillate at least four inches from point to point - - - We are informed that the State House, which is supposed to be 250 feet in height vibrated at least 6 or 8 feet at the top, and the motion was perceptible for 8 or 10 minutes. A number of clocks were stopped and the ice in the bay and river cracked considerably. Some persons, who were skaiting, were very much terrified, and immediately made for the shore. In the lower part of the city it appears to have been most forcible, some people being in the act of abandoning their houses, for the purpose of seeking safety in the open air. It is said that a noise like distant thunder was heard about 3 o'clock in the morning, and a slight motion of the earth observed about 8, but neither were very sensibly heard or felt.

There was nothing extraordinary in the atmosphere, except that it was remarkably calm, and rather inclined to be warm, although there was a deep snow on the ground and for several days past it had been extremely cold.

ANNAPOLIS MARYLAND REPUBLICAN

Friday, January 31, 1812
Charleston, Jan. 24

Earthquake - Yesterday morning, at fifteen minutes after nine o'clock, another shock was felt in this city. The vibrating motion was more severe than any we experienced last month, and continued for one minute. The pavements in several of the streets are cracked, by the loosening of the cement; and a three Story Brick House in King-Street, belonging to Mr. Brownlee, has received very considerable injury. The walls are cracked from the top to the bottom, and the wooken work and the plastering in the inside, are split and broken. Many persons in different parts of the city were sensible of a shock at eight o'clock in the morning- Several families left their beds. Both these concussions were unaccompanied with any noise.

A report prevailed in town yesterday, that a part of the town of Natchez had been sunk by an Earthquake, and that four thousand persons perished.- We trust that this report will prove to be unfounded; but if such a deplorable circumstance has taken place, it could not have been on the morning of the 16th December, as a letter dated on that date at Natchez, and published some time since at the city of Washington says "A considerable shock of an Earthquake was felt here last night", without adding anything further; which most undoubtedly would have been done, had any fatality attended it.

ANNAPOLIS MARYLAND REPUBLICAN

Wednesday, February 5, 1812
Natchez, Jan. 2

Important Arrival - Arrived here on Monday last, the steam-boat from Pittsburgh, which had on account of low water been some time detained at the falls of the Ohio; and is destined to run between this place and New Orleans as a regular trader. She was only 221 hours under way from Pittsburgh to this place a distance of near two thousand miles.

No very satisfactory accounts of the shocks of Earthquake, and their effects, which have lately happened, could be expected; that received from the gentlemen on board, is rather more so than we anticipated.

The shake or jar, produced by the powerful operation of the engine, rendered the shocks imperceptible, while the boat was under way. While at anchor five or six shocks were felt, two or three more severe than the rest. On enquiry at New Madrid, a small town about 70 miles below the mouth of Ohio, they found that the chimnies of almost all the houses were thrown down, and the inhabitants considerably alarmed. At the Little Prairie, 30 miles lower down, they were bro't to by the cries of some of the people, who thought the earth was gradually sinking; but declined to take refuge on board without their friends, whom they wished to collect. Some distance below the Little Prairie, the bank of the river has caved in to a considerable extent, and two islands had almost disappeared.

We also understand that letters have been received from Louisville, Falls of Ohio, which state, that the houses have suffered considerable damage in that place.

RICHMOND ENQUIRER

Saturday, January 25, 1812

Another Earthquake was most distinctly felt in this city on Thursday morning last [Jan. 23] , about nine o'clock. Some persons were rocked in their chairs. Some staggered as they stood. Hanging keys oscillated. Doors and windows flapped. Bedsteads and tall articles of furniture were moved to and fro. Those who were at breakfast saw a violent ripple on the surface of tea and coffee. A few ran out of their houses in great alarm. The convulsion was more sensibly felt on the hill than below it; in high than low houses. We distinctly felt two of these convulsions, within the lapse of 15 or 20 minutes between them.

RICHMOND ENQUIRER

Tuesday, February 11, 1812

THE EARTHQUAKE

The following very interesting communication is from an intelligent friend at N. Orleans. - It is, we presume, the most particular and satisfactory account of the earthquakes on the Mississippi, which has, as yet, been published: And Mr. Pierce being an ear and eye witness to the scenes he describes, the authenticity of his narrative cannot be doubted.

To the Editor of the **NEW YORK EVENING POST**

Big Prairie, (on the Mississippi, 761 miles from N. Orleans,)
Dec. 25, 1811.

Dear Sir,

Desirous of offering the most correct information to society at large, and contributing in some degree to the speculations of the Philosopher, I am induced to give publicity to a few remarks concerning a phenomenon of the most alarming nature. Through you, therefore, I take the liberty of addressing the world, and describing, as far as the inadequacy of my means at present will permit, the most prominent and interesting features of the events, which have recently occurred upon this portion of our western waters.

Proceeding on a tour from Pittsburgh to New Orleans, I entered the Mississippi, when it receives the waters of the Ohio, on Friday the 13th day of this month, and on the 15th, in the evening, landed on the left bank of this river, about 116 miles from the mouth of the Ohio. The night was extremely dark and cloudy, not a star appeared in the heavens, and there was every appearance of a severe rain - for the three last days, indeed, the sky had been continually overcast, and the weather unusually thick and hazy.

It would not be improper to observe, that these waters are descended in a variety of small craft, but most generally in flat bottomed boats, built to serve a temporary purpose, and intended to float, with the current, being supplied with oars, not so much to accelerate progress as to assist in navigating the boats, and avoiding the numerous bars, trees and timber which greatly impede the navigation of this river. In one of these boats I had embarked - and the more effectually to guard against anticipated attacks from the savages, who are said to be at present much exasperated against the whites, several boats had proceeded in company.

Precisely at 2 o'clock on Monday morning, the 16th instant, we were all alarmed by the violent and convulsive agitation of the boats, accompanied by a noise similar to that which would have been produced by running over a sand bar - every man was immediately roused and rushed upon deck. - We were first of opinion that the Indians, studious of some mischief, had loosed our cables, and thus situated we were foundering. Upon examination, however, we discovered we were yet safely and securely moored. The idea of an earthquake then suggested itself to my mind, and this idea was confirmed by a second shock, and two others in immediate succession. These continued for the space of eight minutes. So complete and general had been the convulsion, that a tremendous motion was communicated to the very leaves on the surface of the earth. A few yards from the spot where we lay, the body of a large oak was snapped in two, and the falling part precipitated to the margin of the river; the trees in the forest shook like rushes; the alarming clattering of their branches may be compared to the affect which would be produced by a severe wind passing through a large cane brake.

Exposed to a most unpleasant alternative, we were compelled to remain - here we were for the night, or subject ourselves to imminent hazard in navigating through the innumerable obstructions in the river; considering the danger of running two-fold, we concluded to remain. At the dawn of day I went on shore to examine the effects of the shocks; the earth about 20 feet from the waters edge was deeply cracked, but no visible injury of moment had been sustained; fearing, however, to remain longer where we were, it was thought much advisable to leave our landing as expeditiously as possible; this was immediately done - at a few rods distance from the shore, we experienced a fifth shock, more severe than either of the preceding. I had expected this from the louring appearance of the weather, it was indeed most providential that we had started, for such was the strength of this last shock, that the bank to which we were (but a few moments since) attached, was rent and fell into the river, whilst the trees rushed from the forests, precipitating themselves into the water with a force sufficient to have dashed us into a thousand atoms.

It was now light, and we had an opportunity of beholding, in full extent, all the horrors of our situation. During the first four shocks, tremendous and uninterrupted explosions, resembling a discharge of artillery, was heard from the opposite shore; at that time I imported them to the falling of the river banks. This fifth shock explained the real cause. Whenever the veins of the earthquake ran, there was a volcanic discharge of combustible matter to a great height, as incessant rumbling was heard below, and the bed of the river was excessively agitated, whilst the water assumed a turbid and boiling appearance - near our boat a spout of confined air, breaking its way through the waters, burst forth and with a loud report discharged mud, sticks, &c, from the river's bed, at least thirty feet above the surface. These spoutings were frequent, and in many places appeared to rise to the very Heavens. - Large trees, which had lain for ages at the bottom of the river, were shot up in thousands of instances, some with their roots uppermost and their tops planted; others were hurled into the air; many again were only loosened, and floated upon the surface. Never was a scene more replete with terrific threatenings of death; with the most lively sense of this awful crisis, we contemplated in mute astonishment a scene which completely beggars all description and of which the most glowing imagination is inadequate to form a picture. Here the earth, river, &c. torn with furious convulsions, opened in huge trenches, whose deep jaws were instantaneously closed; there through a thousand vents sulphureous streams gushed from its very bowels, leaving vast and almost unfathomable caverns. Every where nature itself seemed tottering on the verge of dissolution. Encompassed with the most alarming dangers, the manly presence of mind and heroic fortitude of the men were all that saved them. It was a struggle for existence itself, and the mede (?) to be purchased was our lives.

During the day there was, with very little intermission, a continued series of shocks, attended with innumerable explosions like the rolling of thunder; the bed of the river was incessantly disturbed, and the water boiled severly in every part; I consider ourselves as having been in the greatest danger from the numerous instances of boiling directly under our boat; fortunately for us, however, they were not attended with eruptions. One of the spouts which we had seen rising under the boat would inevitably sunk it, and probably have blown it into a thousand fragments; our ears were continually assailed with the crashing of timber, the banks were instantaneously crushed down, and fell with all their growth into the water. It was no less alarming than astonishing, to behold the oldest trees of the forest, whose firm roots had withstood a thousand storms, and weathered the sternest tempests, quivering and shaking with the violence of the shocks, whilst their heads were whipped together with a quick and rapid motion; many were torn from their native soil, and hurled with tremendous force into the river; one of these whose huge trunk (at least 3 feet in diameter) had been much shattered, was thrown better than an hundred yards from the bank, where it is planted into the bed of the river, there to stand, a terror to future navigators.

Several small islands have been already annihilated, and from appearances many others must suffer the same fate. To one of these, I ventured in a skiff, but it was impossible to examine it, for the ground sunk from my tread, and the least force applied to any part of it seemed to shake the whole.

Anxious to obtain landing, and dreading the high banks, we made for an island which evidenced sensible marks of the earthquake; here we fastened to some willows, at the extremity of a sunken piece of land, and continued two days, hoping that this scene of horrors was near over - still, however, the shocks continued, though not with the same frequency as before.

On Wednesday, in the afternoon, I visited every part of the island where we lay. It was extensive, and partially covered with willow. The earthquake had rent the ground in large and numerous gaps; vast quantities of burnt wood in every stage of alteration, from its primitive nature to stove coal, had been spread over the ground to very considerable distances; frightful and hideous caverns yawned on every side, and the earth's bowels appeared to have felt the tremendous force of the shocks which had thus riven the surface. I was gratified with seeing several places where those spouts which had so much attracted our wonder and admiration had arisen; they were generally on the beach; and have left large circular holes in the sand, formed much like a funnel. For a great distance around the orifice, vast quantities of coal have been scattered, many pieces weighing from 15 to 20 lbs. were discharged 160 measured paces- These holes were of various dimensions; one of them I observed most particularly, it was 16 feet in perpendicular depth, and 63 feet in circumferences at the mouth.

On Thursday morning, the 19th, we loosed our cables, with

hearts filled with fervent gratitude to Providence, whose protection had supported us through the perils to which we had been exposed.

As we descended the river every thing was a scene of ruin and devastation; where a short time since the Mississippi rolled its waters in a calm and placid current, now subterranean forests have been ushered into existence, and raise their heads, hard and black as ebony, above the surface of the water, whose power has been so wonderfully increased, that strength and skill are equally baffled. Our boat was borne down by an irrestible impulse, and fortunately escaped uninjured; we passed thousands of areas of land which had been cleft from the main shore and tumbled into the water, leaving their growth waving above the surface. In many places single trees, and whole brakes of cane, had slipped into the river. A singular instance of this kind peculiarly attracted my observation; a large sycamore had slipped from its station on the bank, and had so admirably preserved its equilibrium, that it has been left standing erect in the river, immersed about 10 feet, and has every appearance of having originally grown there.

The shocks I conceive were most sensibly experienced upon the islands, and numbers of them have been much shattered, for I observed where the stratum of earth was fairest, it did not crack, but undulated excessively. At Fort Pickering in the extremity of the fourth Chickasaw Bluff, and 242 miles from the mouth of the Ohio, the land is strong and high; here, however, the earth was extremely agitated, and the Block-house which is almost a solid mass of hewn timber, trembled like the aspen leaf.

The obstructions in this river, which have always been quite numerous, are now so considerably increased as to demand the utmost prudence and caution from subsebuent navigators. Indeed I am very apprehensive that it will be almost impassable in flood water; for until such time it will be impossible to say where the currents will hereafter run, what portion (if any) of the present embarrassments will be destroyed, and what new sand bars, &c. may yet be caused by this portentous phenomenon.- Many poor fellows are undoubtedly wrecked, or buried under the ruin of the banks. Of the loss of four boats I am certain.

It is almost impossible to trace, at present, the exact course of this earthquake, or where the greatest injuries have happened. From numerous enquiries, however, which I have made of persons above and below us at the time of the first shock, I am induced to believe, that we were very nearly in the height of it. The ruin immediately in the vicinity of the river is most extensive on the right side in descending. For the first two days the veins appeared to run a due course from W. to E. afterwards they became more variable, and generally took a N.W. direction.

At New Madrid, 70 miles from the influence of the Ohio, and on the right hand, the utmost consternation prevailed among the inhabitants; confusion, terror and uproar presided; those in the town were running for refuge to the country, whilst those in the country fled with like purpose towards the town. I am happy, however, to observe, that no material injury has been sustained.

At the Little Prairie, 103 miles from the same point, the shocks appear to have been more violent, and were attended with severe apprehensions. The town was deserted by its inhabitants, and not a single person was left but an old negro man, probably too infirm to fly: everyone appeared to consider the woods and hills most safe, and in these confidence was reposed. Distressing, however, as are the outlines of such a picture, the latest accounts are not calculated to increase apprehensions. Several chimnies were destroyed, and much land sunk, no lives however have been lost.

A little below Bayou River, 103 miles from the same point, and 130 miles from the spot where we lay, the ruin begins extensive and general.

At Long Reach, 146 miles, there is one continued forest of roots and trees, which have been ejected from the bed of the river.

At the near Flour Island, 174 miles, the destruction has been very great, and the impediments in the river much increased.

At the Devil's Race ground, 193 miles, an immense number of very large trees have been thrown up, and the river is nearly impassible. The Devil's Elbow, 214 miles, is in the same predicament; below this the ruin is much less, and indeed no material traces of the earthquake are discoverable.

The western country must suffer much from this dreadful scourge; its affects will I fear be more lasting than the fond hopes of the inhabitants in this section of the union may at present conceive. What have already been the interior injuries I cannot say. My opinion is, that they are inferior in extent and effect.

The continuance of this earthquake must render it conspicuous in the pages of the Historians, as one of the longest that has ever occurred. From the time that the first shock was felt, at 2 o'clock in the morning of the 16th until the last shock, at the same time in the morning of the 23rd, was 168 hours. Nothing could have exceeded the alarm of the aquatic fowl: they were extremely noisy and confused, flying in every direction, without pursuing any determinate course. The few Indians who were on the Banks of the river, have been excessively alarmed and terrified. All nature indeed seemed to sympathize in the commotion which agitated the earth. The sun rarely shot a ray through the heavens. The sky was clouded, and a dreary darkness brooded over the whole face of the creation. The stars were encircled with a pale light, and the Comet appeared hazy and dim. - The weather was incessantly varying from oppressive heat to severe cold, and during many of the shocks some rain fell.

I subjoin the ensuing table of the shocks, with the exact order of time in which they occurred, as extracted from my minutes.

16th December - the first shock followed by 3 others at two o'clock in the morning. 7 A.M. happened a very severe shock - 8, nine shocks in quick succession - 9, three more shocks - 10 minutes after 11, one shock - 25 after 11, another - 5 after 12, a violent shock - 25 after 1 P.M. another - 31 after 1, a long and violent shock - 42 after 1, a shock - 10 after 5, a very severe shock - 42 after 5, a shock - 10 before 6 do. - 15 after 7 do- 35 after 7 do. - 10 of 8 do. - 5 after 8 do. - 5 of 9 do. - 25 after 9 do.- 20 of 10 do. - 15 of 10 do. - 10 of 10 do. - 15 to 20 of 11, three do. - 12 of 11, great shock - 28 after 11, severe shock. 17th December, 30 minutes after 5, a shock - 5 in the morning, a great and awful shock followed, with 3 others; 5 after 12 meridian, a long and dreadful shock, appearances extremely threatening; 18 after 11 P.M. two severe shocks - 24 after 11 a shock - 26 after 11 do. - 35 after 11 do. - 48 after 11 do. 18th December, 17 minutes of 3, A.M. a shock; 17 after 3 do. - 30 after 3 do. - 5 of 4 do. - 10 after 4 do. - 10 after 5 do. - 35 after 5 do. very severe - 5 after 6 do. - 45 after 6 do. - 7 of 8 do. - 10 after 12 meridian - 10 after 1 P.M. do - 25 after 2 do. severe - 30 after 2, five shocks in succession - 3 o'clock, a shock - 15 minutes after 3 do. severe - 43 after 4 do. - 8 after 10 do. - 10 after 11 do. very severe. 19th December, 30 minutes after 5 A.M. 4 shocks in succession- 17 of 9 severe shock - 30 after 1 P.M., a shock - 17 of 2 do. - 30 after 8 do. - 30 after 9 do. - 30 after 11 do. 20th December, 30 minutes after 9 A.M. a shock - 10 after 11, a long and tremendous shock. 21st December, several reports of shocks or distant thunder were heard. 22nd December, 11 o'clock A.M. a slight shock. 23rd December at 2 in the morning a very severe shock.

Thus we observe that there were in the space of time mentioned before, eighty-nine shocks - it is hardly possible to conceive the convulsion which they created, and I assure you I believe that there were many of these shocks, which had they followed in quick succession were sufficient to shake into atoms the firmest edifices which art ever devised.

I landed often, and on the same shore, as well as on several islands, found evident traces of prior eruptions, all of which seem to corroborate an opinion that the river was formed by some great earthquake - to me indeed the bed appears to possess every necessary ingredient, nor have I a doubt but that there are at the bottom of the river strata upon strata of volcanic matter. The great quantities of combustible materials, which are undoubtedly there deposited, tend to render a convulsive of this kind extremely alarming, at least, however, the beds of timber and trees interwoven and firmly matted together at the bottom of the Mississippi, are tolerable correct data from which may be presumed the prior nature, &c. of the land. The trees are similar to the growth upon the banks, and why may not an inference be drawn that some tremendous agitation of nature has rent this once a continued forest, and given birth to a great and noble stream. There are many direct and collateral facts which may be adduced to establish the point, and which require time and investigation to collect and apply.

It is a circumstance well worthy of remark, that during the late convulsions the current of the river was almost instantaneously and rapidly increased. In times of the highest floods, it rates from 4 to 5 knots per hour. The water is now low, and when we stopped on the 16th inst. at half after 4 P.M. we had then run from that morning 52 miles, rating at 6 knots generally. This current was increased for two days, and then fell to its usual force. It is also singular that the water has fallen with astonishing rapidity. The most probable and easy solution of this fact, which presented itself to my mind, was, that the strength of the Mississippi current was greater than the tributary streams could support. Either this must have been the case, or some division of waters above has occurred, destruction below has created some great basin or reservoir for the disemboguing (?) of the main body of water. The latter presumption I apprehend cannot be correct, as our progress towards the mouth of this river is marked with little or no injury.

Thus, my dear sir, I have given you a superficial account of this awful phenomenon; not so much to convey instruction upon a very interesting subject, as to gratify the curiosity of the public relative to so remarkable an event. At some more convenient season it is my intention, from facts which I had the opportunity of collecting, to canvas the subject more in detail; you are therefore at liberty to make whatever use you please of this brief sketch; and publish the whole, or extract such parts as you may deem best adapted.

Should other interesting circumstances occur relative to this phenomenon, I will do myself the pleasure of mailing you another communication.

With much respect, I am, sir

Your obedient servant,
WILLIAM LEIGH PIERCE

New Orleans, Jan. 13, 1812

Dear Sir,

Agreeably to my promise, in the last communication which I had the pleasure of making you, I present a further detail of the late earthquake.

Its range appears to have been by no means confined to the Mississippi. It was felt in some degree throughout the Indiana Territory, and the states of Ohio, Kentucky and Tennessee. I have conversed with gentlemen from Louisville and Lexington, (in Kentucky,) who state that it was severe in both of those places. At the latter, indeed, it continued for 12 days, and did some inconsiderable injury to several dwellings. From thence it ranged the Ohio river, increasing in force until it entered the Mississippi, and extending down that river to Natchez, and probably a little lower. Beyond this it was not perceived.

It is a singular, but well authenticated fact, that in several places on the Mississippi, where the shocks were most severe, the earth was rent (as it were) by two distinct processes. By one it was burst asunder, and instantaneously closed, leaving no traces whatever of the shock; by the other it was rent, and an elective flash ran along the surface, tearing the earth to pieces in its progress. - These last were generally attended with an explosion, and streams of matter, in a liquid state, gushed from the gaps which were left open when the shock subsided, and were in many instances of an immense depth.

It is also reported, through the medium of some Indians, from the country adjacent to the Washita, who arrived a few days since at the Walnut Hills, some distance above Natchez, that the Burning Mountain, up the Wichita river, had been rent to its base. This information I received from a settler at the Hills, and his appearance was such as to attach credit to his information. - Your obedient

servant,
    W. L. PIERCE
    FROM OUR CORRESPONDENT

WASHINGTON, DC
United States House of Representatives Correspondence
Friday, February 7

In Washington, February 7, about eight minutes after four o'clock this morning a shock of an earthquake was very sensibly felt here. It was more severe than that of a fortnight ago yesterday. Many people were awakened by it. It continued upwards of two minutes, unaccompanied with any noise.

Wednesday, February 12, 1812

In Alexandria, Feb. 8 - There was another shock of an Earthquake felt at this place, at about 4 o'clock yesterday morning - its motion was about north and south - a gentle undulation about the same in degree with that felt the 23rd ult.

Tuesday, February 18, 1812

In Richmond, Feb. 8, at 4 o'clock in the morning of the 7th inst. this city was again shocked with an Earthquake, which was much more violent than the two which so lately agitated this continent. A gentleman informed us, that he and his family were awakened by the undulating motion of the earth, swinging or rocking of the beds; and that on lighting a candle, the pictures suspended by one hook, were seen to oscillate violently for about fifteen minutes. He hoisted a window, and observed the tops of some Lombardy poplars in the yard to be much agitated, although the air was still. The top of one chimney was thrown down. We have heard of no other accidents.

    At 11 o'clock at night the same day, another shock equally violent was felt. The furniture in the houses, window shutters, &c.

were so shaken as to occasion considerable noise. We are informed that a side board in the house of Mr. Payton Randolph, was put in such motions as to throw off a waiter which happened to be on it. Another gentleman stated to us that he was awaked by shock not long before day this morning, which continued for a minute. These different shocks which have been felt so sensibly by those living in the higher parts of the city, have scarcely affected those who live in low situations and low built houses.

Saturday, February 22, 1812

Yesterday morning about 4 o'clock, there were some very violent earthquake shocks felt here. - Many persons extremely alarmed rose from their beds, and ran to the streets. In some parts of the town, the people were heard to scream with terror. Flashes of light, similar to those seen on the 16th of December, were perceived towards the south-west. The last concussions were greater than any of those that were felt here before.

There was, another slighter shock last night, between 10 and 11 o'clock.

AUGUSTA HERALD (Georgia)
   Feb. 13, 1812
   EARTHQUAKES!

Again we are bound to notice what is very justly considered as among the most astonishing and alarming phenomena in nature.

On Friday last [Feb. 7] at 20 minutes before four o'clock in the morning, another severe shock of an earthquake was experienced here, and throughout the country in every direction from which we have yet heard; and in most places we believe with more severity than any preceding shock, it continued between three and four minutes. About 20 minutes before 11 o'clock in the evening of the same day, a smart shock was also felt, and though considerably less severe, was to many more alarming than the former one - this might have arisen from apprehensions previously excited, and from the repetition of an occurrence so peculiarly calculated to create astonishment and terror. Indeed since the settlement of this place, we venture to say, that a large proportion of our inhabitants, never lay down at night, with feelings similar to those they experienced when going to bed during the past week. Light tremulous motions of the earth continue occasionally to be felt.

By a gentleman from Jefferson we are informed, that on the plantation of Mr. Ephraim Ponder, near Brier Creek, about 18 miles from this place, a body of earth about ninety feet in circumference, sunk, as was supposed on Friday night last - that the earth being held on one side by the roots of a tree at the edge of the opening sunk in a sloping direction, and that the lower part of it was covered with water, in which bottom was not found with a sixteen foot pole. The gentleman saw this opening, but does not know of any other attempt to find bottom was made, there being no pole at hand, when he was there, longer than the sixteen foot one.

From the accounts we have received we believe the Earthquake on Friday morning last was more severe in several parts of the country than in this place - at General Twiggs, about 9 miles below this place, the agitation of the house was so violent as to break fifty squares of glass in the windows, and throughout the neighborhood, the concussion created general alarm.

AUGUSTA HERALD (Georgia)
Savannah, Feb. 10

The inhabitants of our city, had hardly recovered from the alarms excited by the frequent shocks lately experienced, when they were again aroused on Friday morning by a severe and tremendous Earthquake which commenced at about 4 o'clock and continued for two minutes; this awful and most impressive visitation, was preceded by a loud rumbling, resembling the noise of a number of carriages following each other, and the motion of the earth was so violent as to occasion numbers to rush from their beds to their doors, to avoid the danger which might arise from falling buildings. We are happy to state, however, that no injury has been done. The horrizon immediately after the undulation of the earth had ceased, presented a most gloomy and dreadful appearance; the black clouds, which had settled around it, were illuminated as if the whole country to the westward was in flames and for fifteen or twenty minutes, a continued roar of distant, but distinct thunder, added to the solemnity of the scene. A storm of wind and rain succeeded, which continued until about six o'clock, when a vivid flash of lightning was instantaneously followed by a loud peal of thunder; several gentlemen who were in the market at the time distinctly perceived a blaze of fire which fell between the centre and south range of the market. To those who have made the wonders of nature their study, we leave the calculation whether an eruption has taken place in some distant part, or whether we are again to experience still severer trials.

A slight motion sufficient to cause vibrations was distinctly felt at ten minutes before nine on the night succeeding the above, and at eleven another smart shock took place - the clocks, the pendulums of which vibrated North and South stopped, and several rents have been discovered in brick buildings were without doubt occasioned by it.

AUGUSTA HERALD (Georgia)

New Orleans, Feb. 8 - There was another shock of an earthquake felt in this city, yesterday morning about half past 3 o'clock - It is said to have been much more strong than the one felt some time ago.

AUGUSTA HERALD (Georgia)

Wednesday, March 11, 1812

Russelville, (Ken.) Feb. 19 - We have seen a statement made by a couple of gentlemen just from New Madrid, which says that that place is much torn to pieces by the late Earthquake; so much so, that it is "almost" impossible to get along in any way, but entirely so on horseback. The houses of brick, stone and log are torn to pieces, and those of frame thrown upon their sides. The ground near that place for 100 acres has sunk so low that the tops of the tallest trees can hardly be seen above the water; in other places more than half the length of the timber is under water. The citizens have fled to the mountains, and were, when the informants left there, waiting for an opportunity to move to Kentucky. It is said that they are near one-thousand in number! Merciful God! What a horrid situation. ---

THE YORK GAZETTE (PENNSYLVANIA)
Friday, January 24, 1812

Earthquake - The agitation of the earth described in the subjoined articles was sensibly felt, about the same time as is mentioned below, by many persons in this city, tho' not so violent as it is stated to have been in other places.

A considerable shock of an earthquake was felt on the morning of the 18th (?) inst. at Hackensack, (New Jersey.) It took place a few minutes after 8 o'clock, and continued about 30 seconds. Those who were standing, experienced sensations of dizziness & vertigo. Several ladies who were sitting, complained that they felt as if sitting on a poise, and were afriad of falling from their seats. In an upper chamber, something suspended from the wall was observed to flip sensibly against it.

THE QUEBEC MERCURY (Canada)
Monday, January 20, 1812

Dec. 18 - On Monday morning last two shocks of an earthquake were sensibly felt in this town, the first between 2 and 3 o'clock, the latter about 8. We do not find it was attended by any peculiar circumstances of portentous effect, but being a circumstance of that rare kind with us, it excited as much curiosity in the inquisitive and wonder in the credulous, as did the stranger's nose in Strasbourg, so satirically related by Sterne. There appeared to be but one shock each time, and its undulations might have continued nearly 30 seconds - It had force enough to shake the furniture in houses and doors upon their hinges, and we have heard some instances of shocks(?) being stopped by its throwing their pendulums out of their regular course of vibration.

CHARLESTON HERALD (South Carolina)
Monday, February, 24, 1812

A severe shock of an Earthquake was felt at Charlestown, S. C. about the 16th which lasted minutes and caused some of the clocks to stop, the bells to ring and removed houses to such a degree, as to cause the walls to crack.

CHARLESTON COURIER (South Carolina)
Monday, February 10, 1812

We are informed that a smart shock of an Earthquake was felt at William Henry, on the 23 ult.

MONTREAL HERALD (Canada)
Saturday, February 8, 1812

Another Earthquake - On Thursday morning (says the National Intelligencer) about 10 minutes past nine, another shock of an earthquake was felt in this city, by most of the inhabitants. It appears to have affected some parts of the city more than others; for whilst some were seriously alarmed by it, there are many who did not perceive it - The cups and saucers on breakfast tables were heard to rattle; and picture frames, &c. hanging in the walls, were seen to vibrate.

OTHER WORKS BY AMAZON CHARTS TOP 25 AUTHOR BOBBY AKART

New Madrid (a disaster thriller)

Odessa (a Gunner Fox trilogy)

Odessa Reborn

Odessa Rising

Odessa Strikes

The Virus Hunters

Virus Hunters I

Virus Hunters II

Virus Hunters III

The Geostorm Series

The Shift

The Pulse

The Collapse

The Flood

The Tempest

The Pioneers

The Asteroid Series (A Gunner Fox trilogy)

Discovery

Diversion

Destruction

The Doomsday Series

Apocalypse

Haven

Printed in the USA
CPSIA information can be obtained
at www.ICGtesting.com
LVHW091120031023
759781LV00034B/630/J